THE
UNTESTED

Greg Morse

THE
UNTESTED

THE UNTESTED

Copyright © 2021 Greg Morse.

Cover illustration by: Blokosky

Published by: G-JAM PUBLISHING HOUSE, LLC.
Contact at: greg@gjampublishing.com
Website: gjampublishing.com
Social Media: @gjampublishing

Published on: March 2, 2022

Hardback ISBN: 979-8-9855375-0-5
Paperback ISBN: 979-8-9855375-1-2
eBook ISBN: 979-8-9855375-2-9
Audiobook ISBN: 979-8-9855375-3-6

Printed in the United States of America.

THE
UNTESTED

A special THANK YOU to the reader for spending your hard-earned dollars on my book. I hope you enjoy my story...

Greg Morse

REVIEWS

"An ENGAGING Mafia story spiked with some SURPRISES… Courtroom scenes read AUTHENTICALLY… A courtroom reveal, and an UNEXPECTED ending are more than SATISFYING!"

—*Kirkus Review*

"A SMART legal THRILLER with an EDGE."

—*Palm Beach Book Festival*

"Move over John Grisham! The rich, authentic dialogue creates a real PAGE-TURNER. THE UNTESTED is cross between *The Rainmaker* and *The Godfather.* SPECTACULAR!"

—Amy Morse, Esq.

"A FUN ride! The fast-paced writing and INTERESTING characters made *THE UNTESTED* a riveting story that kept me on the edge of my seat!"

—Susan Sherwin

"The Mafia subplot stands on its own! Finally, an ICONIC Mafia story for a new generation! BRAVO!"

—David Morse

"HOOKED from the first page! I happily took a break from reading my favorite author, James Patterson to read *THE UNTESTED!*

—Tiffany Noble

— Contents —

—1—

PRESENT DAY . . .

THE INSIDE OF Jason Noble's head felt like a marching band was performing at the Rose Bowl. He shook it, which only made it worse. The sea breeze blowing through his open balcony door increased his urge to vomit.

His iPhone was on the edge of the sink, blinking, lighting the bathroom in a bluish glow. His trusted assistant was reminding him of a vet appointment: *Caesar, Thursday, January 22, 8 a.m.* "Fifteen minutes," he said out loud, sighing, shaking his head again, trying to get the marching band to take a break. Jason flipped on the light switch, reached for the Listerine and took a swig. Catching a glimpse of himself in the mirror, he instinctively recoiled. He spit out the burning liquid and took a closer look. The person who looked back was almost unrecognizable. Jason's thick, dark brown hair now had streaks of gray showing through and lines had formed around the creases of his now sunken eyes. *Damn, I look like hell for twenty-nine. I've aged twenty years in the past few months!*

Jason grabbed the soap in hope of washing away his weariness when his attention was suddenly diverted to a screeching sound coming from outside. He turned from the mirror, steadied himself on the sink, and made his way to the bedroom balcony, wearing only his boxer briefs. Squinting from the blinding Florida sun, he leaned over the railing and saw a black Lincoln Town Car stopped in front of the guard booth. The driver's side door started to open. Jason quickly ducked down, his heart racing. He didn't need to see the driver to know who owned the Lincoln. *What's Vinnie "The Bag" Respi doing here?* Jason crouched behind the balcony wall, hiding like a rat.

Vinnie began honking the horn as he stepped out of the car, his thousand-dollar Italian loafers hitting the ground—*HONK! HOOOOONK!* Vinnie looked up at the façade of small balconies and replaced the honking with his baritone voice. "Yo! Jason! Let's go! Hurry up, we gots plans!"

The guard booth door opened, and an old man in a perfectly starched uniform shuffled out toward Vinnie. "You can't park there . . . and keep quiet!" Captain Tom scolded, pointing a rolled-up magazine at Vinnie. He wasn't a real captain, but he took his job so seriously that the residents added the "captain" a few years earlier. "Move your car. Now!"

Vinnie leaned into the car and laid on the horn again as the front passenger door opened and a gorilla sized man stepped out. "Eh, old man, get back in ya fuckin' shoebox before I shove ya back in," Chrissie "Meatloaf" Stephini said in a tone that would frighten a professional boxer. "I'll shove dat magazine up ya ass." Captain Tom backed away, trembling.

Jason took a deep breath, pushed aside the fear welling up inside his chest, and stood back up. He rubbed his eyes hoping the hangover was causing his mind to play tricks on him. *No such luck*, he thought. Jason stared at the scene below, using all his energy to focus on *what* was unfolding and, more importantly, trying to figure out *why in the hell are two mob enforcers at my condo? Didn't I give* La Cosa Nostra *enough? . . . What else could they want from me?*

"Quiet! I have neighbors!" Jason finally shouted.

"Yo! Jason, my friend! . . . Come on down," Vinnie said, looking up with a smile.

Jason thought his expression looked more like an evil smirk. "I'll uh . . . uh . . . be right down."

Jason turned and went inside. Grabbing a pair of jeans and t-shirt from the bedroom floor, he quickly got dressed and walked into the living/dining room. His nerves began to explode, a sense of heat overwhelmed his body, and sweat started streaming down his forehead.

His mind raced out of control, mostly with thoughts that resulted in an untimely and painful death. *Why can't I just be left alone to run my small law practice in Palm Beach? Maybe that's frickin' impossible now.*

"Everything okay?" came a soft, female voice from the couch, startling Jason.

He stopped as he was about to open the front door and spun around. Now it was starting to come back—*Inaya! I forgot she came home with me, but I'm glad she did.* He smiled at her. *Wow! She's gorgeous even when she first wakes-up* "Uh, everything's fine. Are *we* okay? Um, I'm sorry you had to sleep on the couch . . . why are you on the couch?"

Inaya sat up. She rubbed her large, brown, doe eyes and ran her fingers through her straight, black hair. "We're good. Your bed was full . . . besides, I'm a respectable girl. I'm not going to hop in the sack on the first night," she smiled.

"Great. I'll be right back and we'll get breakfast." Jason turned and headed out the front door. He quickly tried to clear his head as he thought about going back and getting his gun . . . but decided it wasn't necessary—he hoped.

* * *

"Mornin', Capitan Tom. Sorry about this," Jason said.

"Are they g-gone, Jason?" Tom mumbled, peeking his head out from under his small desk.

"Just stay here. You'll be fine." Jason didn't really know if that were entirely true. He walked toward Vinnie and Chrissie with an air of false confidence, his chest puffed out, and said, "What do you guys want?" He was suddenly mad at himself for not bringing his gun.

"Boss wants ta see ya," Vinnie said.

"Bout what?"

"How da hell should I know? I'm jus' da messenger. Get dressed and let's go."

"I *am* dressed." Jason took a step back, putting more distance between himself and Chrissie.

"You're not wearing dat garbage ta see da boss . . . and shave for Christ's sake. Show some respect. *Capisce*?" Vinnie said, waving his right hand with fingertips together. "Go put on ya bes' suit."

"Put on sumptin' ya'd wanna be buried in," Chrissie added.

"What if I say *no*?"

"Dat's why Chrissie's here." Chrissie stepped toward Jason clenching his big fists. Jason's chest deflated. "You can put a nice suit on and get in the damn car or Chrissie can dress ya and shove ya in da trunk. Your choice . . . eider way, you're comin' wit us."

—2—

A FEW MONTHS AGO . . .

THE CONSTANT THUNK sound that came every few seconds was maddening—*THUNK . . . THUNK . . . THUNK . . .*

Alfonso clenched his thinning, greasy black hair that was wet from the spray off the ten-foot waves. "Enough!" he yelled to no one in particular, as he bent down and unhooked the harpoon gun on the deck next to a shipping container. *This'll stop that goddamn noise once and for all*, he thought, as he lifted the big gun—the razor-sharp harpoon tip sticking out of the barrel.

The shipping freighter began its voyage in Shenzhen, China, on June 1, but Alphonso boarded in Panama on July 2 for the seven-day journey to The Port of Palm Beach. His "special cargo" was already on board when the ship docked in Panama—six days late. Although, he didn't really mind the delay; the prostitutes and heroin had been good company.

Alfonso quickly got used to the loud, whining engines and diesel smell that permeated his nostrils on each trip—this was his fifth. He gently swayed back against the shipping container, his feet stationary, as the freighter rolled over another ten-foot wave. His sea legs were good because of his low center of gravity. At five feet, four inches, and three hundred twenty pounds, Alfonso stuck to the deck like an anchor. But the constant noise coming from the shipping container made him crazy. He had nightmares for days after each trip, and they were lasting longer and longer.

Alfonso bitched to the crew every chance he got, even though most of them couldn't understand a word he said: *If it wasn't fo' da economy goin' in da shitta, I wouldn't have ta do dis nasty work. Earnin's gettin' harder and harder dese days. Years afta dat Great Recession ding and it's still a struggle ta earn good enough for da Boss—greedy bastard.*

Only Alfonso could hear it over the deafening engines and crashing waves that constantly rocked the freighter and swallowed any other sounds—*THUNK . . . THUNK . . . THUNK . . .* He wiped the saltwater spray from his face and placed his hand on the rusty handle of the forty-foot by eight-foot container. It wouldn't budge.

The deck was full of red, blue, and yellow containers stacked five high. From the shadows of the containers appeared a hard-looking Latin guy—probably from some savage hellhole in Central America. The Central Americans built a lucrative, niche industry, thanks in large part to pirates on the high seas, of escorting illegal cargo across the world's oceans. Their paramilitary training made them perfect for the task and they came cheap, which is what Alfonso liked. "What de hell you doin', *gringo*? It ten-foot seas, they gonna slide out if you open de damn door . . . *Whale.*"

"Don't call me that . . . only *friends of mine* can call me 'The Whale' you two-bit wetback."

"*Eh, holmes, tranquilo.* Don't want to lose any de merchandise. Last trip we lose good one—*mucho dinero. Mi jefe* not happy," Raul said, clinging his skinny frame to the side of another shipping container close to the one Alfonso was trying to open.

"Screw your boss. He'll get his *dinero.* I always pay transport, based on what we left Panama with. I gotta stop this banging. I can't take it!" Alfonso lifted the harpoon gun and shook it in Raul's direction.

Raul adjusted his weight from leg to leg to account for the rocking freighter. "Stand over there so you no hear dem bang around." Raul pointed to a black void about thirty feet away.

"I'll stand by my product until we dock. I don't trust any of you greaseballs."

"Whatever . . . *Whale.* You explain to *mi jefe* if lose more. Bad ratin' if don't arrive with full cargo. Had thirty units when left Panama. Better arrive with thirty."

"Ratin'? What ratin'? I pay per unit. I ain't payin' for no damn ratin.'"
Alfonso awkwardly shifted his weight as the ship dove over a sharp
wave much bigger than the previous few.

"People that need me boss 'special' transport want know if what
they shipping arrive in one piece. Right now we best, but *mucho* competition today. Just make sure none damaged . . . *Bastardo*," Raul turned
and walked toward the bow. Within seconds he was lost in the shadows
of the stacked containers.

"The hell with his *el jefe*. He'll get his money. Almost every trip we
lose one or two anyway . . . one more won't matter," Alfonso muttered.
THUNK . . . THUNK . . . THUNK . . .

He turned back to the container handle, put the harpoon gun down,
and tried to open it again. "Damn it!" His hands slipped and his fat
body smashed into the container with a thud. "What the fu—!" Alfonso yelled, as his legs went out from under him. The freighter quickly
pitched to what felt like a ninety-degree angle. Alfonso fell hard on the
wet deck. He rolled backwards, crashing into another stack of containers a few feet away. Water splashed all over.

The boat finally settled, and Alfonso rolled his body around and got
to his knees. He was gasping for air. Raul reappeared, laughing, pointing with another Latin guy who had a machine gun clenched in one
hand, holding on tight to a container railing with the other.

The harpoon gun came sliding down the deck, smashing into Alfonso's knees causing him to fall forward on his belly.

"He really look like whale," Raul said, pointing and howling.

Alfonso finally got to his feet, coughing, shaking his head, trying to
get his bearings. "What the hell! Sonofabitch!"

A stout, chiseled man, in a Panamanian military uniform, silently
came up behind Raul and commanded, "*Vamoños!*" Raul and his *com-
pañero* quickly disappeared back into the shadows.

The man looked at Alfonso in disgust and said, without a hint of an
accent, "Get off your fat ass and prepare to move your cargo. All of it.
We're docking in five." The man turned around and left.

Alfonso slowly made his way over to the container, grabbing onto anything he could for balance along the way. *At least the noise stopped. Finally, something good happened today.*

The engines made a thunderous roar as the Captain put the throttle in reverse. The ship slowed surprisingly fast given its size. A blaring horn sounded three times as it approached the Port of Palm Beach located at the border of West Palm Beach and Riviera Beach. Alfonso had a guy that worked security at the Port, so it was easy to unload the "special cargo." No one would miss one empty container among fifteen hundred full of knitted blankets from China. Alfonso's ship easily got lost among the thousands of *Zombie Ships*, as they were called, roaming the earth with no cargo. Less than one percent of all shipping freighters coming into the U.S. were searched. Great odds for smuggling illegal cargo.

Alfonso grabbed the metal handle on the shipping container and put all of his weight behind it, but it still wouldn't budge. "Jesus Christ. Eh, *amigo*. Get over here. *Rapido!*" Alfonso demanded, as he motioned with his hand to a guy standing by the edge of the ship. The deck was now busy with people preparing the ship to dock.

"*Estás loco, gringo,*" the skinny deckhand said, as he pushed Alfonso out of the way. He took a metal hook about eight inches long from the pocket of his dirty vest and placed it under the handle, and, with little effort, the latch popped open.

Alfonso was responsible for unloading his one container, the most valuable by far on the ship. Thirty units on this load. Twenty-five to one hundred thousand dollars each. The small ones were the most expensive, if they arrived in one piece. Alfonso pulled open the heavy container door—it creaked loudly from the rusty hinges. . . . He recoiled from the rush of putrid air. That smell got him every time. He covered his nose and mouth and looked in—only darkness, but he could hear muted sounds coming from the back of the container.

He turned on his flashlight. The beam cut through the thick, moldy air, sweeping side to side. . . . Then it stopped on a young, Asian girl's face, perhaps twelve years old. The innocence of youth gone from her eyes. She was covered in filth, wearing rags for clothing, holding her hand over an elderly Asian woman's mouth, who had tears streaming down her face. The old lady was clutching a small boy, who was lifeless in her arms. The little girl removed her hand and sank back as far as she could, which wasn't very far because of the twenty-seven other Asian people pressed against each other behind her. The old lady began sobbing, the noise echoing around the container.

"Shut up! Shut up! Not a sound ya dumb bastards! You want your freedom?" Alfonso stepped into the container, shining his flashlight in their terrified faces. The group was covered in excrement, malnourished, and in severe shock from the long, hard trip. Alfonso pushed open the other door. The freighter was almost at a complete stop. The sound of the powerful engines thrust into reverse filled the air.

These poor people were promised a better life in America for a fee of ten thousand American dollars each. In reality, they just became an unknown statistic in the world of human trafficking. They were paid pennies a week to work off the fee, which only increased because of the ridiculously high rent they were charged for squalid conditions even a sewer rat wouldn't live in. The ones they could prostitute were also charged for the heroin they needed to feed their addiction that was forced upon them by their captors. However, Alfonso felt he was a decent guy because he had rules: no infants and none of the young girls could be sold as breeders, although he couldn't promise his "no breeding" rule was always followed. The temptation to get a girl pregnant then rip the baby from her and sell it for around fifty thousand dollars on the black market was too good to pass up for the heartless men and woman in the human trafficking business.

Alphonso walked over to the old woman and grabbed the boy's arm, yanking him away. She sobbed uncontrollably. Alfonso shined the flashlight in the boy's face. "Shit. I lost a good one. I could've gotten seventy-five large for this one. The middle easterners love the young Asian boys," he said, devoid of any emotion. His blood was beginning to boil at the prospect of all the money he lost. The old lady's sobbing grew louder as she covered her face.

"Enough! Goddammit!" Then a deafening BANG reverberated around the container, a plume of white smoke hanging in the air. Alfonso put his gun back in its holster on his fat waist. His ears were ringing from the gun blast. *That's why I wanted to use the harpoon gun.* "Let's go! Everyone out. Now! And someone carry the old lady and the boy."

— 3 —

"*Caio*, Happy Day of Columbus," Mario "Lug Nut" Rizzo said to the two armed guards dressed in white suits, standing at the dock gate. They stood at attention, saying nothing, expressionless, guarding the entrance to a two-hundred-foot super yacht docked at slip number thirteen in Port Everglades, Florida. The mouth of one of the seven natural wonders of the world, and a great place to hide a body. Mario's boss, Antonio "Magic Man" Barrera, always held his annual meeting for a select few "employees" at the beginning of the Florida tourist season—even crime was seasonal in South Florida. He changed the location every year to keep the FBI guessing. And this year it was a super yacht.

"I'a love you boss. You smart man," Mario said, out loud, to himself. He wouldn't dare use the term "boss" in Antonio's presence. If you called him "Godfather," you wouldn't make it home alive. Antonio preferred "sir" or a simple nod of acknowledgment to a question or greeting. *It was good way to be*, Mario thought. *Less to pick up on wire.*

Standing with an expression of wonderment and looking at the massive yacht, he made the sign of the cross, kissing his fingertips at the end. "*Bellissimo*," he said, looking at the guards, as he walked through the open dock gate.

Mario didn't know where the yacht was heading, only the captain and Antonio did. The trip could take an hour or it could take three days. Mario didn't care; from the legendary rumors he'd heard, this was going to be great time.

Mario was a *cugine* (rising star) in the Berrara crime family. He arrived on loan from Italy two years ago. Antonio liked him so much that he told his Italian Mafia family, "Mario is staying in America." Antonio followed up his conversation with a one-million-dollar cash payment.

Everything and everyone had a price according to Antonio.

Carmine Gatto's heavy steps vibrated the dock. "Yo! Mario! You made it!" He yelled, even though he was only a few feet behind. Carmine was already out of breath from the short walk from the parking lot.

Mario snapped out of his daze. "*Eh, amico mio* (my friend)! I'a make it. I'a no miss for nutin', meat-a-ball." Mario turned his head around, his smile growing wider at the sight of Carmine.

"It's Bowling Ball . . . *Capice!*" Carmine raised his fist in the air. "How many times I gotta tell ya . . . if yous ain't careful, I'm gonna show ya why I'm called 'Bowling Ball' and stuff you in a ball bag."

"I sorry, 'Bowling Ball'. I'a get it one day."

"You been here two years for Christ's sake. Everyone in Italy this stupid?"

"I just so happy, I forget." Mario embraced Carmine and kissed him on each cheek. "Guys in Italian mob, no nicknames, just first name. I'a not used to it, but I like'a mine."

They turned and started walking toward the gangway. Mario in front—Carmine was too wide to walk side by side on the narrow dock even with someone as skinny as Mario. "Oh yeah? How'd you get your name 'Lug Nut'? . . . because you got *lug nuts* for brains?" Carmine asked, laughing.

"To weigh down body in ocean, I remove lug nuts from many cars I find around dock, because I forget concrete on first job." He turned back toward the parking lot pointing at the cars. "Parking lot no full so I run around all over town getting lug nuts. I wish I see people in morning drive away with tires fly off."

"Yeah, great story. You yammer on like a broad. Now let's go."

"No one around but security. We must be last ones, hurry," Mario said with a concerned look.

"Relax, I'm not hurryin' for nuttin'." Carmine took another slow step with his heavy foot. "Look, security is still at the end of the dock. We're fine."

"I no want to miss anything. This my first time."

"Oh! You're gonna break your cherry." Carmine slapped him on the back like he was congratulating a high school kid on his way to the prom. "I've been to this party many times. It's the best day on the job. It's the only day of the year ya know ya ain't gonna get whacked." Carmine had a wide smile growing across his meaty face. "Every other day of the year we live with the stress of knowing ya best friend might be takin' ya to dinner to put an ice pick in ya neck." His smile disappeared at the thought.

"I hear Antonio rent out entire Vegas for everyone at party last year."

"He rented a hotel and casino in Vegas . . . moron, not the entire city. Just get on the boat before I chrow ya in."

They approached a security station that was at the entrance to the gangway. Four men, two with AR-15 machine guns, dressed in white, linen suits suspiciously eyed Mario and Carmine as they approached. One of the men stared at them for what seemed like an eternity then said, "Everything in the bin, including *all* weapons and step through the machine with your hands up." *Security was normally tight whenever the boss was around, but this was a whole new level of security*, Mario thought.

"Watch out!" Carmine said, as he elbowed past Mario like a fat kid trying to get cake. Carmine took a silk handkerchief out of his lapel pocket, opened his suit jacket, and lifted his gut to reveal a small re-volver—38 special. He took it out with the handkerchief over his hand and placed it in the gray plastic bin along with a wallet, keys, lighter, cigarettes, and cell phone. "Looks like you guys finally got a bigger x-ray machine. No more small ones like at the airport. Those weren't made for a big fella like me." Carmine stepped into the x-ray machine with his hands up—*still a little tight.*

He walked to the left to grab everything but his gun and cell phone, which were no longer in the bin that was rolling out of an x-ray ma-chine. The first year he was invited to Antonio's party, he had so much anxiety about leaving his gun with security; he kept thinking that it was a trick to frame him by using his gun in a murder. So now, he just cleaned all his prints off the gun and didn't touch it again until he came back from the trip.

"*Dio Mio* (my God)!" Mario said, kissing the tips of his fingers as he stared at the super yacht, made by Italian builder Benetti, that glistened brilliantly against the clear blue sky. It's blue hull with white exterior glistened like a brilliant diamond. Mario estimated it was at least five stories high from the waterline. "Carmine? . . . look, . . ." he pointed to the stacked decks, "four decks for sun. How many girls we can fit?" Mario's grin went from ear to ear, his mouth began to water at the thought.

"Come on. Let's go. We're gonna miss the best part," Carmine ordered, now frustrated by the delay.

Mario looked at Carmine, confused. "The best part is beginning of party?"

"Oh man, fuhgeddaboudit. You better hurry up." Carmine turned and started walking up the gangplank to the yacht.

"I comin', Carmine, wait!" Mario placed two black semi-automatic pistols that he pulled from side holsters under his suit jacket; two small, silver semi-automatic guns from each ankle; a switchblade from a seamless pocket on his right pant leg; a money clip with a wad of cash; and an iPhone. Mario patted his sides, "I think that it."

Young kids with all their guns and shit. All you need is one reliable gun and a strong set of fists to handle any situation. Period. End of story, Carmine thought. "A gunfighter don't charge by the bullet," he shouted to Mario.

Mario could barely hear Carmine because his head was still filled with thoughts of bikini-clad girls on four different sundecks.

— 4 —

MARIO AND CARMINE reached the entrance to the main deck. "Finally," Carmine said between gasps for air. Walking the gangplank was the most exercise his soft body had experienced in a long time. Two men, dressed like admirals with red sashes around their waists, stood on the main deck—no weapons visible.

"We only ones here?" Mario asked, looking around the empty deck made of highly polished teak wood.

"In there and down the stairs," the taller guard said, pointing to blacked out glass doors with ornate gold handles to the right. "You're the last two. We were about to leave you behind."

Carmine's face lit up like a boy on Christmas. "Let's move, Lug Nut. Two years ago we met in Hawaii. Antonio had 'Hawaiian Tropics' contestants, including the winner, dressed in gold latex with Rolex watches up and down their arms for each of us. The best gift ever . . . and the watches were nice too," Carmine said, winking.

Carmine grabbed the shiny door handle and pulled open the door. Mario squeezed in front of him and abruptly stopped, causing Carmine to bump into his back. Mario lurched forward into the pitch black landing. Two men blocked the entrance. A bright light shined from behind them, blinding Mario and Carmine. "Pass." The man on the right said.

"Uh . . . Uh . . ." Mario stammered, shielding his eyes from the blinding light.

"Now."

"Relax," Carmine said, putting his left hand on Mario's shoulder and reaching his right hand around, holding his thumb out for the man. "They run your fingerprint; Antonio don't trust no one."

"Oh. that why Vinnie 'Clear Eyes' tell me, 'bring your thumb,' when I invited."

The man placed Carmine's thumb on a handheld scanner. "We were closing up to set sail. You just made it." A little green light went off. He then took Mario's trembling hand, placed it on the scanner . . . green light. "You're lucky I didn't kill you." He squeezed Mario's thumb extra hard. "You can enter paradise now."

Both men stepped aside, revealing a lacquered rosewood staircase with gold railings descending to a lower level. The bright lights went out, replaced by wall sconces and running lights down the stairs. Carmine and Mario rubbed their eyes as they adjusted to the new light. "Now the fun's gonna start . . . let's go, man," Carmine said, as he bounded down the stairs, Mario right behind.

They stepped onto a black and white marble floor laid out across a larger foyer in a classic pattern. Mario stared in awe at the carved, likely by hand, mahogany wood trim all around the room. "Gentleman, you are the last two to arrive," said the tanned woman sitting behind a small glass desk. She stood up, showing off all of her curves. Mario snapped out of his trance.

"Put your tongue back in your mouth," Carmine said.

"My name is Lola. If you need anything while you are on the ship or at our final destination, just ask me and I will take care of it. Well . . . almost anything," she said with a wink. She walked over to Carmine, who stood like an expectant dog, and pinned a small red rose on his lapel, then one onto Mario's.

"This is your ticket inside. Enjoy. . . ."

* * *

The large mahogany double doors opened in unison revealing an elegant ballroom filled with fifteen mobsters dressed in silk suits. The sounds of a live band filled the cavernous ballroom with Connie Francis' *Who's Sorry Now*. Carmine looked around and proclaimed, "You can dress a pig in silk and put it in a castle, but it's still a pig."

They were greeted by a slender black woman dressed only in high heels and a thong. She didn't look a day over twenty. "Drinks, gentleman?" Mario was fixated on the silver tray that was breast height.

"Johnnie Walker Gold, no ice," Carmine said.

"Peroni, *mi amore.*" Mario finally broke his stare and turned to Carmine. "This great party. I glad I wear dancin' shoes." Mario pointed to his alligator skin loafers and did a little two-step.

"You ain't seen notin' yet."

"Oh! Look who it is! Git ova'ear you greasy bastad!" said Mikie.

"Eh, Mikie 'Two-lips', how the hell you been?" Carmine asked, extending his arms.

Mikie embraced Carmine and kissed him on each cheek. "It's going to be another great time."

"Hey, Mario, you know why day call'em 'Two-lips'?" Carmine didn't wait for Mario to respond. "He was gettin' it on wit dis little ding when he went to choke er and felt an adam's apple da size of a grapefruit. He reached down to confirm it was a dude . . . din't ya? Two-lips, you sick bastard, you." The waitress returned. Carmine grabbed his drink from the silver tray. "He sliced *her* two lips off." Carmine slapped his thigh as he let out a booming laugh.

"Screw you 'Bowling Ball'." Mikie turned and walked away to mingle with someone who didn't always break his balls, which was hard to find in this room.

Mario was laughing as the waitress handed him a Peroni.

The music suddenly stopped. Anyone who wasn't a mobster started to leave the room. "Uh, can I have all you guys attention.," said a male voice through the yacht's sound system. "Listen up, fellas." The voice instructed a little louder. The crowd of mobsters completely ignored it.

"Shut the fuck up and listen!" screamed Joseph, Antonio's trusted driver/bodyguard. "You mooks act like little schoolgirls when you get together." Everyone immediately went silent and turned toward the front of the room.

While standing in the main ballroom, one could easily forget he was on a yacht. The exterior walls were blue tinted glass while the interior had ceilings three stories high. The front wall was decorated in lacquered mahogany and rosewood, so shiny you could see yourself in it. The floor was white marble with gold leaf designs bespectacled throughout. A marble balcony with bronze railings protruded from the wall. The chandeliers and wall sconces were ornate Murano glass.

"Da man who can make any problem . . . *disappear* . . ." Joseph said, like a ring master at a circus. The double doors to the balcony opened. Everyone looked up in unison.

Our great leader, Mario silently mouthed, making the sign of the cross.

Antonio "Magic Man" Barrera stepped onto the balcony. He stood for a moment, surveying his men . . . like the Pope about to give mass in St. Peter's Square. Antonio had dark brown, almost black, thick hair, and blue eyes that immediately drew in his audience. His olive-colored skin always made him look like he had a perfect tan—the benefit of Sicilian roots. He was dressed in a custom-made, silk suit that hung perfectly to his six-three athletic frame and no tie. If he wasn't a mob boss, he'd be a movie star or a professional athlete.

"Welcome, friends of mine," Antonio said, extending his arms like Christ. "It's time to celebrate another great year of business. The great recession is a distant memory and we are all earning again. From the ashes of the economic collapse . . . *La Famiglia* has RISEN more profitable and powerful than ever!" The men let out booming cheers in unison. They were all loosely huddled in front of the balcony now.

Antonio had a relaxed smile as he continued. "Thanks to all of you. . . ." More wild cheers. Antonio glanced over each man in the room as he spoke, making each one feel like he was the only one Antonio was talking to. "Although, by the looks of those five-thousand-dollar suits some of you are wearing, I think you held back a little." The group laughed, some a concerned laugh, too paranoid to believe he was joking. "For the three newcomers to my yearly celebration, what happens here, stays here. Do not even talk about it with your crew. You are all here because you are the best at what you do. I want you to know how much I appreciate your hard work. I will continue to move us into non-traditional businesses that have a lower risk and higher reward . . . God bless the internet!" He pumped his fist in the air. Everyone cheered. "As a thank you for all your hard work, I got each of you some gifts from Brazil that I think you'll enjoy." The men's eyes went wide with anticipation. He pointed toward a golden spiral staircase to his right; a spotlight beamed onto the landing. "I present . . . the Girls-of-Rio!"

Twenty tanned, Brazilian beauties slowly paraded onto the landing and down the staircase. They were dressed in tiny, sheer, bikinis. Their perfectly lean bodies supported by six-inch heels. The men gawked at them, speechless.

Petey "two-time" shouted, "I love you, Antonio!"

"Marry me!" Lorenzo "Baby Hands" Petrini yelled at the girls, even though he had a wife and five kids at home. The mobsters started hooting and hollering.

"Calm down. Calm down. . . . There will be plenty of time for you to enjoy the ladies," Antonio said, moving his arms like a quarterback silencing the crowd. "Each of these lovely ladies is wearing a beautiful emerald and five carat diamond bracelet, which is yours to take home to your loved one. Hopefully it brings a little less bitching when you walk in the door after being gone a few days." Antonio tried to lessen their *on the job* stress level so they'd perform better, although most of the guys in the room were true sociopaths and should never be in any kind of relationship, especially a marriage with kids. "For the guys who don't have a loved one, this will buy you one." The men howled. Antonio knew, sadly, that most of his guys would pawn the expensive bracelet for pennies on the dollar and pay gambling debts or blow the money in a weekend partying. The Girls-of-Rio were now mingling with the guys.

The staff started to reenter. Waitresses served each man a shot of grappa . . . Antonio raised his shot. "No matter what happens to any one of us . . . *La Famiglia* will always survive. *Cent anni* (100 years)! *Salute!*"

— 5 —

JASON NOBLE AWOKE with the same hot feeling enveloping his body that he felt every morning for the past few months. He looked at the clock: 4:30a.m. *No need for an alarm—stress is my alarm*, he thought. His mind swirled like a tornado: finances, career path, his future, no steady girlfriend; but mostly, the stress-tornado was driven by thoughts of his clients—all one hundred and twenty-five of them. Jason spent yesterday, Columbus Day, making a house call of sorts. Most of his clients called the Palm Beach County Jail home for the foreseeable future. Even on a court holiday, Jason worked, which is why his meager salary usually averaged out to near minimum wage. The running joke around his office was that the lawyers should call the U.S. Department of Labor and file a complaint.

Jason's mind wandered to the Intracoastal Waterway as he lay in bed listening to the water lap against the seawall along Flagler Drive. West Palm Beach was his slice of paradise, or so he thought, when he moved to South Florida from New York three years ago. He traded in the concrete jungle for the bright sun and palm trees, but South Florida was a jungle in its own way. Murder, prostitution, drug deals, all taking place within a stone's throw of the Atlantic Ocean.

The heat was back and his mind started to ball up with stress again. Most mornings, he asked himself the same question over and over: *Why did I spend $250,000 to educate myself in college and law school and then take a job making $35,000 a year? Oh, that's right, to save the world and fight against "the man", which apparently didn't pay much.* He rolled over to spoon his companion. It didn't help, the depressing thoughts continued. *I wish someone had told me in law school that, unless you're already rich, don't become a government criminal defense attorney . . . odds are you'll be as poor as your clients.*

Jason worked at the Palm Beach County Public Defender's Office located in the heart of downtown West Palm Beach. "If I hear, *are you my public pretender?*, one more time, I'm going to lose it," Jason whispered, stroking his companion's belly.

"Caesar!" Jason exclaimed, as he sat up in bed and smelled the rancid air. "Good morning to you too." Caesar was his five-year-old English bulldog who stretched out his sixty-five-pound frame across the bed, taking three quarters of it. Caesar slightly picked up his head, half opened his eyes, looked at Jason with his wrinkled face . . . then rolled over, went back to sleep, and was snoring within seconds.

Jason got out of bed, straightened his six-foot, lean body, and walked into the bathroom. He came out of the bathroom a few minutes later dressed to run. "Don't get up on my account, Caesar." Jason walked through his bedroom into the kitchen and grabbed a bottle of water from the fridge. He then made a cup of coffee in a Styrofoam cup from his Keurig coffee machine, added three sugars, a splash of milk, put the lid on, and headed for the front door.

He lived on the third floor of Sunshine Towers Condominium. The main floor had ceiling to floor windows for the exterior walls, with most of the remaining surfaces covered in mirrors—even the square support columns. The white wicker furniture had a few splashes of turquois and orange in the cushions. The design style was a cross between Scarface and a seaside cottage. Captain Tom was sitting in the small guard room just inside the front entrance. "Good Morning, Captain Tom. How's your day going so far?" Jason asked.

"Quiet as always," Tom replied, burying his head back in his newspaper.

Jason walked outside and took a deep breath. He loved to fill his lungs with the fresh, salt air in the morning. Sunshine Towers was situated on the corner of Flagler Drive and Southern Boulevard across the street from the Intracoastal Waterway, on the west side—a two-minute walk to Palm Beach. Condos like Jason's were a dime a dozen after the real estate collapse in 2008. He only paid $75,000 for his unit in a short sale while the previous owner paid $375,000.

As Jason crossed Flagler, the stars were still bright at 4:45a.m. "Morning, General," he said to the man just waking up on the seawall with a crisp salute.

The General sucked in the salt air and yawned. "At ease, soldier. Coffee," he commanded. He stood up and stretched his desert-camouflage-covered body.

"Three sugars and a splash of milk—not a drop more. Like always, Sir." Jason handed the General his coffee. The General's real name was Stanton Riley, a veteran of the first Iraq war. Now homeless, mostly because he chose to be. Jason had found him housing and offered to pay for his ticket home to Iowa, but he refused. He managed his PTSD pretty well with the help of a little Jack Daniels. *At least he has a great view*, Jason thought. "May I be dismissed, Sir?"

"Diiis-missed, Sargent Noble." The General raised his coffee cup in a gesture of thanks.

Jason began his morning jog along the water. Quickly his mind wondered back to work: *Will I get the five-year prison plea deal in Jerome's theft case? Will I be forced to trial on the Bonner rape case that I still haven't really looked at? Can I physically keep up this current pace? Can I make it on my own? I can't keep living paycheck to paycheck. . . .*

— 6 —

"I AM THE greatest," Trevor Wittingham said out loud, as he looked in the mirror and adjusted his red silk tie. He turned and grabbed the bulletproof vest off his bed. He didn't have to wear it often, but when he did, he felt invincible. His vest was emblazoned on the front and back with "DOJ" in bright yellow—Department of Justice. He would put his vest on over his suit once he arrived "on-scene." He wore a dark blue suit that clung a bit too tight to his five feet, five-inch frame. *You never know when the media might be around*, he thought, as he continued to look at himself in the mirror.

Trevor was in the middle of prosecuting Buddy Turner for armed marijuana drug trafficking. It was a high profile case, which Trevor always seemed to sniff out, because the defense was arguing for the first time in a federal marijuana case, medical necessity for personal use. Buddy had a lot of marijuana (211 pounds to be exact) when the FBI, DEA, and Palm Beach County Sheriff's Office raided his small farm as if he were hiding plutonium while his wife, two children, and basset hound Buttercup were sleeping. All Buddy remembered was the way he was awakened that Sunday morning before church. "On the ground, scumbag!" A large agent dressed in all black, including a ski mask, yelled, aiming an AR-15 assault rifle at Buddy's head.

To Buddy's shock and dismay, his high-powered lawyer, Peter Berkley, informed him that he faced a minimum mandatory of ten years in prison for his medical marijuana. "My white country ass won' las' ten minutes in the clink," Buddy said. "But it's legal in most of the country! Heck! I was growing it next to my basil plants. What about all the money I donate to children's cancer research? Ain't there anything I can do?"

"Since you had a hunting rifle in your house, the prosecutor, that asshole Wittingham, is charging you with armed drug trafficking. The boys in Washington won't approve a plea deal below the minimum/ mandatory of ten years hard time. Besides, Wittingham wouldn't plea it out anyway, he wants to use you as an example in the media." Buddy's shoulders slouched . . . he couldn't take the ten, so he chose trial.

Trevor was a Chief Assistant United States Attorney for the Southern District of Florida, which covered the southern part of the east coast of Florida; from Ft. Pierce, a city about sixty miles north of Palm Beach all the way to Key West—the southern-most part of the United States and only ninety miles from Cuba. Every waking moment for Trevor was devoted to removing the *assistant* from his title.

He walked into the kitchen of his modest four-bedroom, three bath house, situated in Wellington, a community about fifteen miles west of the coast in Palm Beach County. It was predominately home to Florida's affluent equestrian scene and some people who desperately wanted to be apart of that scene but didn't have enough money, like Trevor's wife Marlene. Wellington was dotted with gated communities and world class Polo grounds.

Trevor's house was a cookie cutter, open floor plan, Mediterranean design, sitting on a quarter acre. While everything looked nice in the house, under the surface it was cheaply made like so many in Florida during the boom time years from 2000-2008. His wife Marlene wanted something more grand, and she told him so every chance she got.

Trevor walked into the kitchen. "Where are you going so early in the morning?" Marlene asked as she poured him a cup of coffee. "I hope you're getting paid extra for going in so early. You make peanuts as a salary, so we have to live in this shoebox of a house . . . the least they can do is pay you overtime like an over-educated factory worker." Marlene couldn't be happier that Trevor was leaving so early. The thought of spending anytime with him at home was revolting to her.

"I have work to do," Trevor responded as he adjusted his tie. He was going with some FBI special agents to execute a search warrant at Buddy Turner's customer's house; a seventy-six-year-old woman with pancreatic cancer who is supposed to testify for Buddy at trial. Trevor salivated like a hungry dog at the thought of being there when the "bad guy's" door was kicked in. Trevor was forty-eight years old and walked through life with a warped sense of reality. He and his wife should have divorced years ago, probably fifteen years ago right after they got married, but he did not believe in failure and would have no part of a divorce.

For Marlene's part, she liked telling people she was married to a Federal Prosecutor—Chief Assistant Prosecutor at the U.S. Attorney's Office. It sounded more prestigious than it really was. Being from a small town in Texas, you married a cowhand, an oil rig operator, or you stayed single your whole life and were whispered about behind your back by everyone in town. Marlene left when she was sixteen, got fake ID that said she was eighteen, and enrolled in college. She quickly realized that life would be much easier if she focused on getting a *Mrs.* degree instead of one that required her to work hard. So, she met and married Trevor when he was in his third year of law school at University of Miami School of Law and she was a sophomore at the University of Miami's undergraduate college.

Both went into the marriage under false pretenses. Marlene thought Trevor would immediately make large sums of money at a prestigious law firm right out of law school, but instead he chose to work for the Federal government. After a couple years of marriage, they decided to have a child, thinking it would bring them closer. Looking back now— what a dumb idea.

"What type of work?" Marlene asked, as she stood up and walked to the fridge.

"Government stuff. Nothing you'd want to hear about."

"Figures. What do you have to do, go and arrest some drunks? No wait . . . maybe it's real dangerous and you have to arrest some poor, blue-collar worker who took an extra hundred dollar deduction on his taxes. Ohh, big lawman."

Trevor can't remember when every interaction with his wife became an exercise in how nasty and cold they could be to one another. More *her* than him, he thought. For at least five years it had been like this. But he could not fail at his marriage. Plus, he had his thirteen-year-old daughter, Gisela, to think about. She could not think failure was okay in life.

Trevor poured the cup of coffee into a travel mug and said, "Haven't you been reading the newspapers or watching the local news? . . . Where's the paper?" He said, more as a demand than a question. "Am I on the front page?"

"Oh, right, your big marijuana case." She tossed the paper across the counter. "You're not even on the last page. I'm sure you'll screw it up and we'll be stuck in this cheap house forever."

With that, Trevor turned and walked to the front door, closing it carefully as he left. He had stopped slamming it after Gisela was born.

—7—

"I'VE HAD ENOUGH of this life," Giovanni "Snowman" Adrano said to his pet Iguana, Carlito, who was snuggling on his lap. "I'm seventy-four. It's time to leave this life. I've given enough to it . . . Sixty years in this business . . . I'm tired." He took a sip of gin from a crystal tumbler. "Plus, we don't want to push our luck." He gently stroked Carlito's soft, green head. "It's time for us to retire." Carlito bobbed his head in agreement.

Giovanni ran the South Florida mob since 1974 and was considered the *Don* of *Dons*, because he was the longest tenured mob boss in American Mafia history. He took control right after the turbulent 1960s and Vietnam War. The country was ready for a break and a good time—cocaine and disco were just what the doctor ordered. Giovanni first saw the potential for cocaine as a young man in 1955 when he visited his third cousin in Columbia. He noticed all the workers moving at a frantic pace. He asked his cousin Abilene, "Why are they so energetic?"

"*Mira, Mira,*" Abilene said, as she pointed to the horizon at the vast, lush fields of green bushes that went on for as far as the eye could see. The bushes had small green leaves and stood between a few inches to more than eight feet in height. "*De coca planta.*" Abilene reached over to the nearest coca plant to her left and plucked off a few of the small leaves and handed one to Giovanni. "*Comer,*" she instructed then put the leaf in her mouth and started to chew it. He put the leaf in his mouth, but didn't chew at first, he just sucked on it like a lollipop.

"*Masticar! Masticar!*" Abilene said with a laugh. Although Giovanni didn't really know what she was saying, he figured it out and started to chew on the coca leaf. Within minutes he had a rush of energy that he couldn't describe and felt as if he could take on the world!

Giovanni noticed two men sitting at a small table outside in the sun, snorting a white powdery substance through their noses. "What are they doing?"

"They supervisors of Plantation. They cook coca plant and make white powder they put in their noses." She tapped her nose. "They have barrels full of powder all over. So much they laugh when it spill on ground and pigs eat it. They call it *cociana*."

"*Cociana*?"

"*Si*. They look funny when they snort it. It look like mama's powdered sugar she sprinkle on delicious churros she make, but sugar *mucho dinero* then nose powder. The men party for days with it." She had a look of dismay on her face. "I don't like them when they snort it, they get *mucho, mucho loco*."

Giovanni thought about the people at his dad's club in Miami—they always wanted to party forever and this cheap, white powder would let them.

Giovanni seized control of the South Florida Mafia in '74 in one of the most vicious takeovers in Mafia history. His predecessor, Dominic "Snake Eyes" Rappini, wanted nothing to do with the drug business or Latin America, especially Columbia, and resisted any effort to get into the drug trade. He thought there was no money in it. Rappini would kill any of his men caught even smoking a joint. "Booze, cigarettes, gambling, loansharking, extortion, and swag is how we make money for decades and I won't change now!" Rappini would yell.

"Don Rappini, I beg you to let me experiment with selling cocaine," Giovanni pleaded, his hands together as if he were praying. "I will make you more money than you can dream. If I don't make you at least a million dollars in the first month, I will immediately stop. Please . . . I beg you."

"Stop begging before I lose respect for you," Don Rapinni said as he waved his right hand dismissively. "You and your crew will not be happy if you get involved with that junk. Drugs are for the *mulignans* (blacks) and Puerto Ricans . . . Italian mafioso will never become that," he said with pride.

Giovanni continued to plead, "They are disorganized. We can easily take over their operation and keep them as distributors. Let the *mulignans* and Puerto Ricans take all of the risk."

"What then?" Rapinni wasn't expecting an answer. He stepped closer to Giovanni. "I don't think Senator Walton or U.S. Attorney Albright will continue to protect our family if I'm in business with *mulignans*. I said no . . . *capisce!*"

Giovanni knew that was old thinking . . . small money. A major mistake that would ultimately cost Rapinni his life. Mistakes weren't tolerated in this business—there were no second chances. "I didn't mean to offend you. I will always respect your wisdom."

On Halloween in 1974, Giovanni made his move and had Rappini, his underboss, and consigliere eliminated—the men responsible for running the family. The Press dubbed the killings *The Scarecrow Murders* because each man was tied to a cross and set on fire at the exact same time while they were alive.

The rest of Rappini's men immediately followed their new "Don" without question, and Don Giovanni paid them back with more money than they ever dreamed possible. Even the lowest ranking member made at least fifty grand a week. Ninety percent of the cocaine going up Americans' noses passed through South Florida.

In the late 90s, Giovanni saw the handwriting on the wall with the drug business. Too many people were dying, long prison sentences were becoming mandatory thanks to President Clinton, and a lot of guys began testifying for the government.

"I'm not going to spend the rest of my days in prison, Carlito," Giovanni said, as he placed the Iguana on the ground. He stood up and looked out his study window that had a panoramic view of the Atlantic Ocean. His mind wandered to his last trial when the Feds made up a lot of garbage about his running a criminal organization and indicted him under R.I.C.O. (Racketeering Influence Corrupt Organization).

Giovanni turned from the window and looked down at Carlito, who was slowly crawling away over a Persian rug. "But we had Peter 'The

Great' to protect us . . . didn't we? I'm not going to die in prison like Gotti. Plus, I don't think the government will let me take you to prison, and you know I can't live without you." He looked affectionately at Carlito, who went under a couch in the far corner.

Giovanni walked to his study door, opened it, and said to Oscar, one of his trusted bodyguards, "Summon Antonio."

— 8 —

DON GIOVANNI CHOSE his underboss, Antonio "Magic Man" Barrera, to take the reins. Antonio was the son of Sicilian parents who emigrated to Argentina three days after he was born in 1962. Even though he was born in Italy and full Sicilian blood, since he was raised in Argentina, the heads of the five families (Lucchese, Bonanno, Gambino, Genovese, and Columbo) gave Giovanni problems when he made Antonio an official member of *La Cosa Nostra*. They treated him like he was a Puerto Rican.

Antonio didn't care. It just meant he didn't have to deal much with the outdated figure heads from a time gone by. They sure liked the money he made them though. At last estimate by the Department of Justice, Antonio Barrera was worth approximately twelve billion dollars. If Forbes had a *richest mobster list*, he'd be at the top.

Antonio was sitting at his sports bar/strip club, heavier on the stripping, named *In The Hole*, located on Washington Street in South Beach, Miami. He motioned to the girl-next-door type bartender. "Give me another, Gina." He turned back to face his 'guest'. "I don't think so, Chase. The Port and everything around it is mine . . . I get a piece of everything, including what's underground—data also has a tax when it moves through the ports of South Florida."

"Antonio, you're being unreasonable in this matter. You get a tax on the shipping containers, the trains that connect to the ports, the trucking, pretty much everything already. I was the one who figured out a way to tax data and I created all those no-show union jobs. Those fucking cables and server switches always need repair. And your club girls make a killing from all those IT geeks that work at the docks now," State Senator Chase Reynolds responded, reaching for his craft IPA beer and taking a sip.

Antonio visualized smashing the pint glass over Chase's head. He could picture the blood flowing down his blonde hair and lizard-like face. Not because Chase was trying to rip him off and play him for a fool, Chase would quickly realize that was a bad move, but Antonio hated the fact that these young, arrogant politicians always wanted to drink this new age garbage. *What happened to a scotch on the rocks or plain old Budweiser?* "If money comes from any port in South Florida, my backyard, I get a piece. I will take forty percent now . . . I was going to take only thirty, but you must learn to respect my authority."

"This is bullshit! It's because I'm not Italian. You're not the *boss*. I want counsel with Don Giovanni," Chase demanded, standing as if to leave. He realized as he was standing that he likely made a fatal mistake. If only he could rewind life five seconds. Chase saw Joseph approaching from his right. . . .

Antonio took a sip of scotch, then put his glass down . . . he turned and looked at Chase with his icy blue stare. "Fifty percent now. If you say another word, I will take one hundred percent because you won't be around to collect anything. Do you understand me?"

"Uh . . . thirty percent is good."

"Now thank me and get out of here."

"Tha . . . thanks," Chase said, flinching as Joseph stopped in front of them. Chase put his head down, like an obedient dog, turned, and quickly left—not able to finish his IPA.

Joseph leaned into Antonio and whispered, "Don Giovanni wants to see you, now."

"Is he here?" Antonio asked, with a concerned look on his face. Giovanni never traveled unless he was fleeing some indictment or delivering a message that required a personal touch, which usually meant bad things for the recipient.

Joseph answered, "No, but I was told you must leave now. His private jet is waiting for you at our friend's airstrip."

"Meet me out front." Antonio drained his drink and left a hundred-dollar bill on the bar for Gina.

Joseph added as Antonio was about to turn and leave through the back, "I was also told to tell you that *the TV is out*, whatever that means."

Antonio knew it was a pass phrase to authenticate who you were when meeting with the Don. Sometimes the best security was the most low-tech.

When the boss wanted to see you right away in this business, it usually wasn't a good thing. Antonio went over the past few months in his mind to try and remember if he had offended Giovanni in anyway. . . . *Could it have to do with this nonsense with Chase? I sent him his monthly package of ten million cash on time. I didn't kill anyone I shouldn't.*

For a second, the thought to run crossed his mind, but where do you run to and hide when the Mafia has people in every country and city across the globe. Running was futile; he knew he would have to board Giovanni's private jet.

— 9 —

JASON STEPPED OUT of the shower and wrapped a towel around his lean waist. He walked into the living room and grabbed his iPad to check the lotto numbers. "Damn, one number again. I guess I'm going to work today, buddy." Caesar had moved from the bed to the couch while Jason was in the shower. He dressed in a blue, Men's Wearhouse suit that didn't look half bad on him. He picked up his keys and headed for the door. "Don't work too hard today, Caesar."

Jason's commute was only a five-minute drive North on Flagler drive along the palm tree lined Intracoastal Waterway. Jason pulled into the parking garage connected to the Palm Beach County Courthouse. The parking garage acted as a barrier separating the Courthouse from "the Hood." It was built in 1994—HBO did a documentary in the late 80s called *Crack Town USA* that was partly filmed where the Courthouse now sits.

He crossed the train tracks then Quadrille Avenue, walking east. The Courthouse façade was a brown, tan, and green marble with sandstone and bronze accents. The grounds leading to massive archways on the east and westside of the courthouse were littered with partial concrete barriers made to look like art with inscriptions like *Equal Justice for All*—they were added after 9/11 to stop a car bomber from driving up to the entrance. The Judges thought they would be a target of terrorism because the Palm Beach County Courthouse was the site of the *hanging-chad* controversy from the Bush/Gore election in 2000.

"Good morning, Rhonda," Jason said to the security guard standing at the metal detector and x-ray machine.

"Mornin', counselor. You have a good long weekend?" Rhonda responded.

"Better than the Dolphins weekend. They lost again—fourth loss in a row."

"I hear that," the guard said, as Jason approached the metal detector.

Jason grabbed his stuff out of the plastic bin that just rolled out of the x-ray machine and walked to the elevator bank that was between both sides of the security line. "Day after a holiday," he muttered to himself, as he jammed into the elevator lobby with the others, all looking up at the digital, green numbers above each of the twelve elevator doors; the entire crowd ready to swarm the first door to open like a school of fish. *Ding!* The elevator closest to Jason opened. *Must be my lucky day.* As he was pushing into the elevator, he heard a commotion on the *General Public* side. A slurred voice yelled, "I's not goin' inside wi-out me VODKA. . . ." *What an idiot . . . the guy probably had a DUI. I'm sure when he's found guilty it will be his lawyer's fault!* Jason thought as the elevator doors closed.

Jason got off at "the Penthouse". For the past two years he worked exclusively before Judge Georgia Reese—a/k/a "No Release" Reese. Each felony judge's courtroom was assigned three assistant public defenders. The State Attorney staffed each courtroom with four prosecutors—word on the street was that the newly elected State Attorney, Tripp Sanchez, only added a prosecutor to one-up Public Defender Kelly Hudson.

Judge "No Release" Reese would lock a person up for a minor marijuana charge, and she gave new meaning to the phrase "rocket docket." Defendants never had to worry about their constitutional right to a speedy trial being violated in *her* courtroom. A case that should take a year to prepare for trial, Judge Reese would set it for trial in sixty days. She was worse than federal judges, Jason had heard, from lawyers who practiced in federal court. From their horror stories, he wanted no part of practicing criminal defense in federal court. He hated Judge Reese, but at least she didn't routinely lock up the lawyers, like some federal judges. The prosecutors loved Judge Reese, as long as they didn't slow a case down, they got everything they wanted from her.

Judge Reese had one good quality: she caused most of Jason's clients to want to plead guilty instead of going to trial and take the risk of having her sentence them if they were convicted. Which was fine by Jason; even though he was a "trial attorney," he had a debilitating fear of speaking in public causing him to stutter, which didn't help inspire much confidence in him by his clients. In his first trial, he asked the jury to find his client *Guilty* by mistake. Sure, his client was guilty, but his own lawyer shouldn't tell a jury that.

"Mornin', Richard," Jason said to Assistant State Attorney Richard Deal.

"Hey, Jason. Packed house this morning?" Richard replied without looking up from his files.

Courtroom 11H had one of the best views in Palm Beach County—the entire east wall was ceiling to floor glass that looked out over downtown West Palm Beach, the Intercostal waterway, Palm Beach, and the Atlantic Ocean. If you had to go to prison, it was truly a magnificent view to remember as your last one for a while.

"It's already starting to get loud in the courtroom. Should put Reese in a *fine* mood," Richard remarked as he pulled files from a full banker's box. "You know she only likes to hear the sound of her own voice."

"What's with the cameras?" Jason asked, as he opened his iPad to look at his list of forty felony clients set for arraignment—arraignment is a defendant's first court date after the initial bond hearing immediately following arrest; it is the official starting point of a criminal prosecution. The defendant's lawyer simply enters a plea of *not guilty*, requests discovery (evidence state has against the defendant), and gets a new court date down the road sixty or so days. Most defendants with private lawyers didn't even have to show up for arraignment, neither did the lawyers. The lawyer simply filed a written plea of *not guilty* and demand for discovery. *To be a private lawyer,* Jason dreamed.

"Some Palm Beacher's twenty-year-old kid got arrested with a seventeen-year-old and a couple of ecstasy pills," Richard said as he pulled a file out of his box.

"*Four* TV stations for *that*. Must be a slow news day. I've got better than that. Let's see." Jason grabbed the thick court calendar on the table and flipped through the twenty-two pages of defendants. "Here's a good one . . . six counts of exploitation of a minor under twelve for the purpose of prostitution, or this one's even better, attempted murder with a device designed for torture. Give me a break, the media has nothing better to do."

"Rough holiday weekend? What are you ranting about *now*, Jason?" Claudia Perez asked as she sat down next to him, playfully pinching his arm. She was another Assistant Public Defender assigned to "No Release" Reese's courtroom.

"Oh, nothing, just wishing the media would actually report on a case that's important not the crap they usually report on . . . and, I didn't win the lottery again," he answered, frowning.

"You should rethink your stance on the media . . . look back again at that reporter in the white dress . . . mm, mm, mmmm," Claudia said, now staring at the female reporter in white.

Jason and Richard snapped their heads around to look . . . Jason's mouth dropped open. He couldn't help but stare at the reporter in white's natural beauty: straight, long, black hair; tanned, smooth skin, clearly ethnic—maybe Italian or Middle Eastern; and her eyes . . . large, brown, doe eyes that sucked Jason right in. "Um . . ." Jason broke his stare and looked at Claudia. "It would never work . . . she's the most beautiful girl I've ever seen, but she's a crime reporter."

"Hear Ye! Hear Ye! All rise before the Honorable Judge Georgia Reese of the Fifteenth Judicial Circuit in and for Palm Beach County Florida," the courtroom deputy, Cedric Johnson bellowed, as Judge Reese entered the courtroom from a "secret" door behind the bench. "Remain standing!" Deputy Johnson continued, moving his six foot five inch frame from behind Judge Reese's black marble bench to the left where courtroom clerk Katrina sat. The clerk's workstation extended from the judge's bench along the side wall of the courtroom.

Judge Reese sat in her oversized black leather chair and took her sweet time pouring a drink of water from the stainless-steel pitcher on her bench. She shuffled some papers then looked up with her constant scowl and barked into her microphone, "Be seated." The one hundred and fifty people packed into the courtroom like sardines sat in unison. "Madam Clerk, who's first?" She sat up a bit straighter upon noticing the TV cameras.

Clerk Katrina handled all Judge Reese's case files for the day. She made sure every case was called, the paperwork was properly filled out on each one, and that every defendant signed for their next court date, which was vitally important to Judge Reese. When they didn't show up or were ten minutes late, Judge Reese could revoke their bond and have them hauled back to jail for failing to appear in court on time. It didn't matter to her whether the person was late because the security line was extremely long or because their car broke down. Defendants in jail plead out their cases and that's what she wanted—exercising one's constitutional right to a trial took too much court time in her view.

"Vincent Tribolie, charge is throwing a deadly missile into an occupied dwelling," Clerk Katrina said into her microphone. Generally,

Katrina called the names in alphabetical order, but if a defendant was fortunate enough to have a private lawyer, she would call those cases first. The rational was that private lawyers generally had multiple court-rooms to attend every morning, and they needed to get in and out of each one quickly. Assistant Public Defenders were in the same courtroom all morning, so it didn't matter if they had to wait to call their cases. The reality was that private lawyers donated to judges' and the head clerk of court's re-election campaigns, and this was one of the perks.

"Where is Mr. Tribolie?" Judge Reese asked.

The reporters and cameramen snapped to attention. Three lawyers in three-thousand-dollar custom-made suits approached the podium. "Good morning, Your Honor, Thomas Prescott here on behalf of Mr. Tribolie. And with me is—"

"One of you is enough, the other two lawyers sit down, this is an arraignment not argument before the U.S. Supreme Court," Judge Reese sternly informed Prescott.

"But, Your Honor—"

"*But Your Honor* what?" she snapped, peering down at him over her reading glasses. "Is this your first time in court?" she asked, not expecting an answer, as the people in the gallery laughed. She narrowed her eyes and looked at the gallery. "Quiet! Or I will remove all of you from the courtroom and issue each of you warrants for failing to appear." Looking back at Prescott, who was standing at the podium embarrassed, she instructed, "Arraignment is simple, three lawyers aren't necessary. You don't need to play to the cameras in this courtroom." Judge Reese looked down, smoothing out her robe, making sure it wasn't wrinkled.

As the other two lawyers were walking back to the gallery, Prescott said, "But, Your Honor, I'm also moving for the Court to set a reasonable bond for my client."

Deputy Johnson looked up at the ceiling and rolled his eyes, he knew what was coming. "Madam Clerk, enter a plea of not guilty on behalf of the uncooperative defendant and his lawyer and set the case for trial at my next available time slot."

"Judge, our next trial date is in May, seven months from now," Clerk Katrina responded.

"So, set it. The defendant will stay in custody until then or he'll hire a lawyer who knows what he's doing. Next case."

Jason disliked private criminal defense lawyers because their clients usually got all the best deals and they made real money. But he disliked Judge Reese more. He stood up from behind the defense table, walked to the podium and whispered in Prescott's ear: "Tell her your client is a juvenile being held no-bond, and she will briefly let you argue for one—exactly five minutes, so make it quick."

"Are you on this case Noble?" Judge Reese snapped.

"No judge, I was just—"

"Then sit down until you have a case called."

As Clerk Katrina was about to call the next case, Prescott interrupted, "Your Honor, Mr. Tribolie is a juvenile."

"Hold on, Madam Clerk, which one is Mr. Tribolie?" Judge Reese asked with a look of frustration, as she turned and looked at the shackled inmates that were in the jury box. The jury box held fourteen inmates at a time. Out of the fourteen currently in the box: eight were black men, three white men, one Hispanic female, one white female, and one seventeen-year-old Italian kid. The adult men and woman wore blue scrubs with crocs—very trendy. An inmate wore orange scrubs if he was a disciplinary problem. Juveniles charged as adults wore red scrubs, which made them easily identifiable, and thus easy prey to the adult inmate population. All inmates were handcuffed from a chain around their waist and shackled around the ankles with a chain connecting the two. The shackles were removed once the inmates were seated in the jury box and a deputy stood guard on each end.

"Fine, I'll hear your bond motion." Judge Reese begrudgingly agreed. "You should have just told me your client was a juvenile from the beginning, and we would have saved a lot of time. You have five minutes."

"Thank you, Your Honor," Prescott said. *If you just shut up for a minute, I would have told you that.*

Deputy Jennifer O'Malley, who was stationed outside the courtroom, walked over to counsel table, bent down and whispered, "Jason, there's a rough-looking guy, last name Wilson, yelling your name outside in the hall." Jason got up from counsel table in a huff and mumbled under his breath, "I can't take care of everyone at the same time." He walked as close as he could to the reporter in the white dress on the way out. *She's more beautiful up close.* She caught him looking at her as he passed. Jason thought he detected a slight smile.

—11—

TREVOR WITTINGHAM UNLOCKED his office door and walked in at six a.m. He was always the first person in the office—another reason his staff disliked him. He was only at the office so early because he wanted to get out of his house as soon as possible every morning.

Trevor had a corner office on the fifteenth floor of the J. Edger Hoover Federal building located in downtown Miami. The office was typical government drab—light gray walls with mismatched, well-used furniture, and a faded carpet. The focal point was his view of Biscayne Bay—a spectacular view wasted on him. He placed his black briefcase on his desk, sat in his oversized, burgundy, leather chair, and propped his feet up on his dark wood desk. Trevor purchased the chair himself because he didn't like the ones the government provided. He felt the oversized chair made him more imposing to whomever he was talking to, but in reality, it only made him look like a child sitting in a grown-up's chair. From the visitor's side of the desk, it looked like Trevor's feet didn't even hit the ground.

He was reading an article about a conviction of Sonny "Big Pizza" Brasine for money laundering and racketeering. Sonny was a high-ranking mobster in the Pacific Northwest with connections to the NY Ardelo family. He was nicknamed "Big Pizza" because he owned three hundred pizza parlors up and down the West Coast, which was how he laundered his money. *Wow! The mafia is everywhere, even in Oregon*, he thought. The article had a picture of the United States Attorney for Oregon, Robert Evans, standing on the steps of the Wayne L. Morse Federal Courthouse with a quote that read: *I will continue to infiltrate and destroy organized crime . . . regardless of where it hides! The citizens of Oregon can sleep better tonight knowing I made the streets safer with this conviction.*

Trevor thought, *that's what I needed to get to the next level, a good public conviction.*

"Boss! Did you see FOX News!" Assistant U.S. Attorney Tim Barnes said, as he barged into Trevor's office, out of breath. Tim was a butt-kissing new transfer from the Washington, D.C. office. Trevor took a liking to him immediately.

"No. What news?" Trevor quickly put his feet on the floor and his newspaper down on the desk. He looked at Tim suspiciously—*Is he getting to the office before me? Impossible.* "When did you get in?"

"A couple of minutes ago. Hurry, turn on FOX or you'll miss it." Trevor grabbed the remote off his desk and turned on the flat screen TV that was on a credenza to his right. When he flipped to FOX, he saw the Governor of Florida, Stanley Butterworth, speaking to a battery of microphones and cameras—the Governor looked shell-shocked. FOX had the *BREAKING NEWS* graphic in red flashing above him. *Everything seemed to be "breaking news" today*, Trevor thought.

"It is with great sadness and a heavy heart that I announce my resignation as the Governor of the great State of Florida," Governor Butterworth said, as he did his best to act remorseful, which was difficult with the nickname "Steamroller Stan". "I do not wish to put my family through anymore of this investigation . . . they have endured enough."

Trevor's mind was already working overtime on how he could become the next governor of Florida—*This could be my opportunity.* He started to play out scenarios in his head and a smile spread across his face: *Governor Wittingham, the President will see you now . . . Welcome to the governor's mansion, Prime Minister. . . .* He snapped back to reality when he heard Tim's voice say, "Do you think he's guilty?"

"Who cares." Tim looked back at him, incredulous at his response.

The Governor was embroiled in a good old fashion sex and corruption scandal that might actually get him indicted. He was accused of using his software empire to funnel money to the North Korean government in exchange for Korean prostitutes—apparently he had a thing for underage Korean girls. He basically purchased the Florida governor's seat in 2008 when he outspent his opponent one hundred to one. It was the closest vote in Florida's history.

"I knew winning by only thirteen votes was a sign of bad luck," Trevor quipped. Before Tim could open his mouth, Trevor said, "I have work to do, I'll see you at our eleven o'clock meeting." Tim turned and left without saying a word.

Trevor took a deep breath to try and quell the excitement that was bubbling up inside of him at the thought of becoming the next governor of Florida. Sure, he dreamed of running for governor one day, but never with any serious consideration. Ten months until the election and the incumbent, who probably would have run unopposed because nobody could afford to keep up with his spending, just dropped out! The first thing he had to do was call his only family, Luke and Mollie June Maybury.

— 12 —

DON GIOVANNI'S GULFSTREAM G200 landed at Maceo International Airport located in Southeast Cuba. The airport was mostly used for domestic flights and a few "special" international flights. Although most Americans were not allowed to travel to Cuba, Cuba was a friend to the American Mafia and always welcomed them and their money. Don Giovanni held all of his important meetings at his home in Playa Santa Lucia, Cuba. At this stage in his life, he rarely left the safety Cuba offered a mob boss. The Cuban government would never extradite him to America—unless, of course, he ran out of money.

As Antonio exited the terminal, a rush of warm, tropical air splashed over his face. A man approached from his left—a standout at the sparsely populated airport. "Right this way, Sir." The man, dressed in white linen said, as he motioned to a limousine parked in front of a large mural of Che Guevera, the bright sun glistening off Che's head creating a halo effect. He said nothing and followed the man to the limo. Antonio sat in silence for the entire thirty-minute ride to Don Giovanni's oceanfront estate. His mind twisted full of thoughts the entire ride. Each thought leading to the same end—*death*.

The limousine pulled up to ten feet high wrought iron gates. On either side of the gates stood four men, two to a side, standing at attention like guards at Buckingham Palace. While no guns were visible on the guards, no doubt each one had a small arsenal under their suits. "*Hola*," one of the guards said, as he walked to the driver's side window. From the back seat of the limousine Antonio's face was not visible to the guard outside.

Antonio said, "The TV is out." The guard knew better than to even glance into the back of the limousine.

Don Giovanni invited many high-profile visitors from all over the world, especially America. The politicians and entertainment industry executives who were always a friend of the Mafia were recently joined by technology and software startup company guys, venture capitalists, and pharmaceutical executives—thanks to Antonio. All of whom wanted Don Giovanni's help in one way or another, but none wanted to be seen at the home of a reputed mob boss, or in Cuba, for that matter. The guard immediately motioned for the gate to open and let the limo through.

The driveway was about one hundred yards long and led to a twelve-bedroom, ten-bath mansion, sitting atop an oceanside cliff. The grounds were meticulously landscaped with fountains, palm trees, tropical flowers, and limestone walkways. The house exterior was smooth white stucco with extra-large doorways, windows, porticos, and balconies—a masterpiece of Neoclassical design.

The limo drove to the apex of the driveway, around a large white marble fountain with statutes of several nude woman pouring water over their heads from pitchers, and stopped at the entrance. Antonio stepped out of the back seat, looked around, then walked to the front doors, which were twenty-feet high and made of sturdy looking dark, almost black, wood with iron framing. They reminded Antonio of a Spanish Galleon. They opened like it was scripted. No doubt Don Giovanni knew exactly the moment he arrived. He undoubtedly was digitally scanned for bugs multiple times since he stepped foot on the private jet in Florida.

"Please come in, Sir. Welcome back, Mr. Barrera." Carlo, Giovanni's longtime servant greeted.

"Thank you, Carlo." Antonio didn't look at Carlo but scanned the marble foyer, especially in the shadows.

"This way, Sir." Carlo walked toward a sweeping double staircase and through the center of it toward the back of the house. Antonio was led to a back patio that had a majestic view of the Atlantic Ocean. It was made of what looked like a bluish marble that perfectly matched the azure color of the Atlantic. Just beyond the upper patio was an Olympic-sized pool with a colorful Italian fresco covering most of its floor. On the patio to the right was a table with a white umbrella set for two.

"Please sit." Carlo pulled out one of the chairs. "Would you like something to drink or eat?"

"No, I will just wait. I'm fine standing."

Carlo walked off into the house. Antonio walked to the edge of the patio and scanned the palm tree, bougainvillea, and sea grape covered grounds. . . .

"How do you sleep with the demons, my old friend?" Don Giovanni asked, as he entered the patio from the house.

"I sleep sound. How about you, my friend?"

"I'm too old to worry about demons." Giovanni laughed.

He walked over and embraced Antonio and kissed him on each cheek. "So good to see you. How long has it been?"

"Almost a year. I assume you've been getting my monthly packages?"

"Yes, yes . . . it's like Christmas once a month." Giovanni disengaged the embrace and walked to the table that now had sliced fruit, orange juice, and coffee on it. "You're probably wondering why you're here." Giovanni took a slice of pineapple from the table.

"Since you rarely call on me anymore, I was wondering why you needed to see me so quickly. A thought of concern crossed my mind."

"Ahh . . . don't be concerned. Pineapple?" He pointed to a slice. "It's the best in the world."

"No, thanks. Why am I here?" Antonio pressed on.

"This business of ours makes us paranoid. If I wanted to kill you, I wouldn't have sent my private jet for you."

"That's good . . . I guess. Then why did you call me to Cuba? Surely not to eat fruit and stare at the ocean."

"Of course not. Although, this pineapple is worth the trip alone. Let's take a walk on the beach and talk."

They walked down a limestone pathway that meandered through

the lush tropical landscape and opened up to the beach. Don Giovanni noticed a family of four walking and laughing about fifty yards to their left. He pulled a small device that looked like an old beeper out of his pocket and hit a button on it. Within a blink of an eye, Carlo appeared. "Yes? What do you need?"

"Those people are too close, remove them from the area. Don't kill them, just make them to leave now."

"Yes, Sir." Carlo turned and walked toward the family.

"I have to be careful what I tell Carlo, he wants to kill everyone," Giovanni said, smiling. "Useful, but it could create unnecessary problems."

Giovanni and Antonio continued walking side by side down the sand along the ocean break. "I'm getting old, Antonio."

"Nonsense, you are still young, seventy-six is the new fifty."

"No, my time has come and gone. Someone else must guide *La Famiglia* now. This new millennium needs a new leader."

"You're letting your age cloud your judgment."

Giovanni stopped, turned toward Antonio, grabbed him by the shoulders, and stared deeply into his eyes. "Yes . . . yes . . . you are the right one. You can take the pitchfork from the devil. A fearless leader you will become. Actually, a fearless leader you already are."

Antonio couldn't believe his ears; he never heard of anyone *retiring* from the Mafia. You were either killed by your successor or went to prison until you died, but not retire. He breathed a sigh of relief that Giovanni wasn't going to kill him. "You have a lot of good years left," Antonio said as he broke the stare, turned, and continued walking.

"No, it is *you* who has a lot of good years left to lead the Family. I gave the Mafia cocaine . . . and then crack. I made my billions. Today, drugs are a dying business and part of me died with it. It's time to move on . . . hell, you have essentially been running things for the past several years anyway—the formal transition will be easy. The men already respect your leadership. It's time to make it official."

Antonio could hardly contain the jubilation welling-up inside of him. *Finally! My time has come!* "What will the five families say?"

"They will accept you if I say so. Do not worry about those *pazzo vecchio* (crazy old men). They will respect my decision. And, if they don't . . . I will make them." A look of intensity washed over Giovanni's face as he spoke. "They ran like *polli spaventati* (scared chickens) when I made you my consigliere and "inducted" you into *La Cosa Nostra*. The first made member not raised in Italy or America. The Commission never understood the benefits of your unique background—full Sicilian blood, so you have the unyielding loyalty necessary for this business of ours, and raised in Argentina—Latin roots are a must to rule South Florida and take full advantage of the spoils of Latin corruption. . . . I long for the days of *Chaves, Castro, Pinochet, Noriega* . . . these were great men to work with in this thing of ours. Well, maybe using Noriega's banks wasn't such a good idea in hindsight. Send them their envelope every month and they will leave you to run a very profitable business in the sunshine and palm trees."

Giovanni stopped, reached up and put both hands on Antonio's face, and pulled him close, almost nose to nose. "You are about to receive untold power in this world, Antonio, always be true to *La Famiglia*."

— 13 —

"WILLIE WILSON, IS there a Willie Wilson out here?" Jason yelled into the hallway outside of the courtroom. The hallway was full of lawyers; defendants; police officers; random courthouse personnel; and families of grandmas, aunties, and children—sadly, not too many dads or uncles were standing in the hallway, they were usually the ones in blue scrubs and shackles inside the courtroom. To the outsider it looked like utter chaos, but to those working in the criminal justice system, it was how it functioned on a daily basis—*organized chaos*.

"Willie Wilson," he said, again.

"Righ'here," said a hard-looking white guy, wearing a black leather vest with biker patches covering the front. Willie had squinty eyes and a dirty gray beard. He was leaning over on one of the two benches outside the courtroom in the vestibule. "Yoouzz my laaawy-er." His voice slurred and raspy. Either he had a stroke or a few drinks before court—Jason guessed the latter.

"You're Willie Wilson?" Jason recoiled from the strong odor of alcohol emanating from Willie.

"Thhhat's my name, don' weeear it'out," he said through a drunk laugh, then leaned over a bit more like the bench was slowly teetertottering on an imaginary pivot point. "They took me vodkey downstairs . . . I waaaan it back. Go ge-it *public pretender.*" Willie's laughing turned into a coughing fit.

At this rate, Willie won't be society's problem much longer, or mine. I've got to get a new job, Jason thought. He opened his iPad and looked at his case summary for the day. "You've got to be kidding me, Willie. You're here for your fourth DUI . . . and you show up to court drunk!"

"I's ain't dunk."

A DUI (driving under the influence) was normally a misdemeanor charge, but when you accumulated three or more, it became a felony, at the choice of the prosecutor, punishable by up to five years in prison. *This guy should be locked up forever; what a waste of air—new job, new job, new job.* "Move over." He sat on the bench next to Willie, putting his hand on Willie's right shoulder to help him sit upright since he was moving like he was stuck in molasses. The second Jason sat, he felt it. His ass and back of his legs were wet instantly—not a cold wetness but a warm one.

"What the?" Jason jumped up. The people standing in the immediate area turned around to look at him. Thankfully he didn't yell, which would have drawn the attention of the entire hallway and probably a few bailiffs from inside the courtrooms. He looked down at the light wood bench and saw a puddle of clearish liquid. Willie was passed out now, leaning over to the other side. Jason turned around and looked at the back of his tan suit. He touched the wetness on the back of his pants and smelled his hand. *Great! I just sat in a drunk, derelict client's piss. New job . . . new job . . . new job.* His ass and back of his thighs were soaked. The smell of urine started to permeate the vestibule. Some of the people standing around started to laugh.

"Yo . . . that dude just sat in piss!" yelled one onlooker.

Jason put his head down, the last thing he wanted to do was make eye contact with anyone. He took his phone out of his pocket and texted Claudia who was inside Reese's courtroom: *just sat in piss going hm. cover 4 me. BTW tell Dep. Johnson there's a passed-out defendant on bench outside courtroom.*

— 14 —

"HEY, JASON, WHERE'RE you going? I thought you had a trial in front of 'No Release Reese' this morning?" Aaron Moskowitz asked, as Jason, with his head down, stormed past him in the walkway between the courthouse and Public Defender's Office.

"Not a good time, Aaron," Jason said without stopping or looking back.

Aaron turned around and could see the big wet spot down the back of Jason's tan suit. "You know your suit is wet in the back?"

"Thanks for telling me the obvious." He waived his hand in the air in frustration. *New job, new job, new job. . . .*

Jason yanked open the large glass with bronze trim entrance door to the Public Defender's office. Its facade mirrored the courthouse—big slabs of reddish and tan marble with green trim covered the six-story office building. Jason charged into the lobby. "How you doing Moses?" Jason said with an unintended edge. He always said "hello" to the guards and court personnel, some lawyers were rude to the staff, they felt above them, which was ridiculous, because so many lawyers didn't deserve a *hello* from even the devil. Jason learned a long time ago when he lived in a group-home in the bowery neighborhood of New York City that the janitor could be the nicest person to him. The "professionals" who hid behind their degrees always seemed to do everything with their own self-interest in mind. "Good mornin', Jason. Keep your head up," Security Officer Moses Brooks replied. Moses was probably in his eighties and likely couldn't see a bazooka if it went through the x-ray machine, but it didn't really matter. The clients that the Public Defender's office served weren't a threat to the physical safety of its staff. Even though they generally mistrusted and disliked their "free" lawyer, a criminal defendant wasn't going to hurt him or her; they knew they needed that "free" lawyer to have any chance of making it out of the criminal justice system with a possible future outside prison.

Jason walked through the lobby to the elevator. He rode the elevator to the sixth floor instead of the fifth floor where his office was. He'd had it—*New job, new job, new job.* He knew he should go and cool off before he did something stupid, but he couldn't; his mind pushed all rational thought out of his head. Every time he took a step and felt his urine-soaked suit pants rub against his bare skin, his anger exponentially increased.

The elevator doors opened and he quickly stepped out and made a right, bumping into Ms. Elerby, the boss' secretary. "Slow down!" Ms. Elerby said. Jason kept marching with his head down, not hearing her.

He walked directly to Sherman Stills' office at the end of the hall. Sherman was the go-to lawyer when a felony lawyer had a problem.

Jason approached his office door and barged in. "You can't just go in." Jason heard Mary Spencer, Sherman's secretary, say from behind him, but ignored her.

"I've had enough! I was just—"

"Relax . . . and hold that thought," Sherman said, as he closed the law book he was reading. Jason was ready to explode as he stood there impatiently, looking at Sherman for what seemed like ten minutes . . . Sherman looked up from his desk, leaned forward in his chair, and folded his hands in front of him. "Sit down, young Jason."

"I don't think you want me to sit. Trust me."

"Do you want something to drink, Pepsi, coffee, caramel macchiato? Although, I don't think Mary will go to Starbucks and get you the macchiato. I'm not sure she'd get me a cup of water if I was stranded in the dessert," Sherman said with a slight smile. "Why don't you just take a Pepsi." He turned and reached under the credenza behind him and opened a small fridge, grabbed a Pepsi, turned back around, and gave it to Jason. "I like Pepsi, but sometimes it makes me have to pee."

"Thanks, but no thanks. I'm not thirsty."

"Just sit then. You're making me nervous standing there." Sherman knew a young lawyer in distress when he saw one. Many assistant public defenders were in their twenties, most were green and ill-equipped to deal with the stress and horror that was the criminal justice system in America, especially for a defense attorney. Society loved the prosecutors, but defense attorneys were vilified—*How can you do what you do*, which every criminal defense attorney hears at least once at every cocktail party. From Sherman's observation, Jason was just overwhelmed—one too many child sex cases or violent, home invasion robberies, or another ungrateful client who treated you like the lowest form of garbage, even though you saved them years of their life. Most of the time the young lawyer just needed to take a deep breath and vent, maybe a day or two off, and then they were fine for a while and back on the assembly line of justice.

In Sherman's twenty-seven years as an assistant public defender, he had only one lawyer commit suicide by jumping out of her office window. After Mildred Boozeman jumped to her death, the office permanently locked all the windows and made every lawyer wear a circular sticker on their hand that would change color when someone was stressed out. It was the dumbest thing, but it was the eighties. And, as people in high stress or morbid jobs tend to do, they made jokes when a person's dot would turn red, meaning they were about to blow a gasket.

"I quit! This is bullshit dealing with these ungrateful clients. Let's not even talk about the nasty judges who only give a damn about helping the State win every case. Let's not even get into the ridiculous pay! You know . . . I did the math once on my triple rape case—my salary was $10.82 per hour! I can make that at McDonalds or Walmart! I'm done!" Jason exclaimed, rambling on like he was shot out of a cannon.

"Are you *done*?

"I was pissed on this morning!"

Sherman looked at Jason and a smile spread across his face. "That's a first. That was information you should've announced before you sat in my chair. For Pete's sake, Jason, use your head, good furniture is hard to come by working for the government." Sherman slumped back in his chair, letting out a deep exhale.

He pressed the intercom button on his phone. "Mary, get young Jason a towel . . . and see if you can find me a new chair, please."

"*New chair*? Did I hear you right? Why do you need a new chair? I can't get—" Sherman hung up the intercom.

"No, you don't get it, Sherman. I'm done. I'm out. *Sayonara*. I didn't go to law school for this aggravation!"

"Don't be so dramatic, Jason. Fine, if that's what you want to do. Why don't you go home, relax . . . have a beer, smoke a joint, play x-box, or do whatever you young folks do to relax, and we'll talk in the morning."

Mary opened the office door and walked in, a confused scowl on her face. "Thank you, Mary. Please hand Jason the towel," Sherman said.

Jason put the towel under his right thigh and butt. "Thanks." He looked down at the floor, too embarrassed to make eye contact with her.

"What's this about a new chair?" Mary asked, putting her hands on her hips, ready to argue.

"Nothing, it was a joke. That's all. Thank you."

"Not. Funny." She turned and left, closing the door behind her.

Sherman had seen the *look* on Jason's face so many times in his career; heck, he probably had it once too. Although it was worse now and happening much quicker than in the past. The face was creased with the lines of a permanent scowl, hair turned gray well before it should— more common on the men. Just last week Sherman was talking a twenty-six-year-old off the ledge, who had more gray hair than the professor from *Back to the Future*. Jason's right eyelid twitched at random times, something known as "The Stress-Eye."

Thanks to the harsh drug laws enacted at the federal and state level in the nineties, the caseloads for assistant public defenders were out of control. The Public Defender's Office handled most of the cases in the system. Ninety percent of defendants had no money to hire a decent private lawyer—crime really didn't pay. Lawyers in their twenties with no experience were carrying caseloads of more than one hundred cases, each one more serious than the next: murder after murder, beatings, stabbings, rapes, drug trafficking. You name it, an assistant public defender has dealt with it. Some state courts recently declared that, because the felony caseloads of assistant public defenders were so ridiculously high, all the lawyers were *per se* ineffective.

Sherman was reminded of a joke at that moment and he laughed. "Jason, what do dinosaurs and honest lawyers have in common?"

"Huh?"

"What do dinosaurs and honest lawyers have in common?"

"You think this is a good time for a joke . . . I don't know."

"They're both extinct." Sherman chuckled as he delivered the punchline. Jason didn't find it funny. "Jason, you've only been in "No Release" Reece's felony division for nine months. Give it time. You'll get more comfortable."

"Why, so someone can actually take a crap on me and then ask me to apologize for being in his way when he had to take a dump! No, thank you. I'm out. Done. No more public *pretender* for me. If I'm going to be poor, I might as well be happy!" Jason proclaimed, leaping out of his chair, raising his hand with his pointer-finger up. A serene look suddenly washed over his face.

Sherman leaned forward in his chair, concerned about the change in Jason's expression; he looked like he was going to pass out. "Jason, take the rest of the week off. I'll get someone to cover your cases, think about what you want to do."

"I thought about it for a long time now."

"How could you have thought about it for a long time? You've only been at the office for three years."

"Being an assistant public defender is like working in dog years, every year equals seven. . . . Thank you for the opportunity, but I quit. I'm sorry. Feel free to tell whoever takes over my caseload to call me." Jason extended his hand. "Bye Sherman, you've been an excellent mentor."

Sherman shook his hand out of habit. "Jason, don't make a foolish decision, you could—" Jason withdrew his hand and quickly walked out.

He went down one floor to the fifth and walked to his office without saying a word to anyone. He retrieved the only two personal items in his office: a framed poster with one of those inspirational sayings—*you can overcome* with a picture of a guy standing at the base of a lighthouse with twenty foot waves crashing around him, and a book of lawyer jokes his constitutional law professor gave him when he graduated with the parting advice—*Don't take yourself too serious.* Jason thought for a moment and only grabbed the book of jokes.

"Goodbye, Cindy," Jason said to his secretary, who sat in a cubicle right outside his office.

"Goin' home for the day? It's only ten o'clock." Cindy spoke while cracking a piece of gum.

"No, I'm going home for good. I just quit. My files are self-explanatory. Good luck." Jason turned and left.

He'll be back, Cindy thought. *They always come back.* "By the way, the back of your pants are wet. Is it raining out?"

"I'll be a crackerjack! If it ain' lil' T.T. on the teeleephone!" Luke May-bury said. "Mollie June, T.T.'s callin' from tha big ci-tay. Quick, go get a lotto ticket, it must be our lucky day." As he spoke on the phone, Luke stared at his wife of fifty-one years who was standing in the kitchen placing a blueberry pie on the windowsill.

"Gooolly, Luke! I reckon he may have the *wrong* number," Mollie June responded back. She felt bad about using sarcasm, but it was fun to razz Trevor.

"Quit it, *Liquid White*," Trevor said, into the phone with a light laugh.

"What the heck you sayin' that name for on tha phone," Luke's stern voice quickly whipped the smile off Trevor's face.

"*Relax* . . . I'm sure the statute of limitations on bootlegging has runout on any shine you ran back in the day."

Luke cradled the phone in his ear as he stood up from his rocking chair in the wood paneled sitting room and walked over to a window that looked out over his expansive backyard. It was packed with old-growth fir, spruce, maple trees beset by snow-covered mountains in the background. Luke had an amused look on his face. "You can breathe now, 'T.T.' I'm only jokin' wit' ya."

"Stop pokin' fun at poor, 'T.T.', you'll give 'em a heart attack," Mollie June said, as she took potholders off her delicate hands.

"Why are you always messing with me, Dad? And stop calling me *T.T.*; you know I hate that name."

"In't 'T.T.' better than *Tattletale Trevor*?" Trevor let the moment pass; he didn't want to go down the rabbit hole of arguing with Luke—a futile endeavor at best.

Luke Maybury was a seventh generation North Carolinian from Forest City. His family was one of the original settlers, off the Mayflower, in North Carolina when it was founded by King Charles II in 1663. Although, Luke's people added some Cherokee Indian to his blood line in the 1800s. That's why he never got caught up in the racism that plagued the country and particularly the South in his youth. He was a God-fearing Southerner through and through with respect for all of his fellow man and woman. And he was wealthy, beyond imagination.

"Did you see the news about the governor of Florida?" Trevor asked, with a hint of excitement in his voice.

"Well, course I did, what do ya think . . . me and Mollie June live under a rock."

"I'm going to run for governor of Florida," Trevor beamed with pride on the other end of the phone—his smile ear to ear. "With your backing I really—"

"Now I reckon what this call's 'bout. Not a *hello, how ya doin'* call, but a let me reach into your pocket call," Luke said, slumping back in his chair. "I can't help ya, I live on social security."

"Stop lying, Liquid," Trevor said, trying to bait Luke, which was never a good idea. "You've got more money than God."

"Watch your tongue, boy," Luke's stern tone was rarely used unless the Lord's name was taken in vain. "DO NOT slander the good Lord's name . . . am I making myself clear?"

"Yes, Sir," Trevor's voice barely audible.

As a youngster in the 50s and 60s, Luke struck it rich making C_2H_5OH, better known as moonshine. Some of the finest moonshine or *White Lightnin'*, as the locals called it, this country had ever tasted. His family had been in the moonshine business since they came over on the Mayflower. Much to their dismay, he broke the cycle when he was twenty-nine and quit the business, sort of. He gave all his money to the Local Church and went legitimate after he and Mollie June adopted Trevor. Although, he always made a little *White Lightnin'* for family and close friends. He figured that the Lord wouldn't get too mad if he made a little hooch for personal use.

Then, in 1998, he had a brilliant idea. He saw the home brew beer business taking off and thought he could do the same for spirits. *Home brew whiskey* was just a legal way of saying moonshine. He developed a simple copper distillery kit for "home" use and called it *Country Luke's Home Brew Moonshine*. It cost him a total of $9.99 to make in China and he sold them around the world through the internet and infomercials for $109.99. His kits were continually top sellers on Amazon. If anyone could fund a political campaign, Luke could.

Luke and Trevor spoke for about ten more minutes with Luke raising his voice a few times. "Goodbye, Trevor, and I'm sorry I can't help you. Ya know, a visit occasionally to us poor old country folks wouldn't kill ya . . . and don't only call when you need something."

"Yes, Sir," Trevor responded. "Please tell ma, I love her."

"Will do, Son. And we love you too." Luke hung up the phone. "I don't know what that boy's up'ta Miss Mollie, but I tell you what—his constant need to prove himself is fixin' to git him in trouble."

Mollie June was standing in the living room now, looking at Luke. "Oh dear . . . Pride goethe before the fall," Mollie June said, quoting scripture, as she was prone to do when worried.

— 16 —

"Jesus, Mary, and Joseph! It looks like a floating black sun from up here . . ." gasped Coast Guard helicopter pilot, Chief Petty Officer Dakota Jones, who was hovering her HH-65 Dolphin over the Atlantic Ocean at about 1000 feet. . . . The media would later dub it: "THE FLOATING DEATH SUN."

The pilot circled the chopper around, tilting its axis to the right so the copilot and three crew of seamen could get a look. . . . "We're definitely gonna have nightmares," the copilot yelled over the whirling blades. Seaman Li Ko immediately vomited. Lucky for the crew he was closest to the open door.

"Looks like . . . Jamaicans . . . over," Jones finally said into her radio mouthpiece, mesmerized by "the floating death sun."

"How do you figure? Over." responded Captain Terry Johnson of the U.S.S. Teddy Roosevelt, who had an ETA of three minutes to the scene.

Jones held the chopper in a stationary hover. She couldn't take her eyes off the seven black men attached to each other, spread eagle, forming a circle. Lazily meandering over the small, lapping waves. "Well . . . uh . . . Captain . . . how shall I say this . . . they're wearing their country's colors." Tiny green and yellow Jamaican flags were flapping in the light wind as they stuck out of each floating man's eyes. "And . . . the dreadlocks. All of them got 'em. Floatin' like sea snakes, over."

Antonio Barrera awoke from his dream—he always slept with the demons of his past. The Tiffany wall clock showed 10 a.m. Antonio never needed an alarm clock or wake-up call. He slept a maximum of four hours a night ever since he was a kid, no matter when he fell asleep. Growing up in Argentina, he worked all night on the fishing boats and went to school during the day, until he dropped out at twelve-years-old. Sometimes he went days without sleeping and always appeared as fresh as if he had just slept twelve hours. That's why he never got into cocaine; even though, at one time, he was running the largest cocaine ring in the U.S. and probably the world. He couldn't imagine taking something that would make him sleep less than he naturally did.

Antonio put his feet on the ground at the base of his bed, sat for a minute to clear his head, and stood up to begin a new day of running one of the largest and most profitable crime organizations in the world. He could smell the coffee his wife, Marie, was brewing—it was imported from a private estate in Argentina.

Antonio lived in Palm Beach, next to the likes of Howard Stern, Rush Limbaugh, and Donald Trump. It was a heavenly stretch of land bordered by the Atlantic Ocean on the East and the Intracoastal waterway to the West. His ten-acre estate had a main house, three guest houses and ten-car garage. The Mediterranean-styled estate was built with two things in mind—keep people out and let Antonio *get out* quickly.

"Good morning, Hon," Antonio said, as he entered the breakfast kitchen. It was one of two gourmet kitchens in the fifteen thousand square foot home. The breakfast kitchen was an indoor-outdoor area that was built into a massive slate and limestone patio that overlooked the ocean—the ocean naturally energized him every morning.

"Don't *morning* me," Marie said, glaring at him.

He stepped back, put his hands up and smiled. "I didn't do it."

"Don't try and be cute. *Thanks* for coming with me to Michael's school yesterday. Waaay to be a responsible father. You couldn't spare one damn hour from your precious *job* for your son!"

"I'm sorry, Babe, but I couldn't. We will talk about it in five minutes." He took a sip of his coffee, but kept his gaze at the ocean, for he wouldn't let anything ruin the few moments of peace he had every morning while drinking his coffee—not even an angry wife. He took another sip of coffee, swallowed, then took a deep breath. . . . He finally said in a soothing tone, "What's the problem with Michael this time?"

"You never listen! I'm sick of it!"

Antonio stood up from the small round table and stepped toward her. He gently put his hands on her shoulders, staring into her eyes. He thought for a second, *God you're beautiful. After eighteen years of marriage, I still find you breathtaking.* "Stop yelling and calm down. What is the problem with Michael? Whatever it is, I'm sure we can resolve it." His soothing blue eyes immediately calmed her. He was more powerful with his words and stare then a gun. He would've been a great trial lawyer.

Marie took a deep breath, exhaled, and calmly said, "Michael was caught in the girls locker room again . . . kissing TWO seventeen-year-old girls this time!"

"Older women, good for him," he responded with a laugh. "And good for *us* it was the girls locker room. I don't need to tell you what my business associates, with all of their infinite ignorance, would think if I had a *finocchio* for a firstborn son."

"This is not a joke, Antonio. He is sinning in the eyes of the Lord."

Antonio pulled her closer. "Marie, *il mio amore* (my love), relax, Michael will be fine, so what if he likes girls. He's a sixteen-year-old whose hormones are going crazy. He's still on honor roll, right?"

"Yes." Marie immediately melted when he spoke Italian. Words simply became faint sounds as she succumbed to him.

"He's smarter than I ever was at sixteen or even now sometimes. But, I will talk to him about respecting women and staying out of the girls locker room . . . or at least being with only one girl at a time." He pulled her to him and kissed her hard on the lips and whispered in her ear, "*Andiano di sopra a letto*" (let's go upstairs to bed).

—17—

AFTER ANTONIO AND Maria enjoyed each other, he showered and dressed for work. He slipped his Beretta Nano 9mm into the custom-made leather holster clipped on his belt and then put on a gray silk suit jacket that perfectly concealed the Beretta—his tailor cut the left side of his jacket slightly bigger to account for the holster. He finished his impeccable look with an antique gold Rolex that had belonged to Al Capone.

He walked into the main kitchen and took a sip of a protein shake Marie had prepared. "I added kale this time. You need your greens . . . what do you think?" Maria asked, her eyes lighting up, hopeful.

"Better, but still gross. I love you for trying."

Maria half-smiled. "Have a good day and don't forget to pick Michael up from school."

"I'll try. See you later tonight." Already lost in his day's work, he walked down an Italian renaissance painting lined hallway that led to the front door.

"Don't work too hard today, Mussolini," Antonio said to his Doberman Pinscher sitting by the inner front door, as he did every day when his master was leaving. "Here you go, boy." He reached into a crystal bowl and grabbed a treat. Antonio scratched Mussolini's ears and gave him the treat. "I wish all of my employees were half as loyal as you." Antonio's home was more secure than Fort Knox. He approached the front door and looked at the three ten-inch TV monitors hanging on the wall to check if anyone was outside, waiting to ambush him. He touched his thumb to a small black pad below the ornate gold door handles; the multiple locks disengaged instantly and he effortlessly pushed open the twenty-foot high double doors. They were taken from a British Warship that sailed into battle in the War of 1812—Antonio figured if they could stop a cannon ball, they could stop an FBI battering ram.

The grounds were meticulously landscaped with palm trees, hedges, bushes, tropical flowers, and Roman statutes throughout. Antonio had fountains installed to create background noise in case anyone was trying to listen in on his conversations—it sounded like Niagara Falls. The perimeter of the property took advantage of natural security. Palm trees and silk floss trees with their big thorns created an impenetrable wall and bushy bougainvillea filled in the spaces between the trees to stop prying eyes and ensnare an intruder in thorn hell.

"Morning, Antonio," said his driver, Joseph, who was standing outside of Antonio's black custom-made, stretch Jaguar XJ—a nod to Tony "Ducks" Corrallo who was the boss of the Lucchese family in the eighties. Joseph always arrived four hours after he took Antonio home the night or morning before and would wait no matter how long Antonio took to come outside.

Antonio got in the backseat, turned on CNBC, and ordered, "Take me to the Cheese Shoppe."

— 18 —

"That looks perfect . . . thanks," Jason said to the man who just finished attaching his gold-letter sign to his new office front door: Jason Noble & Associates, P.A. It looked impressive set against the faux walnut door. Jason knelt in front of the sign and took a selfie that he immediately posted to his *Facebook* and *Instagram* pages with the tag line: *Open for Business* . He *almost* felt like a success when he looked at the photo. *Now I need to get some associates. But first, I need some clients to pay for the associates.*

Jason rented an office in the Raymond James building a/k/a *Darth Vader Building* situated on Flagler Drive in downtown West Palm Beach across the street from the Intracoastal waterway and Palm Beach with a gaggle of other law firms. The building had a mirrored, black exterior. He liked it because it was only three blocks from the state courthouse where he would be spending most of his time. The federal courthouse was also close by, but he had no need to ever go there.

Jason opened the front door and walked into his office. *Fifteen hundred a month didn't get me much. There's not even enough space to think in here.* The office was four hundred square feet, broken up into two small rooms, one behind the other. The walls were a light beige. The carpet was thin and a depressing gray color. Jason took a deep breath, looked around . . . exhaled, and proclaimed, "This is the first day of the rest of my life."

"Me too," said a high-pitched, female voice from behind.

Jason startled, turned around, "Uh, hi."

"Hi, new neighbor," said the short, squat woman with red hair styled in an old-fashioned bob cut that looked a bit frazzled. "I'm Jeanie Francis, the lawyer with two first names." She smiled as she extended her hand.

Jason shook her hand. "Jason Noble, nice to meet—"

"What type of law do you practice? Are you a solo? Where'd you go to law school? How many clients do you have? Are you married? Kids?"

Jason felt like he was being shot by a machine gun full of questions. He opened his mouth to start answering her interrogation, but she continued. "Sorry, I get excited when a 'newbie' moves into the *Iron side* of the building. No one ever wants to rent office space on this side. The building must be full or you don't have much money."

Jason recoiled a bit. *The lawyer with two first names*—he heard in a squeaky voice inside his head. *Great! She's hopped up on Red Bull.* He noticed her holding a can when she came in—Jason was hyper observant of his surroundings and people; a habit formed by paranoia from years of living in group and foster homes. *She'd have to pause to breathe at some point.* He decided to jump in and asked, "*Iron side?* Why do they call it that?"

"Come here, I'll show you." Jeanie Francis charged past him and walked into his tiny office, paused, and looked around. "You must've come from working for the government—Public Defender's Office or Legal Aid. Wait, I got it, just graduated law school." She turned and looked him up and down and then back to the empty office. "Definitely not the federal government or from a large firm. You don't have any office furniture. Not even a picture on the wall. The lawyers that just left the Feds or large firms always have their offices setup *before* they move in . . . lucky bastards!"

"I wanted to get a good feel for the office before I set it up. Plus, it's only my first day."

"Whatever." She grabbed his arm to hurry him to the back wall of the office. Jason's office had two windows along the wall opposite the door—*Voilà!*" she squealed, opening the cheap vertical blinds.

Outside was a hideous view of rusted iron girders of a five-story parking garage. His office was on the third floor. "Twelve hundred bucks a month for this! Now I know why the blinds were shut and the leasing agent told me *not to touch them because they were broken but would be fixed when I moved in.*" Jason turned away from the depressing view. "It's fine. I'll be in court most of the day anyway."

Jeanie Francis eyed him suspiciously. "What area do you practice? Do you want to refer each other clients? If you're going to be in court all day, you must have a lot of clients."

There she goes again asking multiple questions before I can answer the first. She must get admonished all the time when questioning a witness. It's probably comical—I'll definitely have to watch her some time. Although, I shouldn't make fun of anyone's courtroom style—I asked my first jury to find my client 'guilty'. "Criminal defense. What about you?"

"Good ol' family law and the occasional, anything that walks in the door when business is bad, which seems to be all the time since the *Great Recession* of '08. You must have a lot of money or something, because it sure is stupid to leave a guaranteed paycheck and medical benefits. Ahhh . . . and vacation, how I miss vacation," tilting her head up like she was daydreaming.

Jason started walking toward the front door, hoping Jeannie Francis would take the hint. "What do you mean? I'm my own boss now. I can take vacation whenever I want."

"Ha. Ya can't take no vacation without no money. Besides, all you'll be thinking about on vacation is if you'll get a new client to pay for it. I took a vacation once. I couldn't put my phone down . . . and now I'm divorced. That was the last time I ever took a vacation or had any money for one."

I have to get out of this conversation. This woman is depressing. It was the first day of his new life; he wouldn't let the lawyer with two first names spoil it. "Um, well, it was nice to meet you, Jeannie Francis. I'll see you around." Jason lightly took her arm and walked her to the front door.

"You want to come hang in my office down the hall—I have chairs. I even have a coffee maker and mini-fridge." She looked at him with a genuine smile.

"No thanks, I need to get to work."

"I'll be down the hall if you need anything. And don't forget, I'm the *lawyer with two first names*." She cheerfully waived as she bounded down the hallway.

Jason went back inside, shut the door, and locked it.

— 19 —

"I NEED SOMETHING high-profile, Tim. Something to get my name in the paper . . . better yet, a juicy case to get me on *Oprah*. . . ." Trevor mused, rubbing his hands together like in prayer, his eyes staring, unfocused, through his hands at the cheap red and white checkered tablecloth.

"I think you mean *Ellen*," Tim chirped back, through a mouth full of *arroz con pollo*.

Trevor leaned in closer and glanced around at the other lunch diners, mostly speaking Spanish, to make sure no one could overhear him. Tim leaned in with excited anticipation on his face. "You're an idiot." Tim's expression suddenly deflated.

Trevor grabbed his iced tea and took a sip. They were having lunch at *El Gran Cubano*. For $5.99 you get the best *arroz con pollo* and *frijoles negros* in Miami. The place was no frills. The air was filled with a delightful mash of deep fry, slow-roast pork, garlic and cumin. The loud Spanish being yelled from the open kitchen and spoken at almost every table but theirs, was deafening.

Trevor stared at Tim for a second and contemplated . . . *should I trust this moron? He's "young and dumb." I guess that will make him easy to control and the fall-guy if necessary.* While Trevor was abrasive and vile to most people he interacted with, he wasn't bad at managing people; well, in his case, *using* people. Trevor leaned back over the table, self-importance washing over his face, and whispered—even though there was no need to, "*I'm* going to be the next governor of the great state of Florida."

Tim absorbed the statement for a moment . . . He wasn't that smart, but he knew opportunity when he saw it. He knew absolutely nothing about running for elected office, but, what did he care, maybe it would lead to a better paycheck, which would let him get a nicer place to get better looking guys. "I'm in, Governor Whittingham." Tim said loudly, rice spitting out of his mouth.

"Shh, Shh, I don't want anyone to know yet. This has to be completely confidential at this point."

Tim looked around the room. *No one can hear us, understand us, or gives-a-damn about our conversation.* "What do we do next?"

"Let's get back to how *I* get in the paper and on *Opr—Ellen.*"

"What about a good art heist prosecution? Maybe we can even get one of those Nazi guys who stole a bunch of art in WWII. They're even missing *Van Goghs.* I can solve and prosecute one of these in three to five years." Tim's face lit up like he just came up with the greatest idea ever. He took a big gulp of his Diet Coke in celebration.

"Three to five years! The governor's race is in six months because of the special election. I need a case from arrest to conviction in three months tops. It needs to be a definite trial—an *easy* trial. No plea deal . . . and the higher the profile the better . . . maybe a death penalty case? The national media likes those and all the protesters that will show up every day at the trial will add to the suspense."

"Well, we are in the fastest federal judicial district in the country, but *arrest, trial, and conviction* in three months tops . . . that's gonna be tough."

Trevor's face wrinkled in disgust. "There is no *can't*! I don't *fail* in life—*failure* is unacceptable. I live by the code: *Win at all costs.* If you can't or won't get on board with that then leave now."

Tim thought about the better class of boyfriends he was going to get when he worked in the governor's mansion. "Something that saves little kids would be great for your image. What about a terrorist prosecution. We could rally the voters behind the fires of false hate against Muslims." Tim shoved a fork full of *plátanos* into his mouth.

"Now you're thinking. Problem with all that ISIS crap is the prosecutions take forever. Plus, the New York City boys like all those cases, and we don't want them coming down here to steal our thunder. Something else. . . ."

Tim rubbed his chin . . . thinking . . . "I got it!" He snapped his fingers. "A good mob conviction. The public loves organized crime. They'll eat it up. Before I left the D.C. office, I sat in on an organized crime debriefing, where DOJ got some new intel that this guy Antonio "Magic Man" Barrera was just named the head of the South Florida Mafia. They even put this Antonio guy's picture at the top of the mob family tree DOJ constantly updates. I think Antonio killed the prior *Don*, Giovanni "Snowman" Androdi.

"I was just about to say that." Trevor, already deep in thought, mentally dismissed the idea as Tim's and made it his own.

"I just saw a show on *CNN* that said the mob was now involved in sex trafficking. They showed a fifteen-year-old who was reunited with her family. Everyone was crying like crazy, real touching. They even had an interview with the U.S. Attorney for the Eastern District of Texas, who prosecuted some sex traffickers. It was great PR," Tim added.

"You watch two much TV, but I like it." Trevor had a twinkle in his eye, and the corners of his mouth slowly formed a mischievous smile. "I'm sure there's something in the pipeline at DOJ with all the usual crimes—drugs, guns, murder, now sex trafficking. We'll do a RICO prosecution so it will be really easy to get a conviction—thank you Rudy Gulliani."

The waitress came over to the table and dropped a check and two warm *pastelito de guayaba* (guava pastries)—the pastries were free. The waitress knew exactly when to bring the check—the line was too long to let people linger.

Trevor stood up to leave. He grabbed both pastries with his grubby little fingers. "Now pay the bill and I'll meet you outside." Tim looked up at him, about to protest. Trevor said, without missing a beat, "The *Governor* doesn't pay for his own lunch."

— 20 —

ANTONIO SAT BACK for the fifteen-minute drive to the Cheese Shoppe in Riviera Beach, which bordered West Palm Beach to the North. It sounded like paradise, but it was uncompromisingly violent underneath the sunshine and palm trees. Riviera Beach was a stone's throw from Palm Beach, but the similarities stopped at the palm trees—A ying and yang of cities separated by a small strip of Intracoastal waterway. Palm Beach was one of the richest zip codes in the world and Riviera Beach was one of the poorest. It was the perfect place to run a 21st Century Boiler Room.

"Eh, Antonio, you see dose Dolfuns las' night?"

"No, Joseph, it's bad for my blood pressure to watch the Fins and its Dol*phins*. I didn't look at the daily sheets yet . . . how'd they do?"

"Fantastic! Dey lost by twenty-eight to da Pats. I bet da Pats to cova by fourteen. Fuhgeddaboudit, I love dem Dolfuns."

"What was the balance?" That's what Antonio cared most about the game.

"I'd say, based on da degeneits at Moe Moe's last night, heavy on da Fins—fuckin' mooks . . . they always bettin' wit emotion."

"It's *de-gen-er-ates*. Have you been watching the *Hooked on Phonics* YouTube videos I told you about—they helped my kid before he went to kindergarten." Antonio took a sip of his *bucci*. "I assume you adjusted our position accordingly."

"We made sixty-two cents of every dollar bet on da Fins game last night an averaged fifty-six cents on all sports. Deer was some big badminton tournament in dat China place last night. Dose yellow bastads saw da biggest action. I love da Chinese. I don' know why dey ain't allowed ta use no forks ta eat dey damn pasta. I heard dey use chopsticks as weapons dat's why they always usin' 'em instead'a forks."

"Where'd you hear that?" Antonio asked. *Everyday Joseph says something dumber than what he said the day before.*

"On da radio . . . I dink?"

Antonio knew better than to engage Joseph when he said something stupid. But he was a brilliant sports book handicapper and fiercely loyal protector. He could predict the total action Antonio's crew made on gambling in a given night just by watching the degenerates at one of Antonio's sports bars; he was quicker than the computers and always right. Joseph was also getting good at predicting the action on foreign sports since Antonio branched out his gambling activities to Asia. Antonio's crew now took bets from the Chinese, Koreans, Japanese, and Philippine degenerates—No matter what country they were from, degenerate gamblers were all the same.

"I saw on da news las' night dat de Feds was comin' down on organized crime. Where dey comin' down from, Canada?" Joseph asked.

Antonio looked at Joseph's face in the rearview mirror and shook his head. *I have to get smarter people working for me,* he thought. *At least he knew Canada was North of the U.S.* "Stop watching the news. It's going to make your head explode. By the way, what's the story with our *friend,* Alfonso?"

Joseph looked in the rearview mirror at Antonio, a look of apprehension on his face. "Alphonso is still runnin' slaves from overseas, mostly from China and Korea instead of Brazil. He sells um to pimps up Nort, Texas, and Cali*phone*ia so ya won't find out."

"That worthless piece of shit! I told everyone: *No more human smuggling!* It's not worth the risk and we don't need it . . . he selling kids, too?"

"Dat's da word on da street. I talked to some *Friends of Ours* in those places and they confirmed it. . . . He's also been disappearin' for a few hours each week. Nobody knows where he goes . . . maybe he talking to da Feds?"

Antonio picked up his espresso cup and finished his *bucci.* He stared for a moment in deep thought at the hand-painted cup—this one had a scene of the Colosseum in Rome . . .

Antonio put the cup down. "I think it's time to rent Alfonso 'the Whale' a tuxedo. Give our friend the contract . . . and make sure he sends the *right* message."

"I'll take care of it today." Joseph raised the privacy partition between them. He knew when Antonio was done talking and wanted privacy—he didn't need to be told after twenty years.

—21—

ANTONIO SWIPED DOWN on a screen in front of him—four, eight-inch screens came to life, filling with financial data from different parts of the world. Antonio never directly communicated with anyone about business by phone, email, or text—only face to face. And he certainly didn't use social media—no *likes* or *location check-ins*; imagine: *Antonio checked-in to Angelo 'the Butcher's' basement.* However, he did have to keep track of his global empire through the internet.

Five years ago, he ran a fake rewards scam using *BestBuy*; for ten dollars a year with a ten dollar activation fee, customers would get a minimum of twenty percent off of everything they purchased—It was when everyone and their grandmother were buying flat screen TV's. Antonio's problem was he couldn't find enough people to work the phones, so he got the idea to hire a call center from India, which worked beautifully—it even added authenticity to the scam. He netted twelve million dollars in a little over a month.

While he was in India looking for a call center, he met a computer genius named Yeshi Patel who created an encrypted network, complete with its own satellite, that would make NASA envious. Unfortunately for Yeshi, Antonio couldn't allow him to live with this knowledge. Yeshi's body was eventually seen floating among the endless amount of garbage in the Ghanges River.

Joseph pulled into a covered parking space in front of a nondescript, dilapidated, two story warehouse with a dirty white stucco exterior and few windows—The Cheese Shoppe. Antonio ran a boiler room on the first floor and his Port and energy businesses on the second floor. The warehouse was a few blocks off US Highway One and two blocks from the Port of Palm Beach. Riviera Beach was a forgotten city, the product of forced integration, white flight, and the crack epidemic. It was the perfect place to operate illicit businesses and it was a quarter of the rent of Miami real estate. Antonio was all about the bottom line—he ran his criminal enterprise like a Fortune 500 Company. He quickly realized that even a three percent increase in profit margin on some of his more sophisticated schemes was easy to achieve and produced enormous amounts of money, which made him a top earner in the eyes of his boss Don Giovanni and the NY bosses, moving him up the ranks of the Mafia leadership ladder quickly. He went from associate to solider to capo to underboss quicker than any mobster before him.

Antonio profited handsomely from the Port alone. *Florida Power and Light* (FPL) had a power plant at the border of Riviera Beach and West Palm Beach, and *Ribovich,* a world-renowned mega yacht builder that could accommodate super-yachts, was also in the area. Antonio made hundreds of millions of dollars over the years from just energy, shipping, and luxury boats. Especially when FPL decided to build a new power plant in 2014, he made a fifty-million-dollar profit on the recycling contracts alone. The police didn't go to places like Riviera Beach—the residents had them outgunned.

"Go see Pinto at the docks and pick-up my package, be back in thirty," Antonio instructed Joseph as he exited the car.

Antonio walked through the front, double metal doors and down a long hallway. "We all clean, Sal?" Antonio asked the heavy man dressed in a black suit, sitting next to a set of double doors that had no doorknobs.

"Mornin', Sir. All clean," Sal responded, as he put his hand, palm side up, under the small desk next to the door. The door clicked three times and both double doors swung open. If Sal didn't say "all clean" Antonio would know something was wrong. Every morning the place was swept for "bugs." No one could carry a cell phone or any electronic device inside except for Antonio, Joseph, and Capo Umberto "Mr. International" Stutani who ran The Cheese Shoppe.

Antonio stepped into a small entryway, a polished steel elevator door in front of him with a security keypad to the right. He punched in a seven-digit-code that only he and Umberto knew and the elevator doors opened. He stepped out on the second floor. "How are we doing, Umberto? Are we unloading that XWAC garbage that *you* purchased at the ridiculously high price of one cent a share?"

"It would've been a good company if the EPA didn't conclude the company's water filtration technology actually made water more toxic. Good thing I buried the report. XWAC is trading at seventeen cents a share. We already unloaded ninety-five percent of our hundred million shares, mostly on the Rio De Janeiro stock exchange."

Antonio walked over to the glass balcony overlooking his trading floor; Umberto followed. Fifteen "associates" were working the phones. Each one sat in a cubical that had a Dell laptop computer and a simple black landline telephone. The workers were broken up into three teams by primary language of the target investor—English, Spanish, and Chinese.

There were two conference rooms off the main floor that were used for investor video conferences. Through the internet, Antonio extended his reach of potential investors exponentially. He added green screens to the conference rooms so he could project anything he wanted to the viewer—like a luxurious conference room and large staff in posh offices to trick the viewer into thinking Antonio's operation was legitimate. Bobby Strombolie was currently using one of the conference rooms to deliver his daily recommendations, which of course included XWAC stock. "Buy! Buy! Buy!" he was yelling. *Day traders are such suckers,* Antonio thought.

In the new Millennium, especially after the Great Recession of 08, Latin Americans and Asians, mostly from China, started heavily investing in everything American—real estate, stocks, bonds, and businesses. Antonio saw this trend coming and profited handsomely from it through his "pump and dump" penny stock schemes.

"Are. We. Ready. To. PUMP and DUMP!" Umberto said to the men and one woman who sat in their cubicles looking like they were ready for war.

They all yelled, "HOO-RAH" in unison. While the New York families would never allow a woman to become an associate of the mob and work at a mob business other than as a stripper or server, Antonio was more progressive. He didn't micromanage, he appointed solid Capos to run his businesses and bring him new money-making schemes. He trusted their judgment and allowed them to do unorthodox things if it increased the profit margin. The downside of not producing money in a scheme kept everyone motivated. If you didn't produce, the consequences were much worse than Donald Trump telling you: *You're Fired*! A woman was more likely to convince prospective women investors to open their pocketbooks, he thought, so why not employ one. The one he hired spoke fluent Mandarin and turned out to be the smartest one among her male counterparts.

Tina looked at the list on her computer screen and dialed Ms. Wong Chang in Hunan Province, China. "*Ni hao ma,*"(Hi, how are you) Tina said in a perfect Chinese dialect to the woman answering the phone.

"*Ni hao,*" the woman responded.

"Is this Mrs. Chang?" Tina asked in Chinese.

"*Shi,*"(yes) the woman responded in a soft voice.

"Do you have two minutes to learn about the best decision you will ever make, an honorable decision?" Tina knew the Chinese social customs perfectly and understood that a Chinese woman could not and would not lie, even to strangers, so they never gave an excuse to get off the phone in those first few critical seconds of a sales call—if you can get them to stay on the phone past the first ten seconds, you were seventy-five percent more likely to close the deal. Tina also knew that decisions made in the Asian culture had to have honorable outcomes. "Do you make the decisions for your family?" Tina asked.

"Well, uh, sometimes."

The split-second hesitation was all Tina needed to pounce on her prey like a cheetah. "I'm going to help you make a smart, honorable decision for your family's financial future."

"I'm listening."

"I'm going to guarantee you nine percent on your money, every year . . . you can't lose—Tina knew nine was a lucky number in the Chinese culture. The investment is insured." Since it was a total scam, Tina could promise any percentage and guarantee she wanted. She wasn't restrained by those pesky SEC rules and regulations, or the truth. Within a few minutes, Tina convinced the woman to transfer five-thousand American dollars to a bank account in Hong Kong, then the money would be instantaneously routed through several banks in different countries until it vanished into thin air—*Poof!* The investor wouldn't be the wiser, because they would get monthly e-statements showing their money growing and growing—the statements would never show a down month no matter how the real stock markets around the world performed. Three billion people in China, and at last count, Antonio's organization had two-hundred thousand "investors" from there. *La Famiglia* was swimming in money from this scam alone.

— 22 —

JASON LOOKED DOWN at his phone. *Google maps* told him that the *Paul G. Roberts United States District Court* was just a few blocks southwest of his office. Thanksgiving was just a few weeks away which meant hurricane season was almost over—the sun was shining with almost no humidity in the air. Jason was on his way to take the Federal Bar Exam for the Southern District of Florida. He was as relaxed as could be, even though he only decided two weeks ago to sit for the exam. "Good morning," he said to a passing jogger, as he crossed Dixie Highway. In most Florida cities on the east coast, Dixie Highway was a demarcation line between the "good" and "bad" areas—like any imaginary line, it was crossed all the time, mostly by people from the "bad" side.

Jason never planned to take a federal case. The stories he heard about the intensity of federal court and the overbearing judges scared the hell out of him. Federal judges answered to no one—A federal judgeship was a lifetime appointment. None of that mattered to Jason, because he would never step foot in the federal courthouse after today. He was only taking the exam to get another certificate to add to the sparse diploma wall in his office. Besides, he was bored most of the day. A month into life as a private lawyer and he still had no clients and nothing to do. He sat in his office sending out direct-mailers and playing computer games most of the day.

Jason walked up to the entrance of the Paul G. Roberts United States District Court located at 701 Clematis Street, which was situated between Clematis and Banyan Streets in downtown West Palm Beach. It was a contemporary design in 1973 when it was built—it was a faded sandstone, square building with a multitude of decorative arches. Today it was outdated and badly in need of a demolition crew; after hurricanes

Francis and Jean in 2004, the entire building was infested with mold, which was only discovered because jurors started getting mold poisoning during trials. An Assistant U.S. Attorney thought he was giving such a great closing argument in a bank fraud trial when three jurors passed out; turns out, they passed out from a combination of boredom and mold poisoning.

The front glass doors slid open automatically and Jason walked into the lobby. He could tell immediately that the one woman and four men standing around a single x-ray machine and metal detector in the small well-worn lobby were not ten dollar an hour security guards like at the state courthouse. The badge on their blue blazers said *Federal Protection Services (FPS)*. Jason walked up to the FPS Officer sitting at a desk behind a computer. "Can I help you?" The man asked, eyeing Jason suspiciously.

"I-I'm here to take the Federal Bar Exam," Jason responded nervously. He looked around at the empty lobby and wondered if he was in the right place. *Am I the only one taking the exam?*

"Driver's license," the officer said, as two of the other officers approached the desk. Jason handed his license to the officer.

The FPS officer looked from the license to Jason a few times, his expression never changing. "You an attorney?"

"Yes," Jason said proudly.

"You been here before?" the officer placed his license upside down on a glass screen that was on the top of a big microscope looking thing.

"No, first time."

"I got that from the *no*. You tryin' to be smart," The officer said, looking up from his computer screen, eyeing Jason like he was ready to fight. "Hey, Don? This guy thinks he's a funny man." The larger of the two other officers looked at Jason hard and took a few steps closer.

Jason started to sweat, not knowing what to say. "Um. Um. No, Sir. I, I—"

"Ha. Got you." All the officers started to laugh. The main officer handed Jason his license and said, "Go stand on the 'x' so I can take your picture." Jason's sphincter finally relaxed and he walked over to the 'x'.

Jason's heart was still pounding, but thankfully he got through security without further incident. "Second floor, you'll see the signs to the exam room . . . good luck," an FPS officer said as she took the tray back from Jason.

Jason walked down the bland hallway on the second floor, following the signs to the exam. He stopped a few times and looked around in disbelief at how quiet the courthouse was. *This is nice. In the state courthouse, I can't hear myself think in the hallways.* Another person finally walked out of a room with a sign that read: *Clerk's Office.* She walked past him and pleasantly said, "Good morning."

"Hi," Jason replied. *I must be in an alternate universe of courthouses.*

He arrived at a set of double wood doors: *Federal Bar Exam Room.* He was the first person to arrive. The classroom-like room had several rows of stadium seating with a small folding desk on each seat that was already setup. The front of the room had a desk and large screen. The man sitting at the desk looked up and said, "Here for the bar exam?"

"Yes."

"Take a seat anywhere. DON'T turn over the booklet until I tell you," the man admonished before Jason even had a chance to sit down.

"Thanks." Jason took a seat in the fourth-row end. The room filled up with about fifty other lawyers.

At exactly 3:00 p.m. the man got up from the desk, and instructed, "Alright, everyone, turn over your booklets." Jason looked at the cover: *Southern District of Florida, Federal Bar Exam.* "First thing I'm going to do is swear everyone into the *United States District Court for the Southern District of Florida.* This test is so easy, I will swear you in first, figuring all of you will pass it. Everyone raise your righthand and repeat after me: *I do solemnly swear. . . ."*

— 23 —

"WHAT THE HELL does Trevor want?" Jackson Reed asked Drug Enforcement Agent Lisa Hoyt, looking up from his makeshift workspace that was bare except for an empty business card holder.

"Don't know, just got an email saying he wants to meet at nine thirty this morning in his West Palm Office—'High priority' meeting. Out of business cards?" Lisa responded through gasped breaths. She drank from a water bottle and glanced around at the other three desks in the otherwise empty room, all had nothing but empty business card holders on them.

Jackson Reed was a Special Agent with the FBI currently doing undercover and handler work in the Organized Crime Division, which now included every group of two or more criminals working together from *La Cosa Nostra* to Sur-13. Jackson pushed back from his desk and stood up. His 6'5" solid frame towered above Lisa who stood at 5'5'. "*High priority*? Must not be *that* important if he wants us to drive from Miami to West Palm at rush hour." Jackson's baritone voice reverberated around the empty room.

Lisa wiped the sweat from her brow with the back of her hand. "You know Trevor, he thinks when he takes a piss it's *high priority*. This better be good, though, I just cut my jiu jitsu workout short. You want to ride together?" Lisa picked up the empty business card holder and played with it.

"Can't . . . after the meeting I need to check on a confidential source that screwed me on a human trafficking case I'm working. The Fat SOB bailed on the wire at the last minute when he was about to meet with Antonio Barrera and pay his tribute from a recent smuggling trip where two people died, including a ten-year-old Chinese kid." Jackson took the business card holder out of Lisa's hand and put it back on the desk.

"Ohh. Sounds exciting . . . it's like a movie." Lisa put her hands to her cheeks and contorted her face in mock fear. "Let me tag along, so I can learn from the great 'Reel'em-in-Reed' . . . If your nice to me, I'll let *you* buy dinner on the way back," she playfully winked at him.

Jackson grabbed his jacket off the back of his chair. "Alright, you can tag along. But *you're* buying dinner." He playfully poked her muscular arm.

"By the way, why do the desks only have empty business card holders on them?"

"Us undercover guys are supposed to be ghosts . . . Technically we don't exist, so no calling cards. Now let's hurry up and wait in traffic for three hours."

— 24 —

"Too many leaks in the Miami office. *Y'all* gossip like schoolgirls down there. That's why we're meeting here at my West Palm office until the arrest," Trevor said, standing behind an unnecessary lectern at the front of a small conference room. His short, meaty arms going in every direction as he spoke. Trevor hated when he said a word in his southern drawl; he tried so hard to eliminate any hint that he was raised in the "unsophisticated" South. "Pay attention, all of you," Trevor added, like a schoolteacher scolding his students before they even had a chance to do anything wrong.

Way to start off a meeting, moron. Put everyone on the defensive from the get-go, thought FBI Senior Special Agent Tomas De Cruz. He looked at Jackson Reed, who was no doubt thinking the same.

"Each of you in this room is now reporting to me. Full time," Trevor informed the five people he handpicked to bring down one of the world's most notorious crime bosses—Antonio 'Magic Man' Barrera. The memo in front of you is from Attorney General Hank Boulder reassigning each of you to me for this investigation, arrest, trial and conviction . . . any issue with that? Hearing nothing, we'll move on then. Now, introduce yourselves." He looked down at Herb Rosen, who was sitting to his immediate right.

"For the couple of you who don't already know me, I'm Herb Rosen. I've been an Assistant United States Attorney at this office for thirty-four years, but it seems like a hundred." The rest of the people let out a light laugh. "I've tried my fair share of organized crime cases." Herb was a career man—smart with limited ambition. At 5'7" with a balding crown of curly, gray hair and thick glasses, he didn't have much jury appeal, but made up for it in his relentless preparation and well-crafted legal arguments. It didn't matter, Trevor would do all the parts of the trial that required direct contact with the jury and the major witnesses, but he'd *let* Herb prepare everything.

They were sitting around a plain conference table. Its worn brown, rectangular surface stained and scratched from years of use. The room was small and cramped. A lone, depressing-looking plant was in one corner. Other than some banker's boxes in another corner and a flat screen monitor hanging on the wall, the conference room was empty. Light poured in from the ceiling to floor windows that overlooked Clear Lake—no matter how depressing a room was on the inside, if it had windows, it had a good view in Florida.

Herb looked to his right at Senior IRS Agent Miache Charles, CPA, CFE, LLM. "Hi, everyone. I've been at the IRS for seven years. I emigrated here from Kenya when I was eighteen. I graduated from Columbia with an accounting degree, a law degree from NYU, and then a L.L.M in tax law from Yale." Miache said, smiling at everyone. His African accent only slightly detectable. His appearance was not what people expected for a Treasury agent—he was Denzel Washington handsome. "As a past time, I've been tracking all of Antonio Barrera's and his crew's financial transactions, or, I should say, lack of them. He's like a ghost online. Tracing money to him and his crew is near impossible . . . But, I will get him, eventually. Every criminal makes a mistake." He sat back, looked up at the ceiling, and engaged in a fantasy where Antonio is captured.

"Next," Trevor commanded, looking at FBI Special Agent Tomas De Cruz.

"You all know me," Tomas said. He was a field agent's type of boss— *agents over politics* was his unofficial motto. He gained notoriety, and was deemed "someone to watch" by his superiors, as a young agent when he stayed undercover in a Columbian Cartel for three and a half years.

"Jackson Reed." He looked at Lisa Hoyt sitting next to him.

Lisa sat forward in her chair. "Lisa Hoyt, DEA." She looked at Trevor and asked in a contemptuous tone, "What are we reporting to *you* on?"

Trevor glared down at her. "Be quiet and pay attention. You'll find out soon enough." Lisa sat back in her chair, letting out a deep breath. Herb rolled his eyes.

Trevor pointed the remote at the monitor hanging on the far wall and clicked it on. "That's our prize." Everyone in unison looked at the monitor. Staring back at them was Antonio "Magic Man" Barrera. The photo was a bit older, but his blue eyes were unmistakable. "If you don't think you have the stomach for this, leave now." Trevor said, in unnecessary, dramatic fashion.

You sound like an amateur . . . and, in this business, amateurs get people killed, Tomas thought then asked, "The stomach for what?"

"We're, I mean, *I'm* going to take him down and all of you are going to help. I am going to prosecute him for murder, racketeering, fraud, conspiracy, prostitution, you name it and I'm going to indict him on it—Antonio 'Magic Man' Barrera is our prize." Trevor's eyes seemed to twinkle for a second. A good ol' fashion Mob R.I.C.O. prosecution like Rudy Giuliani did in New York City in the eighties. He became an instant superstar—rode the wave all the way to the Mayor's mansion."

Jackson Reed leaned forward on his elbows and said, "He's not called 'Magic Man' for nothing. He's one slippery SOB . . . and a nasty one too, according to my CS, Alfonso 'the Whale' Tomisini."

Trevor excitedly pointed the remote at Jackson. "See, that's perfect. Call in this Whale guy and we'll have him testify. . . . He'll be our star witness—a guy on the inside willing to testify will make this easy." *And add some real Godfather type drama*, he thought.

"I can't call him in now," Jackson said. "I'm in the middle of investigating Barrera for human trafficking, mostly in young kids and girls who are forced into prostitution. Arresting him now will screw that up." Jackson Reed threw his hands in the air in frustration.

"That's perfect. I'll indict Barrera on human trafficking charges too—add another life sentence on top of the murders, frauds, money laundering, and racketeering life sentences that I'm going to get. And, if I'm lucky, he'll get the death penalty."

Trevor peered down at the group, "You've all been screwing around long enough with one of the richest and most powerful mob bosses in the history of organized crime. He has certainly earned his nick name 'Magic Man,' but his *magic's* just run out. I figured out all his tricks and it's time to haul his ass in." He looked at Jackson directly, "Call in this Alfonso 'the Whale' and let's put him in witness protection . . . now! Call the Attorney General if you have a problem with my orders."

Lisa Hoyt interrupted the tension and asked, "Why Antonio Barrera, and why now?" Everyone looked away from Trevor and focused on Lisa. She was one of the DEAs best agents—a rising star. She had no idea why the DEA was there; the Italian Mafia was mostly out of the illegal drug game.

"Antonio Barrera is unlike anyone we've ever dealt with before," Tomas DeCruz added. He took a sip of his bottled water and continued. "He saw the handwriting on the wall in the 90s—guys getting thirty years mandatory without time off for good behavior for selling even a small amount of heroin or crack. Plus, as an added bonus, Italian mob guys started serving their time in gen-pop with all the blacks, Latinos, and skinhead psychos. It didn't matter how many judges or prosecutors Antonio bought, his guys started going away and doing hard time, so he decided to develop an exit strategy that worked brilliantly."

"Well, let's shut down his exit strategy," Trevor said, trying to focus the attention back on him. They stayed focused on Tomas.

"It's not that easy. Antonio was very smart, especially getting out of the illegal drug business. He started developing revenue streams from low-risk medical marijuana businesses in California—people forget that California legalized medical marijuana in 1996 and Antonio's been in the industry since then. Now he has marijuana businesses in twenty-six other states with more each year as *weed-mania* sweeps through the country. It's a multi-billion-dollar industry still in its infancy . . . there are no rules yet. Hell, the entire business is all cash because there are no banks willing to take deposits. Antonio uses his traditional mob muscle tactics to grab 'legal' territory. These millennial, new age, hippies are no match for a sophisticated and vicious mob family. He also sold off his illegal drug territory to the highest bidder, just like a fortune five hundred company sells off its assets."

Now I know why the DEA's here, Lisa thought. *But DEA doesn't bother with the State legal marijuana business? What does this idiot want to do? Prosecute Antonio for selling legal joints to cancer patients.*

IRS agent Miache chimed in. "From what I can tell—although these numbers are just estimates, Antonio sold his drug territory to a conglomerate of drug lords from Jamaica, Columbia, and China for . . . are you ready for this . . . five BILLION, with a 'B', dollars."

Jackson Reed whistled.

Tomas continued, "The Mexican and Russian cartels had a different plan. The violence that was created by the power vacuum was unprecedented, but that was someone else's problem, so Antonio didn't care."

Miache further added, "Do not forget about all the fraud based activities he started focusing on about a decade before the *Great Recession.* He's a master at using the anonymity of international corporations. Once money hits an account in the U.S., it immediately moves overseas, routed through dozens of countries, anonymous shell companies, and bank accounts. Hell, for all we know, he's collecting the rent on the building we're in."

Trevor jumped in again, leaning forward over the podium, visibly frustrated. "I've reviewed everything we have on Antonio and his criminal enterprise and I think I can easily get a conviction." Everyone in the room thought the same thing—*What a pompous ass! Nothing was "easy" in this business.* "We have to protect the children. . . ."

Oh boy. Here comes the campaign speech. Trevor's true intentions are obvious now, Herb Rosen thought. *A prosecution for any other reason than true justice was usually a bad idea. Although, we do have tons of solid evidence on Antonio's illegal activities. Prosecuting him on any one of a dozen serious crimes is virtually a slam dunk.*

"I stand before you to tell you that the violence and atrocities committed by scum like Antonio Barrera and his criminal gang of thugs has gone on far too long. It is my job to end the suffering of his countless victims, including the children. I want to indict him in two weeks."

— 25 —

Tuxedo Tommy checked his Rolex: 9:00 p.m. "Time to party," he whispered to himself. Tommy looked toward the sky and made the sign of the cross. "Grant me strength, Mother, for I am weak without *you*."

The industrial glass ceiling held Tommy's stare. *The staccato pounding of the rain should work perfectly to drown out the noise to come*, he mused. He filled his lungs with the thick, moldy air. Lightning cracked loud overhead, rattling the cavernous space. Across the room, the outline of the "guest of honor" hung in the air for a second from the strobe effect created by the lightning.

"Chrissie, sit him down in front of the tank," Tommy ordered, matter-of-factly. Tommy, wearing Italian loafers with smooth, rubber bottoms so he didn't leave tracks, silently walked on the cement floor to a table and chair in the center. Running lengthwise across the space, back in the shadows, was a massive tank emitting a low slushing sound.

Chrissie's large hands grabbed the fat man around the collar and dragged him across the warehouse floor. "Let's go Alfonso . . . time for some fun."

Tuxedo Tommy was a sanitation worker for organized crime. His real name was unknown. He loved taking out the Barrera family's garbage. They paid well and he was free to use his creativity. He always dreamed of being a famous artist or sculptor. . . . His mom loved art.

"Ain't you hot in dat tuxedo?" Chrissie asked, as he shoved Alfonso into the chair.

"I'm used to it." Tommy brushed aside his shoulder-length blonde hair. He wore a tuxedo on every job to honor his parents who were gunned down with shotguns in an Iowa church, renewing their vows when he was ten. His mom made him wear a tuxedo that day and he complained the whole time.

Alfonso squirmed in the tiny chair causing the chair legs to make a grinding sound against the cement floor. "Come on guys! It's me, Alfonso 'the Whale'. I'm a *made* guy . . . you can't do this. Call the boss . . . I want a sit-down," he pleaded through bated breath. His face was swollen and bloody like he just went twelve rounds with Mike Tyson.

"The boss already called . . . time's run out for you," Tommy said.

"I'm a Capo, my crew will kill you if you hurt me . . . all of you," Alfonso hissed, with a tone of false authority. Tommy was going to kill a made guy. To whack a *made* guy, the bosses of the five New York families and Alfonso's boss, Antonio Barrera, had to give their unanimous okay. If Tommy and Chrissie didn't have that, they'd be the ones getting whacked.

Tommy chose an abandoned warehouse in Riviera Beach. The warehouse used to be home to a high-flying trapeze and water act—it was perfect for the message Tommy wanted to send.

Tommy put a black leather bag on the small table next to Alfonso. "Get 'em ready, Chrissie. We want to give him an early Christmas present."

"Yeah, a Hanukkah present too," Chrissie added, laughing.

"What the hell do you mean Hanukkah—you're an idiot—he's not a Jew. Just tie him to the chair."

"Come here, Felicia, show Alfonso a good time," Tommy ordered, motioning with his hand, to the attractive, large breasted girl standing off to the side. "Give our friend here his early Christmas present."

Felicia walked across the warehouse, her clear, high heels clicking on the floor. She knelt down between his fat legs and unzipped his pants. Felicia cracked a piece of gum in her mouth, made a look of disgust, and complained, "Come on guys, this is gross, I'm gonna need some more money."

"Just do what I asked," Tommy ordered. In his calm voice, she could sense an evil man that didn't have patience for negotiating. *Oh well*, she thought, *this wouldn't be the weirdest thing I've been asked to do before—*

these mobsters are pervs. Felicia lifted Alfonso's huge gut, sighed, and took his penis out of his pants.

Chrissie began laughing. "You definitely ain't black, Alfonso."

Tommy had a disgusted look on his face. "You have no respect for yourself or the *La Famiglia*. You're a good earner, Alfonso, but your greed caught up with you. You wanted to be the boss, but you're too stupid to run a shoeshine stand." This struck Chrissie as funny and he let out a howling laugh.

"Go to hell, Tommy. Antonio will make you pay for this. I earn too much," Alfonso spit gobs of blood out of his mouth as he spoke.

"The 'Magic Man' wants you to disappear. The boss doesn't care about the pennies you bring in anymore. You just couldn't stop pimping those young illegals. You thought if you switched from Mexicans to Chinese he wouldn't know . . . and, you didn't even pay a full tribute." Tommy grabbed Alfonso by his lapels, leaned in close, and looked him in the eyes. "Even the devil doesn't want what you're going to get tonight," he whispered. The hairs on the back of Alfonso's neck bristled and his eyes went wide. Tommy backed away and Felicia began stroking the exposed penis.

"Stop, Felicia," Tommy abruptly said, putting his hand on her shoulder. "This is a party in honor of Alfonso . . . we should at least have a drink together."

Alfonso knew this was *no party*. He went limp with the realization that his life on earth was about over. He just wondered how painful the end would be. He silently prayed for a quick death.

Chrissie reached into the bag on the table and pulled out a bottle of Johnnie Walker Gold and several plastic shot glasses. "Wow, the good stuff," Chrissie said, looking at the label. "The boss must like you." He poured four shots of the good scotch.

Everyone but Alfonso, who's meaty hands were tied behind his back, raised their glass. Chrissie took Alfonso's glass and raised it to his mouth.

"To the Whale and his business sense," Tommy said. "Wait. Wait.

Let's give the guest of honor something to really have a good time at his *party*." He reached into his pocket and removed three blue pills wrapped in cellophane. Tommy tried to put all three pills in Alfonso's mouth. Alfonso gritted his teeth. "Open your freakin' mouth. . . ."

It happened quicker than a blink of an eye. Tommy deftly produced an old fashion shaving razor from his pocket, and, with one smooth movement of his strong arm, sliced Alfonso's left ear off—it plopped on his shoulder, while blood streamed down his neck, and bounced onto the cement floor making a slight rubbery sound. Alfonso's screams enveloped them in a cocoon of piercing sounds.

"Now can you hear. Open your fuckin' mouth and swallow the pills."

Alfonso opened his mouth and took the three pills from Tommy. They raised their shot glasses again, except Alfonso, and Chrissie said, "*Salute!*" as they drank the expensive scotch. "Here ya go." Chrissie poured Alfonso's shot down his throat causing him to swallow the three blue Viagra pills.

They each had another shot of scotch to give the Viagra time to work. Felicia thought she would need the whole bottle to finish her part. After a few minutes, Felicia went back to pleasuring Alfonso. . . .

"Okay, baby. You can stop . . . he's ready," Tommy said. Felicia got off her knees.

"Thanks, Hon, I'll see you later at the club," Chrissie said, as he gave her five thousand dollars cash.

"Good night, boys," she said, still cracking her gum.

"Let's turn this into a pool party. Now, Alfonso, are you ready to go for a swim?" Tommy asked. "After all, you are '*the Whale.*'"

Chrissie looked like he was about to laugh at some joke he was telling in his head, and blurted out, "Three Viagra pills! If your hard-on lasts more than . . . hey, Tommy, what's three times four?"

I've got to find smarter people to work with. "Twelve, you moron. Now let's go, enough with the comedy."

"If your hard-on lasts more than twelve hours, Alfonso, let me know and we'll call a doctor." Chrissie was the only one who laughed.

"Hoist him over the tank," Tommy instructed. Chrissie grabbed a metal chain that was hanging from the ceiling—it was connected to a track that ran lengthwise across the room. He wrapped it around Alfonso's robust chest and under his arms—the chain immediately swallowed by his fat rolls. His face was redder than a firetruck and soaked with sweat and blood. The blood from his ear was now all the way down his arm, dripping onto the floor.

Tommy slapped Alfonso's face. "Hang in there. Don't die before you go swimming."

The fish tank was thirty feet by fifty feet, ten feet high, and eight feet deep. Alfonso turned his bloody face toward the tank. The water was cloudy, so he couldn't see what was inside through the clear cutouts in the tank wall. *It was probably better that way*, he thought.

Chrissie hit a green button on the control box and nothing happened. He kept hitting it over and over, but still nothing happened. "Did you turn the power on?" Tommy asked, exasperated. He preferred to work alone, but this job required help because Alfonso was such a lard-ass and Tommy surely wasn't going to pleasure him, which was essential to send the right message.

"Now it's on." Chrissie hit the green button again. The winch slowly started to wind up toward the rafters in the ceiling. Alfonso started to scream uncontrollably, and his bowels let loose, which gave Tommy and Chrissie a good laugh. He probably would have pissed himself, but he still had an erection. Alfonso rose in the air until his feet were level with the top of the tank. Chrissie walked up a set of stairs that led to the edge of the tank and wrapped another metal chain connected to a winch around his ankles. Chrissie started that winch and Alfonso's legs lifted up so he was hanging over the tank like a fat Superman flying through the air. Alfonso tried to resist but the pain under his shoulders exponentially increased every time he moved. He started begging for his life between hysterical sobs. "Ca-ca-ca-come on guys! Da-da-don't, kill me! I'll do anything! You can have my daughter . . . She's fifteen and a virgin!"

"For that, the party will last a bit longer," Tommy said, with a look of disgust. He tuned out the rest of the begging and screaming, like he always did on jobs and continued.

Chrissie reached into a cooler that was on the table and pulled out a few pieces of raw chicken. He walked back up the stairs at the edge of the tank. He peered down into the churning, cloudy water. He tossed the chicken into the tank. "Don't forget to throw his ear in too," Tommy said. Within seconds, the tank came alive beneath Alfonso who was now hovering over it like a whale—*fitting*, Tommy thought.

Two alligators burst out of the cloudy water and snapped for the chicken at the same time. They were between six and eight feet in length. "Good girls. Now you're awake. Dinner time," Chrissie said, like he was talking to a puppy. The gators thrashed around right below Alfonso who was bleeding into the tank, his erect penis about five feet from the gators snapping jaws.

"Lower him," Tommy said. The winches made a metallic winding sound as Alfonso was lowered about an inch from the water. "Now my two friends here are going to show you a good time like Felicia did," Tommy said, with a sinister laugh. It would be the last thing Alfonso ever heard besides the snapping sound of the gators' jaws ripping at his fat body and chomping on his penis.

— 26 —

FOLD . . . Stuff . . . Lick . . . Seal. That's how Jason usually spent his mornings. *So much for the "good life"*, he thought to himself over and over again. He stuffed mailers into envelopes from 7 to 9 a.m. *Arrested? Facing Deportation? Facing Foreclosure?* He put a bunch of different things on his flyer just to get his phone ringing. He mailed one to every person arrested the night before in Palm Beach County—between 150 to 300 people. At 9:15 he walked to the Post Office to drop off the day's mailers and then to the courthouse. He didn't have a real reason to go to the courthouse since he didn't have any clients. He mainly went to see if he could snag a client or two so he wasn't forgotten in the criminal justice system—it moved on quickly.

Ring . . . Jason quickly grabbed the phone before it could ring a second time. He cradled it in his ear with an expectant smile at the thought of a possible client. "Hello, Law Office of Jason Noble and Associates." Jason's face quickly turned to frustration. "I can't use your internet marketing services until I get some clients to pay for it!" He slammed the phone down. "Damn telemarketers!" Fold . . . Stuff . . . Lick . . . Seal.

THE PHARMACY WAS housed in a two-story art deco building built in 1955. It was on Washington Street, just off Ocean Drive in South Beach, Miami. It was an old Woolworth five-and-dime when Antonio, through an offshore corporation, purchased the building in the eighties after Woolworth filed for bankruptcy. Antonio liked the nostalgia and kept the five-and-dime façade. The place was really a mob social club that was never open to the public.

Antonio walked up behind Mario "Lug Nut" Rizzo, who was sitting playing poker with four other *made* guys, slapped him on the back, and said, "Don't take all this *cugine's* money. We want him to stay in America." The other four laughed.

"Eh, Antonio, sit wit us fo a while. We need some fresh money in dis game." Pinto "Bird Bath" Ravello pleaded. "I'm gettin' killed by dis *cugine*. I wish you'd send him back to Italy befo' I deal da next hand."

"Luck of beginner. We'a no play poker in Italy club," Mario shrugged his shoulders, smiling.

Antonio drained his drink—Johnnie Walker Gold, no ice. "Not yet fellas, I need to see Maxine first and work off a little stress," he said, winking at them. "Besides, the pile of money in the center looks like this game is too rich for my blood . . . I got a wife and kid to support. Besides, I'd rather spend my money on Maxine." Almost every Friday night, Antonio and his crew met at *The Pharmacy* for a little "medicine". Everyone was forbidden from discussing business while Antonio was at the club.

The club was about five thousand square feet, broken up into two rooms. In the front room, a long bar went across the room on the right side. On a stage next to the bar two strippers were gyrating to electric dance music. Four tables were setup for poker in the center of the room. Opposite the bar, along the wall, was a banquet table with all sorts of Italian and Latin food. A few pool tables and two skeet ball games completed the set-up.

"Thanks, Bobbie," Antonio said to the bartender who handed him a refreshed drink. He went into a back room that looked like a mini-replica of Studio 54—the floor intermittently lit up; colored lights strobed and circled around; couches lined the wall; glass tabletops were littered throughout, some with people snorting cocaine; seventy's disco played loud; and waitresses dressed like Playboy Playmates kept everybody liquored up.

He went up a wooden staircase to the second floor. At the top of the landing stood two waitresses. "Can we get you anything, Hon?" The brunette asked.

"No, I'm all set." Antonio walked past them to the main suite. The upstairs had eight bedrooms that were surprisingly well-appointed for a Mafia social club. He went to the last room on the left. The suite was dimly lit by candles and spa music filled the room.

"Get over here you stud and show me what a real man is like," said a female voice from the shadows.

"Oh, Baby. Your *real* man is coming. He's been waiting for this all week."

"Oh, Sugar. You know just what to say to a girl to make her hot. Now get those clothes off and get over here." Maxine commanded, stepping out from behind the shadows in the corner of the room. She was five feet eleven with long auburn hair.

"My God . . . you're a gorgeous woman." Antonio couldn't take his eyes off her body. She was wearing a sheer, white negligée that fit perfectly to her curvy body. The neckline plunged just below her full breasts.

I'd love to have sex with you right now, Antonio thought. "I wish I wasn't married," he said as he took his silk tie off.

"Who cares if you're *married*." She gently ran her fingers over her now hard nipple. "It doesn't stop any of the other guys. My girls can't keep up with your crew of unfaithful freaks."

"I've got enough stress in my life. I don't need to add to it by cheating. Plus, your massage is better than sex. I fantasize about it all week." He removed his pants and walked over to the massage table in the center of the room.

"You'll make an honest woman out of me one day. For now, I'll have to be happy with rubbing my hands all over this tight, tan body of yours for the next hour."

— 28 —

"I want Antonio in orange in three days!" Trevor said, slamming his fist on the unnecessary lectern. He flexed his hand from the pain. Trevor looked to the back of the once sparsely filled conference room, which was renamed the *Antonio Barrera War Room*, above his trial teams' heads, which was now plus two since their last meeting; paralegal, Jana Wisp and Senior U.S. Marshall, Wade Tome joined the team—not by choice. Trevor, subconsciously, straightened his posture and adjusted his tie—always preparing to be in front of the cameras. "The longer Antonio Barrera is on the street, the less safe our children are."

DEA agent Lisa Hoyt rolled her eyes and whispered to FBI Special Agent Jackson Reed, "He looks like he's talking into a damn TV camera."

"Sir, federal inmates wear blue jumpsuits when they're locked-up pretrial at FDC (Federal Detention Center)," U.S. Marshall Tome corrected. He was added to coordinate the ultimate apprehension and arrest of Antonio.

"Whatever . . . just get ready to arrest Barrera." He commanded, pointing at each one of the team. "I want Barrera off the streets by *this* weekend. Is that understood?"

They each nodded in agreement. None of them thought he would actually arrest Antonio Barrera this soon, especially since he wanted to seek the death penalty.

"What are you going to arrest him on at this point? . . . Parking violations?" asked IRS Agent Miache Charles.

"If your department bothered to share once in a while, then you'd know what we have on Barrera," Trevor said dismissively. "We have him linked to murder, gambling, stock fraud, human trafficking, sex trafficking . . . you name it and he's 'trafficked-it'. . . especially kids."

Jackson Reed cut-in and explained in his baritone voice, "You have information connecting Barrera's *Crew* to those crimes, *not* Barrera. No one in his crew is talking. Trust me, I know. Once Confidential Source One-six-six-five, Alfonso 'the Whale' Tomisino, went radio silent . . . we lost our only mole inside. Everyone else is too scared to talk, especially with the rumors of how Alfonso died. . . ." Jackson's face contorted to a look of disgust.

"I heard he was slowly tortured for a week. They even made him eat his own genitals," Lisa said, covering her crotch at the horrifying thought. "That's one time I'd be glad I'm a woman . . . much less to eat." Everyone but Trevor laughed at the notion.

"Gross," Jana Wisp said, pretending she was throwing up.

"That's street gossip to keep the soldiers in line. We believe he went to Thailand to satisfy his need for really young boys," Sr. FBI Agent Tomas De Cruz corrected. "We know Barrera was just officially made the boss when he went to Cuba to meet with The Godfather, Don Giovanni and his Iguana, Carlito, according to our sources there."

"Who cares where this *Whale* guy is or when Barrera was officially made the 'boss,'" Trevor said, trying to refocus them. "Just put together everything you all have on Barrera and his crew. I will get the Indictment; trust me . . . I can indict a ham sandwich."

"Our evidence on the Whale's death is about as good as a jailhouse baloney sandwich," Tomas DeCruz interrupted. The only potential lead we have is a stripper whose a meth freak with a five-page rap sheet . . . zero credibility—I wouldn't even build a possession of marijuana case around her testimony if she was the one smoking the weed." Everyone except Trevor laughed.

"So, I'll indict her too. Charge'em both with conspiracy in this Whale guy's death—who cares where he really is—he won't come into court and say he's alive. When this whore is facing a murder charge, she'll get in line real quick and testify the *right* way. I'll have her looking like a choir girl by the time of trial. That's another murder to ensure I give Barrera the chair. Thanks for the idea, De Cruz. Good thinking." De

Cruz leaned back in his chair with that *are you fucking kidding me look.*

"Sir, Braxton Murphy is here from the Department of Defense," Trevor's secretary interrupted through the phone intercom that was in the center of the conference table.

"DOD, here? For you?" Jackson asked, looking suspiciously at Trevor.

"Uh-it's-uh . . . nothing . . . different case. Alright, everyone, let's get to work. Remember, I want to see Antonio Barrera in orange or blue or whatever, as long as he's in handcuffs, in three days."

"HAVE A SEAT, Braxton," Trevor offered. He got up from behind his desk and walked over to the interior office wall and closed the blinds.

"Morning, Trevor," Braxton Murphy from the Department of Defense said. He looked around the sparsely furnished office. "Two corner offices. One here and one in Miami . . . nice."

"My West Palm office is a little more private—no one at DOJ cares what happens in the West Palm office, might as well be the Alaskan office. This meeting requires the utmost secrecy and confidentiality, right?" Trevor affirmed.

"Of course," Braxton responded, staring hard at Trevor.

"So, what do you have for me and how did you know I needed it?" Trevor smiled and took a sip of coffee from his *Big Boss* mug.

"When I heard through the grapevine that you were about to take down mob boss Antonio Barrera, I wanted to help."

Trevor leaned forward and fixed his eyes on Braxton's . . . searching . . . "Why do you want to help me? And who's the leak? Is it Herb? . . . that bitch from DEA?"

"Don't worry about the leak—I know everything, I catalog surveillance audio and video for every law enforcement and spy agency the Feds have. Other than the president, I have the highest security clearance in the government. I don't really care about helping *you*, as much as I want Antonio convicted. He's scum of the earth in my book. My niece overdosed on some bad heroin and I traced the supplier back to someone from Alphonso Tomisini's crew."

"His name just came up in my meeting about the takedown of Barrera." Trevor leaned all the way back in his chair now, his feet slightly dangling. "They call him 'the Whale'. Apparently, he was an FBI informant and is missing—either dead or off with an underage boy in some Asian country. No one seems to know for sure. I think he's a capo in Barrera's crime family."

"Well, wherever he is, I hope he's suffering. This is my chance to get back at Antonio for killing my niece with that poison he makes his guys sell."

A man committed to the same cause by tragedy and revenge . . . this should work out perfectly, Trevor thought. "Continue."

"First, if I help you convict Barrera, what are you going to do for me?" Braxton leaned forward in his chair as he asked his all-important question. He was about to retire after a twenty-eight-year distinguished career, until the end, at the DoD. He didn't want to retire but had no choice after the government made him the fall guy for the Wikileaks scandal.

Trevor stood up, put his hand to his chin like he was pondering a very serious question. . . . "You're going to come with me to the governor's mansion—a cabinet level position . . . then maybe the Whitehouse." Trevor's face broke into a smile. "How does National Security Advisor sound? You can put those two PhDs in computer science from Harvard and Princeton to good use."

Braxton contemplated this for a moment. . . .

"Plus, maybe you can get a little revenge on the DoD for the Wikileaks *thing*." This was Trevor's gift: he figured out how to tap into people's desire for revenge and heavily leveraged it to get what he wanted. "It must be frustrating to a Full Bird Colonel that your job now is to catalog surveillance video . . . isn't that how you found our little gem on Antonio? Lucky for me you got transferred."

Braxton smiled. "The CIA was testing out some new surveillance tech on an anti-terror operation. They literally 'bugged' a few warehouses at the Port of Palm Beach with mosquito cams—high definition cameras and mics built into a bug the size of a bug. Antonio was having a secret meeting to motivate his guys to earn more money for him. Since he wasn't talking about committing a terrorist act, the CIA ignored the footage and tagged it for archiving."

"So . . . what's on the video? It better be something good for a cabinet position."

"Trust me, it'll make your job convicting Antonio easier than an open layup." Braxton stood ramrod straight, extended his hand and announced, "I'm in." They shook hands to seal the deal.

Trevor held on to Braxton's hand and demanded, "Now, let's see the video."

— 30 —

THE TWO CRABS were in a death match over a Cheeto. Their little legs scurried on the hot sand like a choreographed dance—three steps forward . . . three steps back. They stayed just out of reach of the gently breaking waves.

Jason was sitting in his beach chair at the ocean's edge on Palm Beach, which was five minutes from his condo. It was a Tuesday afternoon and he just opened his second Corona. The sun was at its peak—not a cloud in the sky. A few boats dotted the horizon—the glistening waves smooth and calm. *I live in paradise*, Jason thought, as he looked out, pretending to crush one of the boats between his fingertips. *Now, if I can just figure out how to afford to stay in paradise.*

The tornado of stress he felt every day right before he quit the PD's Office was back; only this time, it was fueled by one thought—*will I ever get a paying client!* He'd been on his own for a few weeks and still didn't have a paying client—private or court appointed. He received some phone calls for traffic tickets, but that was it. At this point, he refused to become a traffic ticket lawyer—toiling away with hundreds of cases for a hundred bucks a case. *No thank you.* He was determined not to work on volume. He wanted to give each case the attention it deserved. Not like when he was at the Public Defender's Office with too many cases to properly prepare any one of them. Plus, he could try an armed robbery and attempted murder case (he never had an actual murder case, yet), but he had no idea what to do with a traffic ticket. The Constitution didn't guarantee an accused the right to an attorney for any crime or infraction that was punishable by less than six months in jail, so he never had to handle one as an assistant public defender.

Jason picked up his phone and checked his email: *USDCSD-OFFI-*

CIAL was the subject of the first one. He tapped his screen and read the email. *Bar Exam Results.* He kept telling himself that he was never going to practice in federal court so the results didn't matter; but suddenly, with the results in front of him, he got a little nervous. *What if I failed!* He held his breath and tapped on the attached file: *PASS.* He exhaled deeply, a broad smile spreading across his face. He picked up his Corona and said, to no one in particular, "Cheers to me." He took a long swig of the beer and savored the view for a minute.

He turned his attention back to his emails. The second one more exciting that the first: *NEW CLIENT LEAD FROM WEBSITE SERVER.* Jason almost pushed his finger through the screen he was so excited to tap the email. *Wash Sampson, dob: 11/3/74, charge: Driving Under the Influence (DUI).* His smile slightly diminished. *Oh well, at least it's not a speeding ticket.*

"Hey! Anyone here!" yelled the greasy-looking man standing, more like leaning, on the empty reception desk in Jason's office. "Not much of a law firm, especially if it ain't got no lawyers." The man grumbled to himself, as he slowly looked around the office.

"Hello, Mr. Sampson?" Jason said, as he walked out to the desk. He resisted the urge to recoil at the foul odor, a mixture of booze and BO, that emanated from his potential new client—Wash Sampson. Wash was slight with a lifetime of alcohol abuse and poor nutrition written all over his face. Jason extended his hand, making sure he made direct eye contact—Jason read that direct eye contact was a sign of confidence, although Wash's eyes seemed to struggle to stay in one place.

Wash looked down at Jason's hand for a moment, then limply shook it. "You the lawyer that's gonna get my bullshit case dismissed? This an easy case for any lawyer, so don't go chargin' me an arm and leg. I know all about you lawyers," squinting his eyes now.

What an ass. How about a "hello" before you tell me you think I'm a slimeball. "Please, Mr. Sampson, we'll get to all that in a minute. Why don't you come into my office and sit down." Jason moved to the side and extended his arm pointing into his office. Sorry about no receptionist, uh, uh, Mary is out sick. Would you like some coffee or water?"

Mr. Sampson stood up straight, looked at Jason for a second, "I'm *watching* you," then walked into the office. "I'll take a coffee. You got any breakfast?" Wash's face lit up at the thought of a good breakfast.

It's three in the afternoon and this guy wants breakfast! Great! I'm betting this guy has no job, and therefore, no money. "The coffee I can do . . . sorry, but I don't have breakfast for you. You'll love the coffee though, a special blend from Columbia."

Jason went into his file/storage/kitchen closet-sized room and put some cheap instant coffee and hot water into a mug. He walked into his office. "Here you go, Mr. Sampson. Columbia's finest." Jason sat down behind his desk. "Now, how can I help you?"

"I'm gonna help you make a name for yourself with my high-profile case."

Jason looked at him, confused. "You're Wash Sampson, right? The guy with the DUI charge?"

"Never heard of me? Huh? You must not have practiced law here very long. Everyone knows me in Palm Beach. I'm a *V.I.P.—very important prick.*" Wash cracked himself up over his little joke.

"Ha. Ha. Good one." Jason looked down at his yellow legal pad, picked up a pen and scribbled—CRAZY. "Do you have any paperwork on your case?"

Wash picked up the Christmas edition Starbucks coffee mug and took a long sip of the hot coffee. He closed his dancing eyes. "Mmmm. This is gooood stuff." He put the mug down, opened his eyes, and reached into his heavily worn, green sport coat and pulled out some crumpled papers. As Jason took them, Wash said, "Now make sure you give me the *high-profile* discount. Hell, after you learn who I am, you'll probably take the case for free." Wash's shaky hand let go of the crumpled papers.

Jason later learned that Wash Sampson was anything but a *VIP*. He was an on-again/off-again—more *on-again*—alcoholic who hit it big then lost it all to his drug of choice: huffing canned air. Wash won a three million dollar settlement after he was hit by the *Diva Duck*, which caused him to have the tremors in his eyes. The *Diva Duck* was a huge amphibious vehicle that took people on tours around West Palm Beach and Palm Beach, both on land and water; it quacked every few minutes, which was maddening when it passed through a neighborhood on a Sunday morning.

Jason flattened the crumpled papers: two yellow, carbon copy court event forms and one traffic citation that was made of that plastic-like paper. He scanned them. "Is this your first DUI?" he asked Wash, testing his truthfulness.

Wash was now leaning forward, "Yes, Sir. Never been in trouble before."

Jason frowned. "Then why are you charged with felony DUI?" Most crimes are classified by different levels of misdemeanors or felonies based on the maximum jail or prison sentence: *jail* is a facility where you go pre-trial and serve a sentence of one year or less and *prison* is where you serve a sentence of a year-and-a-day or more. Jason learned this distinction the hard way in front of Judge Georgia "No Release" Reece when he told her his client had been to "jail" before when it was technically prison. She accused him of misrepresenting to the court and almost held him in contempt his first day in her courtroom. DUI was either a misdemeanor or felony depending on if the defendant has been arrested for DUIs in the past. "You have at least two prior DUI convictions within the past ten years because you're charged with felony DUI, which is punishable by up to five years in prison and cares a minimum mandatory sentence of thirty days in jail."

Wash looked back at Jason with a blank stare. "Must be a mistake." Wash shrugged his shoulders. "Yeah, gotta be. I ain't never been in no trouble before. And, don't you go chargin' me—"

"We'll get to my fee in a minute." Jason knew it likely wasn't a mistake, but he'd humor Wash. His goal was to finally get a paying client. *And now a little salesmanship by fear.* "The prosecutor is probably going to want to send you to prison for the max—five years DOC (Department of Corrections). . . ." Jason waited for the thought of *prison* to sink in. "But, don't worry, I know all the prosecutors—*technically true.* If you hire me, I can get rid of the prison time." Jason didn't even know who the prosecutor was, but it sounded good. *It was sales puffing, not lying,* he rationalized in his head. By the way, how'd you get here? You know you can't drive? Right?"

Wash looked at Jason with confidence in his eyes. "I *can* drive. This is all an attempt to frame me by the government because of what I know.

Besides, I drove here very, very slowly, so no problem . . . slow people don't get pulled over. If you really cared that much about me, you'd have made a house call, well, actually a *bridge call*—my current housing is under the Palm Beach Lakes Blvd. Bridge."

What a waste of time. This guy is more broke than me!

"Just tell me how much this is going to cost."

"Normally I charge five thousand dollars to handle a felony DUI; but, I like you, so I will reduce that fee to twenty-five hundred dollars— which is a steal for my services." Jason had no clue what to charge, but he knew twenty-five hundred was his monthly salary as an assistant public defender, so getting that amount for one case sounded good to him.

Wash reached into his pocket. *That was easy*, Jason thought and started to smile at the anticipation of getting his first private fee. Wash slapped four, crumpled fifty-dollar bills on Jason's desk. "This should get you started. There's a bonus in it for you if you get the case dismissed."

Jason's smile quickly faded. "Mr. Sampson, I'm not taking your felony case for—" Jason thumbed through the fifties, "Two hundred dollars."

"I'll have the rest soon." Wash got up and turned to leave. "This case is easy, just get it dismissed."

"Wait! Mr. Sampson?"

"You'll do a great job as my new lawyer. You'll thank me for this someday." Wash didn't look back as he headed out the door.

Jason sighed, swiveled his chair around and looked out the window. *I don't know what's more depressing: the horrible start to my law practice or this view of the rusted parking garage.*

— -32 —

Luke entered his office, which was also the main control-room for the entire production line. It was a simple, ten-thousand square foot open industrial room. A small, enclosed office was in the back corner. The "control console" was situated to the right of the entrance. It had a bank of six, twelve-inch monitors, each dancing with its own digital activity. Painted on the light gray, rubber-coated floor around the console was a five-inch red boarder with the words: *AUTHORIZED PERSONNEL ONLY*.

Luke looked down at Darla who was sitting at a metal desk in the center of the room, facing the entrance, and requested, "Darla, get me a coffee and Mollie-June some eucalyptus tea, please?" Luke learned a long time ago that you could never *order* Darla-Jean Ruiz to do anything; he had to *request* something be done—she would grant the *request* if she felt like it. Around her entire desk was a five-inch red boarder with white bold lettering that read: *CROSS THIS LINE AT YOUR OWN RISK!*

"I don't need tea, thank you." Mollie-June said through the open office door.

Luke rolled his eyes and mouthed to Darla, "Get the tea . . . please."

Luke walked into his office and took off his white hard hat and placed it on the edge of the desk. Mollie-June turned from staring out at the production floor and immediately focused on the hardhat. "Is that where your hardhat belongs?" She walked over to the desk, picked it up, and placed it in its proper spot on a coat rack in the corner.

"Why don't you sit down, dear." Luke pointed to a chair around a little metal table in the middle of the office. There was a plain gray, metal desk off to the side with only an un-opened, Dell computer box on it. Luke's production facility was state of the art, but he still hated computers and refused to put one in his office. He'd say: "Ain't nutin' a cooomputer can do that this here brain can't do with some pen and paper." And he had proven it on more than one occasion over the years.

She stared at him for a moment, then walked over to the chair and sat down as if she weighed a thousand pounds. Before Luke could sit next to her, she unloaded her troubles: "I'm concerned . . . I think Trevor is going mad." She fiddled with a paper clip, looking down at her hands as she spoke. "He called today . . . talking crazy."

"Trevor called? What did he want?"

"He wanted money. I'm concer—"

"Trevor called *you* about *money*." Luke's tone getting louder with each word.

Mollie-June looked up at Luke, tears welling up in her blue eyes. "I'm concerned our boy may have a drug problem. The devil's poison may be running through his veins. He kept saying: 'Wouldn't it be great if I became the Governor of Florida . . . then you and Dad would be proud of me.' I told him we were very proud of the man he's become, but he just continued: 'I need one hundred million dollars. The time is right. Tell Dad to give me the money. I need it now. I can't wait. I'm going to be in the news soon for a high-profile case and I want to announce right after I get a guilty verdict.'" Mollie-June looked back down and moved on to fiddling with a pen after she mangled the paper clip.

Luke reached out his weathered hand and gently took Mollie-June's delicate hands. "Look at me, my dear. Trevor will be fine . . . he doesn't have a drug problem, he has a *vanity* problem. He's always been a little too high on himself. God knows I tried to work the vanity out of him when he was a boy, but no matter how many fields he plowed or horse stalls he cleaned, he always thought he was better than everyone around him."

— 33 —

TREVOR SLAMMED THE phone down on his desk. Even though he loved his mom, Mollie-June, her constant worrying made him crazy. He saw it as an insult that she didn't just say: *Of course I will tell Luke to write you a check for millions of dollars for your campaign, or I will write it myself.* He had no doubt she never wrote a check for anything in her life.

Money was a matter exclusively handled by the man of the household. *My Mollie June don't need to worry herself 'bout no money, I've got her taken care of, you hear, boy?* Luke chastised Trevor whenever he mentioned a word about Mollie-June not being an independent woman with her own bank account, or at least access to their joint accounts. Although, for his own marriage, Trevor wished he had followed Luke's policy with Marlene. Unfortunately for him, Marlene controlled the money and spent ten times what he made.

Trevor was back in his Miami office staring out the window at Biscayne Bay daydreaming about International headlines: *OPERATION CANNOLI A SUCCESS . . . TREVOR WHITTINGHAM SAVES THE CHILDREN . . . If I'm lucky, the Mafia will put a contract on my head—that'll get a lot of media coverage.*

He named the investigation against Antonio Barrera *Operation Cannoli* because he thought it would look good as a newspaper headline. No one else on the "team" liked the name.

"Herb is here to see you," his secretary announced through the intercom, interrupting his daydreaming.

"Uh, send him in." Trevor sat back down at his desk.

Herb sat down in one of the black, cloth chairs in front of Trevor's desk. He paused for a moment, looking at Trevor, a slight smirk curled at the corners of his mouth. Herb wanted to bust out laughing at the sight of Trevor's chunky, short frame sitting in his oversized chair. "Hi, boss," he finally said. "What do you want me to do with Antonio's information for the grand jury? When are you going to review it? I don't think we'll make it for tomorrow's grand jury. You're probably going to want to push it off a few weeks, so you're more prepared."

Trevor sat back in his chair and put his hands behind his head. "I'll be prepared, like always. You do most of the questioning. It's just a grand jury proceeding. You know the saying: *You can indict a ham sandwich.* You can't screw this up."

"Thanks for the vote of confidence." Herb sighed.

"Just make sure you defer all media to me. Don't make any statements. I'll handle that."

"I'm not worried about the media. I'm worried about our weak case," Herb responded with dismay.

"Weak case?"

"So what, we get an indictment. Proving the case at trial, *beyond and to the exclusion of all reasonable doubt,* won't be an easy task based on my assessment at this point. Especially since you want to seek the death penalty."

Trevor eyed Herb hard. "So, what's *your* assessment?"

This guy's the worst kind of idiot, Herb thought as he tried to hold back the disgust that his face was fighting to show. *You don't know the first thing about the case and you want to put someone to death.* "Well, let me explain," Herb said, his face now showing a condescending smile.

"Hurry up, I have things to do."

"The case against Antonio is full of speculation, hearsay, and weak connections to low-level associates. Our main witness on one of the murder counts where you're asking for the death penalty is a junkie stripper. Frankly, when informant Alfonso 'the Whale' Tomisini was killed, we lost our best witness that would have made this case a slam dunk. . . . It would take years to develop another informant inside Antonio's crew."

Trevor grabbed his pen and wrote something on a yellow legal pad. . . . He showed it to Herb: *I DON'T CARE!!!* "You got it! And we don't have *years.* Antonio Barrera has been a criminal his whole life. The amount of evidence connecting him to serious crimes must be overwhelming. You're just not smart enough to see it I guess." Trevor looked away from Herb, dismissing him with his body language.

Herb swallowed his pride and thought, *Only one more year until retirement. Keep it together.* "I'll look harder to see the connections, Boss."

"That's my boy. Be more positive . . . and appreciative. This case will be a good career advancer for you. You're welcome."

What a douche. "Right. Yeah. Thanks, I guess. But I'm pretty sure I don't need anymore career advancement since my career is only going to last about one more year."

"Whatever." Trevor looked down at some irrelevant papers on his desk.

"By the way, the video you claim will bring everything together and make this case a slam dunk would be really helpful. Where is it?" Herb pleaded.

"Don't worry about it. By the time this case goes to trial, which will be in a few weeks, you'll have it. Government exhibit number one will be the video, so start tagging the trial exhibits with number two. You don't need the video to get the Indictment. If you think you need it for the grand jury, let me know and I will get another assistant to help me with this ridiculously easy case."

— 34 —

"STRIKE!" YELLED THE ten-year-old; her red pigtails bouncing as she jumped with joy. "In yo' face, Conner." She pointed at her brother as she skipped back to her seat.

"Lucky shot . . . should'a been a gutta ball . . . I'm still gonna beat you. Suzie's gonna luzie." Conner chided in a singsong voice. His gangly, sixteen-year-old body was hunched over the scorer's table.

"Mom, tell Conner to stop making fun of me," Suzie complained. "He's going to break my *Zen*." She closed her eyes, put her hands together like she was praying, took a deep breath, and exhaled hard.

"Zen? What? Stop being dramatic, Suzie . . . and, Conner Roy, stop making fun of your sister. Nice shot, baby," Mom said, winking at Suzie, a big smile spreading across her face.

Wise Guy Lanes in West Palm Beach on Old Okeechobee Blvd. was busy for a Thursday night—tourist season was underway. Barrera Capo, Alfonso "the Whale" Tomisini opened the place a few years ago in the forgotten industrial district of downtown West Palm Beach. The front was a bowling alley, one of the few left in Palm Beach County, with ten lanes and a bar. Adjacent to the bar were five pool tables and two dart boards. Off to one corner was a DJ playing the latest pop hits. The bowling alley was dark except for the glow of large screen TV's spread throughout, scorer's table screens, and pulsating colored disco lights. The TV's were broadcasting sports from the U.S. and around the world—for Alfonso and his crew to keep track of their sport books and for the degenerate gamblers who occasionally had to spend quality time with their kids. The place made good money on the gambling alone—Alfonso's guys took action on everything: bowling, darts, pool, and worldwide sports.

The back room was the crew's hangout. Alfonso had it sound-proofed. It was the size of a large living room with a bar, several poker tables, a few couches, and two stripper poles rounded out the decorum.

"Alright!, Everyone! Time to GO! The lanes are closed," yelled Bobbie "the Whistle" Frateli—who got his nickname because of his loud voice. He was a large man with a pockmarked face and jet black hair, slicked back. His voice was fighting with the music to get everyone's attention.

Bobbie looked over at the DJ station, which was about twenty feet away on the other side of the lanes. "Shut that shit off!" The DJ had no reaction due to the red *Beats* headphones over his ears. Bobbie's face turned red and his eyes narrowed on the DJ as he made a beeline for him across the lanes, which got all the bowlers' attention.

He stopped in front of the DJ who was looking down at two Apple computer screens. His bushy blonde hair spilling out of his black hoodie. Bobbie grabbed him by the hoodie and smashed his head into one of the Apple computers. His headphones came partially off. Bobbie ripped them off his head as the DJ stood up. He stepped back and looked at Bobbie, his face showing confusion and fear as blood poured out of his nose. "I said, SHUT THAT SHIT OFF!" Bobbie spat on the kid as he yelled.

The DJ extended his shaking hand and depressed the *off* button on his equipment and said between gasps of air, "Why'd . . . you . . . do . . . that?"

Bobbie ignored the kid and turned away from him. "Everyone ou—"

"You're gonna pay for anything you broke. And my nose! I think you broke my nose! My dad's a lawyer; he's gonna sue this place."

For a big man, Bobbie turned surprisingly quick and hit the D.J. square in the jaw with a right hook. The kid fell like a sack of potatoes, unconscious before he hit the ground. Bobbie shook out his right hand, turned around to the customers and calmly said, "Everyone, time to go. On your way out, pick up a gift certificate for a free game and popcorn."

No one moved a muscle.

"Get the hell OUT! NOW!"

Everyone in the place packed up their stuff and rushed to the counter to return their multicolored bowling shoes. Most people that came to *Wise Guy Lanes* knew exactly what type of place it really was and they wanted no part of whatever was about to happen.

"Jimmy, get this little punk out of here. Toss 'em in his car," Bobbie instructed.

"How do I know what car is his?" Jimmy asked, as he walked over to the DJ, who was starting to regain consciousness.

"Figure it out, you moron." Jimmy was the low man on the totem pole in Alfonso's crew—he was an associate, not a made-guy. And from his level of intelligence, he wasn't likely to go very far, but he was loyal. Bobbie walked into the back room.

"What the fuck was all that racket?" Tim "the Duck" Bellini asked. He had a genetic disorder that caused the skin between his feet and hands not to separate at birth so it looked like webbing.

"Just turning off the music," Bobbie answered with a smirk. Bobbie was Alphonso the Whale's second in command. The other four guys in the room were Alphonso's lieutenants—good earners with leadership skills: there was Tim "the Duck" Bellini; Phil "the Pick" (last name unknown), who got his nickname because he only used an ice pick on jobs; Luca "the Latin" Pompeo, who got his nickname because of his connections to Central America; and Robert "No-No" Romano, who hated his nickname because it came from kids in school teasing him—*No, No Romano* they used to say when he wanted to play with them; that's why he left school in the sixth grade after he set it on fire . . . with everyone in it.

Jimmy returned, he was out of breath. "That DJ woke up, had to crack his skull again."

"Eh. Jimmy, get us some drinks. Scotch and sodas work boys?" Tim asked.

"Yeah, but add a lime to mine, will ya." Romano said.

"A lime? . . . Huh," Luca said, looking at Romano with one eyebrow raised.

"You got a problem with dat, Luca?" Romano's eyes narrowed.

The stare down was broken by Tim's hearty laugh, as he slapped his thigh with his webbed hand. "You guys are ready to kill each other over a lime. . . I love it. Do it! Do it!"

Luca broke the stare first. "I'm just bustin' balls, *rilassare*."

"Be careful who's balls you bust," Romano said in a whisper as he leaned toward Luca, not breaking the stare.

"Enough, guys, we have serious business to discuss," Bobbie said, refocusing them. "Jimmy, also make sure all the staff out front is gone and lock the doors." That's why Jimmy was at such a high-level meeting of Alphonso's crew. They needed someone to get them drinks. "Tim go wit'em and sweep for bugs one more time. Me and Phil will sweep this room again."

Luca took a cigarette out of his pocket and lit it. He blew a large plume of smoke. "God damn, Luca; you still smoke? Haven't you seen that commercial where the broad has no legs from smoking?" Phil said, waving his hand in front of his face

"Those commercials are bullshit. Ain't no way smokin' makes you lose no damn legs—smoke goes in my lungs. That's just government propaganda." Luca took another long drag of his Camel unfiltered cigarette and blew it at Phil.

"Enough with the surgeon general warning, let's just sweep the room again. We gotta make sure the Feds or Antonio ain't listenin'," Bobbie said, putting them back on task. Antonio was so paranoid about disloyalty he was known to bug his own guys' hangouts and cars.

Jimmy and Tim entered the room. "All clear out front," Tim confirmed. Jimmy placed a tray of drinks on the table in front of the guys then left.

"Alright. What's the word on the street about Alphonso?" Bobbie asked Luca first.

"Haven't heard from him in over two weeks. I have no idea where he is. My contacts in Panama told me he left on the cargo ship happy and healthy a few weeks ago—they lost two, an old lady and young boy, on the trip, but that's expected . . . no big deal," Luca answered.

"Last I heard, he was supposed to meet that fuckin' gorilla, Chrissie, to talk about some union problems at the Port." Tim offered. "Then poof—he disappeared." Tim took a drag of his cigarette and blew the smoke on his fingertips and opened them in mock *poof.*

"Sounds like the work of a magician. Who do we know that's a *Magic Man*?" Romano added while he chomped on an ice cube.

"We need to deal in facts, not school-girl gossip. We have no idea if Antonio had him wacked," Bobbie scolded.

"Is he on another run for 'cattle' over in that shithole Panama?" Romano asked.

"Watch what you say about my adopted homeland *hombre*," Luca warned. "No, Alphonso's not made another run since the one I just mentioned. My contacts there would know for sure."

After about thirty minutes and two scotch and sodas each, they circled back to Antonio Barrera as the reason Alphonso was missing. Bobbie looked at each man and said, "Listen up, fellas. We don't know shit, yet. Keep your ears to the street and let's find out where Alphonso is—even if it's at the bottom of the ocean, *capisce*. For now, tell everyone who asks: 'Alphonso's away on business and it's none of their damn business where the fuck he is.' Direct all business through me." Bobbie let that last statement hang in the air for a minute . . . then added, "Anyone have a problem with that?"

They all responded *no,* but when it came to Phil, he hesitated . . . thinking he should take Alphonso's place, but he ultimately said *no* too.

"Good," Bobbie said, "Now, let's get back to earnin'. Act normal, but tell everyone to go into protection mode—carry extra guns, never be alone, and start saving money. I will hold back some cash from Antonio when I kick upstairs to him at the end of the week. That money will be for us in this room . . . in case this is a long drawn out war."

— 35 —

AN ALPHABET SOUP of federal and local law enforcement agencies descended on Antonio Barrera's Palm Beach mansion at 5:00 a.m. on Friday, November 1. Trevor called in everyone: FBI, ATF, DEA, DOJ, Coast Guard, Homeland Security, Postal Inspectors, IRS, U.S. Marshals, Palm Beach Police and Palm Beach County Sheriff's Office (PBSO). Trevor knew all of this was probably unnecessary, but it looked better on TV for him to stand in front of the cameras with dozens of agents from a multitude of agencies. All he really had to do was call Antonio's lawyer, Peter Cohn, and tell him to surrender to the Marshal's office in Miami. *But what fun would that be*, Trevor thought when he was planning the arrest.

"Everyone in place?" Trevor squawked over the radio . . . no response back. "I say again, everyone in place? . . ." Still nothing.

U.S. Marshall Tad Rutherford was standing next to Trevor, who was as far away from the action as possible. "Turn the radio to channel three," Tad said, rolling his eyes.

"Uh. Yeah. I knew that . . . I just forgot, probably from all the adrenaline pumping through my veins." Trevor turned the dial to channel three. "Everyone in place?"

"Roger that. We've been waiting with our thumbs up our asses. What's taking so long?" FBI SA Jackson Reed whispered through the radio—he was lead on the entry team at the front of the house.

"Um . . . nothing . . . ready . . . GO! GO! GO!" Trevor yelled, clinching his whole body, especially his sphincter.

SA Reed pointed with two fingers at the hinges at the front double doors. Even though Trevor was overall "lead," no one was going to listen to him when the stakes were life and death. Two DEA agents immediately moved to the door and placed little silver stickers on each hinge. Behind Reed and the two agents were a group of six police officers and various federal agents ready to explode into the house and capture their prey.

Reed's team was duplicated at each entryway around the mansion—eight total. The team knew there was a person on the first floor in the kitchen and two people on the second floor in separate rooms by real-time thermal imaging of the house. Everyone had a watch-like device on their wrist with a split screen: on the left side was the real-time thermal imaging and on the right was real-time video of what SA Reed was seeing. The few seconds it took to depress the call button on a radio, say *Go. Go. Go*, let the radio go, and pick up a weapon could mean the difference between life and death, so everyone reacted to Reed's actions not his words. The other breach teams silently placed silver stickers on the hinges of the doors they were at and the windows of the occupied rooms on the second floor.

Lisa was crouched behind a row of hedges that ran along the northside of the mansion. She was North and East side containment—if anyone got past the breach teams, she was responsible for taking them down. She saw the hinges on the front doors explode through her watch. She moved silently, but swiftly, toward the east side of the mansion—her eyes constantly scanning the grounds. Lisa rounded a corner and came face to face with a Doberman Pinscher that looked ready to defend the house at all costs. It stood like a statue, intensely staring at her, bearing its teeth—*grrr*. "Good boy . . . I'm your friend . . . see . . . I have some food for you." Lisa stood tall and held out her hand with a wet piece of meat she took out of the cargo pocket of her BDUs. Within seconds the Doberman was eating out of her hand. She threw another piece of meat about ten yards away and the Doberman ran to get it. She always carried food on raids, better to feed a dog and calm it down then shoot it. She heard a woman scream and glass-breaking sounds coming from the mansion.

Lisa locked eyes with the two officers that had *PBSO SWAT* emblazoned in yellow across their bullet proof vests coming across the back of the house from the South side. She motioned down what appeared to be a stone entrance into the home's cellar that the breach teams overlooked. Along the shoreline were three Coast Guard Cutters ready to provide marine support. Overhead was a local police helicopter for arial support. She heard a dog yelp in the distance.

Lisa extended her hands in front of her that held a Glock 22, forty caliber semi-automatic pistol with nuclear sites. As she stepped into the entryway, she clicked on the flashlight attached to the barrel of her gun. The stone steps were moss covered and slippery. They led to a set of double steel doors. She carefully descended the stairs. A dank smell hit her in the face. As she stepped on the landing, the double doors smashed open. Her gun went off as she was knocked backwards the gun and flashlight now pointing skyward. Her head hit the stone stairs. Her eye site started fading to black. She felt a heavy foot on her chest as a man ran over her. She grabbed his ankle just enough to cause him to stumble up the stairs. *Get down now! NOW! . . . You're gonna pay for that.* Was the last thing Lisa heard before she went totally black.

Antonio Barrera was apprehended by the two SWAT team officers. Three other FBI agents arrived and tended to Lisa. She finally got to her feet, but her head ached like it was about to split open, her vision still a bit blurry. Antonio was lying face down on the ground, hands cuffed behind his back. Numerous agents and officers were standing around him, guns drawn.

"Where's Antonio? Did we get 'em?" Trevor asked through the radio.

"Roger that. He's in the backyard," one of the agents said.

"Don't move him, I'll be right there."

"Thanks, guys, for having my back," Lisa said, as she walked between the agents surrounding Antonio. Lisa looked around then came down hard with her knee into Antonio's back. She leaned close to his ear and whispered, "We got you, you son of a bitch."

He let out a groan. "Bitch. I want my lawyer," he managed to choke out in a low voice, full of pain.

"What happened to Antonio?" Trevor asked, as he came running to the back of the mansion, huffing and puffing.

"He tripped up the stairs, fleeing, after he assaulted me," Lisa said.

"Yeah, the idiot tripped." One of the local police officers confirmed.

"Well . . . get him up so I can walk him to the car. Doesn't look good for the cameras if we have to carry him out."

"There aren't any cameras here, they couldn't know about the raid yet," SA Jackson Reed said, glaring at Trevor as he walked out a back-patio door of the mansion.

"Uh . . . well . . . someone must've tipped them off, because they're here." Trevor looked down as he responded to Jackson.

"I WILL SEEK the death penalty in Antonio Barrera's case," Trevor announced, brimming with joy, pausing to let his proclamation sink in for the battery of reporters. He was looking directly at the cameras—*to the voting public*, he thought. "*I* made the streets of South Florida, really the nation, safer today by capturing Antonio Barrera; one of the world's most notorious, and . . . vicious crime bosses."

Trevor was standing just outside of where Antonio's front doors used to be periodically motioning to an antique foyer table with handguns, rifles, shotguns, AR-15s, five-hundred thousand in cash, and an ounce of pot from Michael's room.

Lisa Hoyt was standing behind and to the left of Trevor with a swollen nose and racoon eyes. After about five minutes, Lisa turned and walked away. "What an asshole. He was nowhere near the real action, but he takes credit for everything," she whispered to Jackson Reed who was standing behind some tropical plants in large ceramic pots, away from the reporters' view. He was not a man who spoke to the media or really anyone else for that matter.

"I hope he chokes on one of the microphones," Jackson responded.

"He's about to choke on his own bullshit," Lisa quipped back, a slight smile forming on her face for the first time all day.

They walked to Jackson's undercover car just outside Antonio's main gate, which was now twisted metal. Antonio was long gone, taken in handcuffs to the Palm Beach County Jail for booking by the U.S. Marshalls. Antonio would remain there for at least forty-eight hours until he was brought before a federal magistrate for a pretrial detention hearing. "Think Antonio will get a bond?" Lisa asked.

"No way. Trevor's seeking the death penalty. I've seen defendants get held no-bond for having a kilo of cocaine." Jackson answered.

"Let's flip to see who will have to sit with Trevor during the trial . . . I call heads," Lisa said, as she took a quarter out of her pocket. They passed an ambulance with an FBI agent getting his arm looked at by two EMTs.

"There'll be time enough later to decide who has to suffer through a trial with Trevor. Why don't you get checked out before we go." Jackson said, pointing to the EMTs. "You look like Rocky Balboa at the end of *Rocky I*."

"Gee thanks, but I'm fine. I look like a beauty queen compared to when I was blown up in Iraq taking down Qusay Hussein. I just want to go home and drink a nice Tequila on the rocks . . . or maybe three."

They reached Jackson's car. He opened the passenger side door and helped her in. "Fine, have it your way. After I take you to the hospital to get checked out you can have all the Tequila you want . . . I may even join you for a few, if you're lucky." He winked at her, a slight smile forming at the corners of his mouth—a rare sight.

"Fine." Lisa relented. "But after the hospital, we're flipping that coin. I need to know if my life will be miserable for the next few months or if I will be sitting on a beach in Key West while you sit with that demeaning little gas bag."

"Trevor's going to face stiff competition from Antonio's lawyer who will probably be the best money can buy," Jackson said as he started the car.

—37—

PETER'S CUSTOM SUIT pants creased as he sat behind his black granite desk. The gray pinstripe vest tensed around his slight belly. Peter "the Great" Cohen put on a few pounds as he neared retirement. Although, at seventy, his mind was as sharp and nimble as when he was at Harvard Law School. The international media dubbed him Peter "the Great" after he walked Prince Henry of Bittenberg, the world's most popular member of British Royalty and Palm Beach fixture, on a triple homicide—a case that included two eyewitnesses and a confession. He was relentless in trial, controlled chaos that rained down on the government like a B-52 bomber.

"Senator, I've had plenty of clients in worse situations than you," Peter assured. *Not many, though*, he thought. *Time to start looking for another job, Senator Moron.* "Calm down, I will get you through this."

Senator Wesley Minton thought about Peter's words for a second . . . then with his shaky hand he reached for the crystal tumbler in front of him on Peter's desk. He drained the clear liquid in the tumbler—this was his second vodka since he'd been in the office, which was only fifteen minutes. "Calm down! Easy for you to say . . . you didn't wake up in a drug den three days ago with an OD'd sixteen-year-old and two local and one national media outlet in the lobby asking for you," Senator Minton responded, exasperated.

"Meth and hookers . . . not the first time a married politician has been caught up in such a scandal and survived," Peter reassured. "Hell, I bet the first caveman politician got himself jammed up in a cave-hooker and drug scandal." Peter reached for the hand-painted, porcelain espresso cup and took a sip. He stared at the map of Italy on the cup before he put it down. "Take a vacation for a few weeks . . . go visit Italy. The story will blow over."

Senator Minton snapped his head up and stared at Peter, eyes going wide. "Vacation! Vacation!" Minton started to think he hired the wrong lawyer. He leaned forward, elbows on the desk. "She was sixteen AND from a wealthy family AND she OD'd on fentanyl-laced meth AND she had a DICK!" Minton slumped over more placing his head on the desk. With his head still in his arms, he moaned, "My platform for re-election is *Family Values . . .* I'm doomed."

What a hypocritical prick, Peter thought, *only concerned about yourself.* Peter slapped his hand on the desk. "Listen. Stop bellyaching and compose yourself." *Oh boy, if you have to do some time Minton . . . I have a feeling you're going to be picking up a lot of soap in prison.* "I will get you through this. For the moment, I've convinced the State and Feds to hold off on filing criminal charges . . . they both want a piece of your ass. The most important thing right now is to make sure no one else tries to take a *piece of your ass*, like six four, three hundred pound Bubba, who's doing life in every prison in America." Peter was a master at hooking the big-fish. "So, you'll transfer my standard retainer of two million dollars today?"

Senator Minton sat up ramrod straight and wiped the tears from his eyes. "Absolutely." The Senator fiddled with his phone for a second. "I just texted my financial girl. She's calling your assistant right now for the wire instructions."

The thought of repeated anal rape in prison worked every time. Peter smiled.

* * *

"Peter, it's Joseph. He says it's 'code red' urgent," Meredith, Peter's long-time assistant, said through the intercom on Peter's desk. *'code red' . . . these mobsters watch too many movies,* Peter thought. "Go ahead, Meredith, put him through."

"This. Line. Is. Now. Encrypted," said a computerized voice through the phone.

"Yeah, Peter, this is Joseph . . . we gotta a big problem. Antonio was jus' arrested."

Peter rubbed his temples. "By whom?"

"Whatta you mean *by whom*. Who's *whom*?"

Even after all these years, Peter still let himself get surprised by how stupid most of these mobsters were—he shook his head in disbelief. "Local police, FBI, the Marines . . . who the fuck arrested him?"

"Why didn't you jus' ask dat? From what I'm told, every federal and local police agency was involved. Hell, da Marines might 'ave been there. It was a big takedown. They went in hard, like they was arrestin' Bin Laden."

"Where did they arrest him at?"

"I dink his house on that Palm Beach. I was told his wife and kid was there . . . for Christ's sake, Peter, is dis bad?"

"Thanks for the info, Joseph," Peter hung up the phone. "Get Tim Murphy with the U.S. Marshall's Office on the phone for me," Peter instructed Meredith.

— **38** —

Jason walked into Rocco's Tacos for his third networking event this week. *Networking is a job by itself*, he began to realize. Rocco's Tacos was a popular tequila bar/restaurant for the white collar crowd; which, after a few minutes of small talk, made him realize the financial gap between *blue collar* and *white collar* jobs was really indiscernible today—everyone was struggling to stay afloat financially except for a select few in America. This event was sponsored by the Better Business Bureau and Life Growth Therapies: *An Alternative Lifestyle*, was its motto. It was a residential drug rehab facility. The only requirement to entry was private medical insurance.

Jason was already seeing the same people over and over at these networking events, or *excuse to go home late event*, if you have kids, as Jason learned. He was bored and growing impatient—still no good paying clients. He was finally on the court appointed list, but no appointments yet.

"Hi, I'm Doreen. Grab your name tag and head on into the *fun-zone* and here's your free drink ticket," said the overly cheery volunteer. She was homely looking with straight brown hair and precision cut bangs. "Wait, wait," she called, as Jason began to walk toward the bar. "Drop your business card in here for a chance at a *Kome-shot—*"

Jason turned around, a confused look on his face and responded, "Huh? Did you just say cu—"

Doreen just realized what he thought and gasped, "Oh no, Silly. A K-O-M-E-shot, a shout-out on The Palm Beaches number one radio station for Christ."

"Riiight," Jason said. He quickly took a business card out of his brown suit jacket pocket and dropped it in the fishbowl. "Thanks. Bye."

He quickly left, putting his name tag on as he walked away directly to the bar.

Before Jason could get to the bar and order a drink, a man with bad hair genes stepped in front of him and said as though he'd been waiting all night to say, "Hi. My name is Mark Bidwell. Want to bump?" He held up his phone.

WTF! Jason thought. *I'm in networking hell. "Bump?" What the hell is this guy talking about. Maybe I should just punch him.* Jason instinctively recoiled a bit. "Bump? What do you mean?"

"You know 'bump' our iPhones to air share our contacts." Mark said as if this was universal knowledge.

"I'm good, Mark, I'm going to get a drink. We'll talk later." Jason saw a small opening and squeezed up to the bar. He looked up at one of the many muted TVs—it was broadcasting CNN. The scroll across the bottom caught his attention: *MOB BOSS ANTONIO "MAGIC MAN" BARRERA HIRES POWERHOUSE LAWYER, PETER COHEN.* Jason frowned after he read it. *Great, I can barely get five hundred dollars from a client and Peter Cohen is probably getting a Brinks truck full of money to represent this mob boss.* Instead of the beer he intended to order, he upped it to a Jack Daniels on the rocks.

— 39 —

PETER PARKED HIS black with chrome trim Hummer H2 in visitor parking by the sally port of the Palm Beach County Jail (PBCJ). The sally port was an arrestees first stop on the way to "Lockupsville." It was one of the most dangerous *points of contact* at a jail for a correctional officer. Most arrestees were a volatile bunch: tweaking, amped-up, sometimes bloody, and most of all, scared of what lies beyond when the steel gates close.

"Good morning, my little friends. . . ." Peter said to the cats and raccoons lying in the grass together like best friends. *If cats and raccoons can live in harmony, world peace is possible.* He smiled at the thought. Peter ascended a set of stairs and walked over a footbridge to the visitors' entrance of the jail, which was on the second floor. For the most part, a lawyer can see his client seven days a week anytime during the day except feeding times.

The PBCJ was on Gun Club Road in West Palm Beach. The PBCJ was part of the Palm Beach County Judicial Complex (Sheriff's Office, bond/misdemeanor court, and the jail). It was situated between an ultra-luxurious Trump International Golf Course and a low-rent strip club. Some inmates actually had a view of one of the world's nicest golf clubs from their tiny cell windows—cruel! The jail itself was a cement fortress built to keep people in—a central tower (South-side) that had twelve floors and two wings of six floors each (East and West sides).

Peter walked through the two sets of heavy, steel doors into the jail lobby. The lobby was sparsely decorated: a gray semi-circle counter took up about a quarter of the room; it was in between the entrance and exit facing into the lobby. The walls were a dingy white and dark gray painted cement block and the floor was a cheap, well-worn gray-speckled linoleum tile—clearly, the interior designer went with a *depressing* theme. Peter stopped right inside the inner lobby door.

"Good morning, Dep., you look radiant this fine, sunny morning," Peter greeted Palm Beach County Sherriff's Deputy Marsha King with a smile.

"Mornin', Peter," Deputy King said, returning the smile. "I figured I see ya here this weekend."

"Now my Saturday is complete—I get to see a beautiful woman in uniform with a gun belt."

"Don't tempt me . . . I have the power to strip search your fine ass." Deputy King winked.

Peter placed his keys, wallet, watch, and belt on the counter and walked through the metal detector into the rest of the lobby.

"Too bad ya didn't beep, I'd get a chance to pat you down."

The lobby was an open space with nine blue, well-worn, rubber chairs bolted to the floor off to the right—on occasion rival gang families would fight waiting to visit their loved one and use the chairs as weapons, so they got bolted to the floor—problem solved. Across the far wall was a control room, steel framed with thick plexiglass windows and a tan door on either side—a guard sat inside eating breakfast. Two public bathrooms were off to the left, which Peter still, thankfully, never had to use in his forty years of practicing law in Palm Beach County. A small TV screen hung on the wall which continuously broadcast "jail house" programing. This morning it was broadcasting a show that informed inmates how to avoid sexual assault in prison.

Peter walked over to the counter and looked at the master list of where all the inmates were housed: East, West, or South Tower. "I'm here to see—"

"Let me guess," Deputy King interrupted, "our newest superstar, Antonio Barrera."

"Bingo, you're so perceptive."

"Where's he at?"

"Probably South-8B. He's a federal inmate," Peter answered, flipping through the master list to confirm. "Wait . . . I'm wrong, he's in West-3C. Must've been a problem to put him on the West side."

"You're all set, Sugar." Dep. King said, as she handed Peter ID badge L-1.

Peter clipped the badge onto his polo shirt. "Thanks, Darling," He walked over to the door to the right of the control booth, passing under the TV—*Don't become in debt to another inmate, sometimes sex is used as currency*, said the voice from the TV. Peter stopped in front of the steel and plexiglass tan door; he turned his chest, showing his ID, to the female guard, dressed in a gray and black uniform inside the control room.

"Thank you," Peter said, nodding his head; he never actually knew if the guard could hear him in the fortress-like control room.

A CLICK sound came from the door and it sprung open slightly. From this point forward, a person had no control over any door. The first few times Peter came to the jail as a young lawyer, it took some getting used to. He almost freaked out once when a riot started in the mental health pod as he was speaking with a client. But now it's old hat to him. He pushed open the heavy door and walked through it; it made a loud CLANG when it closed behind him.

About twenty-five feet in front of him was another steel-framed door that led into the bowels of the jail and was the entrance non-lawyer visitors used to use before the jail went to video-visiting where the loved one goes to an offsite center and speaks via video conference—a very sterile experience. To Peter's left was a heavy steel door that led to the bond processing counter, property room, and elevators. The door CLICKED and sprung slightly open. He pushed the door the rest of the way open and walked through; it closed behind him—CLANG.

"Thanks for holding the door," a scraggly, ultra-skinny woman, holding a 5" by 7" index card (*the get-out-of-jail-card*), as it was known, said sarcastically; she just bonded out. Peter knew never to hold a door for anyone inside of a jail or prison—normal societal conventions did not apply on the inside. As he passed her, he could tell she was tweaking from a night spent without her beloved heroin. *She was probably pretty at one time*, Peter thought.

The interior of the jail followed the same depressing motif as the lobby, except no ugly linoleum tile, just a bare cement floor with years of ware on its surface—linoleum tile could be used as a weapon. Peter continued through the maze of steel doors to the west-side.

"Tower! Gate on one please!" Peter yelled to the small control room with blacked out windows inside double steel gates. The look of the jail changed on the westside. It was even more depressing then the lobby and southside—it was evident that this was the oldest part of the jail, Peter always expected to see Cool Hand Luke when he was on this side of the Jail.

CLICK, the heavy gate began to grind open at a snail's pace. Peter walked into a small elevator "lobby" with two elevators. "GOING TO THREE, PLEASE."

The elevator doors opened. "Move back," said a hulk of a guard in a deep baritone voice that immediately let you know she wasn't going to ask twice. The six male inmates (four black, one Hispanic, and one white). *A good representation of the racial make-up of any jail in America*, Peter thought, as he stepped onto the tiny elevator. The inmates were all dressed in oversized, well-worn, brown uniforms—signifying that they were *trustees*; trusted inmates that helped the jail staff run the jail. The inmates had two plastic carts stacked with trays of the slop that qualified for breakfast in a jail. The entire elevator smelled like cheap, wet dog food. The button for three was already lit—only the guards in the control rooms had control of the elevator, unlike the elevators on the South-Side.

The West-side had five floors of cells or *pods*—the change in terminology was implemented in the 90s to sound less harsh. The elevator opened on three—the odd numbered floors had guard rooms. "TOWER! GATE ON THREE!" The battered steel blue gate made a grinding sound as it slowly opened. Three black inmates were inside the gate with no guards. The gate clanged closed behind Peter.

One of the inmates was on his hands and knees scrubbing what looked like a good size pool of fresh blood on the steps to the control room. One was standing close to him holding a mop and the other guy was leaning against the wall—clearly the supervisor.

"Hey. Man. You a private lawya or *public pretender*?" The inmate holding the mop asked; he was tall and skinny with twists in his hair—he was swimming inside his dirty brown scrubs stamped with "5X" on the front. "Take a look at my case. The Po Po done me all wrong . . . Theys violated my rights, man."

"Only if you have a lot of money," Peter responded with a pleasant smile. He stepped toward the guard door and up one step, making sure to stay away from the pool of blood.

The guy leaning against the wall chimed in, "He a big time lawyer, repin' the new *Boss* in here, I bet. Them shoes he wearin' cost at least a grand—Bruno Maglias or some shit." He was bald with a black bushy beard. Tattoos, mostly jail tats, covered both arms. His scrubs also had a "5X" stamped on the stomach area but it looked like it was trying to jump off the shirt as it strained under his enormous belly. "Dog, you ain't got no doe stacked. So it's a *Public Pretender* fo you." His belly shook as he laughed.

Peter looked at each of the sad men, all at different stages of the cycle of life growing up in any ghetto in America. He stopped on the kid with the mop. "Don't be a pain in the ass to your P.D.—they work real hard for their clients . . . I know, I used to be one." His look turned serious. "Stop coming in this hellhole or save some money and you won't have to worry about dealing with a Public Defender."

The heavy guard door creaked open. "What are you looking at?" The Puerto Rican-looking guard in gray shirt said with a nasty tinge to his voice to the inmate scrubbing the steps. "I don't want to get some type of Hep-C or shit like that. Clean that nasty crap up . . . fast."

No need to be a dick, Peter thought.

"Who you here to see?" The guard asked Peter.

Peter handed him the little slip of paper. "Antonio Barrera."

The guard looked at it . . . unclipped his keys from his belt and handed them to Peter. "Bring them back right away," he commanded.

"Of course," Peter responded, with a hint of contempt and a fake smile.

* * *

Peter unlocked the door to the attorney's room, which was chipped royal blue heavy steel with a plexiglass window. He put a chair in the door jamb to keep the self-closing door open while he returned the keys—he once forgot to return the keys, and it caused a brief lockdown until he returned a few hours later in the day.

Peter returned to the attorney's room. About ten feet from the door were two sets of steel gates that ran lengthwise across the room and led into the *Pod*. The Pod was about the size of a large living room—Twenty inmates were cramped into the space where they ate, slept, shit, and showered. In about an hour, the Pod would come to life with lots of noise and commotion as the inmates woke up. A visitor could see right into the bathroom and showers—most inmates didn't care, they were happy to show their junk while catcalling all the disgusting things they wanted to do to a female lawyer—many would just masturbate for all to see.

Peter moved the chair he placed in the door jamb and walked into the small, six by six, white, cement room. On one wall was a small video monitor with a pay phone like receiver—for the Public Defender's Office, so they could video conference with their clients to save time, but no one trusted that the line wasn't being recorded, so it was rarely used. On the back wall was a small, dirty window with bars over it, about the size of half a pizza box—not much of a view. In the center of the room was a small, square table with God-knows-what on and under it and three molded peach-colored plastic chairs, like you see in a high school classroom.

Peter put a leather portfolio on the table but waited to sit. Being locked in a small room with a person accused of all manner of vicious crimes, with no one around to help if he yelled, never bothered him—he always figured a client wouldn't hurt him since he was the only person fighting for them on the outside. Only one time was he concerned; years ago, he represented the son of a wealthy make-up heiress in a multi-rape case. Every time he met with the client, the client would just stare at Peter with the most sinister eyes he ever saw and ask him to "cuddle" over and over.

Antonio appeared in the door window; Peter opened it. Peter was about to hug Antonio when he stopped midway in extending his arms. "Whoa." Peter stepped back. "I don't have many clients who come to attorney visits with a cup of coffee."

"While it's not like the jail scene in *Goodfellas*, I'm still respected enough to get good coffee from the guards, but I have to use this cheap plastic cup—no fine china in here," Antonio said like he was sitting outside at a street-side café. He certainly didn't look like he just had his house raided and his face repeatedly slammed into the ground by almost every federal and local law enforcement agent in Florida and spent a night in jail. If it weren't for the jail scrubs, Antonio looked like he was ready to go out with his wife for the night. Even the jail scrubs hung on his athletic frame somewhat nicely.

Peter sat down at the table. "How are you holding up in here."

"Fine . . . but I'll be better when you get me out of here today."

"It's Saturday, that won't happen until Monday at the earliest at your PTD hearing."

"I thought I paid you so much money so I wouldn't have to wait until the Pretrial Detention Hearing to get a bond." Antonio put the coffee cup to his nose and took in a deep breath; he closed his eyes and sat silent for five minutes, which seemed like five hours to Peter.

Antonio opened his eyes. "Why didn't you see this coming? You're slipping, Peter. Maybe I should give the five-million-dollar retainer, I'm sure you're going to ask me for, to a younger lawyer. Hell, I can probably get better representation for much cheaper." Peter leaned back in the plastic chair, getting ready for the verbal assault. He knew better than to respond. After all the years representing criminal defendants, he knew they needed to vent in the beginning, and most of the venting consisted of how much he sucked as a lawyer or how easy the case would be to get dismissed and he should do it for free.

When Antonio finished telling him this was an easy case to defend and the Feds have zero evidence, Peter leaned forward, opened his monogrammed leather portfolio and took out a two-page document and a thirty-seven-page document.

Peter focused on the thirty-seven-page document first; the front page read: *UNITED STATES vs. ANTONIO BARRERA a/k/a THE DON, THE BOSS, THE GODFATHER, and THE MAGIC MAN.* Underneath was: *CRIMINAL COMPLAINT.* A criminal complaint was the Federal Government's version of the local police probable cause affidavit—it was the "articulable facts" that formed the base for probable cause to arrest someone. *Probable cause* was less of a standard than what a prosecutor needs to secure an indictment, and a ham sandwich can be indicted. Peter thumbed through the Complaint. "You were arrested for the murder of three people, one of them is a child—"

"What *three* people?"

Peter put on a pair of reading glasses and turned to the fifteenth page, scanned it, and replied, "An Alfonso Tomisini a/k/a 'The Whale'; Jane Doe, an elderly Asian woman—cause of death: gunshot wound to the head; and John Doe, a ten-year-old Asian kid—cause of death: malnutrition, basically that means starvation."

Antonio picked up his coffee cup, took a sip—he didn't flinch at what Peter just read. *Oh. The Whale, I forgot about him. I should get a medal from the Feds for getting rid of that piece of trash.* "That's crazy, I don't even know any of those people."

"Shall I continue?" Peter asked.

"Go on." Antonio waved his hand in front of him like he was yielding the floor.

"Human trafficking of adults and children for the purpose of slavery and prostitution with multiple deaths, and possession of bomb-making materials—they found some volatile chemicals in your garage."

"Bomb-making materials . . . in my garage . . . those chemicals are to get rid of the damn gophers that are destroying my backyard. I tried to shoot them, but the little bastards are fast."

Peter continued, "Those are the highlights . . . the rest of the Criminal Complaint alleges your run-of-the-mill, R.I.C.O., running a criminal enterprise, money laundering, drug trafficking, fraud, and possession of assault weapons." Peter looked at Antonio over his reading glasses with a deadpan expression on his face. "This is serious stuff and my sources inside the DOJ tell me that prick Whittingham is desperate for media attention, and he's going to make an example out of you."

Without missing a beat, Antonio responded to Peter's warning. "So . . . the Feds type up a few pages of bullshit and you're scared all of a sudden . . . can you recommend another lawyer I can hire that isn't scared of bullshit like this?" He pointed to the Criminal Complaint.

"The last thing I am is *scared* of the Federal Government, especially Trevor Whittingham. I've kicked his ass plenty of times. As I recall, a few of those ass-kickings were your cases. But before we talk more about this case, let's get the business of my retainer fee out of the way."

"Ah, yes . . . your fee. That's all you lawyers care about."

"I have to eat too." Peter handed Antonio the two-page document he took out of his portfolio. "This is the same retainer agreement you've signed in the past."

Antonio quickly scanned the agreement. His eyes lingered briefly on the section that read: **NONREFUNDABLE RETAINER $5,000,000.00**. The Florida Bar requires the word *nonrefundable* to be in bold and all caps, so the client knows that the second he signs the agreement his money is earned in full even if the lawyer quits or is fired the next day.

Antonio absently signed the agreement. "I'll have the money wired today."

"I'm sure there won't be a problem with the source of the funds?" Peter asked. "Trevor is going to crawl up my ass trying to prove my fee is from illegal profits so they can get me off your case."

"No need to worry about your *precious* fee. I have some very wealthy friends in Silicon Valley who look at five million dollars like lunch money. Now, let's talk about how you're going to get me out of this shithole on Monday morning."

— 40 —

PETER EXITED THE back seat of the black Cadillac Escalade at the Paul G. Rogers United States District Court in West Palm Beach. His associate and daughter from his third ex-wife, Jennifer Lopez, exited the front passenger side. Jennifer was smart and fearless with just the right amount of fire to be a great criminal defense attorney. Thankfully, she had her mother's good Cuban looks and, much to Peter's dismay, her last name after the divorce.

It was a Monday morning in November—the sky was blue, sun shining bright, low humidity, and a light breeze meandered through the air. Peter stepped onto the sidewalk and looked up at the courthouse and thought, as he always did before battle, *I must break you, Trevor Whittingham*—it even sounded like Ivan Drago from Rocky IV in his head. He carried only his monogrammed leather portfolio—he never went to court without it; a client had given it to him as a *thank you* for winning his quadruple murder with an explosive device (grenade) case. Peter's thoughts were quickly interrupted by a gang of reporters stampeding toward him from the entrance. Jennifer was now standing beside him with a black, leather briefcase over her shoulder. "Here comes the circus," Peter said with a mischievous grin.

The Paul G. Rogers Courthouse was a neomodern, for 1973, building named after the late congressman. Its four stories were accented by a multitude of off-white and beige decorative arches. It looked like it could withstand a nuclear blast.

"Is Antonio innocent? Is this the end of the South Florida Mafia? Did he really kill a child and grandmother? Does the 'Magic Man' have any *magic* left?" The various reporters shouted out.

Peter flashed his million-dollar-smile that made many a jury melt in his hands and answered, "Folks, please, give me a break? This is a simple bond hearing—"

"And arraignment, didn't you know that?" A reporter from CNN shouted. Then others followed suit shouting over each other, "Didn't you know Antonio had an arraignment today also? Don't you have a copy of the Indictment? Geez, for what Antonio's probably paying you, you'd think you'd have the Indictment before the media—Maybe Peter 'The Great' is no longer *great*," A reporter from the Shiny Sheet (*Palm Beach Daily News*) quipped to no one in particular.

Arraignment, also? Peter thought. *Why the fuck didn't I know about this? The grand jury meets on Tuesday and Thursday, Antonio was arrested Friday, and today's Monday. How could there be an Indictment already. That snake Trevor must have convened the grand jury on Sunday, claiming an 'emergency'.* Still smiling and always quick on his feet no matter what was thrown at him, Peter said, "Of course I know today is also arraignment, but it's such an insignificant hearing in the grand scheme of a criminal case, I didn't think any of you were that low on the totem pole to have arraignment duties. Isn't that what interns cover?" He looked right at the *Shiny Sheet* reporter as he finished his comment. "Excuse us now, we don't want to be late for court."

Now, we're really gonna kick your culo (ass) today, Trevor, Jennifer thought, as they walked through the center of the media gang to the automatic front doors of the courthouse.

TREVOR SAT WITH his feet on top of the cheap table inside the Igloo, drinking coffee, with Herb Rosen, Jackson Reed, Lisa Hoyt, and Tim Barnes. In the center of the table were six bankers' boxes labeled in black marker: **ANTONIO BARRERA DOJ ATTORNEY WORK PRODUCT**. The Igloo was a three-room office on the second floor of the courthouse for use by the U.S. Attorney's Office. Just to make sure that the prosecution had every advantage in a trial, the judiciary gave them an office right inside the courthouse so they wouldn't have to waste time going back and forth between their actual office and the courthouse, like defense lawyers had to do.

"How come you're not downstairs talking to that gang of reporters? I hear CNN, MSNBC, FOX News, and the BBC are covering this case," Lisa asked Trevor.

"I'd rather make my first statement after I win the PTD hearing and Antonio is held no-bond pending trial."

"Did you call Peter yesterday and tell him you got an Indictment so we can do the arraignment also this morning?" Herb asked.

"Call Peter about the Indictment?" Trevor rhetorically asked, taking his feet off the desk. "Why would I do that?"

"How about professional courtesy," Herb responded. "Hiding the fact that we got the Indictment yesterday on Sunday doesn't give us any advantage . . . why not tell him. It will make the hearing go a bit quicker."

"Don't go soft on me, Herb. This is *war* and we take no prisoners." Trevor stood up.

Everyone at the table looked at one another.

"What time is it?" Trevor asked the room at large.

Tim, looking at his phone, said, "9:45."

"Fifteen minutes until the hearing, let's go . . . and bring the boxes," Trevor ordered.

— 42 —

JASON SAT AT his desk, dressed in a tan suit, staring at his phone . . . praying it would ring with a new client. He had no idea why he was at his office Monday morning when he had absolutely nothing scheduled. *I should be home in bed with Caesar,* he fondly thought.

He already resolved Wash Sampson's DUI case—case number one at Jason Noble & Associates, P.A. was a success. Jason got the case dismissed on a technicality—the traffic stop was bad. Wash still owed him money, and, of course, he thanked God for the dismissal instead of Jason.

"Ring . . . ring," Jason pleaded with the phone.

— 43 —

THE PAUL G. Rogers Courthouse was in serious need of a wrecking ball. The interior was drab, highlighted by antiquated fluorescent lighting throughout the building. The architecture was choppy—the courtrooms on each floor were haphazardly located in a disconnected pattern throughout the maze of hallways. A dank smell always hung in the air from years of mold buildup.

Peter opened the left side of the solid mahogany doors that were recessed from the hallway—above the doorway in bronze was: COURT-ROOM 1. Across from the double doors in the hallway were a few mahogany benches to match—Peter had seen many family members over the years weeping on those benches.

Jennifer walked through first, across a small vestibule, passing a plain, tiny conference room on the right, and opened the interior mahogany double doors. She held the door for Peter. Courtroom 1, like most courtrooms, had obscenely high ceilings, unless, of course, giraffes were the litigants. The room had a clean look. The high ceiling was white with recessed lighting and simple white chandeliers. The walls were floor to ceiling large panels of golden oak. Oil portraits of sitting and retired district court judges adorned the walls—all white men that looked like possible plantation owners.

Courtroom 1 had no windows. Some defendants literally never saw the light of day after they entered Courtroom 1. Peter and Jennifer walked on the once plush deep red carpet. On either side of them were five rows of golden oak pews. A bar of the same wood, separating the *unauthorized* and *authorized* courtroom participants, ran lengthwise.

"Good morning, Murph," Peter said, as he walked to the bar with Jennifer.

"Not open yet," replied the hunched over Federal Protection Services Officer Sean Murphy—retired NYPD detective. Federal Protection Services (FPS) was the government agency responsible for protecting every building leased by the federal government; the officers were mostly retired from other law enforcement careers.

Peter swung open the well-worn bar and asked, "Did you find a bomb?"

Murph's head snapped up and he looked at Peter ready to take action. . . . "Peter, how you been? Haven't seen you in a while." Murph's expression calmed with a slight smile.

"Still fightin' the good fight."

"Well, don't fight *too* hard." Murph let out a hearty laugh that began deep in his big belly. "Courtroom's not open yet, I have to finish looking for bombs. You can come in though."

"This is my daughter, and really my *boss,* Jennifer Lopez. She's a much better lawyer than me." Peter beamed with pride. "But, I wouldn't let her in before you're done; she's not that trustworthy." Peter winked at Murph.

"Nice to meet you, Ms. Lopez," Murph said, tipping his head of gray hair, like he was meeting a Southern belle. "There's only one joker I have to keep my eye on in this room," Murph narrowed his eyes at Peter when he spoke. . . .

"It's nice to meet you, Murph." Jennifer walked through the bar to the defense table.

Peter placed his portfolio on the well-worn table on the left side of the room—farthest from the jury box. The defense had two large tables forming an "L" shape with burgundy leather chairs. The prosecution table was next to the jury box, as it always was in every courtroom in America. The jury box had fourteen white, modern style leather chairs. A computer monitor was between each chair.

In the center of the courtroom was a wooden podium stuffed with electronic equipment. Several feet in front of the podium, running lengthwise across almost the entire courtroom, was the judge's bench and in front of that was the clerk's desk—the judge's bench was much higher than the clerk's. Directly behind the judge's high-backed chair was a large bronze seal of the United States with: *U.S. District Court for the Southern District of Florida* around the outer rim. Flanking the bronze seal was the American flag on the left and the Florida state flag on the right. The witness chair a/k/a *hot seat* was to the left when facing the judge.

On the bench was a placard that read Magistrate Karen Smith. Peter was glad he would be arguing before Magistrate Smith; he knew her well. They used to sit on the Criminal Justice Commission together.

"Well, hello, if it isn't my worthy adversary, Peter Cohen . . . or is it Peter 'the Great' now," Trevor bellowed, as he strode into the courtroom. Herb Rosen, SA Lisa Hoyt, SA Jackson Reed, and Tim Barnes in tow—each, except Trevor of course, carrying a banker's box.

"He even sounds like a douchebag when he says *hello*," Peter whispered in Jennifer's ear as he stood up and turned around. "Trevor, how have you been?" Peter asked in a soft voice with a hint of condescension. "I haven't seen you since the Buddy Turner trial."

"Whatever," Trevor retorted. "It's the death penalty for your guy this time."

Peter ignored Trevor. "Good Morning, Herb, nice to see you. What is it . . . one more year until you're living the good, retired life? I should've stayed with the government."

"Hello, Peter, three hundred days from today," Herb responded, as he walked through the bar, holding the banker's box above it. *You're such a dick, Trevor, you couldn't even hold the bar for us,* Herb thought.

"Hi, Lisa, hello Jackson," Peter said as each one walked through the bar that Herb was now holding with his foot.

"Peter." They both said in near unison, nodding. Everyone Peter ever dealt with in law enforcement usually respected him win or lose after a case.

"Who's the new guy?" Peter asked.

"Tim Barnes, from Washington," Lisa said, rolling her eyes.

"Hello, Tim Barnes, nice to meet you," Peter greeted.

"Hi, Mr. Cohen, it's a pleasure," Tim said.

Peter looked at the four banker's boxes on the prosecution's table and remarked, "Wow, four boxes full of stuff, I feel *out-boxed*. I didn't even bring one box. But, I do have my secret weapon." Peter turned and pointed to Jennifer who was reviewing some notes. "This is my daughter, Jennifer Lopez. She's the senior partner at Cohen & Associates—I just do what she tells me."

Everyone but Trevor said "hello".

The back of the courtroom started to fill up with a gang of reporters and two sketch artists—cameras were prohibited in federal courtrooms much to Trevor's dismay.

Antonio's wife, Maria, took a seat in the galley right behind the defense table. Guys from Antonio's other *family* wanted to come to the hearing, but Peter told them a stern *no*. He knew he'd have no chance to get Antonio released if the benches behind the defense table were packed with known mobsters dressed in silk suits. As it was, he didn't think he had any real chance of getting a bond for Antonio anyway.

Peter walked over to Trevor and asked, "Where's my copy of the Indictment?" Although he was frustrated that Trevor didn't call him yesterday and tell him about the Indictment, he didn't show it.

Trevor turned around, went into one of the boxes, pulled out a thick packet of papers, handed them to Peter with a big smile on his face, and said loudly for the reporters to hear, "Get ready for war."

Peter took them, leaned in close to Trevor, and said—so the reporters wouldn't hear, "That's the problem with you. Your job is not about *war*, it's about *justice*." As he was walking away, Peter turned back to Trevor and said, "Want to agree to a bond, it's your last chance."

"*Agree to a bond*, you must be kidding. I'm seeking the death penalty."

Before sitting back down, Peter turned to the first row in the galley and said, "Hello" to Maria, warmly shaking her hand. He leaned over the railing and whispered to her, "He'll be home with you soon." It did no good at this point to crush her hope. Maria nodded politely, pulling the shawl tighter around her shoulders.

Peter said into Jennifer's ear, "I can't wait to kick Trevor's pudgy ass in trial." Just then, the hidden door on the wall to the left of the bench opened. Peter and Jennifer looked at the door, as did everyone else in the courtroom.

Two marshals, dressed in ill-fitting suits, the marshal's Silver Star attached to their lapels, walked into the courtroom with Antonio Barrera, handcuffed and shackled, between them. Antonio had no expression on his face. He did the shackle-shuffle to the defense table. Before sitting down in-between Peter and Jenifer, he looked at his wife and mouthed, "I love you." Maria's eyes started to well up with tears. One of the marshals removed the handcuffs but not the shackles.

"Hi, Justin, how are you?" Peter asked, as he stood and shook the marshal's hand.

"Good morning, Peter. Good to see you."

Jennifer leaned forward and asked Peter, "You know *everyone* in this courthouse?"

"How do you think I get what I want all the time," Peter answered with a wink. He was about to speak with Antonio when Antonio turned toward Jennifer.

"Good morning, Jennifer, thank you for working so hard to get me back home and out of this *fashionable* outfit," Antonio said with an engaging smile, pulling at his worn, blue prison shirt for affect.

"Don't mention it . . . thank you for your kind words." She leaned closer. "It will be a pleasure kicking that prick, Trevor's ass—excuse my language." *He even smells good for being in jail,* Jennifer thought. As she pulled back from his ear, she got lost in his eyes and handsome face. *Mm. Mm. Mm . . . with that charm and those young Humphrey Bogart looks, what fun we'd have—too bad you're accused of being a vicious mob boss and face the death penalty.* She broke her stare and went back to reviewing the contents of her briefcase that was now on the table in front of her.

Antonio now turned to Peter, his smile gone, replaced by an intense seriousness. "Get me out of here, today."

"Good morning, Antonio," Peter responded. "I'm working on it." Peter looked up, saw the clerk and court stenographer enter the courtroom, which meant Magistrate Smith would be out momentarily. He mouthed 'hi' to them; they waived back. Peter quickly scanned the last two pages of the fifty-page Indictment, which gave a summary of all the charges and the minimum and maximum sentences—he explained the highlights to Antonio.

Thirty seconds later, a FPS Officer entered the courtroom through a side door to the left of the judge's bench, Mag. Smith behind him, and bellowed: "ALL RISE BEFORE THIS HONORABLE COURT AND CALL TO ORDER ANY BUSINESS BEFORE THE HONORABLE UNITED STATES MAGISTRATE JUDGE, KAREN SMITH.

"Please be seated," Magistrate Smith instructed. She was a frumpy woman in her late sixties. Her blonde hair was short and spiky. Her chubby face always had a look of disdain that scared many inmates and lawyers alike. Peter liked her because she was one of the fairest and smartest judges he'd ever been before and she was nice to him, mostly because he represented her life-partner's son to great success for free.

The gang of reporters in the back of the courtroom knew better than to make a peep or suffer her wrath, which, if you were lucky, meant you got banned from the courthouse for only a year, not a lifetime— Magistrate Smith had no patience for interruption.

"Gloria, call the first case," Mag. Smith ordered the clerk.

"We have only one case on the docket for a pretrial detention hearing this morning and it is: *The United States of America versus Antonio Barrera.*"

"Will the parties announce themselves for the record," Mag. Smith commanded.

Trevor jumped up like he was called to attention at an Army barracks. "Good morning, Your Honor, Trevor Whittingham for the People of the United States of America. At counsel table with me is Herb Rosen and Lisa Hoyt from the DEA. Thank you." He sat back down.

"Good morning, Mr. Rosen and Special Agent Hoyt."

"Good morning, Your Honor," they replied in unison.

Trevor began to seethe inside because she acknowledged Herb and Lisa first, especially in front of the reporters.

"Good Morning, Mr. Wittingham." She then turned toward the defense.

"Hello, Your Honor. Peter Cohen and Jennifer Lopez on behalf of Antonio Barrera who is present and sitting to Ms. Lopez' left."

"Good morning, Mr. Cohen, Ms. Lopez, and Mr. Barrera." Her face almost looked like it had a slight smile when she said good morning to Peter. "Are both parties ready to proceed?"

"Yes," Peter replied.

"Yes," Trevor replied.

"Is there an agreement on bond?"

"No, Your Honor," Peter said.

Not to miss a chance to speak in front of the reporters and stand so the sketch artists can get a good view to draw—the middle eastern artist was drawing Trevor on the corner of her pad as a pouty monster—Trevor added, "We can also do the arraignment if it pleases the court."

Mag. Smith glared at Trevor. Herb wanted to go under the table—he'd seen that look before and it usually meant a tongue lashing was about to spew out of her mouth. "Mr. Wittingham, I don't have an Indictment in front of me . . . Gloria, do you?"

"No, Your Honor, and I don't see one being filed on PACER." PACER was the federal courts' electronic filing system.

"Mr. Barrera was arrested on Friday and today's Monday . . . the grand jury doesn't meet until Tuesday . . . How do you have an Indictment already and, more importantly, why are you asking me to consider a matter not on the calendar?"

"Uh, given how dangerous Mr. Barrera is, I thought it best to get him under indictment as quickly as possible. May I remind you that

I'm seeking the death penalty in this case." Trevor was hitting his verbal stride. *That quote will play great on the evening news*, he thought.

"Let me remind you, Mr. Wittingham," Mag. Smith's voice started to quiver. "Mr. Barrera is presumed innocent and I'll be the judge of whether he's dangerous."

"Yes, Your Honor. The Indictment was issued by the grand jury sitting in an emergency session—all proper procedures were followed. We can set the arraignment in the normal course. I was just trying to save the Court time." Trevor sat back down, knowing he would get nowhere continuing to argue.

Mag. Smith hated lawyers who tried to call matters not properly placed on her calendar, but she hated wasting court time more—*why have two hearings when one would do*. She turned to Peter and asked, "Do you object to doing the arraignment today?"

Peter stood up, "No, that's fine, Your Honor. Mr. Wittingham's attempt to ambush me and deny my client his due process rights have not prejudiced the defense. My client and I are ready to proceed with the arraignment."

"Thank you, Mr. Cohen and Mr. Barrera for being so accommodating in the interest of judicial efficiency despite the government's attempt to pull a fast one on the defense and this Court." She looked at the reporters as she spoke, knowing they would quote her on the evening news. "Let's do the arraignment first." She turned to Trevor, "Ready to proceed with arraignment?"

"Yes," Trevor responded, remaining seated.

She turned back to Peter. "You may proceed."

"Come to the podium with me and just say *yes* when she asks you questions," Peter instructed out of habit. They stood and walked to the podium, which was on center with Mag. Smith and about three feet in front of the counsels' tables—the marshals stayed right behind their prisoner.

"Good morning again, Your Honor," Peter began. "I filed a Notice of Permanent Appearance on Saturday. I've received and reviewed the

Indictment with my client, Antonio Barrera."

"Is that correct, Mr. Barrera?" Mag. Smith asked, as if on cue. All the reporters and two sketch artists focused on the star of the courtroom.

"Yes."

Peter continued, "We waive formal reading of the Indictment."

Mag. Smith turned to Trevor. "Mr. Whittingham, a *brief* summary of the charges and minimums and maximums."

Trevor stood and read a litany of charges that quickly blended together: murder, conspiracy to commit murder, conspiracy to commit a conspiracy to commit murder, every manner of trafficking (humans, drugs, exotic animals), R.I.C.O. Antonio basically faced *life* on top of *life* on top of *life* for each charge. But, Trevor saved the best for last. He stood a little taller, his head a little higher and said, "Murder of a child under the age of twelve . . . minimum sentence, twenty-five years . . . maximum sentence . . . death." *Take that, Peter,* Trevor thought as he sat down.

Mag. Smith turned back to Peter who absently recited: "I will enter a plea of Not Guilty on behalf of Mr. Barrera, request the Standing Discovery Order, and demand a trial by jury." *Discovery* was what evidence the government intended to use at trial; Trevor had fourteen days per the standard order to make everything available to the defense—the definition of *everything* was surprisingly limited in the criminal context. It was always *trial by ambush* for the defense in federal court.

Mag. Smith said, "I will accept your 'Not Guilty' plea, enter the standing discovery order, and set this case for a status conference on . . . Gloria, what is Judge Quarter's next available date?"

"Next Monday, November 8."

Mag. Smith continued, "I will set the status conference on Monday, November 8 before Judge Calvin Quarter in Miami."

Trevor's head perked up. Judge assignments were random. Trevor knew Mag. Smith would handle the preliminaries because she was the Duty Magistrate this week, but the judge was randomly assigned after the arraignment. Trevor couldn't believe his luck—United States Chief

Judge Calvin Quarter, a/k/a Chief Judge "Drawn and Quartered". He was older than dirt, had a penchant for being irritated with everyone, and hated delay. He was a Civil War buff and never minded acting as Robert E. Lee, who he kind of looked like with about fifty extra pounds, when he did reenactments a few times a year out in Belle Glade. *This case will be easier than I thought*, Trevor mused.

"Now, let's turn to the pretrial detention hearing," Mag. Smith said as she organized some papers. "Since there's no agreement, I'll take evidence. Mr. Cohen, do you want to cross the agent."

Peter stood, excited inside for the first battle of the case. "Yes, Your Honor, we are ready to proceed today." Peter and Antonio went back to the defense table.

She looked at Trevor. "Is the government ready to proceed?"

Trevor stood. "Yes, I am ready to proceed." He walked up to the podium with some papers and a yellow legal pad.

"I assume the government is requesting pretrial detention due to *a danger to the community*, since you indicated your intent to seek the death penalty. Are you also alleging Mr. Barrera is a *risk of flight*?"

"That is correct, Your Honor."

"Fine, make your case." She took a sip of water and sat back.

Trevor looked down at his legal pad. "I would ask the Court to take judicial notice of the sworn Criminal Complaint, Indictment, and Pretrial Services Report."

"Any objection, Mr. Cohen?"

"No, Your Honor."

"I will take judicial notice of government's composite exhibit one."

Trevor put a check on his legal pad and called FBI SA Zachary Platt to the stand.

Peter looked over, he assumed Lisa or Jackson would be the agent to testify—he'd cross examined them dozens of times and won more times than he lost. He never saw this kid before, who looked like he just arrived from Oklahoma.

"Raise your right hand and repeat after me," Gloria said, right before SA Platt sat in the witness chair: "Do you solemnly swear to tell the truth, the whole truth, and nothing but the truth, so help you God."

SA Platt responded "I do," then sat down.

Mag. Smith said, "Please state your full name and title for the record.

"Uh . . . Zachary Platt, Special Agent for the Federal Bureau of Investigations."

"You may proceed, Mr. Wittingham."

"Thank you, Your Honor," Trevor said from the podium. All SA Platt had to do was verify his signature on the arrest warrant affidavit and criminal complaint then he was off the stand—*What could go wrong?* In his rush to get a Magistrate to sign the warrant, Trevor sent all the other agents to the field to prepare for the raid leaving only SA Platt to sign the affidavit and complaint. Trevor began his direct examination.

"Please restate your name?" Trevor started with the easiest question he could think of.

"Zachary Platt."

"Current Employment?"

"Federal Bureau of Investigation." Special Agent Platt took a sip of water.

"How long with the Bureau?"

"One year, tomorrow."

"Were you involved with the investigation and apprehension of the Defendant, Antonio Barrera?"

"Yes."

Trevor then went through the Criminal Complaint and Arrest Warrant Affidavit with Platt—he didn't sway too far from nuts-and-bolts facts questions—no opinions; that would only get this green agent in trouble and cause Peter to object to every other question. "I respectfully ask this Court to take judicial notice of the Criminal Complaint and the Arrest Warrant Affidavit and all the facts contained therein," Trevor concluded.

"Any objection, Mr. Cohen?" Mag. Smith asked, thoroughly bored at this point from the routineness of the process.

"No objection," he said without standing.

"The Court will take judicial notice of government's composite exhibit number 1. Any other questions for the witness Mr. Wittingham?"

"No further questions or evidence, Your Honor." Trevor went back to his seat."

"Mr. Cohen, you may inquire."

Peter and Jennifer were taking notes—Peter had one ear on the questions and answers. He put a line down the center of the top page of his yellow legal pad. One side was for key facts the witness testified to—written in blue, the right side was for cross examination questions written in red.

Antonio was staring intently at SA Platt. Antonio had a photographic memory and he leaned over to Peter and Jennifer and whispered, "I know that guy. I took a, what is it called . . . *selfie* with him."

Peter looked at him confused. "A selfie? With an FBI agent?"

"It was about six months ago. I was out to dinner with Maria at the Forge in Miami and he was tailing me. He was by himself for some reason and got a table by us. He was the most obvious agent I'd ever seen. So, just to fuck with him, I got up from dinner and went over to him and told him, 'let's take a selfie, it'll last longer.'" My son just happened to show me what a selfie was the week before. SA Platt stood up from his table, his eyes went wide with embarrassment, and I put my arm around him and snapped a few selfies—he didn't seem to have a sense of humor about the situation like I did. I'm sure the photos are still on Maria's phone. I—"

"Mr. Cohen," Mag. Smith asked with impatience. "Are you here with us? Do you want to cross the agent?"

"Uh, yes, Your Honor. One minute, please."

"You have thirty seconds. Let's move this along. This isn't my only case today."

Peter ignored her. He thought a moment about how to use this information. "Jennifer, have Maria email you the photos and let me see them on the iPad." As he stood up, he leaned into Antonio, a slight smile crossed his face. "This should be fun."

Peter walked to the podium and looked down at his legal pad, stalling for time to ponder the selfie and how he could use it to his advantage.

"Good morning, Special Agent Platt," Peter said.

Be suspect of every question a defense lawyer asks, he remembered from one of his classes at the FBI Academy in Quantico. "Uh . . . good, uh, morning . . . Sir."

"You've been with the FBI for almost a year now?" Peter kept it conversational to get SA Platt comfortable, although, he looked so tense, you could probably turn coal into a diamond if you shoved it up his ass.

"Yes." He took a sip of water.

"Congratulations on your almost year anniversary. *Good sign*, Peter thought, *he's starting to relax. A few more easy "yes" questions and he'll be eating out of my hand.*

"And before joining the FBI, you were a deputy sheriff in Coal County, Oklahoma?"

"Yes."

"For five years?"

"Yes." SA Platt leaned back a little in the chair, relaxing a bit further.

"And, recently, you were assigned to a task force investigating organized crime? About six months ago?"

"Yes, Sir, and before that I was a trainee."

Perfect, Peter thought, *he's offering information I didn't ask for.*

Jennifer placed the iPad on the podium in front of Peter. There was Antonio with a big smile and his arm around SA Platt, who had a look of shock on his young face. *Bingo*, Peter thought.

"Your primary job on the organized crime task force was to investigate allegations of organized crime, correct?"

"Sort of . . . I was mostly stuck doing boring surveillance and getting coffee sometimes."

"You were the low man on the totem pole?"

"I guess you could say that."

Herb leaned over to Trevor and whispered, "Peter's setting him up for something."

"I know, I wonder what was on that iPad," Trevor whispered back.

"We'll soon find out," Herb said, raising one eyebrow.

"Now," Peter continued, "You swore to the allegations in the Criminal Complaint, correct?"

"Yes."

"I'd like to show you Government's Exhibit number one." Peter walked to the front of the courtroom and picked up Exhibit 1 off a wooden table right in front of the clerk's bench. He walked back to a low cart in front of the jury box with a computer screen and an Elmo on it. The Elmo was like an overhead projector on steroids. Anything placed on the Elmo would show on every computer screen in the courtroom. Peter flipped to the last page of the Criminal Complaint and placed it on the brightly lit Elmo glass and asked, "SA Platt, is that your signature?" It appeared on the monitor next to the Elmo. Mag. Smith leaned closer to her monitor.

SA Platt turned his head and looked at the wall behind him, clearly expecting a movie screen. He turned back around and looked at Peter, confused.

"Turn the monitor on in front of you?" Mag. Smith instructed.

"Oh, okay . . . Yes, that's my signature."

"Have you ever been tasked with following Mr. Barrera?" Peter shifted topics quickly to keep the witness off balance.

SA Platt thought for a moment. "One time, a few months ago."

"Date?" Peter always tried to work a one-word question into his cross examinations. If he could do it, it meant the witness was totally under his control.

"Uh . . . I believe it was in June—I don't remember the exact day."

Peter couldn't believe his luck. The only time SA Platt surveilled Antonio was when he wasn't "working" and out to dinner with Maria. *Perfect*, he thought.

"When you surveil someone, they are generally considered a target, correct?"

"That's correct, Sir. If I'm surveilling an individual, it's because there is a founded suspicion that they are involved in criminal activity." SA Platt managed a confident smile at his textbook answer.

"Back to government's Exhibit one." Peter walked over to the Elmo and put the cover page on the glass.

SA Platt didn't like these questions. He barely read the Complaint and Warrant when Trevor grabbed him and asked him to swear under oath that each and every fact was true and correct, and he had personal knowledge of the facts contained therein. He was holding a tray of coffee at the time for the tech guys monitoring the wiretaps.

"You never actually witnessed any one of the facts contained in this document, correct?"

Um, Um . . . it was relayed to me by other sworn agents . . . I relied on the *good-fait-officer rule*."

"So, that's a *yes*—you never actually witnessed Mr. Barrera committing any of these acts? Correct."

"Correct," SA Platt reluctantly agreed.

Peter walked back to the podium, looked at his notes and asked, "Would you agree with me that a husband and wife out to dinner pose no threat—"

Trevor bolted upright. "Objection! Your Honor. This has no relevance to this proceeding. What does a husband and wife out to dinner have to do with—"

"No speaking-objections, Mr. Wittingham." Mag. Smith chastised.

Mag. Smith turned to Peter. "Mr. Cohen, where are you going with this?"

"Just a little latitude, Judge, and you'll see the relevance in a minute."

"Okay but get there fast. Objection overruled."

"Special Agent Platt, let me ask that again: "Would you agree with me that a husband and wife out to dinner do not pose a threat to society?"

His face had a confused look. "Generally, no."

Peter leaned forward as he dictated, "Would you further agree with me that people you suspect of crimes don't normally take selfies with the agents following them? Correct?"

"Um. . . ." Was all he could initially muster at the question. The confused look on his face growing by the second.

Peter added, "It's the FBI special agents, like you, who do the picture taking? Right? The "dangerous suspects" usually run and avoid having their pictures taken . . . that's what your *extensive* experience has taught you? Correct?"

"Um . . . yes, I guess," SA Platt answered, shrugging his shoulders. *He's just going on a fishing expedition, he's got nothing on me . . . Antonio faces the death penalty—he ain't gettin' a bond*, SA Platt thought as he answered, gaining a bit of confidence again.

"Now, you never observed Antonio," Peter picked up the Criminal Complaint for effect, "commit a murder? Correct?"

"Um, correct." SA Platt responded the same way for each charge against Antonio listed in the Criminal Complaint.

"In reality," Peter finished, "the only time you actually observed the defendant, Mr. Barrera, he was eating dinner with his wife at The Forge restaurant in Miami? Correct?"

"That's a nice restaurant," Mag. Smith quipped involuntarily.

"Huh? I don't understand the question," SA Platt answered.

Really, Kid, you're gonna play dumb with me . . . suit yourself. "What's not to understand? In your capacity as a special agent for the Federal Bureau of Investigation you surveilled Antonio Barrera? Correct?"

"Yes. Not very often though."

"One time, you told us earlier. Do you remember that answer?"

"Right, only one time I followed Mr. Barrera."

"When you followed him that one time, all he did was have dinner with his wife. In fact, you didn't even witness him commit a traffic infraction? Correct?"

SA Platt glanced at Trevor and answered, "I don't recall . . . but, when I surveilled the defendant, he was definitely associating with known criminals."

Peter loved *I don't recall* answers—it usually meant the witness was concerned about the question and didn't think Peter could challenge his suddenly faulty memory. "One moment, Your Honor," He walked back to the defense table, leaned over and whispered to Jennifer, "Let me see the photo." Jennifer handed him the iPad. A smile spread across his face. "Can you put this on the monitors?"

"Sure, I can easily plug the iPad into their system. The HDMI port is right there." She pointed to the computer thing in the base of the podium.

"The HDM—what?" Peter asked, like Jennifer was speaking Japanese.

"Don't worry, I'll take care of it." Jennifer took the iPad back.

"Let's go, Mr. Cohen," Mag. Smith Chided.

"Coming, Your Honor," Peter said. Jennifer walked over to the podium and plugged the iPad in and placed it on top of the podium. "Thank you," Peter said as he took his place behind the podium. He looked at SA Platt who now had numerous breeds of sweat on his brow.

As soon as the selfie of Antonio and SA Platt appeared on everyone's monitors, Trevor was on his feet. "Objection! Your Honor. What is this? This is inadmissible."

Mag. Smith looked closely at her monitor then looked at Trevor, "I don't think *what is this* is a proper objection, Mr. Wittingham. Besides, this looks like a picture . . . actually a selfie of . . . your agent here and Mr. Barrera with big smiles on their faces. So you can obviously *see* what it is—the picture speaks for itself. I will overrule your objection, because Mr. Cohen has not sought to introduce this photo, so there's nothing to object to. Sit down, Mr. Wittingham." She looked at Peter. "Mr. Cohen, are you seeking to introduce this photo into evidence?"

"Yes; however, right now I'm just introducing it for identification purposes and we'll mark it as *Defendant's Exhibit One* for identification purposes only."

"You may proceed with authenticating the photo, then I will take up your premature objection Mr. Wittingham."

"Thank you, Judge," Peter said, looking at SA Platt now who had sweat glistening all over his face. "Special Agent Platt, do you recognize this photograph?"

SA Platt stared at the selfie in disbelief. He glanced at Trevor and Herb a few times with pleading eyes.

"Special Agent Platt, Mr. Wittingham and Mr. Rosen can't help you answer my simple question?"

"Uh . . . can you repeat the question?"

"Of course," Peter said with a smile, knowing SA Platt was in a mental free fall by the site of the photo he surely never put in a report for fear of embarrassment and violation of FBI protocol when surveilling a "Target". "Do you recognize this photo?"

"Yes . . . Yes I do." He finally muttered.

"Do you recall when it was taken?"

"Uh, Uh," he stammered, knowing exactly when that picture was taken, but he needed time to figure out a way to fix this, so he didn't get in trouble for not putting this encounter in his report. *In a million years, I never thought this would be relevant.* "It was taken a few months ago, on or about June 20 of this year. You see, I was surveilling Mr. Barrera, and per department policy, I'm supposed to—I didn't eat or drink anything; my partner was waiting in the van . . . I don't know why I didn't put it in my report."

"Objection!" Trevor said.

Peter made a note on his pad, in red: didn't put in my report.

"Nonresponsive," Trevor continued, not that he really had a legal objection, but he needed to stop SA Platt's sudden diarrhea of the mouth.

"Overruled. He's your witness."

Peter continued, "Now, back to the selfie. Does this photo fairly and accurately depict you and Antonio Barrera at the Forge restaurant on or about March 23 of this year around dinner time?"

"Um, yes."

Peter turned to Mag. Smith. "I'd move Defense Exhibit 1 into evidence."

She turned to Trevor. "Now you may make your objection."

"No objection," Trevor said, still seated. *Where the hell is Peter going with this?*

"Defense Exhibit 1 is admitted without objection."

"Are you a *known criminal*?" Peter abruptly asked SA Platt.

"What, me, no, of course not—no."

Peter's questions came fast now. "The night of the selfie, was Mr. Barrera having dinner with any known criminals?"

SA Platt looked up and to the left as he thought for a moment. Peter knew that looking up and to the left was a sign someone was trying to access their brain for the truth. "Uh, no," SA Platt finally answered. "He was with that nice lady sitting behind him." He pointed to Maria.

"And you later learned that that lady was his wife, correct?" Peter was now testifying in his questions—one of the benefits of being able to ask leading questions on cross-examination.

"Yes."

"In fact, Mr. Barrera wasn't with any *known criminals* when you took the selfie, correct?"

"I don't know that." SA Platt answered.

"So, I guess you're the *known criminal* Mr. Barrera was with that night, because Maria Barrera is an honest, upstanding citizen who devotes her time to raising a family and doing charity work in the community. In fact, I think she recently attended a charity event for federal agents injured in the line of duty."

"I'm not a criminal. I'm a sworn, federal agent."

"Are you saying it's impossible for federal agents to be criminals?"

"Well, no, but . . . I was just sa—"

"Actually," Peter, with a twinkle in his eye, pounded on, "you violated FBI rules that night. Isn't the selfie proof of an unauthorized picture with a suspected target violating FBI rule section 8.35?" Peter looked at SA Platt with intense eyes.

"Proof? What? No. I didn't violate any laws."

"Wait . . . is that a beer on your table? Are you allowed to have beer when you're working?" Peter looked closely at the monitor with the selfie. He really didn't care what was in the photo—he knew SA Platt probably wasn't drinking on the job, but just by asking the question, he put his credibility in doubt.

Indignant in his response, SA Platt answered, "Absolutely not."

Now for the crescendo. "You never put this encounter with Mr. Barrera and his family in your investigative report, correct?"

SA Platt's shoulders were now dropping a couple inches lower then when the cross examination started and his head was hung, eyes looking at the floor. "Correct."

"In fact, you never mentioned this encounter to any of your superiors. Correct?"

"Correct."

"And your surveillance team that night never put this encounter in their reports? Correct?" Peter was really taking a chance now.

"Correct." SA Platt said, now on autopilot. He wished he could run and hide back on the farm in Oklahoma.

I could probably get this guy to admit to the Kennedy assassination, Peter happily thought. *What a shame though, another good cross and Antonio has zero chance for a bond with his charges. One more question* to start manipulating the potential jury pool. "Isn't it true that you never reported this encounter with Mr. Barrera and his wife because you knew it *disproved* the allegations in the Indictment, correct?"

"Correct . . . wait, I mean, n—"

"No further questions. I'm done with this witness."

"No. I meant to say NO!" SA Platt blurted out, but no one cared at this point.

"Any further witnesses or evidence, Mr. Wittingham?"

"No," he said, standing, with a little more confidence, knowing he was about to proceed with legal arguments and, regardless of SA Platt's testimony, he was confident Antonio wasn't getting a bond in a death penalty case.

"Do you have any other evidence besides Defense Exhibit 1, Mr. Cohen?"

"One moment please." Peter quickly consulted with Jennifer and Antonio. "Anymore photos with FBI agents . . . maybe at *Disney World*?"

"No, just that one," Antonio whispered.

They all agreed there was no other evidence to offer. Peter stood. "No, Your Honor, just argument."

Mag. Smith sat up straight. "Okay. I'm going to save you some time, Mr. Wittingham. Even though the government has the burden of proving the defendant is a flight risk and danger to the community, which means you argue first. Given the sworn allegations in the Criminal Complaint, even though SA Platt wasn't the greatest witness, he did testify that it was in fact his signature on the criminal complaint and arrest warrant affidavit, and that the allegations contained therein were observed by other sworn agents, relying on the *good faith officer rule*; given that a grand jury issued an Indictment; given the fact that the government indicated that this will be a death penalty case; and given your client's considerable resources and international ties, I am initially finding that Mr. Barrera is a *flight risk* and *danger to the community* and thereby not entitled to a bond. Convince me otherwise, Mr. Cohen."

Peter argued why a bond should be issued in this matter for thirty minutes. Trevor responded for ten minutes. Peter spent five more minutes having the last word.

Mag. Smith looked at each of them. "After that, I need to think about my decision. I will issue a written order by the end of the day. Each party may email my clerk within two hours any additional case law you want me to consider." Jennifer already texted several associates to do more research and find more cases in addition to the fifteen Peter already provided. "This Court is in recess," Mag. Smith said and banged her gavel.

Peter leaned into Antonio, who was standing with both marshals now standing behind him, ready to take him out of the courtroom, and said, "Surprisingly, I think we have a chance." The marshals took Antonio back to jail.

Trevor walked over to the defense table. "Can I help you, Trevor?" Peter asked with indifference.

Trevor walked over to Peter with a smug look and proclaimed, "Your guy isn't getting a bond. By the way, here is government trial exhibit number one." He dropped a DVD in a white paper sleeve on the table then turned and left.

"What an obnoxious prick," Peter said, handing Jennifer the DVD.

— 44 —

THWACK ... Thwack ... Crack. ... "Will you knock that damn noise off! I'm tryin' to dink," yelled Bobbie "the Whistle". He threw down the *Palm Beach Post* and rubbed his fingers tightly through his hair.

"I thought I saw smoke coming outta ya head," Tim "the Duck" chimed in.

"How about I reach across this table and rip your brain outta ya head." Bobbie's hard look from across the small card table was enough—Tim looked away and didn't say another word.

Phil "the Pick" and Luca "the Latin" were off in the corner huddled around a large butcher's block, blood dripping down the edges onto the stone cellar floor into a drain—they were at Luca's mom's house.

Phil was holding an industrial-sized meat clever; he stopped his taught arm midway. "Come on," he pleaded with Bobbie, "one more *chop*. I bet Luca I can cut the thigh bone in three chops—it just cracked. One more chop and this prick is payin' me five hundred bucks." Phil said with a large smile, clearly already counting his money, as he pointed the bloody meat clever at Luca, blood dripping off its edge and splattering on the floor.

Bobbie looked at Phil and Luca, exasperated, and bitched, "Little Richie Wilson can wait. That degenerate-fuck isn't worth the trouble of chopping him up. You should'a left 'em outside his kid's school after you ice picked 'em in the parking lot." Bobbie spit on the dank floor. "We gots more serious problems."

Tim reached down and picked up the newspaper Bobbie threw down. "Give me that," Bobbie ordered as he snatched it from Tim's hand. Phil and Luca were now sitting at the small metal card table; their rubber aprons, clothes, and skin covered in blood—Phil's face looked like he had bad acne from the bespectacled blood on it. Bobbie laid the *Palm Beach Post* on the table and pointed hard to the front-page headline. "Look . . . I told you that son of a bitch Antonio was going to flip . . . *Magic Man*, my ass."

They all read the headline to themselves: *THE "MAGIC MAN" DOES IT AGAIN! JUDGE GRANTS BAIL IN DEATH PENALTY CASE OF MOB BOSS, ANTONIO BARRERA!*

Phil finally said, "So much for dis ding of ours."

Luca added, shaking his head, "No way Antonio's flipping. He would never do that—he lives and dies by *omertà*."

Bobbie picked up the newspaper and threw it at Luca. "What else you need to see? It's right there in black and white." Bobbie looked around the table. "Where's Jimmy and Robert? I said, *emergency* meeting."

"They's off doin' dat thing, at dat place, wit dat guy, ya know what I means," Tim answered.

"Oh. That's right . . . that *thing* at that *place* takin' care of that *guy* in Chicago—"

"Luca? . . . Luca? . . . You and your friends want some nice gravy and rigatoni I made this morning." Luca's eighty-seven-year-old mama interrupted. She was standing on the dark landing at the top of the cellar stairs—she never descended the stairs.

"Pasta and gravy sounds good right now," Phil said as two blobs of blood dripped off his ear.

Bobbie was about to lose it. "Are you fuckin' kiddin' me . . . your mom is home. Why did you say to meet here for Christ's sake."

"Phil and I were a little busy when you called," Luca said, pointing to the partially hacked up body of Little Richie Wilson. "Besides, you're the one that said it was an *emergency*. Don't worry, this place is clean—the stone walls are too thick to get a signal from a wire. My mama don't care what we do neither and she cook real good, like in the old country." Luca rubbed his belly through the bloody apron and licked his lips.

"Whatever, just get rid of her," Bobbie said.

"Yeah, Mama. That would be great, we be up soon." The door closed.

Tim said, "I don't understand, Bobbie, why do you think Antonio is flippin'? A lot of guys get bail . . . and his is real, real high." He looked closer at the front page of the paper. "Ten million plus house arrest."

Bobbie sighed. "No one makes bail when they are charged with murder, sex trafficking, R.I.C.O, and all that other shit he's charged with. Then add on the DEATH PENALTY! He's decided to flip on us all," he pointed at each of them, "and the rest of the family."

"Probably New York too," Phil added, slumping his shoulders.

"Look, I know I'm right. Right now we watch and wait. No one do notin' . . . and let's all keep a low profile. And don't fuckin' tell anyone else about our suspicions, we don't know where the other guys' loyalties lie yet. Agreed?"

"Yeah," they all said.

"Now, let's go eat," Luca said.

Phil pointed to Little Richie Wilson. "No one better touch 'em'. I'm gonna take that thigh off with one more whack and win my money."

— 45 —

TREVOR CRUMPLED THE newspaper and threw it in his garbage can. Marlene snickered under her breath as she slid a cup of coffee across the table.

"You screw up another case?" she asked.

He glared at her . . . then said, "It was this idiot FBI agent who screwed-up . . . but I'll win the trial. That moron agent has been reassigned to a field station *graveyard* in Guam." He took a sip of his coffee.

"From what I read, it seems like that Peter guy is going to win this case pretty easily." Marlene slurped her green drink through a straw. "Great, now I'll have to listen to people at the club talk about the bad headlines you're going to get every day." She sighed.

Trevor thought it best to try and change the subject, like he always did when Marlene was belittling him. "How's Gisele doing in school?"

"Not that great. She's skipping a lot . . . She's got a lot of stress. Most of her friends are traveling to Aspen or the South of France for the holidays . . . The fact that her father doesn't make much money is really wearing on her." Marlene slurped her drink some more.

What a selfish bitch. "Don't you mean it's wearing on *you* that I make a government salary . . . which by the way isn't that bad—a hundred and eighty thousand a year plus benefits should be enough to live a comfortable life."

"It's not that bad if you want to live next to plumbers and cops. But, since you mentioned it . . . I think it would be good for Gisele and me to spend Christmas in Aspen—it would really help *our* daughter a lot. You don't need to go, just stay here and work on your case . . . we'll get out of your hair and let you focus on winning." She softened her eyes and looked at him.

He stared back for a second. *Those cute puppy dog eyes don't work anymore, babe.* "I'll think about it."

"Well, while you think about it, I need some money to go Christmas shopping." Marlene put her smoothie cup in the sink hard.

"So, use the money in the Christmas account. I have to go to work." Trevor took another sip of his coffee, turned, and quickly left before Marlene continued belittling him about money.

In the distance, as he was almost at the front door, he heard Marlene say something about there wasn't even enough money to buy one person a good gift in that account.

— 46 —

PETER PACED THE length of his office balcony. The crashing waves of the Atlantic helped him think, especially at sunrise. Brilliant bursts of yellow, orange, and red filled the sky over Palm Beach. It was his therapy—much better, and cheaper than a therapist Peter always found. He was currently staring at the old sandstone clock tower at the entrance to the beach at the top of Worth Avenue—a/k/a *the Avenue*. He could not get the video Trevor gave him at the end of the pretrial detention hearing out of his head. . . .

How could Antonio be so stupid? He must be slipping . . . he's never even been recorded saying "hello" to a stranger on the street before . . . and now this video! I'm going to be responsible for killing my client. No way I can win . . . if the video didn't exist . . . maybe I could win . . . at least I could avoid the death penalty. After Trevor presents all of the horrific circumstantial evidence that he alleges in the Criminal Complaint, and then plays the video, the jury will want to shoot Antonio right there in the courtro—Peter's concentration was interrupted by three pelicans, flying in formation in front of the clock face—it was 6:25 a.m. Suddenly, the *2* and *5* on the clock face stood out to him . . . *Bingo.*

He went back inside his office and sat behind his desk of black onyx with inlaid jade borders, which was a gift from an Indonesian prince he walked on an exotic animal smuggling case. The sheer size of his office was intimidating. The walls were large panels of light-colored silk. The floor was covered by expensive Turkish rugs. He took out a yellow legal pad and began formulating a defense strategy.

Peter's office was at 100 Worth Avenue in a four-story building with floor to ceiling windows, French doors, and balconies. To the East was the clock tower and the beach and to the West were shops like: Gucci,

Hermès, and Cartier lining both sides of Worth Avenue. The law firm of Peter Cohen and Associates had five other lawyers and fifteen support staff.

"Mr. Barrera is here to see you," interrupted his assistant through the intercom. Peter was normally by himself this early, but Antonio wanted to meet at 7:30 a.m., so he had Meredith come in early. Most of his high profile clients preferred to meet real early in the morning or later at night; less chance someone with a camera would notice them walking into Peter's office, which everyone knew meant you were in serious trouble.

"Good morning, Antonio. How are you?" Peter asked.

Antonio looked at Peter like he just asked the dumbest question ever. "How do you think? . . . I've been better, Peter." They shook hands.

"I know, but at least your walking into my office instead of me coming to see you in the clink."

"That's one way to look at it, I guess." Antonio walked over to the white leather chair in front of Peter's desk—his custom-made, olive-colored silk suit creased perfectly as he sat.

Peter sat and took a sip of his coffee. He stared for a few seconds at Antonio then asked, "Are you alright?" *I've never seen Antonio with such a worried look on his face.*

"How bad is it?" His stare never leaving Peter's eyes.

Peter raised an eyebrow, *these meetings never started with* that *question,* and replied, "Well, you face the death penalty and the evidence is—"

"Don't give me that canned legalese bullshit. I pay you three thousand dollars an hour and God knows how much for your ever-growing staff."

Peter recoiled a bit at Antonio's intensity. He had been doing this so long he didn't take offense to his clients' irrational rants—they were highly stressed. He could win ten times for a client, literally give them their freedom back, and on the eleventh time, he was the worst lawyer on the planet because he didn't produce the same magic results.

Peter dealt in a very high stakes business—a criminal defense lawyer's product was years in prison and sometimes actual life. This job could mentally crush a person quickly, lawyer and client alike.

"For Christ's sake, Peter, the Feds kicked in my front door and came from the fucking ceiling while I was making love to my wife. My kid was home—he pissed his pants . . . and they found weed in his room and threatened to arrest him." Antonio's eyes briefly flashed compassion at the thought of his son. "I had no chance to leave. I paid you two million dollars last year and I didn't even get arrested. You did nothing to earn that fee."

"Why do you think that is? I more than earned my fee last year." When it came to money, no lawyer lets their client get away with saying they didn't earn a fee.

"Save me the sanctimonious crap. I was still arrested this time with no warning . . . I should be on a beach somewhere far away from the Feds' jurisdiction. Am I wasting my money?" He slammed his hand on the table, jolting Peter.

Sensing Antonio was done bitching, Peter calmly said, "This was different . . . the FBI and U.S. Attorney used the Pentagon for assistance on this one for some reason. Someone with very powerful friends has a problem with you. I'm in the process of finding out—"

"Excuses. That's what I hear from you. I want answers. It's been two weeks already since my arrest." In Antonio's world answers were provided immediately, or people died.

Peter still marveled at the fact that most clients, whether a small contract dispute or death penalty case, believed that lawyers just snapped their fingers or wrote a letter and got the case dismissed. "Antonio, look over at the TV screen . . . I want you to see something."

"A first-year law student could've protected me better than you," Antonio grumbled, as he turned and looked at the eighty-inch TV hanging on the wall to his right, which currently displayed an animated African safari scene. Peter tapped the wireless Apple keyboard on his desk. The safari scene dissolved just as a lion was about to catch a gazelle.

The screen now displayed, in high definition, a picture of Antonio sitting around a card table with three of his Capos and driver: Alfonso "the Whale" Tomisini, Vinnie "the Bag" Respi, Carmine "Bowling Ball" Gatto, and Joseph sitting to his right. Antonio recognized when and where the video was taken immediately. He was in the back office at *In the Hole*. He had several meetings that week. Antonio never met with all of his guys at the same time to discuss the family business; he compartmentalized all of them, just like the military—everyone was responsible for their specific part, no more, no less. Only Antonio knew everything. He watched the 2:37 video with a stoic look. . . .

When the video ended, Peter said, "What the hell were you doing that week, holding an adult education course on *the best mob businesses to turn a huge profit*. The human and kid sex trafficking stuff will be a big hit with the jury."

Antonio had a look of disbelief on his face. He turned from the TV to Peter. "I remember that meeting, I told the guys, especially that fat fuck Alphonso, NOT to make money doing that human trafficking shit . . . we were making enough money from our other business that the risk wasn't worth it. Plus, any political capital would have been completely lost if I got into that shit—adult prostitution was fine, but human smuggling and pimping kidnapped kids—I'm not a monster, I'm a simple businessman. Why do you think Alphonso 'the Whale' isn't around anymore . . . he wouldn't listen."

Peter raised an eyebrow at that last statement. "Word on the street is someone made Alphonso eat his own penis."

Antonio ignored the comment and continued. "How the hell did someone get a video like this. It's so fuckin' close and crystal clear. The sound quality is better than IMAX for Christ's sake. . . . It looks like the camera is attached to a bird flying around the room, not attached to one of the guys or stationary. Plus, I have the club, especially the back office, swept twice a day for bugs—always comes up clean. It must be a fake . . . has to be . . . no way the Feds got this type of video on me . . . no God damn way." He was shaking his head now.

"I can guarantee you it is not a fake. I spent two hundred thousand dollars of your money over the past two weeks having the video analyzed by the best in the business." Peter searched his desk, which was a mess of papers, and located the one-inch-thick report and handed it to Antonio. "Here are the results of the video analysis and receipts. Oh, and by the way, I'll need a separate wire of five hundred thousand dollars to cover costs thus far. But I did save you about a hundred thousand, because I have a friend at Lucas Light and Magic who tripled checked the video for authenticity and, bingo, one hundred percent not doctored. The video is as real as it gets, so you must have forgotten what the hell you said in those meetings." Peter's voice never had a hint of emotion when talking to a client; everything was business—the good facts and the bad.

Antonio just looked at the report in front of him, then looked at Peter with intensity and calmly said in a low voice as he leaned across the desk, "Then who flipped, they're dead. Right now." Antonio took his cell phone out of his jacket pocket to punctuate how dead serious he was.

Peter raised his hands in front of him making a stopping motion. "Whoa, whoa, whoa. You know you can't do that, Antonio, or at least you can't tell me you're going to do *that*. Remember, I have ethical obligations."

"Screw your ethical obligations! The Feds just indicted me on thirty felony charges that I didn't commit."

Peter could sense Antonio wasn't only angry, he was scared. He didn't have to hear anything from Peter to know he was screwed this time. The Feds had finally gotten audio and video on him. *But how did they get such good audio and video?* Peter kept asking himself. "I don't know who, if anyone flipped, but I'll find out soon enough."

"Alright, so what's the game plan on this one. Let's prepare for war like in the past. You're Peter 'the Great' . . . this case should be easy for you."

"Not so for this one. But I have an idea that may work."

— 47 —

"SLAM DUNK. THAT'S what this case is. A slam dunk by Shaquille O'Neil—KA BOOM!" Trevor mimicked an explosion with his stubby hands. "It's a standard Mob R.I.C.O. with some really nasty human trafficking and a child murder as a cherry on top." Trevor's mouth widened into a smile at the thought of how perfectly he set up the charges to get maximum sympathy from the jury. *I can't wait until the jury hears from my surprise witness who was on the freighter when the old lady and kid were killed . . . I love trial-by-ambush.* He rubbed his hands together in excited anticipation.

Lisa interrupted Trevor's happy thoughts, "We still don't have any direct—"

"Or *credible*," Herb added.

"—witnesses to link Antonio to the murders or human trafficking counts." Lisa finished, with the exasperation of someone who said the same exact conclusion a thousand times already.

Miache put down his coffee mug that read: *Don't Mistake Google for My Accounting Degree,* and said, "And from the IRS' perspective, I still can't directly tie the flow of money from all of Antonio's known businesses, which are twenty-seven at last count, to him—I get close . . . with some creative inferences I can link him to most of the business revenue streams, but this isn't a game of hand grenades where *close* counts. Using offshore accounts in unorthodox places like India and China, to name a few, his money vanishes once it's wired out of the U.S. In the past I would call my contacts in Panama or the Cayman Islands to follow the money, but places like communist China tell me *Qu si ba* (go to hell) when I ask for banking information."

Trevor stared at Machie and thought, *actually, it is like a game of hand grenades . . . all I have to do is lob a few really nasty facts at the jury and loosely link Antonio to them, and voila . . . a GAC (guilty on all counts).*

Jackson Reed finally broke his stoic look and spoke, "Unless the video you still haven't shown any of us has a smoking gun on it, I think we should push the trial off as long as possible to lock down some of the circumstantial evidence we have connecting Antonio to the counts in the Indictment. Once we lost confidential source–Alphonso 'the Whale' Tomisini, we lost our best witness to really make this case a *slam dunk.*"

Trevor looked at Jackson. "No way this case is getting pushed off." *I need the conviction in the media now, so I can begin my assent to the governor's mansion.* Then he looked at the entire team. "I want this case tried as quickly as possible. Trust me when I tell you, the video will make this case more of a *slam dunk* than it already is. I will show you the video before trial, but I don't want my best piece of evidence leaked to the media before I play it for the jury. Now, get to work and stop bitching."

— 48 —

"Meredith, two espressos," Peter ordered into the intercom. "Antonio, listen to me. I haven't steered you wrong yet. We have to think big picture here . . . this is your *life* . . . literally. This is about stopping the government from killing you or sending you to that Supermax hellhole in Florence, Colorado for the next ten lifetimes." Meredith placed the espressos on the desk, then left.

"Where's my *target letter*?" Antonio asked.

"The Feds didn't send one this time, nor the past ten times they indicted you." Clients always grasped at straws when confronted with the overwhelming evidence against them: *The date on the police report is wrong, the case has to be dismissed; I was too tired to sell drugs, the State can't convict me*—seriously, a client caught on video selling opioids told Peter to argue that defense at trial.

Antonio pressed further, truly believing he discovered a technicality Peter didn't see. "Why not? Don't they have to? It must be in the Constitution."

Peter sipped the espresso and looked over the tiny mug with a raised eyebrow at Antonio. "No, of course not. That's an absurd notion. Sure, the Feds are going to send the largest crime boss in the world, allegedly, a letter reading: *Dear Mr. Barrera, when you have a free minute, we would like to discuss the murders we think you committed while shipping twelve year olds to South Florida for forced prostitution. Signed the FBI and DOJ*. The Feds send a target letter to minor leaguers or witnesses they want to scare into testifying for them when they have nothing on them. You're considered a 'hard target', which means 'extremely dangerous' and 'extreme flight risk', so the Feds come heavy and definitely *unannounced*." Peter let out a slight laugh to break the tension. "I bet that prick Wittingham crapped his pants at the first sound of gunfire—I was told it was actually microwave popcorn that made a loud POP! Trevor jumped behind a big flowerpot—I wish there was a picture. . . ." Peter mused.

"It wasn't funny from where I was, in bed, with Maria . . . my son was making *that* popcorn. He had to see me hauled away like an animal."

"These charges are different than the last time the Feds investigated you for wire and mail fraud in that price-fixing commodities scheme—I'm glad the jury saw it my way. Plus, if I remember correctly, I also got the seventy-five million dollars back that the Feds seized."

"Minus forty percent for you."

"Anyway," Peter continued, "you're charged with multiple counts of racketeering, murder, fraud, tax evasion, sex trafficking minors—and that's just the first few pages of the Indictment. From what my sources tell me, that little prick Trevor Wittingham is lead on this one—he cherry picked it himself. Knowing him, he needs the massive press coverage this case will get . . . probably wants to run for governor or something. My sources also told me that Wittingham moved pretty quick, and out of nowhere, on ordering the Alphabet Boys to wrap-up their investigations, arrest you, and prepare the Indictment. Which is not that difficult when, realistically, some federal agency is always investigating you and your guys."

"*Alphabet Boys?* What the hell are you talking about?" Antonio asked, confused.

"You never heard the term 'Alphabet Boys'? Don't you have a teenage son? I overheard the rap star Jay-z use the term to generically describe federal law enforcement agencies in one of his songs my grandson was listening to. Actually, the song wasn't half bad—it had a nice groove."

"My life isn't a Jay-z song."

"I'm not saying it is . . . move past the anger, and focus," Peter directed. "Although Wittingham isn't a great trial lawyer, he doesn't have to be. The conviction rate for the DOJ is about ninety-eight percent . . . and, with the video we just watched, I'm sorry to say, I think there's virtually a one hundred percent chance he'll get his conviction and kill you."

Antonio sat ramrod straight in the chair, his eyes turning to a confident stare. "So what. We've beat them before, we'll do it again and this one should be easy, because I had nothing to do with sex trafficking, human trafficking, or any other kind of trafficking, let alone the *intentional* murder of children. Piece of cake."

He's acting like he got arrested for misdemeanor pot, Peter thought. "Did you *read* the copy of the Indictment I gave you . . . the last thing this will be is a *piece of cake,* Antonio. Now listen—"

"Damn lawyers! You're always looking for more money. Although you should do this for free given all of the money you've already made off me and my guys . . . don't worry, I'll pay whatever it takes. You don't need to justify charging me more by telling me how difficult the case is going to be."

"You need to listen for a few minutes—calm down and listen. What I'm telling you isn't about *more* money. I haven't steered you wrong yet, and I don't plan to start now."

* * *

Antonio sat back and relented, "Fine, I'll listen to your *great plan.*"

Peter ignored the condescension and decided to just come out and admit it—no sugar coating to increase his fee: "I can't win this case for you, Antonio . . . not this one. No lawyer can—not even *Perry Mason.* Trial is too risky for you. I can virtually guarantee you will spend the rest of your life in prison, or worse, get legally killed by good ol' Uncle Sam."

"I don't like what I'm hearing." Antonio wasn't accustomed to hearing things he didn't like. Antonio's shoulders slumped even further, and the look of disbelief was back on his face. His handsome tanned face drained to white.

Peter got up and walked over to the large built-in bookshelves lined with all sorts of impressive leather-bound legal books. . . . "Here it is," Peter said out loud as he grabbed a thick blue book with gold engraved writing: *Federal Criminal Code and Rules*. He walked back to his desk. "28 U.S.C. 2255," he muttered as he flipped through the pages.

Antonio's face lit up slightly. "Now we're talking. See, I knew you'd figure out how to get me out of this mess. Once we got the *increase the fee dramatics* crap out of the way, I knew you'd come around, Peter my boy. After twenty-five years of representing me, you'd think I'd know your game by now."

Peter ignored him and turned the book around for Antonio to read. Antonio, now with a confident smile, leaned over the desk. Peter pointed to the title of the federal criminal statute—*18 United States Code section 2255. **INEFFECTIVE ASSISTANCE OF COUNSEL.***

Antonio scanned the page . . . He sat back and clapped his hands together, a big smile on his face like he had just solved a Rubik's Cube. "Brilliant! You're so damn brilliant . . . worth every penny."

Peter was surprised Antonio was so agreeable with his unorthodox, and *risky* defense strategy. "You like the strategy?" Peter asked.

"Of course, I do . . . You get the case dismissed because the prosecutor is, what is the phrase?" Antonio looked at the federal statute and pointed to it, *ineffective*. That Wittingham guy did such an *ineffective* investigation, it has to be tossed because it's all bullshit created by dirty FBI agents and prosecutors. How quickly can you get it dismissed?"

Peter sighed; *I knew that was too easy.* "No, Antonio, the prosecutor or FBI is not *ineffective*, we hire *you* an *ineffective* lawyer to defend you."

"You on fuckin' drugs, Peter? You drunk? . . . *Me* have an ineffective lawyer? . . . In a death penalty case? . . . Aren't you my damn lawyer. Are you telling me *you're* going to be ineffective? You can't handle this case? What the—" Antonio stood up, his anger and confusion building like a steam whistle. "I'll pay off some jurors or the judge. It's worked before."

Peter continued. "Not that I *can't* handle this case; you don't want me to . . . Hear me out."

Antonio was starting to pace. "This sounds crazy! Fuckin' great!

You've finally gone nuts and right when my life is on the line." He walked back over to the chair and plopped down, the look of hopeless despair spreading across his face again.

Peter stared at his client for a few seconds, a compassionate expression on his face—like every great lawyer, Peter was a chameleon with his facial expressions. "Trust me and listen. I haven't steered you wrong yet, and I'm not about to when you're life is literally on the line.

Antonio inhaled deeply, looked intently at Peter, then exhaled. "I don't trust *anyone* in life except Maria, but fine, I'm listening."

"Thanks for the vote of confidence," Peter said, tapping his finger on the statute. "The law requires a lawyer to possess a basic level of competence and experience when representing a client. Even though that standard is so low that once a lawyer who kept falling asleep at his client's murder trial was not found to be *ineffective*, there is a standard."

Antonio raised his eyebrows. "So . . . I'm going to hire a lawyer to fall asleep at my death penalty trial?"

"Of course not, the court wouldn't find that lawyer ineffective. Now, when you have a civil matter and your lawyer is a moron and screws up, you can sue him or her for malpractice and get money. You with me so far?"

"Go on. And don't patronize me, I'm not a moron."

"However, when you're a criminal defendant and your lawyer sucks, your conviction gets tossed and you get a new trial. Now, I'm over simplifying things, and like anything in the law, rules of law are subject to interpretation and application to a given case, but to prevail on an *Ineffective Assistance of Counsel* claim you have to show: one," Peter held up one finger, "Your lawyer fell below a 'reasonably objective' standard of basic competence and two," he held up two fingers, "if your lawyer was not *ineffective* then the outcome of the trial *probably* would have been different. The main case is *Strickland v. Washington*. Here is the best part. When the case comes back on appeal, Wittingham will be gone and the new prosecutor will offer a very reasonable plea—they always do."

"But you're one of the best lawyers in the country, unless you plan on throwing my case?"

"You're right, I am one of the best lawyers in the country—really the world. No court is going to believe *I* was ineffective. Plus, I wouldn't ruin my reputation on any case. I'm not going to be your lawyer on this one. I'm going to find a young, no-name, untested lawyer to represent you."

"Great, I get all the money back I paid you on this case."

"We'll talk about that in a minute." Peter quickly responded, knowing he would never give a penny back of his *nonrefundable* retainer fee. Besides, the way he saw it, he earned his money already by putting this plan together and getting Antonio out on bond in a death penalty case.

Antonio stood up again, paced for a minute and said, "No one will believe that me, Antonio Barrera, would hire a second-rate lawyer."

"There are people today that actually believe the Earth is flat; you can make people believe anything. I make a living at convincing people things aren't what they seem. How many times have I had you found *not guilty* now?" Peter knew the answer, he just wanted his clients to remember it so he made them say it from time to time.

"Eight . . . no, wait, nine times—I forgot about that thing in Italy. So, what's your point?"

"My point is, I know what I'm doing and I'm telling you this case is completely unwinnable. From what I can tell, the government has a lock solid case this time. I've looked at most of their evidence already, and, frankly, even without the video it's a very hard case to win. But, with the video, it's impossible."

Antonio, still standing, leaned over the back of the chair. "I'm *not* intentionally throwing my own case. This isn't some NBA game that I fixed."

"No, it's not. It's the ultimate, real time decision-making game where one wrong move will get you the electric chair . . . this is the only chance you got. I'll call some colleagues and get a recommendation for a young lawyer, preferably someone green and untested who just left the Public Defender's Office."

"I'm not using some untested, lawyer schmuck. Johnnie Spinolia's kid just got ten years for selling some weed because Johnnie was too cheap to pay for a lawyer—weed's legal in most states for Christ's sake. No way."

"He or she won't be *free*. *Used to* work for the Public Defender's Office—even I was a *free* lawyer once."

"Well, you're sure making up for lost time on fees. How come I never got the *free* Peter?"

"You're going to lose anyway, so we might as well get someone we can blame for the loss, so you get a new trial and then a reasonable plea—maybe do a few years in the long run . . . You can do that standing on your head. You'll hire me to do the appeal, for a separate fee of course, and I can probably keep you out of jail until the appeals are over, which will be a few years down the road."

"What if your plan doesn't work? Forget it. . . . Besides, the judge and Wittingham aren't going to allow some untested, inexperienced idiot to represent me when I face the death penalty."

"I'm glad you said that. I agree."

Antonio got a confused look on his face. "You do? Then why are you wasting my time telling me about this strategy?"

"Sorry. I probably should have explained this part in the beginning." Peter shrugged his shoulders and continued. "The only type of case a lawyer has to have additional qualifications than just a valid law license is in death penalty cases—you can't hire the type of lawyer we need. Trevor seeking the death penalty is just a political ploy. He thinks it will bring him more media attention. I will convince him to waive the death penalty before I turn the case over to a new lawyer. As long as it's not a death penalty case, under the Sixth Amendment, you have a right to 'counsel of your choice' . . . even if it's a bad choice. And Trevor won't say a word, he needs the conviction, so he'll be thrilled to get me out of the case—I've kicked his ass so many times he won't risk it given the option."

"How much of my five-million-dollar retainer do I get back if we do this? How much could a shitty lawyer cost . . . a hundred grand?"

"My fee is nonrefundable, you know that. Same as it's always been. Besides, isn't literally saving your life by getting the death penalty waived worth a measly five million bucks—that's lunch money to a guy like you."

"Don't count my money," Antonio snapped.

"I'm not. I'll tell you what I'm going to do, just because I've always liked you. I'll pay the new lawyer out of my fee . . . deal?"

Antonio sat back in the chair, looked into Peter's eyes for a full two minutes. . . . "It's like a *bad beat* in poker—you lose, but still win. Let's do it."

— 49 —

"As I LIVE and breathe, I don't believe it!" The Public Defender Kelly Hudson said in a mock, surprise tone. "Is this the famous Peter 'the Great' Cohen?"

"Stop. You're embarrassing me. Besides, didn't I just read about you in the *New York Times* where they dubbed you *The Terminator of False Convictions*?"

"It was a slow news day; they had nothing else to print."

"How are you, Kelly?"

"You know. . . trying to run an office full of lawyers who are highly overworked, overstressed, and massively underpaid on a shoestring budget . . . But enough about my problems, what do I owe the pleasure of this call to?"

Peter and Kelly went to Harvard Law School together. They graduated number one and two in their class, and Kelly never let Peter live it down. Although Kelly worked for the government, she was one of the best criminal trial lawyers in the country. She was the elected Public Defender for Palm Beach County—*Honorable Kelly Hudson*. She just won her fifth term.

"As you may know, my client Antonio Barrera was recently indicted for a slew of charges and the DOJ is seeking the death penalty," Peter said.

"Yes, I know, your *uber-rich* mob client. From what I read in the news, it looks pretty bleak for your client, but then again, it's always bleak for our clients. Remember when we said in law school we'd only represent innocent people when we became criminal defense lawyers," She laughed at their youthful naïveté.

"We'd both still be trying to find our first client if we stuck with that ridiculous notion. Life seemed so much easier when we were young and idealistic," Peter reminisced. "Well, this time, my client didn't like what I had to tell him, so he's firing me."

"Your client is clearly a moron." Kelly wasn't surprised. "Whether it was a poor client from the ghetto with a rap sheet a mile long or Bernie Madoff, they were all the same—life was one bad decision after another. I hope you at least got paid something for your time in the case already."

"I got a small fee for what I did so far—"

"*Small fee*! Humph, so that means at least six or maybe even seven figures. However, will you feed those beautiful children of yours." Kelly mocked.

"I made enough to pay some bills. Listen, I need to find him a lawyer, preferably a young one . . . and cheaper."

"What's your angle here, Peter? Isn't this a death penalty case? I don't know any *young* and *cheap* lawyers who are qualified to handle a federal death penalty case. Besides, most of the death penalty lawyers in the county still work for basically minimum wage at my office—people that commit the most atrocious crimes never seem to save any money for a damn lawyer, you know that."

"I'm pretty sure I can convince the AUSA Wittingham to waive the death penalty, so that won't matter. Antonio thinks I'm too jaded and old at this point and wants a young lawyer who's hungry. No one produces great, young trial lawyers better than your office. I also told him he has to let me try and plea him to life because the case is impossible to win—the DOJ has audio and video of Antonio this time."

"That sucks. I still think you're bullshitting me; I know you too well, but I think I can help you. Two lawyers just quit. One, Jason Noble, couldn't handle the stress and the other, Charlotte Brinson, left for a job that doubled her salary, which isn't that hard to do."

"How are they as lawyers and does either one have any federal experience?"

"Ha, *federal experience*, I don't think so. If any of my younger lawyers had federal experience they wouldn't have taken a job at a State Public Defender's Office for thirty-four grand a year."

"Are they at least competent lawyers?" Peter laughed to himself as he asked. It just dawned on him, for the first time in his career, he was seeking a referral for an *incompetent* lawyer.

"Charlotte Brinson is a smart, aggressive young woman. I was sorry to lose her. She clerked for Florida Supreme Court Justice Jorge Leonardi for two years before she came here. She was a good lawyer on her way to becoming a great lawyer."

"What about the other?" Peter asked.

Kelly thought it odd that Peter didn't want to know more about Charlotte. "Well, I don't know much about Jason Noble. He didn't really make a lasting impression on anyone for his great trial skills. In his first trial, he asked the jury to find his client *guilty*. Can you believe that? Apparently, he gets nervous speaking in public and then stutters. He left that off his resume when he applied for a job."

"Not a good trait to have as a trial lawyer," Peter said, knowing he found his man.

"And," Kelly said, through her sudden laughter, "he really made a lasting impression for why he quit—his client pissed himself on the bench outside of Judge Reese's courtroom and Jason sat in it . . . poor guy."

Peter now joined in the laughter. "That story will last in the courthouse forever."

Kelly continued, "I don't think he's your man. Especially for a federal case as serious and complex as yours. Talk about having *ineffective counsel*; he'd get eaten alive in a second."

Peter had a wide smile on his face, *that was easier than I thought.* "Well, I'll give them both a call just to do my due diligence. Do you have their cell numbers?"

— 50 —

PETER WAITED A few days before calling Trevor. He needed to think his plan through and make sure he was doing the *right* thing for Antonio. Clients always wanted certainty in their decisions, especially when their freedom or life was at stake—it's what caused the most stress in the attorney-client relationship. At the end of the day, all decisions were based on *risk* of a *guilty* verdict by a jury. With the evidence against Antonio, Peter knew this was the best option . . . the only option with a chance to save Antonio's life. He got the idea after watching *Rocky*—Rocky lost the first fight with Apollo Creed but won nonetheless. Peter wondered what that situation would look like in a court of law—*Ineffective Assistance of Counsel*. He never tried the strategy, but there was a first time for everything he figured. *Probably should have tried it first in a misdemeanor case*, he thought, as he sat behind his desk staring at the monogrammed golden gavel given to him by a Dutch princess he represented.

"Meredith, call Trevor Whittingham for me." *Time to convince this gasbag not to kill my client.* He depressed the speaker button. "Trevor, my friend, how are you?" He greeted with a fake jovial tone. "Ready to dismiss all these ridiculously weak charges against Antonio Barrera? I doubt you'll get past my *Rule 12* Motion at trial."

"What can I do for you, Peter. I'm preparing to kill your client, so I don't want to waste time talking to you about a plea that I'm never going to offer—not on this one . . . I got your client dead to rights and I'm going to do society a favor and send him to Death Row."

"Good morning to you too. Listen, you're going to waive the death penalty in exchange for me withdrawing from the case. Then, maybe, you'll have a chance to win."

"Huh? What? What the hell are you talking about? Why on earth would you withdraw? . . . And I'm definitely not waiving the death penalty." Trevor stammered in response, clearly expecting this conversation to go somewhat differently.

"My client wants cheaper and younger—doesn't think I'm worth the money anymore at sixty-seven years old."

"That's horse shit. Are you drunk? You're not making any sense."

"No, and what's *horse shit* is your belief that the flimsy circumstantial evidence you have against my client supports the death penalty. I've spent my career representing people accused of the death penalty *pro bono* and I'll represent Antonio for free unless you waive it." Peter leaned back in his chair and twirled the golden gavel in his hand.

"Haven't you watched the video yet? I'm not—"

"Besides," Peter interrupted, "the death penalty isn't going to bring you any extra publicity that this case isn't already going to get. You'll still get plenty of face time with your future constituents with at least a dozen life sentences . . . I'll even call my contacts at *CourtTV* and get them to follow the case gavel to gavel."

"Future constituents? What are you talking about?" Trevor replied, his voice cracking slightly.

Peter smiled, knowing he was winning this negotiation. "I know you indicted this case because it will get your face all over the TV and in the paper and social media for weeks and weeks. My guess is that you want to run for governor given the unfortunate situation the current governor of Florida got himself into, which I can't really discuss because 'Steamroller' Stan is a current client of mine. Much easier to run when there isn't an incumbent—Am I hitting the mark?"

How does Peter know I want to run for governor? Trevor wondered, then blurted out, "Even if that were true, how do you know that?"

Peter ignored the question. "Thanks for confirming that for me."

"I'm not waiving the death penalty whether you're on this case or not. Period. Now, if that's all, I have to go." Angry that his true motives were so easily detected by Peter. *I really want him off this case, but I can't waive the death penalty—it will surely add to the media coverage.*

Peter glanced at an oil painting on the far wall that depicted a Boston fishing trawler taking a massive wave head-on—like in the movie *The Perfect Storm*. *Time to pull out the big guns and attack Trevor's Achilles heel—vanity.* "The way I see it, Antonio's case is way easier than the *Benitez* case. You get rid of me, you have no chance of getting the same highly embarrassing and public result . . . I must say, as far as *Not Guilty* verdicts go, that was one of my best."

Trevor pulled at his collar and swallowed hard at the memory of the *Benitez* trial. The case gained international media attention and was supposed to be an easy slam dunk for Trevor. Peter's client was accused of kidnapping, torturing, raping, then "accidentally" killing the Treasury Secretary's teenage son. *No way can I have that happen again . . . it will surely derail my path to the governor's mansion . . . I already picked out the furniture,* Trevor thought, a smile breaking through the corners of his mouth. "You'll withdraw right away?"

BOOM! Peter thought, *mike drop, thank you ladies and gentlemen.* "Of course."

—51—

Look at these guys . . . They're the best . . . Jason didn't recognize the number showing on his cell phone as it rang to the theme song from the A-Team. He filled with anticipation every time the phone rang. *How should I answer it—"Law firm of Jason Noble and Associates" or just my name. Maybe . . . "Partner, Jason Noble" . . . answer it before it goes to voice mail, dummy.*

"Hello, Law Firm," Jason's mouth suddenly went dry.

"Hello, Jason Noble, please," said the pleasant, female voice on the other end of the phone.

"Uh, uh, this is him," Jason stammered.

"Hi, Mr. Noble, please hold for Peter Cohen. . . ."

Hi, Jason, this is Peter Cohen. Do you know who I am?"

Of course, I do. You're the envy of every criminal defense lawyer in Palm Beach County and probably the country.

"Hello? Jason?"

"Um, the best criminal defense attorney around," Jason finally said, trying to suppress his nervousness so he wouldn't start to stutter.

"Stop, you're too kind . . . maybe top three. Listen, I'd like to take you to lunch and talk about a case I may want to bring you in on. You came highly recommended by your former boss, Kelly Hudson."

"I did. I mean, sure, I'd l-l-ove to have lunch. W-when?"

"How about one o'clock today? I'll meet you at Cafe L'Europa on The Island. Do you know where it is?"

"Um, let me check my calendar, hold on a minute," Jason said, as he simply held his cell phone down by his side. *Peter Cohen wants to hire me to assist HIM with a case—today might be my lucky day.* Of course,

Jason didn't have to look at his calendar; he was definitely free. *Get back on the phone before he hangs up, dummy.*

Jason put the phone back to his ear. "Sure, I can make it happen. I just have to change a few things around. I-I know where it is," Jason lied.

"Great, I'll see you there."

— 52 —

THE TITANIUM ROPE was specially made for beheading steer at slaughterhouses that offered a more *humane* way to kill your steak without machines—it was weaved together in a way that created micro-razor edges on the surface of the thin titanium rope. Antonio Barrera's front gate man, Johnnie Brenzini, silently crept up behind the skinny figure removing scuba gear on the private beach in front of Antonio's Palm Beach Estate. *Who the fuck is that . . . Aquaman?* Johnnie thought.

Johnnie was a shadow in the night—a whisper lost in the crashing waves and wind. He expertly slid the titanium razor rope over Aquaman's head and tightened it just enough to break the skin. Johnnie whispered, "If you struggle, your head will come right off." Aquaman went limp with fear.

"What are you doing here?" Johnnie asked.

Aquaman tried to speak, but nothing came out. He swallowed hard, which caused his adam's apple to extend slightly and the titanium rope slice further into his neck . . . the pain was searing, but he finally managed to choke out, "Freelance reporter."

"What do you mean, *reporter*? What the hell are you reporting? . . . And to who? Talk fast."

"Pictures of Antonio Barrera are in high demand and worth a lot of money right now to every major news outlet in the world," Aquaman said, his throat starting to lubricate.

Johnnie slightly relaxed the titanium razor rope. "What do they want pictures of Antonio for?"

"Antonio's mob trial has all the makings of the trial of the millennium—death, sex, bribes. Hell, most polls show, people thought the Mafia was dead, the interest is surprisingly overwhelming. The *Magic Man* is bigger than the *Teflon Don*—Gotti never had social media." Aquaman had a sudden confused look on his face. "Don't you guys monitor your online presence? Antonio could really benefit from a good social media PR person—probably make a bunch of extra money endorsing . . . like . . . olive oil on his *Twitter* account."

Johnnie had no idea what he was talking about, but he didn't seem like much of a threat. He took the titanium razor rope off and pushed the kid forward onto the sand, shining a flashlight in his face. . . . "What are you, fifteen? Get on your feet. Give me your wallet."

"Huh? What?" Aquaman hesitantly started to get up from the sand.

"Now! I generally don't ask twice—that's your freebie for inexperience. Don't make me ask again?"

Johnnie's tone and eyes eerily penetrated the darkness. Aquaman reached into a side cargo pocket and pulled out his Press ID—he remained on the ground and handed it up to Johnnie.

Johnnie snatched it and looked at it with his flashlight. "Well, Tad Smith, if that ain't the whitest name I ever heard. Give me your driver's license. Why ain't you with the reporters hangin' around out front?"

"I thought I'd get a better chance at a picture from here." Tad handed Johnnie his license.

Johnnie looked at it for a few seconds—committing Tad's address to memory. "Stand-up." Johnnie took a step toward Tad so they were face to face. "You were never here tonight and you're never going to come back—*CAPISCE?* I know where you live." Johnnie tapped Tad's license on his head as he spoke.

"You'll never see me again, Sir."

"How much do they pay you for a picture of Antonio?" Johnnie asked, suddenly curious.

"Uh, it depends, but for a good picture I could get up to five hundred bucks."

Johnnie reached into the inside pocket of his jacket. Tad winced, expecting a bullet any second. He watched Johnnie's hand come out of his jacket in slow motion. *Dear Lord, please forgive me for my sins,* Tad thought. He turned away and covered his head, as if that would protect him from a bullet.

Johnnie smiled and extended his hand. "Here's a grand to cover the band aids for your neck. Like I said, you weren't here and don't ever come back. Now get the fuck out of here."

Tad couldn't move at first . . . then he turned his head around with his body still in the standing fetal position, facing away from Johnnie.

"Ha, Ha, Ha," Johnnie laughed. "You look like a flamingo. Stick your head in the sand for me. You're too much kid. Hurry up, I got things to do. Take this grand and scram."

Tad didn't know what to think, but he definitely wasn't going to make this guy tell him again to leave. He sheepishly took the money in Johnnie's outstretched hands. Johnnie then handed him his Press ID and license back. He started gathering his scuba gear. "Can I leave from land, please?" Tad asked, his voice still shaky and hoarse.

"I don't think so. Get back in the ocean, *Aquaman* . . . and write nice things about Mr. Barrera. What the government says is bullshit. He's a hardworking family man as honest as the day is long. Don't make me take a walk down thirtieth street to the Charmer's Apartments."

— 53 —

JASON HAD A mini panic attack as he drove over the Royal Palm Bridge to Palm Beach, a/k/a the Middle Bridge, because he only had twenty bucks in his wallet. Hopefully, Peter didn't expect *him* to pay for lunch. He had a few hundred dollars available on a credit card, but Cafe L'Europa on Palm Beach sounded real expensive.

As he descended down the bridge over the Intracoastal waterway into Palm Beach, the crisp breeze snapped him out of his panic . . . for a few seconds. Florida was having a "cold front"—low sixties. Florida's winter sky was a picturesque clear, blue and sunny. When the temperature dropped below seventy most Floridians break out their sweaters, puffy jackets, and boots much to the amusement of the northern and mid-west tourists who walk around in t-shirts, shorts, and flip flops basking in what is a heatwave to them.

"*Next. Right. Onto. South. County. Road. In. point. One. Miles.*" His iPhone said in a pleasant female voice with a British accent. Jason looked down at his google maps app—he was represented by a pulsing blue dot and his destination was a red dot on the map. The two dots were close to colliding.

"*You. Have. Arrived. Destination. Is. On. Your. Left.*" Jason looked left and spotted *Cafe L'Europa* right next to the Palm Beach Police Station. He pulled up in front to the valet stand. *If it's more than twenty bucks, I'm going to have to steal my own car back.* Jason put his car in park, stepped out, and walked to the valet stand. A large Rolls Royce pulled in behind him. The driver's door opened and an elderly man wearing a blue blazer, fuchsia pants, and ascot tie stepped out. He walked over to Jason and said in a voice like he just sucked in some helium, "It's about time this place made the valets wear suits, even if they're cheap suits.

Here's a buck kid, make sure you take care of *daddy's little girl*."

For a second, Jason thought about taking the keys and just driving off in the guy's three-hundred-thousand-dollar car. Just when he was about to tell this guy off—a man in a red jacket with a gold emblem of some sort of crest approached and said, "Sorry Mr. Willbanks, it won't happen again, we're just a little busy." He took Mr. Willbanks' keys while another valet showed him to the front door and opened it. Both valets said nothing to Jason and left him standing there.

"Can I help you?" said a valet who showed up a minute later.

"No, I feel like standing here in front of my car all day," Jason said in a sarcastic tone. "I'm eating lunch here. My money's just as green as Willbanks." Jason snatched the valet ticket from the valet's hand and walked to the ornate front doors of *Cafe L'Europa*.

* * *

Jason stopped in the foyer and looked around. Suddenly, he felt way underdressed. *Cafe L'Europa sure is a lot nicer than Applebees.* The Bistro Room to the left was filled with brilliant rays of sunlight streaming in from the French doors with half moon windows on top that lined two of the walls. The bar was an earth-toned marble with a gold colored railing etched with scenes of Panama Jack. The decorum was simple Palm Beach elegance. The floor was Brazilian cherry wood with luxurious Persian rugs. The tables were covered in white linens with an orchid on each one. The room was filled with people in suits and dresses that looked like they were designed by companies with a lot of vowels in their name—*Gucci, Armani, Versace,* and the like. The only people not dressed in designer swag was a table of four police officers sitting in the back corner. *So much for a donut shop*, Jason thought, *the police are even rich on Palm Beach.*

"Can I help you, Sir," a blonde hostess said, interrupting Jason's daydreaming of a better life.

Jason turned and looked at her . . . and said, "Uh. I'm here for lunch. I'm—"

"Do you have a reservation? You can't eat here without a reserva-tion." The hostess snapped with a tone that said: *you're clearly lost, only rich people can eat here and you ain't one of them by the looks of that cheap suit and those Payless shoes.*

"As I was trying to say, I'm meeting someone here for lunch, Peter Cohen."

Her face went from vicious hawk to embarrassed sloth. "Oh, why didn't you say so . . . right this way. What is your name again?" She regained her composure, flashed Jason an effortless smile that showed her perfect teeth, and gently touched his shoulder.

He totally forgot how rude she was ten seconds ago and responded, "Um . . . Noble, Jason," he flashed a goofy smile, "I mean, Jason Noble."

"Well, nice to meet you Noble, Jason. Right this way, please." She escorted Jason to the more formal dining room. This room didn't have any sunlight, but it was over the top elegant: crystal, mirrors, mahogany wood framing everywhere, and the floor was an orange Mexican tile that was polished to a mirror finish—Jason could actually see himself in the floor.

"Your guest, Jason Noble," she playfully winked at Jason when she said his name—just to make sure he wouldn't complain to the manager.

Peter stood up from the table, extended his hand, and said, "Hello, Jason, nice to meet you in person."

Jason shook Peter's hand. "Hi, Mr. Cohen, very nice to meet you. Th-th-thanks for the opportunity, whatever it is." *Don't get nervous now and stutter . . . relax.*

"Great. I need you to help me hide a body . . . ready to go, or do you want to fill your belly first?" Peter said, his face turning dead serious.

"Uh, um . . . well . . ." Jason started to sweat.

"Just kidding . . . a little criminal defense humor." He had a private table in the back corner—clearly a regular.

"Oh, okay . . . ha ha," Jason said as he sat down.

"This is a great place to eat. Have you ever been here before?"

"No, I don't really get a chance to eat on Palm Beach very often."

"Great! You're going to break your cherry. I'm glad I'm the one to do it. Everything on the menu here is world class. Your taste buds are in for a treat."

The table was set with fine china, crystal wear, and gold leaf silverware. Jason unfolded the embroidered, silk, white napkin in front of him. *This silk napkin probably costs more than my suit. I sure hope I don't have to pay for any of this.*

A waiter came over. "Please, Sir, use the black napkin." The waiter unfolded a black, silk, embroidered napkin and handed it to Jason and took the white napkin.

"Uh. Thank you," Jason was confused.

Peter added, "It's because you're wearing a dark suit—don't want any white thread getting on your pants. They think of everything here." Peter picked up a crystal martini glass and took a sip. "Ahh, seltzer with olives . . . fantastic. The olives and the glass trick my brain. I try not to have a martini before five."

"Clever, I guess."

"Thank you for helping my associate Prescott in Judge Reese's courtroom a few weeks ago. Reese has always been an uptight asshole, especially when we were law partners years ago."

This guy is thanking me—*he must be buttering me up to pay the bill.* Jason took a sip of water and said, "Anytime. You were law partners with that woman!"

"She always busts balls when it's one of my newer associates. She's not actually a bad woman. She was a decent lawyer, but the power of the bench went to her head a bit over the years."

"Good afternoon, Sir, would you like a drink?" The waiter asked, looking at Jason.

Peter cut in and ordered, "He'll have the passion fruit iced tea, unsweetened." Peter looked at Jason, "It's the best on the Island, really the world . . . you'll love it, trust me."

"Very well, gentleman," the waiter replied and left.

"So, Jason, how do you like private practice? You have that *I don't work for the government anymore glow*. You age in dog years working as an assistant public defender. PD offices around the country are rites of passage for a criminal defense lawyer."

"Private practice is okay so far," Jason said, finally relaxing a bit.

"You hung your shingle at the Darth Vader Building . . . hopefully you have a better view than *Old Ironside*. When they built that Darth Vader Building, that rusty parking garage wasn't there. You could see clear to Palm Beach. It's a good place to start. It's an easy walk to the state and federal courthouses."

"Yeah, I like it. My view is a little better than *Old Ironside*." *Note to self: don't invite Peter to my office.* "But, I don't practice in federal court, so I really only have to walk two blocks to the state courthouse, which is somewhat doable in the unbearable summer heat."

"Are you at least admitted in the Southern District?" Peter asked, a bit concerned. *Shit, my whole plan will be over before it begins and I'll have to find some other crappy lawyer to trick if he's not admitted in federal court!*

"Yea-yes, I took the test about a month ago because I had nothing better to do." *What a dumb thing to say. Great! now he knows I have no clients.* "But, I don't plan on practicing in federal court—too intense from what I hear." *What if he wants to hire me on a federal case for, like . . . twenty thousand dollars, I'm such an idiot. I should just stop talking.*

"Are you from Florida?" Peter asked, already knowing the answer to the question—he knew everything about Jason "the Orphan"—his investigator gave him the nickname. Peter liked to test people's truthfulness.

"No, New York. I moved here four years ago for a change of scenery. But, I came to South Florida for two weeks every summer until I graduated high school."

"Family vacations as a kid . . . that's nice," Peter said through sips of his faux-martini.

"Something like that," Jason replied, looking down.

The waiter came back with the passion fruit iced tea, placed it in front of Jason, then left sensing they weren't ready to order.

"Go ahead, take a sip, let me know what you think."

Jason picked up the tall, hand-etched, crystal glass—no straws at this place—and took a sip. The smooth, sweet, cold liquid coated his mouth and throat. He thought for a second then blurted out, "Wow, that's dynamite. The best iced tea I've ever had, period." He took another sip and put the glass down staring at it for a second.

"Told you so. The passion fruit is handpicked from the Amazon Rain Forest and flown here immediately—probably why it costs fifty bucks a glass," Peter said, smiling at the memory of his last passion fruit iced tea. "I think I'll have to get one after lunch."

Jason about passed out. *I already spent the money I have on those two sips.*

Peter sensed Jason's anxiety. "Order as many as you want, lunch is on me . . . well, really, my client, Antonio Barrera. He's the person I want to talk to you about."

"Have you decided on lunch, gentleman," the waiter politely asked. Jason had a look of uncertainty on his face as he reached for the menu that neither had opened yet.

Peter took charge. "Of course, Jason will have—Jason, do you have any seafood allergies?"

"Uh, no."

"Good, we'll each start with the Adriatic Sea crab salad . . . then we'll have the Wagu steak, prepared as Chef Vigo recommends."

"Any sides?" the waiter asked.

"Sure, I'm hungry," Peter responded. "How about today's special side—don't tell us what it is, we'll be surprised."

"Very well, Sir."

Peter looked at Jason with an expectant smile. "Now, back to why I asked you to lunch. Have you read the papers recently or heard the courthouse gossip about my client, Antonio Barrera?"

Jason took another sip of the iced tea. "Yes, I've been following the case on a news app I read."

Young people! Peter thought. *News app . . . can't get the flavor of a community from an app.* "The Feds just indicted him on some bullshit charges—all circumstantial evidence. Anyway, I was thinking of bringing you in to the case to assist . . . I need some help and I heard good things about you from the PDs office."

"You did-Uh-I mean. Thank you. I try and, uh, work hard." *Great answer you idiot.*

"Do you have any experience working in federal court?"

"When I was at New York Law School, I did an internship for a year in the Eastern District Federal Court in Brooklyn for Chief Magistrate Marcelo Cook . . . I learned a lot," Jason said, remembering the experience and gaining some confidence.

Antonio faces the death penalty, and I was trusting his fate to a kid who did an internship! "It doesn't really matter. You've tried felony cases in state court I assume, it's basically the same thing. The courtroom's just bigger."

I almost tried a burglary case once—I guess that counts as state felony experience, Jason sadly thought, realizing how inexperienced he really was. "You don't get to ask the jury questions in *voir dire*?" *I might like federal jury selection. I hate talking to the jury anyway.* "Who asks the questions?"

Christ, this kid knows nothing . . . perfect. "The judge, but a few days before trial you can submit questions you want the judge to ask—sometimes they ask a few of them for you."

"Um, okay," Jason responded, confused. "Aren't you going to be the one doing jury selection in Antonio's case?"

Peter leaned forward, lowering his voice . . .

Tommy the bartender could still hear Peter clearly. Once he heard Antonio Barrera's name, he called Vinnie "Clear eyes". Vinnie told him to listen closely and call him after they leave. Vinnie said he would knock ten grand off Tommy's gambling debts for any useful information.

"Here's the other reason," Peter continued, "I have a conflict of interest. I used to represent one of the snitches, Alfonso 'the Whale' Tomisini, so I'm out. The Assistant US Attorney on the case, Trevor Wittingham, won't let me near this one with a ten-foot pole—bastard! Wittingham always looks for a way to conflict me out of a case because I've beaten him so many times. Word on the street is my former client is deceased, but that blowhard, Wittingham won't agree he's dead and strike him from the witness list." Peter laid it on heavy for effect. "Now you'll just beat him. Plus, Antonio wants a young lawyer representing him on this one. Thinks I'm too old . . . can you believe that!"

"I can't represent him."

"Sure you can, Jason. I'll assist and be available anytime you need it . . . you'll just be the front man for the client's sake."

Jason added, "I don't have the staff or resources to defend Mr. Barrera. I'm not the right lawyer for you."

Now the carrot. "You'll get a nice fee, probably more than you made all last year as a public defender. You can hire as needed. Cost money won't be an issue. Also, like I said, I'll be there assisting you in the background. My office is your office."

Jason was sweating again. "Isn't this a de-de-death penalty case?"

"Don't worry about the death penalty," Peter said like he was having a relaxing fireside chat with an old friend. "I'll stay on until it's waived. The death penalty is a huge stretch in this weak, circumstantial case. Whittingham is just using it for extra media attention."

"Scary to think a federal prosecutor can play with someone's life like that so easily for a little extra coverage on the five o'clock news."

"Right . . . *scary*, anyway, how about it? You want to make some great money and start growing the legend of Jason Noble with an easy win?"

Jason took another sip of iced tea. *This guy must be crazy . . . ME? a federal case? I barely know how to find the courthouse! I'm a nobody! I don't even have a copy machine in my office. But, he'll pay well . . . I should take the case . . . I'm completely unqualified . . . untested . . . But I know I can be a great trial lawyer . . . maybe this is my chance? Nah . . . I'd definitely be ineffective.* "Yes," he finally blurted out.

Peter, surprised at how easy that was, said, "Great, you're on board. Come by my office at nine tomorrow morning and we'll finalize everything and you'll meet Antonio." Peter looked at Jason, raised his martini glass, "Cheers, to the new generation of great lawyers like you, Jason." They clinked glasses and Peter drained his faux-martini. *Poor kid doesn't know what's coming.* Peter *almost* felt sorry for him.

The waiter and two helpers appeared table side. The helpers put two small silver domes on the table; in perfect unison, they removed the silver domes and the waiter softly announced: "Gentleman, your first course—Adriatic sea crab salad with misted truffle oil, *bon appetite.*

— 54 —

"HE'S A RAT, I tell ya. The walls is closin' in on Antonio and he's gonna dime us all out if we don't take care of him NOW!" Bobbie "The Whistle" said, then shoved half of a triple cheeseburger into his mouth. He was at the Port of Palm Beach meeting with his guys. He was the default boss of Alphonso "the Whale's" crew since he went missing.

"I dunno, Bobbie, if we're wrong, we'll be the ones buried in the Everglades," Carlos "Shakes" Vento said; his hands were in a perpetual shaking motion—a doctor once told him that he's in a state of constant withdrawal since his mom was a heroin junkie when she was pregnant. He hasn't seen a doctor since he killed that one for speaking bad about his mama—he had to use a shotgun on jobs because his aim was terrible.

"Relax, my friend, nutin' to worry about if we're smaat," Vinnie "Clear eyes" said, putting his hand on Shakes' shoulder who was sitting to his right. "No one's gonna be gator bait, except maybe that pig of a boss, Antonio. Paulie, what the hell you doin' on that computer thing? Get ove'ear. What's the word on Alphonso?"

"Give me a sec. I'm checkin' my weed," Paulie replied not looking up from the laptop screen.

"What you talkin' bout, *checkin' your weed*?" Vinnie asked.

"My weed stock. Don't you remember Antonio told us to invest in that medical marijuana company, The Plant Doctor . . . I've already made a few hundred thousand," Paulie "Lead Foot" Dounata explained. He got his nickname when he was fourteen after he beat two of his classmates with a sneaker filled with lead pellets—that was his last day attending school of any kind. "We make lots of *moola* with Antonio . . . and I think Alfonso's dead." Paulie hit enter on the keyboard, stood up, and walked over to the table with Bobbie, Vinnie, and Carlos.

"Son of a bitch!" Vinnie said, slamming his fist on the table. "We'll make more without that bastard. We'll be free to do what we want, when we want; no more bullshit moral code he imposes on us. He lives in that mansion on Palm Beach like he's a king, but he forgets who keeps him there. US, dammit! And now he's gonna dime us out to the Feds—I'm not gonna let that happen! And we have to avenge Alfonso—I know Antonio had something to do with his disappearance."

Shakes interrupted, "Paulie, what's on ya shirt?"

Paulie looked down at his white t-shirt splattered with deep red dots. "Ha. I like the design—that's from me doin' tha thing, wit the guy, from tha place, you know. That's where I was before Vinnie texted me. I had to hurry up and finish, I guess I didn't notice. Anyone got an extra shirt?"

"Enough with that shit, I'll get you a shirt. You guys hearin' what I'm sayin'? ANTONIO IS GONNA RAT US OUT OR KILL US!" Bobbie yelled in their faces. "Why do you think he's hirin' that young, dumb lawyer."

They looked back at him with blank stares.

"Idiots!" Bobbie shook his head in disgust. "Antonio's gone into protection mode—he don't want to spend no money on that high priced lawyer since he decided to flip . . . get it!"

"What the fuck you doin' Shakes?" Vinnie suddenly asked. "Put the damn cup down and use the straw I gave you. You're lucky you're a bookmakin' genius or I'd a wacked you years ago for always makin' a mess."

Bobbie instructed, "Follow the new lawyer. Don't let him take Antonio for the plea allocution . . . wack'em on the steps of the U.S. Attorney's Office when he goes in with Antonio. Killing his lawyer will send the right message that Antonio better keep his mouth shut."

— 55 —

"I'm WAIVING THE death penalty," Trevor said without much explanation to Herb. "You file the notice of waiver right before the Status Conference hearing . . . hopefully the media won't pick up on it right away."

"What? Why?" Herb asked. "While I agree this is a tough case, especially since we can't locate our main informant, Alphonso Tomisini, but based on what we've alleged that vicious, psychopath Barrera is responsible for, this is a death penalty case without a doubt, and it should be if you believe all roads lead to Barrera like I do."

Trevor looked suspiciously at Herb and put his coffee mug down on his desk. "*Tough case*, you sound like a first-year lawyer. I will win this case with my eyes closed. It's going to be an easy sell, especially when we play the video. If this case is too much for you, let me know now and I'll probably get an intern to replace you."

Less than a year to retirement . . . less than a year to retirement, Herb thought with increasing frequency, mostly when he was around Trevor. "So, why waive the death penalty?"

Trevor turned toward his computer screen, already bored with Herb. "Not that it's any of your business, but when I convict Antonio, he'll get multiple life sentences . . . so I figured no need to add the extra work and risk of looking bad in the media with the penalty phase in case one of those overly religious jurors who whines about *sitting in judgment* of one of *God's children* slips by you and gets on the jury—those pain-in-the-ass jurors never vote for the death penalty no matter how much a defendant deserves it." Trevor turned away from his computer screen and looked at Herb, evaluating whether he wanted to trust him with the real reason he's dropping the death penalty. *Once the waiver is filed, Cohen is gone*, Trevor gladly thought.

He turned back to whatever was on his computer screen. "Don't worry about it . . . don't you have some exhibit stickers to place on our exhibits? Get to work and stop wasting time asking me questions that don't concern you."

Herb stood up and left Trevor's office. *Less than a year until retirement.*

— 56 —

"GOOD MORNING, MR. Noble," Meredith said with a pleasant smile. "Would you like some coffee or tea? Or maybe a macchiato? I just purchased a new machine that makes them in ten seconds."

"Good morning . . . um, I'm here to see—"

"Mr. Cohen will be with you shortly," Meredith politely interrupted. "Please have a seat and I'll make that scrumptious macchiato." Meredith got up from behind her desk and walked into a room to the right.

Jason took a seat on the plush leather couch in the reception area. He looked around and depressingly thought, *this lobby area is at least five times bigger than my entire office.*

"Here you go." Meredith handed Jason a tall, white coffee mug. The foam on top had a palm tree imprinted in it. "Isn't that palm tree delightful? The machine came with all these little stamps to dress up the drinks."

Jason looked down at the foam palm tree. "Yes, it's nice, thank you."

"Jason, nice to see you again," Peter said with a warm smile, extending his hand as he walked toward Jason from his office.

Jason stood up and walked over, suddenly feeling nervous, and awkwardly shook Peter's hand. "Good-uh-morning, Mr. Cohen."

"Please, like I told you at lunch, call me Peter. We're going to be working together. Come this way, into my office."

"That's right, Peter, good morning, Peter."

Peter closed the door behind them. "Please, take a seat."

Jason looked around at the cavernous office with magnificent views that was bigger than the lobby. *This is what success looks like.* He sat in one of the two chairs in front of Peter's desk and placed his macchiato on a coaster with Peter's smiling face on it.

Peter plopped down in his chair. "So, how do you feel? Are you energized? Ready to kick the government's ass!"

"Uh. Sure. Yup . . . ready to go . . . Let's hit'em with the Hein." Jason made a weak *go get'em* motion with his fist.

"Hit'em with what, who?"

"It means 'to give it your best.'"

"Right. Whatever. *Christ, I'm definitely leading this kid to slaughter,* Peter thought. "Antonio will be here shortly. Why don't we get the business side out of the way. Antonio hates talking about money, so don't mention what we discuss about the fee. You have money problems come to me. Okay?"

"Good. Now . . . your fee. How much did you make as a public defender last year?"

Jason thought for a moment, took a sip of his macchiato—the palm tree dissolved by now. "Thirty-nine-thousand."

Peter balked at the absurdly low salary. "I spent more than that on suits last year. I forgot how little the PD paid. When I started there in 1974, my annual salary was twelve thousand dollars a year. Imagine that? But it was a much more fun time to practice—I was idealistic and full of piss and vinegar, so the money didn't really matter to me," Peter fondly reminisced. "Now, I'm not going to make much money on this case since I wasn't in it long. So what do you think is a fair fee for you?"

"Well, I've thought about it, and it's going to be a lot of work . . . A lot of hours, so . . . maybe . . . like," *just say it, dummy, he'll go for it,* "thirty-thousand-fee," *that sounded great to say,* "and five thousand for costs to get started."

"Wow. You did give it a lot of thought. I'll tell you what . . ." Peter was starting to pity this kid. "Why don't I give you fifty thousand total fee, which will also cover trial, and an extra twenty thousand for costs. Plus, you have access to my office and resources." *I won't even notice fifty-thousand out of my five-million fee. Antonio will pay the cost money,* Peter happily thought. "And, as an early bonus, because I know we're going to work well together, go to my tailor, Ricardo, he's just down the street at 200 Worth. He'll set you up with five new, custom made suits and shirts on me."

Jason's eyes lit up. *Holy crap! That's more than I made all last year and, if you add in the cost of the suits, probably more than I made my entire time as a PD.* Jason pushed his hand across the desk. "Deal." They shook on it.

"Great. I'll have my office wire seventy thousand to your trust account today."

Jason's jubilation turned to dismay. "Um. Wire?"

"You have received a wire before?"

"Of course . . . I'll give your assistant my bank information before I leave."

"Okay, then—"

The intercom interrupted with Meredith's voice. "Mr. Barrera here to see you and Mr. Noble, Sir."

"Bring him in," Peter responded.

* * *

"Good morning, Antonio. This is the lawyer, Jason Noble, that you wanted me to hire for you," Peter said as he came around the desk, extending his hand as he approached Antonio.

Antonio didn't accept the extended hand. "Let's get this over with, I have things to do." Antonio's handsome, tanned face was tense as stone.

Peter glanced over at Jason. "Sure, why don't we sit at the conference table."

Jason got up and walked over to Antonio. "Hello, Mr. Barrera. I'm Jason Noble. Nice to meet you. How are you?" *Ugh! What a dumb first question with the client—He's not doing well, in fact, he's probably feeling pretty shitty with the death penalty hanging over his head.*

Antonio extended his hand. Jason clasped it. Antonio gripped hard and stared into Jason's eyes, saying nothing . . . to Jason it felt like Antonio was staring into his soul.

They sat around the small round conference table made of dark birch wood inlaid with Ivory and Jade carved Chinese battle scenes. "Jason, this table was a gift from a Chinese diplomat who found himself at the Delano on South Beach with four dead hookers and a pile of bad meth. A little bonus after the not guilty verdict."

"Are you done reminiscing," Antonio interrupted. "Let me sign whatever I have to sign and get on with it."

"Right. Like I explained, Jason here is going to take over as lead counsel for me because of the conflict of interest I have. He's an excellent lawyer and came highly recommended."

"I want you to know, Mr. Antonio, Sir, that I will do everything in my power and work really hard to get you found *not guilty.*"

"Right," Antonio said. "Now, what do I have to sign."

Peter slid a Stipulation for Substitution of Counsel in front of Antonio. "This says you consent to Jason taking over for me. Sign right here," pointing to the bottom of the stipulation. "Great, I'll file this next week at the status conference and make it official."

Antonio was already standing up to leave before Peter finished. "That it."

"That's it," Peter replied.

Jason stood up too and said, "Alright, Antonio, we'll meet again soon to discuss your case. We have plenty of time. Call me anytime on my cell. Bye." Antonio was already at the office door with his back to Jason and Peter.

Jason looked at Peter. "Antonio is surely a man of a few words."

"Don't worry about him. He's like that in every case. In fact, the less you keep him informed, the happier he is. Now, let's get you my file and get you paid and you're on your way."

After Jason left, Peter turned to Meredith and said, "If Jason ever calls or comes to see me, I'm not in."

"DROP THE MIC! BOOM!" Jason exclaimed, as he mimed dropping a mic then spreading his fingers apart in mock explosion. He picked up the bottle of champagne he purchased on his way back from meeting his new client, Antonio Barrera, and poured some into a plastic cup. He splurged—$19.99 for the bottle. He picked up the cup and said aloud in his empty office, "Cheers! Or should I say *Salute!*" He took a celebratory sip and thought, *I guess I was a really good PD after all . . . For a guy like Peter Cohen to take notice, I must be damned good.* He took another sip and said aloud, "To my first *real* client." Jason turned to his computer screen and stared at the page: $70,000.00 wire transfer from Peter Cohen & Associates, P.A. Trust Account. Jason's smile almost reaching his ears every time he looked at his online banking account screen—

"*Mazel tov!* What are we toasting? You win a case? Ohh, I bet it's a big fee. How exciting. I remember my first big fee." The lawyer with two first names, Jeannie Francis said, excitement bubbling up in her squeaky voice. "Sad thing is, that was my one and only decent fee in twenty-five years," her excitement quickly tamping down to sadness.

"Geez, you scared the heck out of me." Jason snapped his head up from the computer screen. He quickly clicked out of the webpage. "You really have to start knocking or at least announce yourself at the front door."

"Okay, got it. Announce at the front. What are you doing here so late? And why the sad party?" She pointed to the single plastic cup on his desk.

Jason took another plastic cup out of his desk and poured some champagne for Jeannie Francis. He raised his glass. "I was just hired to defend big time, I mean *alleged*, big-time crime boss, Antonio Barrera."

He thrust his glass forward.

"Wow! Congratulations . . . I guess." She tapped his glass then threw the champagne over her shoulder.

Jason stopped mid swallow and spit out his champagne all over his desk. "What the hell did you do that for!"

"What?" she asked, covering her mouth with her hand and looking over her shoulder.

"You threw champagne on my floor and wall . . . you're supposed to drink it, not throw it."

"Oh. Right. Sorry. Ha Ha. Last time I toasted with champagne I was at a BBQ and threw it on the grass. I don't drink. Too much Boone's Farm Wine when I was younger, you know what I mean," she said with a wink. "You should've asked me if I drank alcohol before you gave me that."

Jason let it pass. "I'll clean it up later. Anyway, I'm Antonio Barrera's new federal lawyer."

She eyed him suspiciously. "I thought you didn't practice in federal court? Isn't this a death penalty case? Don't you need a staff for that kind of case?"

Jason started not to like celebrating with Jeannie Francis. "I didn't and I will for the right price, and Antonio Barrera paid the *right* price. The state—I mean, government is going to waive the death penalty. Besides, I will work with his current lawyer Peter Cohen and have access to his office and staff."

"I worked in federal court a few times . . . years ago, and it was nooooo picnic." Jeannie Francis scrunched up her face at the memory.

"I'll be fine . . . trust me. It's a criminal case, I have almost four years of experience—state court, federal court, it's all the same."

"I hope so for your sake. Cheers!" she said, raising her now empty glass.

— 58 —

"THAT BITCH GONNA shoot'em," Paulie "Lead Foot" said as he adjusted his prone body on the parking structure across from Jason's office.

"Dat's good, she gonna do are job for us, so I ain't gotta waste a bullet—dese new hollow points ain't cheap." Tim "the Duck" whispered, as he looked through his night vision binoculars. . . . "No. Wait . . . she just tossed dat champagne on da wall . . . crazy bitch, why she do dat?"

"Dunno, but she must be pissed. Who trows champagne against the wall unless theys angry. Maybe she's Jason's associate—the sign on the door said *Jason Noble & Associates*—and he didn't consult her before he pled out Antonio's case."

Tim took the binoculars from his face, the overhead fluorescent lights in the parking garage shined on the webbing between his fingers, and looked at Paulie. "*Plea*? He ain't even been to court wit Antonio yet."

Paulie looked back at Tim in amazement that he didn't see what Paulie thought was so obvious. "Don't be a moron. Why do you think he got that champagne—he's celebrating . . . and what else would a criminal lawyer celebrate before trial?"

Tim thought for a moment, but the blank look on his face said it all.

Paulie shook his head. "Trust me and let me do the thinking. He's celebratin' a plea deal—case closed. Fuhgeddaboudit."

"So, should we wack'em now?" Tim picked up the sniper rifle that was lying in a black rifle case between them. He sighted Jason through the high-powered scope—the center dot of the red cross hairs stopping on the back of Jason's head. "I can maybe take them both out with one shot. I packed extra grain in these here rounds . . . it'll probably go threw his head and right into the bitch's forehead if I line it up correctly." Tim adjusted the cross hairs slightly to the right of the back of Jason's head.

Paulie pushed the barrel of the rifle down and shook his head. "Don't you ever listen. We can't kill 'em yet. We have to wait to send the right message. Put that rifle away. Remember the bitch, we'll probably have to kill her too since she works for him," he said as nonchalantly as if he were telling Tim to add milk to a shopping list.

* * *

Mario "Lugnut" Rizzo lowered the Benelli Pro Big Game bolt action rifle he had trained on Tim "the Duck's" head. Mario was fast on the reload, so he would've easily taken out Paulie too.

Carmine "Bowling Ball" Gato tapped Mario's shoulder and whispered, "They ain't gonna kill the kid lawyer yet, but there's some broad their makin'a mess of the place . . . they look like they packin' up. Let's get outta here."

— 59 —

JASON VEERED HIS car to the right, across four lanes of traffic. "Damn, I thought the exit was on the left, stupid *Apple Maps*," he grumbled to himself. He noticed the graffiti and grime covered, green street sign on the right at the last second: *FEDERAL COMPLEX EXIT 3A*.

For the past two weeks, since he's been on the case, he planned on walking up the street to the Federal Courthouse in West Palm Beach for Antonio's status conference. But, yesterday, Meredith from Peter's office called and told him the case was moved to Miami for some unknown reason.

He drove down the exit ramp, made a left at the light, under I-95, and passed a green street sign, barely visible through the graffiti, grime, and bullet holes—the loops in the '*B*' and '*R*' were shot out with precision: *LIBERTY CITY*. Jason immediately double checked that his doors were locked. He got caught at a light—rush hour traffic was in full swing. Liberty City is a forgotten place. Decades of poverty and crime still on full display in the crumbling, but valuable little city because of its location. Liberty City sat in stark contrast to the ever-growing Miami skyline that blotted out the sun from shining—the new skyline was rising faster than the tide. The Freedom Tower, once the crown jewel of Miami's skyline, is barely visible now. Tyrants, dictators, corrupt government officials, and cartel members, fleeing the anarchy that has descended on Latin America in the new millennium, have brought massive cash investments to Miami. The gargantuan, modern glass and steel structures just waiting for the *okay* to swallow up Liberty City and continue the development-march across Miami.

Jason parked three blocks west of the federal courthouse on North Miami Avenue. The courthouse was in Brickell situated between American Airlines Arena, where the Miami Heat play, and Bayfront Park. He looked at the clock in his dash: *9:00.* "What to do for the next hour." Jason was never late—he was late once for dinner at his group home when he was six; he didn't eat that night, but he was never late again.

He stretched after the two-hour drive. His new, navy blue suit, shirt, and shoes made for him by Peter's tailor, looked and felt great. Jason looked around. He'd been to Miami a few times in the past, but only South Beach for the night life, never this section of Miami. He grabbed his leather folder, straightened his tie in the car window, and headed southeast.

He walked past the Federal Detention Center (FDC) on his left—to the passerby it looked like another off-white, cement office building, maybe a building that housed computer servers because there weren't many windows—it even had a revolving door at the entrance.

Jason continued down North Miami Avenue. The street was lined with independent shopkeepers preparing for the day's business—Brickell had mostly resisted the big box stores from taking over multiple city blocks like in New York City.

Jason walked onto the expansive grounds of the Wilkie D. Ferguson, Jr. United States Courthouse. He stopped and looked up at the courthouse from the sidewalk; the bright sun was beginning to glisten off the curved blue glass facade. He used to dream of being an architect when he was growing up—a kind security guard at one of the many group homes he lived in as a kid gave him a copy of Ayn Rand's classic novel *Atlas Shrugged*, which he read a thousand times because it was the only book he had, and he dreamed of being Howard Roark. The courthouse was designed to look like a "great ship's hull" with two limestone towers connected by a blue glass prism, creating a total of 577,000 square feet of interior space—much more than necessary for the twenty five or so district court judges who used it.

The sprawling grounds that comprised two very valuable city blocks were mainly grass and palm trees with stone pathways and benches throughout. The grass areas were created to appear like lapping waves to complete the architect's vision of a building that looked like a ship cutting through the ocean. The "wavy" grass also provided added security to stop a car from driving up to the front entrance and exploding.

The first thing that struck Jason as he walked through the grounds to the front entrance was how few people were going in and out of the building. At the State courthouse, the line would already be out the door. Congregating to the right, across the vast portico, on the opposite side from the front entrance, was a mass of what looked like news reporters and camera people milling about—paying absolutely no attention to Jason as he walked to the entrance and pulled open, with surprising ease, the giant-sized glass door.

The lobby was awash in natural sunlight coming in from the four-story high, tinted blue glass walls. It had a clean, sterile look—off-white tile floor and minimally accented walls in natural beach tones. Off to the right, was a non-intrusive white and chrome guard desk. About twenty feet past that was one X-ray machine.

"Can I help you?" asked the Federal Protection Services officer who was sitting behind the white desk by himself.

"Hi, um, Judge Quarter, criminal court."

"It's all the same court here, civil, criminal, kangaroo court," FPS officer O'Brien said with a slight chuckle at a joke he probably told a hundred times a day. You an attorney?"

Jason was too nervous to laugh. "Um, yes." He finally responded.

"License and bar card," O'Brian pleasantly commanded.

Jason reached into his pocket, pulled out his money clip and handed over his license and bar card—*they must not believe me. It would take three hours to get through security in state court if the guards checked everyone's credentials.*

O'Brian handed Jason back his credentials after he scanned the black strip on the back of his DL—instant federal background check was performed every time someone walked into any federal building. "Stand to the right and look here." O'Brian curtly instructed, pointing to a camera lens . . . he looked at the screen to make sure Jason's digital picture was clear, before he said, "Go over there to the metal detector. Judge Quarter is on the eleventh floor, Courtroom 1."

"Thank you."

* * *

"Chief Judge Quarter's courtroom is on the far side of the rotunda," explained the woman, who's badge read *Chief Clerk*, as the elevator slowed to the eleventh floor. The gold elevator doors opened and Jason stepped out. "Thanks, have a day—I mean, a *nice* day." His mouth was suddenly dry.

"Oh, don't be nervous, Judge Quarter is a teddy bear . . . as long as you don't disagree with him," she said with a wink and a smile as the elevator doors closed.

Jason reached into his back pocket, grabbed his handkerchief, and wiped his brow. He looked around: the outer walls were all glass with panoramic views of Miami in every direction. Miami looked like an erector set from this height with all of the "tiny" cranes dotting the sky-line—Jason stopped counting at twenty-three. He walked around the rotunda. This was nothing like the controlled chaos of the state court-house hallways . . . this was civilized. A few people dressed in business attire milled about. He stopped at a set of large mahogany double doors that were emblazoned with large gold letters: *CHIEF JUDGE CALVIN QUARTER*. Just reading the name made Jason nervous. He tried to open the doors, but they were locked. He looked at his watch: *9:35.*

"Deputy Bernardo opens the doors at ten sharp. What case are you here on?" Jason turned and looked at the short, disheveled-looking man.

"Uh. Uh. Antonio Barrera."

"Wow, I thought you'd be older to have a case like that. How'd you steal that case from Peter 'the Great' Cohen?"

"I didn't steal anything from anyone. I'm Peter's co-counsel. Who are you?"

"Sorry, I'm Herman Tinsdale, originally Tinowitz. I'm a Jew, but my grandparents changed the name to avoid persecution when they came over from Poland in forty-four. It sucks too, because I'd get more clients if I still had the Jew last name." He shoved his hand at Jason.

"Jason Noble, nice to, uh, meet you, Herman Tinsdale, formally known as *Tinowiz*."

"So, how'd you land Barrera? Nice job. You probably got . . . at least a million-dollar-fee for a case like that from a guy like that. I'm sure Peter "the Great" got at least a million just for the PTD and arraignment. Imagine that . . . a million bucks for like an hour of time—that's better than Michael Jordan money."

"Just lucky, I guess. I did fine on the fee." *A million for just the bond hearing? I should've asked for more money.*

"Or unlucky," Herman said, pointing at the courtroom door. "Quarter pounces on lawyers like a wolverine."

"Well, I need to use the men's room, nice to meet you." Jason started turning around to walk away.

"Wait, take my card in case you need anything during your case. I know everyone in the courthouse."

"Thanks." Jason took the card from Herman and put it in his pocket and walked away.

The lights automatically went on when Jason walked into the bathroom. He didn't really have to use the bathroom, he just wanted to get away from Herman. He looked closely in the mirror and saw how much he was sweating. *Calm down, this is a routine court hearing—how much different could it be from state court? Peter said "it would be easy. Just like a status check hearing in state court that you've done a million times. No need for me to be there."* Jason reassuringly thought. He splashed some cold water on his face and took a deep breath. He dried his hands and when he moved toward the garbage can the top automatically opened. *Now I've seen everything. The Feds have garbage cans that open for you.*

Jason walked back over to the Judge Quarter's courtroom and opened the colossal double doors, which opened to an equally large set of interior double doors. Jason stopped just inside the inner doors and absorbed the grandness of the courtroom.

"Excuse me", said a man dressed in a suit who almost bumped into Jason as he stopped.

"Sorry," Jason said. He scanned the largest courtroom he'd ever been in. It had five large, dark wood tables—four tables to the left set in an 'L' pattern and two tables pushed together lengthwise on the right. In the middle of the courtroom was a podium with all sorts of digital equipment tucked into it. To the right was the jury box—twenty-four comfortable chairs arranged in three rows, each chair with a computer screen in front of it. The bench was majestic; Jason almost had to squint it was so far away. In front of Judge Quarter's bench, sitting above the litigants, but below the judge, was a desk with several computers and phones for the clerks.

As Jason approached the bar, his chest swelled up with pride. He felt like a lawyer for the first time. The state courthouse he worked in didn't have a bar separating the public from court personnel. When he was a kid at the group home, he would sneak up to the guard station and watch the TV show *Law & Order*—the guard was usually sound asleep—the characters that could cross the bar into the "holy" area seemed so cool and important to him. The moment was short lived. *What table to sit at? Not a good start, I don't even know where to sit. I got a 50/50 shot of picking the right table.* The general rule of thumb was that defendants and their lawyers sat at the farthest table from the jury box. The court didn't want the defendant sitting too close to the people judging him. In some courtrooms, the prosecutor's table was so close to the jury box, it gave them a huge advantage—they could leave damaging, inadmissible evidence on the corner of the table for the end jurors to see during a trial.

Jason chose the table on the left. His ass hadn't even hit the plush, black leather chair when the double doors opened and in walked four people dressed in dark navy and gray suits. One woman and three men walked down the aisle followed by several reporters. He craned his head around. *The short, chunky guy must be the boss because he was slightly ahead of the other three.*

Most of the reporters sat in the back row, but two of them, who were holding large notepads, split off and sat in the second row. Jason knew they were here for his case, which was one of only four cases on the docket. He stopped and stared at the female reporter with the large notepad in the second row—*where do I know her from?* . . . She briefly locked eyes with him and smiled, at least Jason thought it was a smile. *Oh right, she's that stunning reporter who was in Judge Reese's courtroom the day I sat in piss.*

"And you are?" Trevor asked. Now standing over Jason. The other three people were standing behind him, each holding a banker's box.

"Uh, Jason Noble." Jason laughed to himself as he was sitting and almost eye to eye with Trevor.

"Nope, doesn't ring a bell," Trevor responded back with a sarcastic grin from ear to ear. The people in the courtroom, which was almost full now, were all focused on Jason now. He could feel it and it made him sweat.

"I represent Antonio Barrera. Are you the prosecutor?" Jason responded dryly.

"I am the *prosecutor*, Trevor Wittingham, who's going to send your client to prison for ten life sentences." He extended his hand to shake Jason's, no doubt for the reporters. Out of the corner of his eye, Jason noticed both reporters with the notepads feverishly writing or drawing. *Oh, they must be sketch artists . . . I read that no cameras of any kind were allowed in federal courtrooms.*

Jason reluctantly shook Trevor's fleshy hand.

Trevor's condescending look turned to a smug glare and he said loud enough for everyone in the courtroom to hear, "I know your client's guilty, but you don't have to sit on the United State's side of the courtroom." Everyone in the courtroom laughed except the sketch artist he recognized from the state courthouse—she appeared to have a look of empathy.

Jason pulled his hand back. A hot feeling came over him.

"At least put up a fight," Trevor continued with a laugh, which one of his minions mimicked. "You're sitting on the wrong side, kid, move. Judge Quarter has us sit on reverse sides during all pretrial hearings, until trial." Trevor pointed his thumb over his shoulder at the other table closest to the jury box.

Jason wanted to split Trevor's head open at that moment, but he was frozen with embarrassment . . . he knew his sweat level was at defcon five and rising. "M-My bad, I-I was just ka-ka-keeping the seat warm for you," Jason mustered, forcing a smile, as he stood up, towering over Trevor, which gave him a little satisfaction.

— 60 —

"ALL RISE! THE HONORABLE CALVIN QUARTER OF THE UNIT-
ED STATES DISTRICT COURT FOR THE SOUTHERN DISTRICT
OF FLORIDA PRESIDING!" The courtroom deputy, Bob Dente, said
as he walked through a door behind and to the right of the judge's
bench—It looked as if he walked through the wall.

Judge Quarter followed directly behind; his thick mane of gray hair
looked like it was a Lego cutout on top of the much smaller Deputy
Dente's head. He pulled his black robe up a bit and sat in his chair
making it look small with his grizzly bear-sized frame; he resembled
a giant Colonel Sanders with a tan. Judge Quarter was framed by the
United States Flag and The State of Florida Flag—a red saltire or 'X' on
a white background with the state seal in the center. Directly behind
Judge Quarter, partially blocked by his large, round head, was a gold,
embossed seal of the United States.

"Defendants remain standing, everyone else may sit," Judge Quarter
said in his baritone voice with a hint of southern twang. His deputy
clerk, Lawanda Higgins, a Jamaican immigrant who didn't look close to
her sixty-three years, sat at her desk, smaller than the judge's, but still
imposing, three feet above everyone else. That put Judge Quarter eight
feet above the litigants before him, which only made his six, five, three-
hundred-and-fifty-pound frame that much more imposing.

"For those of you new to my courtroom . . . don't speak unless asked
a direct question by me. Madam Deputy Clerk will call each case in
the order I want." He paused, sucking in a breath. *Clearly a lifetime
smoker—probably pipes*, Jason thought. Judge Quarter looked around
the room, his eyes like concrete stopping on the reporters in the back.
"It appears that somebody on my docket is special. I can't wait to meet

the fine gentleman or woman."

Oh, shit, Jason nervously thought, *Peter said Antonio's appearance was waived for this hearing.*

"Excuse me," whispered a plump woman taking a seat next to Jason.

"First case, Madam Higgins," Judge Quarter instructed.

"Raul Perez," she said in her Jamaican accent looking out at the gallery . . . "Raul Perez?"

"Hi. I'm Courtney Brennan, haven't seen you in here before. First time before Judge 'Drawn & Quartered'?"

"Yes," Jason whispered back.

"I wonder who the media is here for?" Courtney asked. "Sketch artists too. Must be an important case. I hope the lawyer doesn't get embarrassed by Quarter . . . he likes to do that to lawyers in high profile cases just to show them he's the star in *his* courtroom."

Jason stole a glance at the sketch artist he recognized from the state courthouse. *She's so radiant . . . way out of my league.* Jason swallowed hard with visions of Quarter making him beg like a dog to not put him in jail for some minor misstep playing on every news station and website in the country. "Hi, I'm Jason Noble—unfortunately, they're for me."

The first three cases went smoothly—each defendant requested a change of plea date instead of a trial date. "I'm taking a five-minute recess before the last case," Quarter announced and banged his gavel.

* * *

"COME TO ORDER, REMAIN SEATED, Deputy Dente said as Judge Quarter took the bench again. Jason, Trevor and his flunkies, the media, sketch artists, and courtroom personnel were the only people left in the courtroom.

Clerk Higgins called out: "The case of United States of America versus Antonio Barrera, a/k/a Antonio 'Magic Man' Barrera . . . All parties state your appearance for the record."

Jason swallowed hard. He didn't know if he should go to the podium or not. He hoped to follow Trevor's lead. No such luck.

"Counsel for the defense are you going to make an appearance? And how come no one is sitting next to you or in the galley making their way up to counsel table?" Judge Quarter asked with a stern look on his face.

"Uh, Uh, Jason, uh, Noble here on behalf of Antonio Barrera. I-I, uh—*relax*—filed my notice and stipulation for substitution of counsel two weeks ago through the PACER system." He stood at the table instead of making the walk to the podium, which seemed so far away now. *That wasn't so bad*, he thought, gaining some confidence. "My client, Mr. Antonio Barrera's presence was waived in writing by previous counsel . . . I was told—."

"You were told . . . You were TOLD!" Judge Quarter leaned forward in his chair as if he were about to pounce on Jason from across the courtroom.

Even though they were far away, Jason distinctly saw Quarter's eyes narrow in on him. "Um, yes, Your Honor. I have contact with my client. I thought this was just a—"

"Well, don't think. It'll git you in trouble. Are you even admitted to the federal bar, son?" A question meant to embarrass and belittle Jason, Judge Quarter knew full well no one would dare try and appear before him without the proper credentials. One lawyer tried it after he was disbarred. Quarter found out two years later and had the Department of Justice charge the lawyer with perjury and he was sentenced to three years in prison.

The sweat faucet had turned on inside Jason. Trevor and his cronies were snickering. The reporters exchanged confused looks. "I thought Antonio would be at his own hearing. That's why I'm here," the NBC reporter whispered to her counterpart at CBS.

"Me too. At least it looks like we're about to get a good show." the CBS reporter said with a wicked smile.

"Judge, I represent Antonio Barrera. All the necessary pleadings have been filed well before today's hearing and previous counsel filed a waiver of Mr. Barrera's appearance." Jason's heart was pounding.

Clerk Higgins announced into her microphone, "He is right, Your Honor." She gave Jason a confident wink and smiled.

"I didn't ask *you* if he was *right*," Judge Quarter snapped. He turned his wrath back to Jason. "Since *you* didn't file a new waiver of your client's appearance, I am going to revoke his bond and hold him pretrial . . . so ordered." He banged his gavel hard.

Jason, desperate now, blurted out, "The law and rules allow for new counsel to adopt previous counsel's filings, which I will do *ore tenus* (orally) and follow up with a new written waiver of appearance right after court." You would've thought Jason just told Judge Quarter that his wife was cheating on him—Quarter's eyes opened wide, his eyebrows stretched up as far as possible, and his mouth opened.

You go kid, I like you . . . you got moxy, Clerk Higgins thought.

"Mr. Wittingham, can you explain to this young lawyer what normally happens when a defendant is not present at my hearing and the lawyer does not file a signed waiver of appearance?"

Trevor stood tall, welcoming the attention. "Good morning, Your Honor and members of the court." Clerk Higgins and Deputy Dente rolled their eyes. "Well . . . the defendant goes back to jail and the lawyer goes to jail for contempt of court. Trevor looked down at his buzzing phone and read the text that popped up on the home screen.

"Something more important on your table, Mr. Wittingham?" Judge Quarter questioned.

"Uh. No. Judge. Um, I do not have an objection to Mr. Boble wav—"

"It's Noble," Jason frustratingly interjected.

"Whatever, I do not have an objection to Mr. *Noble* waiving his client's presence. I say we welcome this young lawyer to the federal bar with open arms," Trevor said then sat back down and cleared the text message from Peter Cohen: *u better not let Q revoke AB bond!*

Maybe this Trevor guy is okay after all, Jason thought.

Judge Quarter finally relented. "I'll accept the waiver, but a new one better be filed by lunchtime, or you and your client will have warrants for your arrest . . . Understood, Mr. Noble?"

"U-U-um, yes, J-J-Judge."

The sketch artist from state court was staring at Jason and feverishly sketching on her pad.

"Now, Mr. Noble, I assume you're going to request a continuance even though this case is no longer a death penalty case—isn't that correct, Mr. Wittingham?"

Trevor half stood now and spoke in a low voice. "Yes, that is correct, Your Honor. I filed a waiver of the death penalty this morning."

All the reporters exchanged surprised looks.

It hadn't occurred to Jason to ask for a continuance; he never got one in "No Release Reece's" courtroom. "No, Your Honor. I will just go with your calendar at this point. I haven't received discovery yet from previous counsel, so maybe after I review it, I will need a continuance. But, right now, you can set it for—" *what's the next court hearing in a federal case? . . . probably the same as state court—*"calendar call."

"I will provide Mr. Noble a copy of all the discovery after court, Your Honor." Trevor added.

"Thank you, Mr. Wittingham. I don't think I've ever had a lawyer in a case like this *not* ask for at least one continuance. You must be some type of super lawyer, Mr. Noble, or you're a fool. I hope it's not the latter—we set matters right for trial from the first status check in this courtroom. This was your only chance to ask for a continuance. Madam Clerk please give me a trial date in sixty days."

"January fifth," Clerk Higgin's offered.

"Trial set January fifth. No continuances will be granted for either side, no matter how unprepared you are." Judge Quarter was looking directly at Jason as he said the last part. "If you want me to ask the jury questions, submit them to my chambers at least three days before trial. And, Mr. Noble, make sure your client is here for trial—you can't *ore tenus* waive his appearance. Court's in recess." Judge Quarter banged his gavel and was about to get up and walk off the bench.

"Your honor? I apologize, but one more matter, please?" Trevor said.

"Make it quick," Judge Quarter said shifting his weight back down in his chair.

"Since Mr. Noble is new to this case, I'd like to request a *Nebbia* hearing on his fee."

What the hell is a "Nebbia" hearing, Jason thought.

"So ordered. Hearing shall be in one week unless the parties agree otherwise." He banged his gavel and left the bench.

Jason was shell-shocked—his mind was spinning. Trevor interrupted Jason's panicked thoughts and handed him a shoebox. "Here you go—three two terabyte hard drives of data mostly recordings of your client and how guilty he is and one DVD . . . I'd watch the DVD with popcorn, it's a fabulous movie . . . Oscar worthy." Trevor smiled as he turned and left with his flunkies.

As Trevor and his team left, Tim Barnes handed each reporter a DVD with a wink and whispered, "You didn't get this from me."

— 61 —

JASON WAITED UNTIL everyone left the courtroom. *That wasn't so bad.* He watched the luxurious, long black hair of the sketch artist/reporter from the state courthouse go out the double doors; she was the last one to file out besides him. She kept sketching while looking at him well after Judge Quarter left the bench—he thought it was a little creepy. He gathered his leather folder from defense table and said, "Have a good day."

"Good luck, Kid." Deputy Dente replied.

Jason pushed open the double doors to the rotunda and was immediately bombarded with an avalanche of questions.

"Is your client guilty? Why would Antonio hire you? What happened to Peter Cohen? Are you even old enough to practice law? Who are you? Have you ever had a federal case before? Is this some kind of joke or setup by Peter Cohen?"

Jason froze like a cat dropped into a room full of rocking chairs. The questions were swallowing him. All he could focus on were the cameras that were now in his face instead of Trevor's who was standing a few feet to the right. *I guess no cameras in the courtroom doesn't apply to right outside the door.* Coming at Jason, like they were leaping off the sides of the video cameras, were the network names: *CNN, FOX, MSNBC, BBC, ABC, NBC, CBS, CNN International.* He finally choked out, "My name Jason. I-I-I innocent."

She came through the center of the cameras like Moses parting the Red Sea. Her large, brown, doe eyes immediately sucking Jason in and calming him. Her smile was warm and effortless. "Come with me," the sketch artist whispered while taking his hand.

Your skin is sooo soft, Jason thought. *I'll follow you anywhere.* Jason obeyed. She led him away, to a door about ten feet to the left.

Trevor's voice trailing off. "Come back over here. I wasn't done telling you how I'm going to save the children. Forget about Jason Boble . . . he's running like a scared chicken."

They were standing in a stairwell. Jason was panting.

"Hi, Jason, my name is Inaya Nuqi. Are you okay?"

Jason stood up straight. "Yeah-yes, I'm good, just wasn't expecting all that and, a, thanks for saving me." He extended his hand, hoping to feel her velvety touch again.

She gently took his hand. "Your welcome. My colleagues questions were stupid. Weren't you, like, an assistant public defender a few weeks ago?" She disengaged their handshake and sheepishly looked down.

"Um, yes, I started my own firm after I saw you in No-Release Reece's courtroom that day. Antonio Barrera's one of my first clients . . . yay for me." He said mockingly. He couldn't stop looking at her—she was breathtaking. Her skin was light brown and liquid smooth with subtle, but prominent features. Inaya's dark brown eyes beset by full eyelashes were hypnotic and inviting—like a doe's. *Probably a mix of Middle Eastern and . . . Sicilian, exotic,* Jason excitedly thought.

Inaya broke the uncomfortable silence. "Let me go down, I mean," she blushed, "*let's* go down one floor and get on the elevator to the lobby."

Then to get a drink, then dinner, then marriage. "Sounds like a good plan," Jason offered.

When they reached the lobby, they headed out the front door—they beat the media downstairs. "I'm sure Trevor is still boring everyone outside the courtroom with how great he is," Inaya said, flashing her radiant smile.

"Yeah, he seems like a pompous ass. So . . . thanks for getting me out of the lion's den. Are you a reporter or sketch artist?"

"Both. Since cameras are allowed in state court, I'm a reporter, but in federal court, I switch to a courtroom sketch artist because no cameras allowed . . . I enjoyed sketching you today." Inaya batted her eyelashes.

Ask her out, dummy. "Can I see the sketch of me?"

"You'll have to wait until the five o'clock news," she coyly replied.

"Um, okay, I can't wait. . . . Well . . . *ask her out, dummy* . . . would you like to . . . I mean do you want to . . . share twelve inches with me?"

"Huh?"

"Oh, OH! a twelve-inch *Subway* sandwich for lunch. You thought I meant, oh no, sorry about that." He offered an uncomfortable laugh.

"You're funny, Jason Noble. Maybe another time. I need to get these sketches to my boss. Besides, I think you have a lot of work to do. Trevor is going to try and overwhelm you."

"Too late, I'm already overwhelmed. Win one for me."

Inaya took his hand, that was sweaty, turned it over and wrote her number. "Call me and we'll share that *twelve-incher* another time." She winked. She turned and looked into the courthouse vestibule. "You'd better go before the vultures come out with their cameras."

"Thanks again for your help today; it was really nice meeting you. I'll give you an exclusive if you want."

"Sure, that will make my boss happy, lay it on me."

"My client Antonio Barrera is innocent and I'm going to prove it in court."

"Thanks for the exclusive. Enjoy the rest of your day, Jason."

"You too, Inaya." Jason watched her go before he left and walked back to his car with a spring in his step.

— 62 —

JASON SAT AT his desk staring at the box full of hard drives and the DVD Tim Barnes handed him at the end of court. He had since turned off his TV and stopped surfing the internet for stories about his court appearance—he wished the internet never existed. Every national and local media outlet was following the story and the headlines were brutal—*CNN* ran a "Breaking News" scroll across the top of its website that read: *MOB BOSS OUT OF MONEY . . . HIRES "FOOL", JASON NOBLE FOR A LAWYER.* That was one of the nicer headlines.

"Can I use your microwave? I want to make popcorn," Jeannie Francis' voice squeaked from the front door.

Jason looked toward the front door. "Huh, what? Popcorn?"

"Popcorn. It's like a movie watching all the news stories on your case . . . it's so exciting. I really like the action shots of that gorgeous girl helping you run from the reporters—Fox News ran it in slow-mo. I watched it a dozen times already. You're a superstar." She smiled ear to ear as she sat down in his office.

Jason sighed and slumped his shoulders. "Yeah, right, I'm a 'superstar' idiot."

"Who cares that the judge said you're a fool and you didn't look like you knew what you were doing . . . you're famous now. The clients are going to start rolling in. Wish I were you."

"I have enough to do with Antonio's case; I don't need any more clients."

"Oh, look. You're the lead story on the six o'clock news too." Jeannie Francis pointed to the muted TV on a small credenza to her left. That's a great pic of you in action. With no sound, we can pretend the anchor is saying what a great job you did. I thought no cameras were allowed in federal court? How'd a reporter get such a great picture of you at the podium?"

Jason stared at the "photo" on the TV screen. He took some art classes in college and recognized the style of drawing as he looked closer at it. Since he left the courthouse, all he could think about was Inaya's infectious smile, soothing voice, and . . . soft hands.

"Why are you smiling? You look weird."

"Oh, nothing. That is a hyper-realistic drawing that Inaya, I mean, one of the courtroom sketch artists did of me. It's very hard to sketch someone and make it look like an actual photo. You must be very talented to do it . . . like, only a few artists can achieve such perfection and she did it under extreme time pressure . . . She's awesome."

Jeannie-Francis' eyes lit up at the smell of romance in the air. "You know her name already. Is she single? Where does she live? Did you ask her out? Did she say *yes*? Can I go on your date? I'll sit at another table and text you good lines to say—oh, please, please, please."

Jason ignored Jeannie Frances' barrage of questions about Inaya. "It's nothing. I don't even know her and I'm too busy for a date."

"Well, she must really like you . . . she made you look way more amazing than you really are. I'd ask her out if she drew pictures like that of me."

"Gee, thanks." Jason sighed. He went back to the discovery on his desk and thumbed the DVD.

"Let's make this popcorn and watch that DVD you keep playing with."

— 63 —

ANTONIO SAT AT his son's Apple G4 computer playing the fifteen second JPEG video over and over on CNN's website.

"Michael, time for breakfast!" Maria yelled from the kitchen.

Michael shot up in his bed. "Yo, mornin', pops. What you doin' in my crib?" He grunted then rolled over toward the wall and pulled his blanket over his head.

Antonio turned around from the computer toward Michael. "You must be on drugs to speak to me like that," his tone creating a chill in the air. "I'm not one of your friends. If you ever speak to me like that again, I will send you off to an all-boys boarding school in Buffalo."

"Sorry, Father. It won't ever happen again." Michael was now sitting up in his bed, realizing he crossed a serious line. "Good morning, Father."

"Good morning, Son."

"Why are you using my computer?"

Antonio got up from the chair and walked over to Michael. "Since I pay for everything you have, it's really *my* computer." He was standing over Michael now, a most serious look on his face.

Michael looked like he was going to pee himself.

"I'm just kidding—not about paying for everything you have." The corners of Antonio's mouth curled up. "I was just checking some stocks and watched a trailer for a mob movie coming out this summer. Maybe we'll go see it together."

"That would be great. What's the name of it?"

"*The Trial of the Century.* It takes place right here in Florida."

"Cool."

Antonio messed up Michael's hair and said, "Now get ready for school and come have breakfast . . . and make sure you tell your mother you love your smoothie." Antonio winked, "And remember, stay OUT of the girls' locker room. You can get arrested and thrown in prison for that today. Love you, Son."

"Love you too, Father."

* * *

Antonio walked into the kitchen and looked at his wife—he read the concern all over her face. He walked over to her and gently stroked her cheek. "Don't worry, we will get through this. You and Michael are taken care of for the rest of your lives and Michael's kids', kids' lives."

"I don't care about having money . . . I want you." Maria struck him on his chest and was overcome with emotion. That video of you telling those men to kidnap kids and traffic them for sex! Please tell me that's not you."

"That video is fake. Period. You know I don't need to, nor do I make money that way. I make plenty of money from legal marijuana and investments. That is the last time you need to ever question me about that."

"But, but," Maria's bottom lip quivered as she spoke.

Antonio tenderly held his wife by the shoulders. "I know what I'm doing. Trust me."

"Do you? You have a lawyer who is barely out of law school. Who doesn't seem to know the simple procedures in court. He's the laughing stock of the internet: *The Magic Man hires a 'fool' according to Judge.* That was the headline in the *Miami Herald.* THIS *idiota* is who you've trusted with your life. Please, baby," she pleaded with her eyes, "tell me why can't Peter help you, like always? A week ago the government wanted to actually *kill* you! You need Peter!"

"He has some sort of conflict of interest, sounds like legal bullshit to me. Peter highly recommended Johnson—I mean Jason, I'll be fine.

Besides, Peter will be in the background pulling the strings and doing most of the work. I paid him five million dollars so far and he better do most of the work. Jason will come through when he needs to."

Maria plopped down into a kitchen chair, slumping her shoulders and hanging her head. "I wish I knew someone that worked in the jury pool room at the courthouse. I would get them to fix the jury for you, so they'd guarantee a *Not Guilty* vote." She looked up at Antoino. "I would risk prison for you, I love you that much."

Antonio held his wife's face. "Thanks, baby, that's why I love you more than life itself. I will remove the sadness from those beautiful, angel eyes soon enough."

— 64 —

THE FIRST THREE weeks were over before Jason knew it. He barely looked through the six terabytes of discovery the government provided. He was doing the ostrich—burying his head in the sand because he was already too overwhelmed. One hard drive alone had five thousand wiretap recordings. He went to the law library at the courthouse and looked at the fifteen-hundred-page federal sentencing guidelines book to see if he could figure out a reasonable plea to try and negotiate. He didn't understand the guidelines at all—the book was filled with charts and tables that looked almost like a foreign language to Jason.

His mind went to the video of Antonio and his guys talking about human trafficking. *Antonio is adamant it's a fake. Could it be? Would the government really do that? Based on the allegations in the criminal complaint and the few wiretaps I listened to, the government doesn't need to fabricate evidence. Maybe that Wittingham asshole is concerned that a lot of the evidence is too circumstantial? Maybe the video is a sign that I'm supposed to bring down the government and expose its slimy behavior? Like a real-life David and Goliath . . . nah, Wittingham wouldn't risk his career on a case this easy to win.* He decided to call Trevor and talk about a plea and to set depositions of the government's witnesses, whoever they were.

"United States Attorney's Office for the Southern District of Florida, how can I help you?"

"Uh, hello, Trevor Wittingham, please."

"Who's calling?"

"Jason Noble."

"Please hold. . . ."

"Jason, how are you my young friend?" Trevor said.

Jason was glad Trevor couldn't see him, he wiped blobs of sweat from his brow. "H-H-Hi, Trevor, I-I," *deep breath* "I want to see if you have a plea offer for me."

"Plea offer? In a case like this. I don't think so youngster—"

"Stop calling me that, my name is Jason Noble."

"Whatever," Trevor said dismissively, already losing interest in the conversation. "Anything else you want to discuss, I'm busy getting ready for the holidays and to send your client to prison for ten lifetimes. . . . You watch the video yet? This case is a slam dunk for me."

"Yeah, I watched the video, and I'm not worried about it," Jason lied. "However, I want to set some depositions of your agents."

"Depositions? *Depositions?* . . . really? This case is going to be easier to win then I thought. Antonio must not care about his freedom hiring an idiot like you."

"*Idiot!* What! You sonofabitch . . . hello . . . hello . . . that asshole hung up on me."

— 65 —

JASON GOT READY for his morning run. Three weeks had passed since he called Trevor about a plea. He was about to start the first day of the biggest trial of his life and he was woefully unprepared. Peter was nonexistent to assist him like he said he would—so much for, *My office is your office*. Peter's assistant Meredith gave Jason every excuse in the book as to why he wasn't available when Jason called for help.

He called his old supervisor at the PDs Office, Sherman Stills, for advice—that's when he learned you don't automatically get to take depositions of government witnesses like in Florida felony cases. No wonder Trevor called him an "idiot". Apparently, according to Sherman, the defense won't even get the government's witness list until right before trial and won't know who they actually intend to call as witnesses at trial until they call them—Jason's head was swimming when he hung up with Sherman. He wanted to jump out a window. He thought of Sherman's last words: "Play for the fumble." *What the hell did he mean?*

Jason thought the stress-tornado he felt inside as an assistant public defender was overwhelming, but it was nothing compared to the nuclear-stress-tornado he was now feeling. He stared at his *Transformers'* watch that he only wore for special occasions or when he needed good luck—*Optimus Prime* was battling *Megatron* and the digital face was shaped like *Cybertron*; the red digits read *3 a.m.* He won the watch at the local fair when he was six—it was his only good memory growing up in New York City's foster care system.

Jason was trying to keep his heaving chest under control as he reached out and set the microwave to *45 sec.* then pressed *start.* He turned to the coffee maker. *I am so not ready for this . . .* he thought *. . . but I have no choice . . . I have to show up and defend Antonio . . .*

Optimus give me strength!

"What do ya think, Caesar? We gonna win, lil'buddy." Caesar picked up his head, let out a big snort, stretched his front paws and rolled over onto his side. "Thanks for the vote of confidence. Who asked you anyway." Jason got the General his cup of coffee and egg sandwich from the microwave and then left for his run.

— 66 —

THE GENERAL RARELY slept. Most of the night, he lay still on the sea-wall, sandwiched between the Intracoastal Waterway and Flagler Drive. He stared at the sky until sunrise battling with his mental demons from twelve tours of duty between three wars (Iraq times two and Afghanistan) for good ol' Uncle Sam. He always kept his head to the north because in Iraq in 2006, fireballs of liquid metal rained down nightly always coming across the night sky from the north—the brilliant stars acting as camouflage for the little fireballs. He would lay on a wall of sandbags, like he lay on the seawall, and refused to take cover—*God will shield me*, he would chant until the raining fireballs stopped. And God did shield him, except he took a break once: the General got a fireball through his left eye.

He did not move a muscle and slowed his breathing at the sound of the boat pulling up to the seawall . . . he heard two guys bickering.

— 67 —

Phil "the Pick" and Tim "the Duck" drifted their little rowboat into the seawall by a ladder. "I'll just ice pick Antonio's lawyer and we'll be done with it," Phil informed Tim.

"Fuhgeddaboudit, I wanna try out dis new silenca I gots, let me shoot'em in da head . . . much easier than an ice pick to da brain," Tim pleaded.

"Whatever wes do, wes gots to kill Antonio's lawyer so he don't let'em plea and dime us all out today."

The General was about five feet away from them. He silently rolled off the retaining wall onto the sidewalk. He crawled on his belly to the ladder and silently waited.

Phil was the first one to climb over the seawall onto the sidewalk . . . Tim right behind him.

The streetlights were out thanks to the General—he couldn't sleep with them on. They reminded him of the lights the Taliban used to shine in his face during the brutal interrogations he underwent as a POW for three years.

Neither man saw the General's right hand coming. He first chopped Phil in the neck and followed it up with a lighting fast knuckle punch to the temple. Phil dropped instantly on the sidewalk—either unconscious or dead, the General didn't care.

Tim tried to pull his gun that was tucked into his waistband. The General spun around, placed his hand on Tim's hand and rapidly fired the gun three times. Not a sound from the gun. "Good silencer," the General said, smiling, staring into Tim's now wide open eyes.

The front of Tim's white pants began to soak red with blood. Tim screamed for only a nano-second before the General knuckle punched him in the temple. Tim dropped onto Phil. The General quickly tossed them both back over the seawall into their rowboat and pushed them out to sea.

* * *

"Good morning, Sir. Private Noble reporting for duty. What are you looking at?"

"Nothing, Private Noble. Just thought I heard a Manatee, a/k/a 'the sea cow'. . . beautiful mammal of the sea, isn't she?" The General turned away from the Intracoastal toward Jason.

"Uh, sure. You're a little sweaty and out of breath, you sure you're okay, Sir?"

"Don't ask too many questions Private Noble. Thank you for the coffee and egg sandwich." The General took them from Jason's hand. "Diiiisssmissed, Private."

— 68 —

JUDGE QUARTER TOOK the bench promptly at 9 a.m. "Are the parties ready to proceed?"

"The government is ready to proceed, Your Honor," Trevor stood and announced. Herb Rosen and SA Lisa Hoyt remained seated at the prosecution table.

"The defense is ready to proceed, Judge," Jason announced as he stood up with his client Antonio Barrera who were the only two at the defense table.

"Good morning, ladies and gentleman," Quarter bellowed to the prospective hundred jurors filling all but the front row of the large galley. He got right to the point: "Courtroom Deputies Dente and Ruiz handed each of you a sheet of paper with a series of questions; when your name is called, stand up and answer the questions. Speak loud and clear. If anyone needs assistance standing let one of my bailiffs know . . . all right?"

Most judges also told the panel that if they needed a break to simply raise their hand and ask. Judge Quarter did an informal study years ago and determined that jurors asked for way more breaks if you told them they could. "Any questions? Seeing no hands, the parties may turn and face the panel now." Until that moment, Judge Quarter had the parties face the bench instead of the galley, so the jurors got the backs of their heads.

Trevor, Herb, and SA Lisa Hoyt moved their chairs around the table. They now sat facing the jury pool.

Jason stood up to move his chair and knocked his laptop on the floor and then tripped over his briefcase . . . nearly falling to the floor. Everyone in the courtroom was now focused on him. Trevor snickered.

"Damn computer," Jason muttered. He finally got situated facing the jury, beads of sweat already starting to form on his forehead.

Who am I trusting my life to, Antonio thought, as he moved his chair around the table without incident. *Peter better know what he's talking about or he will answer to me.* Antonio sat facing the jury; his face had a relaxed, neutral expression, which he would maintain throughout the entire trial. Some of the female *and* male prospective jurors were already drawn into Antonio's movie star looks.

"Government introduce yourself to the panel," Quarter instructed.

Trevor stood, paused for a moment like a seasoned pro, the corners of his mouth slightly curled, his eyes opened a bit wider. "Good morning, fellow citizens. . . my name is Trevor Wittingham, I'm a Chief United, uhm, Chief Assistant United States Attorney for the Southern District of Florida. Basically, I work for you, the taxpayer."

"Move it along, Mr. Wittingham," Judge Quarter chided. "We have a trial to get to."

Trevor continued, unfazed, "My client is the United States Government." He casually scanned the galley as he spoke, making sure he made perceived eye contact with each prospective juror from *Hello*. "To my left is my assistant, Herb Rosen, who will be sitting with me throughout the trial. Please introduce yourself, Mr. Rosen."

Herb stood, almost straight, his head slightly bowed, and offered a quick "Hello." *What a pompous ass—I'm an attorney, not an "assistant", Less than a year to retirement.*

Trevor continued. "To Mr. Rosen's right is special agent Lisa Hoyt with the United States Drug Enforcement Agency. Please introduce yourself."

"Thank you for the permission," Lisa said low and casual, looking at the panel with a relaxed smile. "Good morning, my name is Lisa Hoyt and I'm a special agent with the DEA. Thank you." She sat down.

Trevor finished. "Thank you for your time, ladies and gentlemen, we'll talk again soon." He sat down. Several of the jurors rolled their eyes.

"Defense," Quarter instructed.

Jason stood, his right knee buckled momentarily on the way up, the beads of sweat on his forehead had doubled, "Uh, g-g-"—*deep breath*—good, morning, gentleman and ladies. My name is Jason Noble and I have the pleasure of representing Mr. Antonio Barrera, seated to my left, well, my right now." Jason stole a glimpse of Inaya, who was sitting in the back row, which was reserved for all media. Inaya caught his eye and smiled.

Antonio casually stood, almost floated up, and offered a "Good morning." His expression never changed except for the facial movements associated with speaking.

"Now, if any of you think you know any of the parties that just introduced themselves or anyone else part of the courtroom staff, including me, let us know when you answer the questions. Juror 1-1 (first row, first juror), please stand and answer the questions."

A gangly kid with red curly hair, who didn't look old enough to be out of high school, stood up, focused on the laminated piece of paper in his hands. "Um, question (1) Seth Brounsonstein; (2) like, one week of college; (3) like, in-between jobs, (3)a. like, Arbys was the last place I worked, but, um, like, they fired me for no reason, man. . . ." He switched his gaze to Judge Quarter, as if looking for him to do something about this injustice. (4) "No way am I married, I'm single." He looked at SA Hoyt. (5) "No kids, like, that I know of, ha ha. (6) *Do I know any friends or family in Law Enforcement?* Well, my dad's a cop."

Jason and Trevor both made a note on the seven-page jury pool chart that had each prospective juror's full name, age, city of residence, and juror number.

"The rest of my family are accountants . . . boooring." The panel chuckled. (7) No, I, like, ain't never been called for jury duty before; (8) *Ever been convicted of a felony?* Is, like, possession of a joint a felony. Last year me and my homeboy got caught by the cops when we was just blazin' up—that wasn't cool, man." He was looking at Judge Quarter again.

"Did you have more than the joint on you when you were arrested?" Quarter asked.

"Um, no, I gave the rest of my stuff to my other homeboy to hold before the cops came." The entire courtroom, except for Judge Quarter, laughed. His gavel came down quick to quell the laughter uprising.

"Just answer the last two questions and sit down," Judge Quarter instructed.

"Like, okay, I was just being honest. (9) *Is there any reason why I can't serve on the jury?* Like, I'm free all week. Plus, don't we get paid for this gig? And (10) *Any reason I can't be fair and impartial if I were selected on the jury?* I don't know what 'impartial' means, but I'm, like, the *fairest* guy around." Juror 1-1 finally sat down.

The questioning continued throughout the rest of the day until 7:45 p.m.

Judge Quarter, who looked bored to death, like the rest of the courtroom, said, "Ladies and gentleman, we're done with the preliminary questions, be here at 8 a.m. tomorrow morning outside the jury room so we can get started right away." He further admonished them: "Don't read or watch any news stories or *Facebook*, or any social media posts about this case or I will hold you in contempt and send you to jail . . . understood?" The jury panel nodded in unison. He banged his gavel. "Court is in recess."

— 69 —

THE JURY PANEL was in their seats by 8:15 a.m. Judge Quarter took the bench promptly at 8:30. "The parties approach," he ordered.

As Trevor, Herb, and Jason walked up to the Bench, Antonio stayed at the defense table with the same neutral expression he had the day before. A white noise filled the speakers in the courtroom. The bench conference needed to be on the record but not heard by the prospective members of the jury.

"Mr. Noble, you submitted forty proposed jury questions you want me to ask."

"Yes, Judge, that is correct."

"I'm not asking forty questions to this panel of one hundred prospective jurors. We'll be here all week just picking the jury. Why don't you go back to the defense table and pick out a few you want me to ask."

"Uh, okay, Your Honor."

After a few minutes, Jason retuned to the bench having cut his questions in half to twenty. The courtroom was pin-drop quiet. Jason could feel everyone staring at him as he walked to the bench which seemed like a mile away.

"Still too many . . . try again." Judge Quarter shoved back the questions.

Jason approached again, cutting the questions down to ten.

Judge Quarter looked at the questions. "I'll tell you what I'm going to do, you've waisted enough of our time and the prospective jury's time being unprepared." He crumpled up the questions and threw them in the garbage can under his bench. "I'll just ask the questions I want and pick a fair jury for your client."

Jason couldn't believe that not only would *he* not be allowed to ask the prospective jury any questions during *voir dire* like he became accustomed to in state court, which is where the trial lawyer wins his case, but this asshole judge wasn't going to ask any of *his* proposed questions either—not one! *How is Antonio expected to get a fair trial if I can't question the prospective jurors and begin planting the seeds of 'reasonable doubt'?* "Okay." Jason responded, shoulders slumped a bit, head bowed slightly. Jason wanted to knock the smirk off Trevor's face as they walked back to their tables.

Judge Quarter cleared his throat and took a sip from a teacup. "Okay, ladies and gentlemen, I'm now going to ask you some questions to determine if you can be fair and impartial. There are no right or wrong answers. I will ask you to respond by raising your hand, and if I want to follow up with anyone of you individually, I will. Any questions? . . . Seeing no hands, let's begin."

"I'm going to read you what the law is on *Plea of Not Guilty, Reasonable Doubt*; and the *Presumption of Innocence: The defendant, ANTONIO BARRERA, a/k/a Magic Man has entered a plea of not guilty. This means you must presume or believe the defendant is innocent. The presumption stays with the defendant as to each material allegation in the Indictment, through each stage of the trial unless it has been overcome by the evidence to the exclusion of and beyond a reasonable doubt.*

To overcome the defendant's presumption of innocence the government has the burden of proving the crimes with which the defendant is charged was committed and the defendant is the person who committed the crimes.

The defendant is not required to present evidence or prove anything.

Whenever the words 'reasonable doubt' are used, you must consider the following:

A reasonable doubt is not a mere possible doubt, a speculative, imaginary or forced doubt. Such a doubt must not influence you to return a verdict of not guilty if you have an abiding conviction of guilt. On the other hand, if, after carefully considering, comparing and weighing all the

evidence, there is not an abiding conviction of guilt, or, if, having a conviction, it is one which is not stable but one which wavers and vacillates, then
the charge is not proved beyond every reasonable doubt and you must
find the defendant not guilty because the doubt is reasonable.

It is to the evidence introduced in this trial, and to it alone, that you
are to look for that proof.

A reasonable doubt as to the guilt of the defendant may arise from the
evidence, conflict in the evidence or the lack of evidence.

If you have a reasonable doubt, you should find the defendant not
guilty. If you have no reasonable doubt, you should find the defendant
guilty."

Judge Quarter scanned the galley for a few seconds to let what he
just read sink-in. . . . "Is there anyone who does not think they can
follow the law as I just read it? . . . Seeing no hands, means everyone can
be fair and impartial in this case."

He can't really be done with his questioning! Jason incredulously
thought. Jason jumped up. "I object Your Honor! I—"

Judge Quarter quickly turned toward Jason. "Overruled, sit down."

"But, I-can't-pick-a-fair—" Jason stammered.

"Mr. Noble, I've overruled your objection and instructed you to sit
down. If you disobey me again, I will hold you in contempt and then
the U.S. Marshalls will have to bring you to court every morning from
the jail. Understood?"

"Ye-Ye—*deep breath*—yes, Judge."

Judge Quarter took another sip from his teacup and instructed,
"Ladies and gentlemen, follow my courtroom deputy into the back. The
lawyers and I need to discuss a few matters."

* * *

"Alright, you can turn your chairs back around," Quarter said. Everyone
but Jason moved their chair around. He was too stunned to move. *That
was the biggest joke of* voir dire *I ever witnessed—this is why I didn't want*

to practice in federal court! Jason finally joined his client on the other side of the table.

"I will recess for five minutes while you go through your notes. Court's in recess." Judge Quarter banged his gavel and left the bench.

Jason looked down at his notes from *voir dire."*

Antonio glanced at Jason's legal pad, slightly smiled at the fact that not much was written. When he had been in trial with Peter before, a team of people had countless pages of notes on every prospective juror. "I want a copy of your notes for my file," Antonio said. Peter told him not to participate in anything, so Peter could argue on appeal that Jason didn't consult with his client and the jury selected wasn't one he agreed to—evidence that Jason was *ineffective.*

Jason glanced at Trevor who was huddled with Herb, Lisa, and Tim Barnes, who joined them from the galley, reviewing their notes. He turned back to Antonio, leaned in close. "Let's go over the juror chart—who do you like?"

Antonio looked at Jason with contempt and said, "There's nothing to go over, you didn't ask any questions or take any notes."

Jason was getting frustrated. "Well, the asshole judge wouldn't let me ask any—" as he spoke he realized his mistake, he hadn't turned off the mic in front of him. Everyone in the courtroom turned toward Jason. The two clerks and Deputy Ruiz had a look of shock on their faces. Inaya gasped.

Trevor finally said, "You know, these hot mics go into chambers . . . this should make for a fun trial." Jason could visualize knocking the smirk off his face.

"ALL RISE, COURT IS NOW BACK IN SESSION!" Deputy Dente bellowed.

Judge Quarter sat behind his bench and looked at Jason and Antonio, his expression neutral. Jason was expecting the worst. "Mr. Barrera?"

"Yes." Antonio responded, staying seated. He could not bring himself to show any respect to this process unless forced to.

"Are you sure Jason Noble is your lawyer of choice? Because now is the time to change back to Peter Cohen or someone with maybe more experience than a lawyer who doesn't even know the mics are on." Judge Quarter was now staring directly at Jason.

Jason felt like Quarter's eyes were searing into his skull; he looked down.

Of course, I don't want this idiot to represent me—it's embarrassing, Antonio thought. *But thank you for asking and putting on the record that he's an ineffective moron.* "Yes, I want Mr. Noble to continue representing me."

"Okay, your choice under the Sixth Amendment of the United States Constitution. Mr. Noble, I'm holding you in contempt and fining you one thousand dollars and requiring you to complete a minimum four-hour CLE (continuing legal education) seminar on *professionalism in the courtroom*, tonight, and bring proof tomorrow morning. Now, let's move on."

Jason thought about objecting, but figured it wasn't worth the fight. *At this rate, I will burn through my fee in contempt fines before trial is over!*

"Each side gets ten preemptory challenges and, since there is only one defendant, you get all ten, Mr. Noble." Either side could use their preemptory challenges to strike a prospective jury for any reason; for example, if Trevor did not like the way a prospective juror looked at him, he could strike them. But, a preemptory challenge can't be used to strike someone because of their race or sex.

After twenty minutes of going back and forth, Jason and Trevor picked the jury that would decide Antonio Barrera's fate—a panel of eight men and eight women (four were alternate jurors), three black woman, one Asian woman, four white women, one black man, three Hispanic men, and four white men, including juror 1-1—the red-haired kid.

The jury was seated in the jury box and the remaining people not chosen were dismissed from the courtroom. "Will the jurors stand, face the clerk and raise your right hands . . . Administer the oath, Madam Clerk," Judge Quarter instructed.

The clerk swore in the jury—the legal start of the trial. Jason wrote on his legal pad:

4:15 jury sworn, double jeopardy attached.

"You may be seated," Quarter told the jury. "Mr. Wittingham, how long do you think your opening statement will take?"

Trevor stood and announced, "There is a lot of evidence establishing Mr. Barrera's guilt for all of the charges that I need to talk about in opening—"

"So, how long do you need? It's a simple question that requires a simple answer."

"Um, about two hours," Trevor answered, annoyed he couldn't say his full rehearsed answer to a question he knew was coming in front of the jury and media.

"Thank you, that's what I needed to know." Judge Quarter turned toward the jury. "I'm going to dismiss you a bit early again, but don't get used to it, we'll work until 5 p.m. starting tomorrow. Now, you have been selected on the jury, it is vital that you DO NOT do any outside research regarding this case—no TV news, newspapers, social media, *Google* searches, or the like. Stay off the internet! If I find out that any of you read any news stories about this case or *Facebook* comments, I will hold you in contempt and send you to jail . . . Any questions?"

The jury answered in unison, "No, Your Honor."

"Good night then. Be back at eight tomorrow morning outside the jury room." Judge Quarter waited until the jury left the courtroom. "Both sides get an hour for opening, which we will start promptly at 8:30. Mr. Noble?"

"Yes, Judge?" Jason began to stand.

"You can stay seated. Don't forget, I want proof of completion of the four-hour CLE tomorrow morning *before* we begin. Is that understood?"

"Yes." Jason sounded dejected. Inaya looked at him with compassion.

"Court dismissed." *BANG!*

Jason leaned into Antonio and asked, "Want to go over my opening and talk about who I think the government will call first back at my office?"

"Can't, I'm busy tonight. See you tomorrow morning." Antonio stood, turned around and walked toward Maria who was sitting behind the defense table in the second row.

Lisa Hoyt walked over to Jason. She was holding a stack of manila folders in both arms. She dropped them on the defense table—*Thud!* Jason snapped his head around from looking at Antonio leave the courtroom like he didn't have a care in the world. He looked at the stack of files then looked up at Lisa. "What's this?" Jason asked.

"*Jencks Act* material for tomorrow. You do know what *Jencks Act* material is? Right?"

"Uh, Uh, of course I-I-I d-d-do." Jason pulled the pile of material closer like he was expecting it.

"Great, see you tomorrow."

Jason counted fifteen manila folders. *What the hell was all this? Jencks Act? Shouldn't I have received this information before trial?* Jason packed his stuff and had to carry the additional folders under his arm because they wouldn't fit in his briefcase—*note to self, bring a bigger briefcase tomorrow.*

— 70 —

"Hey, stud. You called the judge an *asshole*. Good for you. You're on your way to becoming a legendary lawyer or disbarred—either is exciting," Jeannie Francis said with a big smile as she barged into Jason's office.

"How'd you know that?" Jason said from behind the stack of *Jencks Act* material now on his desk.

Jeannie Francis sat in front of Jason's desk. It was the only surface in the office that wasn't stacked with documents from Antonio's case.

"Please, have a seat . . . I've got nothing but time." The corners of Jason's mouth curled down as he pointed to the stacks of documents littered around his small office."

"Great, thanks. Don't mind if I do. This is so exciting to be involved in such a big case. I feel like I'm trying it with you. Practice your opening on me . . . please, please, please."

"First, let's focus on how you know I called the judge an *asshole* and second, do you know what the hell *Jencks Act* material is? Then we can get to my opening."

"Oh, it's all over the internet and the top story on every news station. Over five million views on *YouTube* alone. You're a superstar!" Jeannie Francis twisted her red hair in her fingers as she spoke.

"*YouTube*? There's a video?"

"No, just a split screen sketch of you and this Judge Quarter—he looks mean—with the audio behind it. I also saw it on the five, five-thirty, six, and six-thirty news. CNN, FOX and MSNBC are running it in the 'Breaking News' scroll, so exciting for you," her chubby face lifting in a wide smile.

Jason groaned loud and put his head in his hands.

"I recorded the Miami local news broadcast if you want to see it, but I really recorded it just to look at that gorgeous sketch artist/reporter, Inaya. Mm, Mm, Mm, I'd go gay just for her. . . and she's so talented, she drew you so handsome again like a staged photo. She made that Trevor look like a mean troll. She's got a serious crush on you."

Jason took his head out of his hands, blushed, and said, "She does not . . . stop it."

"Yeah right, you're so lucky you get to see her up close. The news also showed your statement after court: *No comment, but my client, Mr. Barrera is innocent of all charges.* It looked like you ran away fast after you said that—funny visual. What's all this?" Jeannie Francis changed the subject by pointing at the stack of folders on Jason's desk.

"Something called *Jencks Act* material. It seems to be written statements on these forms numbered '302' of potential government witnesses, but I can't figure out why I'm getting it after trial started. I feel like I should have received this stuff well before trial . . . I'll probably object to it tomorrow before opening."

"Oh, I wouldn't do that. *Jencks Act* material is what makes a federal trial a 'trial by ambush.'" Jeannie Francis grimaced at the thought. "I'm surprised Wittingham gave them to you today."

Jason looked at Jeannie Francis like she was crazy. "What do you mean *surprised I got them today*? When am I supposed to get them, after the witness testifies on direct? That can't be the law."

"That's exactly the law."

"No way that would comply with due process under the Constitution." Jason shook his head in disbelief.

"Look it up. I think it's . . . 18 U.S.C. § 3500—I can't help but remember obscure sections of law. I think it's why I graduated law school number two in my class—*summa cum laude*. I remember, this one time, in Con-law—"

"Can we get back to me and this *Jencks Act* stuff . . . please."

"Sure, whatever, but it's a good story. The government has to provide you with any statements of a prospective government witness in its possession *after* the witness testifies."

"How can I review the statements for impeachment purposes if I have to get up and cross the witness in real time—no way that darn Judge Quarter would give me a continuance for every witness until the next day." Jason squinted his eyes and furrowed his brow trying to figure out a way around this impossible dilemma.

Jeannie Frances reached across the desk and patted his arm. Cheer up, you got the information *before* they testify tomorrow—consider yourself lucky."

"Lucky, lucky! I'm in way over my head already! I was held in contempt on the *first* day in my *first* federal trial, I have a client who seems to hate me and wants nothing to do with his defense other than to repeatedly say the video is a 'fake' made by the government, I just got fifteen folders of important stuff on witnesses to review tonight, and . . . the cherry on top . . . I have to do a four-hour CLE, TONIGHT! So, forgive me if I don't feel lucky!" Jason banged his head on the desk a few times. "I wish I was still an assistant public *pretender*."

"Bam!" Jeannie Frances gleefully yelled as she smacked a piece of paper down on top of some other papers on his desk. Who's lucky now."

Jason lifted his head up, looked at her with bewilderment, and read the piece of paper. "OMG!" Jason got up from his chair, walked around his desk, stood over Jeannie Francis—she flinched a bit—and bent down and kissed her on the lips.

"Uh . . . sorry about that, but you're the best. You did the four-hour CLE for me . . . but, how did you know I had to do it?"

"That's okay, you're not that good of a kisser. I saw it on the news, so I did it waiting for sweet Inaya to come back on each half hour. I figured you had enough to do, and I wanted to help. My mother always told me to help nice people and you seem like nice people, Jason. Besides, you haven't thrown me out of your office yet like most people do."

Jason was now sitting on the edge of his desk. "That's so nice. Thank you from the bottom of my heart for helping me. If you want to help more, take some of these and go through them." Jason half turned to the stack of *Jencks Act* material—CRASH. "Shit, now it's going to take twice as long."

— 71—

"ALL RISE! THE HONORABLE JUDGE QUARTER PRESIDING!" Deputy Ruiz bellowed with a thick accent.

Judge Quarter took the bench. "You may be seated. Are the parties ready to proceed with opening statements."

"Absolutely, Your Honor," Trevor said, appearing completely rested and refreshed.

"Uh. Yea-Yes, Judge," Jason said, half standing, leaning on the table. His eyes were red and puffy. Antonio looked perfect with his constant neutral expression.

Judge Quarter turned to the jury and cautioned, "You are about to hear the opening statements of the parties. It is their chance to tell you what to expect from each side—it is their initial arguments. However, what the lawyers say is not evidence and you should not treat it as such. You may proceed, Mr. Wittingham."

Trevor stood and walked over to the jury box without any notes. "May it please the court . . . good morning, ladies and gentlemen of the jury. First, let me thank you for the time you have already put into this very important case and the time you are going to put in over the next few weeks. My name is Trevor Wittingham and I have the pleasure of representing the people of the United States of America, which are you people—"

Jason stood fast, "Objection, golden rule violation. Move to strike from the record."

Judge Quarter, half-listening, said, "Sustained, Mr. Wittingham don't ask the jury to put themselves in the shoes of your client. You may continue."

Wow, maybe this thing is turning around, I won an objection, Jason thought, gaining a bit of confidence.

Trevor didn't miss a beat as he slowly moved back and forth in front of the jury in his navy-blue suit and red tie with horizontal stripes, making sure he turned occasionally toward the sketch artists and reporters in the back of the courtroom. He continued with his opening for every bit of the hour he was given. He outlined how he would prove Antonio was the scum of the earth and a guilty verdict would be easy for the jury to decide, especially after they saw and heard from Antonio himself on a video directing his men to traffic in young children so they could "earn more money" for him. Trevor paused, crocodile tears forming in his eyes, and described how Antonio ordered the murder of a little boy and his grandmother after they were held captive on a ship for weeks in deplorable conditions "not fit for a rat." Trevor showed the jury a *PowerPoint* slide through the Elmo depicting a South Florida mob family tree with Antonio at the top—the background of the slide showed machine guns, drugs, and money that weren't even a part of the case. Former New York City Mayor and U.S. Attorney Rudolph Giuliani was famous for prejudicing the potential jury pool at press conferences announcing mob arrests by speaking behind a table full of guns, drugs, and money—it was discovered that the stuff was staged and not a part of the case Giuliani was announcing.

"Objection! That slide depicts facts not in evidence. The guns and drugs are not from this case." Jason remembered some caselaw cited on this issue in an article that he recently read in the New York Law School Law Review: *TechnoJury: Techniques in Verbal and Visual Persuasion*—since the advent of Microsoft's *PowerPoint,* prosecutors were creating extremely prejudicial slides to go with their arguments.

Judge Quarter snapped his head up from whatever he was reading, looked at Jason, and said without missing a beat, "Overruled." Then he turned to the jury. "Remember ladies and gentlemen, opening statement is not evidence it is merely a lawyer's argument, which is like hot air, it leaves a bad smell in the air." The juror's laughed, welcoming the break in the heavy tension that always hung in the air during a criminal trial. "And, Mr. Noble, I'm holding you in contempt of—"

Jason jumped up, "For objecting?"

"For making a *speaking* objecting when I clearly informed you at the beginning of trial that I do not allow speaking objections . . . and for interrupting me just now."

Jason, already resigned to the fact that he wasn't going to get any love from Quarter on any legal rulings, couldn't believe he was being held in contempt for objecting. *This must be some courthouse record, a lawyer held in contempt twice before the first witness was even called.* He sat and slumped down in his chair, clearly recognizing the futility of arguing and he might as well be comfortable sitting when he's sentenced to jail for the first time in his life, which he fully expected were going to be the next words out of Judge Quarter's mouth.

"I am going to sentence you to complete an eight-hour CLE on professionalism before the start of court tomorrow. Maybe you'll get it after eight hours. You may continue Mr. Wittingham."

Trevor, pointing to each picture on the screen with a laser pointer, methodically described each person's role in the "criminal enterprise" and the heinous crimes against humanity they committed. "Like a marching band, all of these men worked in perfect unison and at the sole direction of their conductor, who in this case, the evidence will clearly show, is that man." Trevor turned from the jury, his face tightened into a crinkle, and pointed at Antonio—the jurors' eyes followed like they were on a string, "Antonio Barrera . . . I respectfully ask you, ladies and gentlemen, to join me in protecting the children of America . . . really the world . . . and find Antonio Barrera GUILTY on all counts. You, I mean, society will sleep better at night knowing the Defendant, Antonio Barrera is off the street . . . thank you."

"Objection, Your Honor, golden rule violation."

"Sustained. Watch yourself Mr. Wittingham, don't put the jury in the shoes of your client. Mr. Noble, you may proceed," Judge Quarter instructed.

After listening to Trevor's opening, any little bit of confidence Jason had in his defense was gone. He slowly stood, grabbed his yellow legal pad, and walked to the jury box. *You got this, no need to be nervous,* he nervously thought. He could already feel the sweat building on his forehead and the back of his neck.

"G-G-G-G—*deep breath*—Good Morning, ladies and gentlemen, on b-b-b-behalf—*deep breath*—of myself and my innocent client Mr. Antonio Barrera, we thank you for taking the time to listen to us." Jason's mind suddenly went blank. He looked down at his legal paid, got tunnel vision, and all he could focus on were the words NOT GUILTY. He swallowed hard, his throat was dry and tight. He looked at the jury . . . the silence and his stare were becoming uncomfortable—the sweat was now at maximum flow down his forehead and the back of his neck . . . "G—Not Guilty. Antonio Not Guilty. Um, thank you." He sat down, blobs of sweat dripped on his legal paid as he stared at it, refusing to make eye contact with anyone, including his client. The jury exchanged confused looks, some clearly pitied Antonio for his bad choice in lawyers, which was evident already.

Trevor leaned over to Herb and whispered with a smile, "This is going to be easy."

"Mr. Wittingham, call your first witness," Judge Quarter ordered.

— 72 —

THE GOVERNMENT'S CASE proceeded with slow efficiency. Trevor started out by calling twelve special agents and one security guard: Eight special agents from the FBI's organized crime unit; two special agents with the DEA; two IRS agents; and William Jefferson, a security guard at Phillips Point. Trevor may not have much jury appeal, but he knew how to organize and present a devastating case, one block at a time.

Jackson Reed testified for two days about Antonio's crime family based on his interviews of Alphonso "the Whale". Jason objected, "hearsay", but he was quickly overruled. Judge Quarter held that Jackson's testimony was an exception to the hearsay rule because it explained his *state of mind* during the investigation. "Bullshit," Jason mumbled to himself as he sat down after objecting.

"You say something, Mr. Noble?" Judge Quarter asked.

"No Judge."

"Well, if you did say something, it would be the most talking you've done thus far. You might want to consider turning your mumbles into actual questions and cross examine a few of the government's witnesses. You may proceed Mr. Wittingham."

IRS agent Machie Charles spent twelve hours methodically explaining an intricate web of global financial transactions that he believed was how Antonino and his crime family laundered their money—Machie extrapolated that Antonio's crime family made over one trillion dollars in the past fifteen years since 2000. Judge Quarter involuntarily whistled when Machie said "one trillion dollars". While all paths of the financial transactions led to Antonio's front door, Machie could not directly push them through his front door. However, that did not stop Trevor from making that leap. Machie finished his testimony by saying, "It's clear to me, based on my extensive training and experience, that all of the money I traced was for the benefit of Antonio Barrera and the Bonanno, Colombo, Gambino, Genovese, and Luchesse Mafia crime families."

"Objection! Speculation!"

"Overruled," Judge Quarter was on autopilot at this point.

After the agents finished testifying, Trevor called William Jefferson, who, from the look on his face as he walked to the witness stand, had no idea why he was being called to testify in a mob trial.

Trevor began, "Please state your name and where you are employed."

"Um, hello. My name is William Thomas Jefferson." William looked straight at Trevor, too nervous to look anywhere else. "I am the nine to five doorman at Phillips Point. No one can enter during the day without passing by me. I know everyone that comes in and out. Been workin' there twenty-five years." Phillips Point was the cornerstone office building in downtown West Palm Beach at 777 South Flagler Drive. Its pink hued façade glistened magnificently in the rising sun.

"Thank you, Mr. Jefferson. You—" Trevor started to say.

"But I ain't never seen no one in this court room. Not sure why I'm here."

Trevor and Jason both smiled wide. "I'm counting on that Mr. Jefferson." Trevor responded. Trevor only kept Mr. Jefferson on the stand for roughly five minutes. He merely established that Mr. Jefferson has "never seen Antonio Barrera enter Phillips Point and go to the Penthouse office."

Alright, I may gain a point here! Mr. Jefferson could not identify my client! So, whatever heinous crimes occurred out of the penthouse office at Phillips Point, can't be directly connected to Antonio. All Jason did on cross examination was solidify that Mr. Jefferson never saw Antonio Barrera enter Phillips Point. Jason would later learn through Trevor's closing argument that he wished Antonio had gone to Phillips Point every day. On his tax returns, which were buried in the hundreds of thousands of pages of documents, Trevor produced in discovery that Jason had no time to look at before trial, Antonio listed the Penthouse at Phillips Point as the office where he ran his internet empire, which was how he showed legitimate income. He deducted expenses on his tax return such as a driver and daily parking at Phillips Point. According to the deductions on his return, Antonio had a very expensive lunch every day at Morton's Steakhouse located in Phillips Point.

Trevor was done setting the table, it was now time to serve the meal.

— 73 —

IN EVERY TRIAL, a lawyer knows the moment he's either won or lost. Jason experienced that moment for the third time in trial already—hope of a *not guilty* was disappearing quicker than spit in the ocean. *This will probably be the fastest GAC (guilty on all counts) of all time*, he thought, as he wrote Day fifteen in red ink on his yellow legal pad.

The first moment came yesterday after Trevor put on a ten-year-old Chinese girl, Li Jing, who was brought into the U.S. illegally with her twelve-year-old brother, Zhang Wei, by her *Nainai* (grandma) with twenty-seven other Chinese Nationals in a shipping container by a man they called Alphonso "the Whale". She sat on the witness stand and told the jury, through an interpreter, about her horrific trip to America—her tiny body swallowed by the adult-sized chair. Her voice was surprisingly strong as she recounted her trip without a hint of emotion. Li Jing's black eyes appeared dead from what they've witnessed in her short time on Earth—no signs of childhood innocence and wonderment left. Her account did not end with a glorious citing of the Statute of Liberty from a ship's bow at dawn's early light. Her *Nainai* paid a man one hundred and forty thousand *yuan* ($20,000) for the three of them and was tricked into thinking that they were coming to America for a better life; instead, they were beaten, given no or rotten food, and forced into slave labor, prostitution, or both. "The Whale man sell me to group of Spanish men who make me do lot of sex on camera." An FBI computer analyst would testify later in trial that he discovered forty videos on the Dark Web depicting acts of a "sexual and sadomasochistic nature involving oral, vaginal, and anal penetration of Li Jing. Jason wisely did not argue to force Trevor to play the videos as "best evidence".

Li Jing described how her ten-year-old brother, Zhang Wei "died on trip from no food, no water, infection." How her seventy-five-year-old grandmother was "shot in head by fat man they call 'Whale.'" She ended her testimony by recounting how the fat man named "the Whale" and four other men raped her for hours at a bowling alley later in the day . . . then they made her mop the floors.

There was not a dry eye in the courtroom after Li Jing was finished telling her story. Jason was smart enough to realize that any cross of this sweet, innocent child would only make it worse for him and his client, so he asked the first question that popped into his head: "Have you ever seen the man sitting next to me, Antonio Barrera, before today in this courtroom?" Jason actually wasn't sure what her answer would be, but he needed to ask her something, she was a main witness for the government, so he took a chance—breaking the first rule of cross examination: *don't ask a question you don't know the answer to!*

Li Jing turned and stared at Antonio, her emotion not changing . . . "*Meiyou* (no)."

— 74 —

THE SECOND MOMENT Jason knew all hope was lost in trial was when Trevor played recordings of the wire Alphonso "the Whale" Tomisini wore for two years—the last recording was from the day he disappeared.

"Objection!" Jason shouted.

"Overruled."

"May we approach?" Jason asked.

Judged Quarter stared at Jason then finally said, "You may approach, but you better have something extremely important to tell me."

Jason, Trevor, and Herb approached the bench; Judge Quarter put on the white noise. "Go ahead Mr. Noble."

Jason plopped his evidence book on the bench and opened it to a pre-marked page.

Quarter raised his eyebrows. "Remove that book from my bench immediately."

Jason knew he had to speak fast, "But Judge, there are four cases right on point that support my position." Jason pointed to the middle of the evidence book that was still on the bench. "Allowing these recordings is a clear violation of my client's Sixth Amendment Constitutional right to confront the witnesses against him. Unless this Alphonso "the Whale" guy walks or swims into this courtroom, Mr. Barrera can't *confront* him, so the recordings must be excluded."

Quarter looked like he was about to blow a gasket. He turned off the white noise. Trevor couldn't suppress his smile. Quarter turned toward the jury. Please go into the jury room." The jury got up and did as instructed. Quarter then told Jason, Trevor, and Herb, "Go back to your seats."

Antonio leaned over to Jason after he sat down and asked, "What did you do to piss off the Judge this time?"

"Fight for your rights."

"Mr. Noble, the rules of evidence are what *I* say they are in this courtroom, is that understood?"

The benefits of a lifetime appointment, Jason thought. "Yes, Judge," Jason responded, numb to continually losing each objection at this point. "I just wanted to make my record for the appellate court."

"Your objection is overruled. I'm also holding you in contempt of court again."

"For what?"

"For not removing your evidence book from my bench after I instructed you to. Maybe after a twelve-hour CLE course on professionalism you will understand how to act in my courtroom, since the four and eight hour courses didn't get through to you."

I sure hope this is on the news and Jeannie Francis is watching, Jason thought.

"Please bring the jury back in." After the jury came back, Quarter said, "You may proceed Mr. Whittingham."

Li Jing's entire trip on the shipping freighter plus a whole lot more damaging information about *La Famiglia* was captured on the wire: For three days Alphonso is bitching about how he had to kick so much money upstairs to "his boss, Antonio Barrera. . . ." How he wouldn't even sell these "dirty, oriental bastards if he didn't have to give Antonio so much money, fuhgeddaboudit. . . ." Trevor strategically ended the highly compressed recordings right after *Nainai* is shot and killed. Li Jing's wails hung in the courtroom air, swirling around in everyone's head, no one was able to move a muscle for a full twenty seconds. . . .

Antonio sat expressionless throughout all the testimony. *He was probably a great poker player,* Jason thought when he looked at him at various times in the trial to see his reaction.

— 75 —

THE THIRD MOMENT: Government Exhibit One, the Video. Trevor saved it for last—he "introduced" it into evidence on the first day of trial through Jackson Reed for "identification" purposes only, now he was "publishing" it to the jury—they were all leaning forward staring at Antonio on their monitors.

You and your crews need to earn more . . . this is not a forty-hour-a-week job. You should be earning twenty-four, seven. There's plenty of businesses you can get into to earn more for the family. However, do that human trafficking shit or I will kill you where you stand . . . Now! Get out there and Earn! Antonio commanded his Capos like some depraved general, banging on a metal table, which caused some on the jury to flinch.

"This is such bullshit," Antonio whispered into Jason's ear. It was the first time all trial he showed any emotion.

After the video was finished and the lights in the courtroom came back on, all sixteen jurors glared at Antonio like they wanted to hang him right there in the courtroom. They then glared at Jason—*how could you defend such a horrible person,* he knew they were thinking.

Jason knew the video was the nail in the proverbial coffin. Yet, something nagged at him, something about the video he couldn't quite place. He'd watched it a hundred times by now but watching it in open court made him hear it differently. *It made no sense for Antonio to say, "However".*

— 76 —

TREVOR STOOD AND announced in jubilant fashion, "The government rests, Your Honor. As he scanned the jury, he thought to himself, *I saved the best for last. If these God-fearing folks could hang Antonio and his lawyer right now in the middle of the courtroom, they would without hesitation. Job well done, again . . . governor's mansion here I come.*

"Okay, It's 4:45 p.m., ladies and gentleman of the jury, I'm going to do you all a favor and let you go early today. Since Monday is the Martin Luther King holiday, you won't come back until Tuesday at 8 a.m. Remember, DO NOT look at the newspaper, local or national TV news, *Google* search, *Facebook*, or whatever or I will throw you in jail. Is that understood?"

"Yes," the sixteen jurors answered in unison like they did every day during the trial.

"Any questions?"

"No, Your Honor," they answered again in unison.

"You are dismissed. Enjoy the holiday weekend and take some time to celebrate the life of a remarkable man." The jury filed out of the courtroom.

Judge Quarter turned to the defense and government and informed, "We'll begin with the defense case on Tuesday morning. How long do you think it will take, Mr. Noble?"

What defense case? Jason thought. He was sitting in his chair too exhausted and beaten down by Trevor to stand. He blurted out the first number that popped into his head. "Five days."

Jason suddenly stood up. "Excuse me, Your Honor, when can I argue for a judgment of acquittal?" Jason knew the motion had a snowballs chance in hell to succeed—in state and federal court the denial rate of defense judgment of acquittal motions is ninety-nine percent, but he had to at least go through the motions.

"Denied. Anything else, Mr. Noble?"

"No." Jason responded as he sat back down.

"Court's adjourned." BANG!

77

JASON GRABBED HIS briefcase, backpack, and sunglasses. He was heading out of town for the holiday weekend in search of some help. *'However'... why does Antonio say that? It sounds weird ... out of place somehow ... but Peter spent three-hundred-grand having the best in the business check it out ... It has to be authentic, right? ... Besides, all the other evidence basically corroborates what my client says in that twelve seconds ... Zach will be able to help.* "Come'on, Caesar, time for a road trip to Key West (a/k/a *The Conch Republic*). We're going to see your best bud." Caesar cocked his head, a wide bulldog grin formed on his wrinkled face, slobber immediately started to flow like Niagara Falls. He half jumped, half fell off the couch and bounded over to Jason.

Jason buckled Caesar into the front seat, got in, and pushed the *Start* button on his Audi TT—a graduation gift to himself that he purchased when he thought he'd be making a lot more money as a lawyer. He looked at Caesar as the engine revved to life. "Top up or down?" Caesar continued to stare straight ahead, tongue wagging like he just ran a marathon, drool dripping on the beach towel under him. "*Up* it is, and I'll put the A/C on high for you, lil'buddy."

The stress tornado always present inside of Jason started to slightly slow down as he drove South on U.S. Highway 1 (a/k/a Overseas Highway), a two-lane road for 160 miles through the Keys—one of the most scenic drives in America. The crystal-clear water on either side of the highway was almost close enough to reach out the window and touch.

Jason made a right at the bottom of the Cow Key Bridge that connected Stock Island to Key West. Like a GPS knowing they were almost at their destination, Caesar perked up. Jason patted his head. "About an hour until sunset ... we have plenty of time to check in, grab a beer, and take a stroll to Sunset Pier." A Key West sunset was a peak into heaven on earth.

Jason curved around at Mallory Square, a live band was filling the air with Jimmy Buffet. The Cat Man, a Key West fixture, was extolling the greatness of his two cats—Puff-Puff and Smoke, that just jumped through rings of fire to a mesmerized and drunk throng of tourists.

Jason pulled into a parking spot at the Pier House Resort and Spa at the Northern end of Duval Street. It was a three-story, beige and white stucco building that blended in seamlessly to its tropical surroundings. It is one of the historic hotels on Key West with the most iconic bar not named Sloppy Joe's—The Chart Room, where Truman Capote penned his final novel and Jimmy Buffet and Bob Marley played their first gigs.

"Thank you," Jason said to the doorman. He subtly scanned the lobby for goons in suits—only hotel clerks, bellhops, and a sun-drenched couple in parrot head t-shirts, shorts and flipflops. "Come on, Caesar. Let's get you to the room so you can take your fifth nap of the day."

The lobby was bright and simple, with an understated seaside motif.

"Good afternoon, Sir. Welcome to Key West—the island of magnificent sunsets."

"Hi. I'm checking in."

"Name, Sir?"

"Jason Noble."

The clerk typed his name into a computer. "Oh, Mr. Noble, you're booked for two nights in our best suite. The balance paid in full and anything on the grounds are free for you as a VIP guest. Would you like something refreshing to drink?"

"Uh. I am? It is? . . . I mean, right. No thank you on the drink. Although Caesar here," Jason said pointing down at his feet where Caesar was already splayed out sleeping, "could use some water. *Thank you, Zac, for the free accommodations. You're the man.*

"Stewart." The Jamaican clerk summoned, in her island accent that evoked relaxation, "Get Caesar some water and take Mr. Noble's bag to the Ernest Hemingway Suite."

Jason and Caesar walked through the property grounds: stone pathways meandering through all types of palm trees, Key West mango trees, which is the perfect fruit, a rainbow of bougainvillea, and dozens of other tropical fauna. They passed the turtle pond then the pathway opened up to the bar, pool, and private beach area. "Buddy, take a look at THAT." Jason bent down and gently turned Caesar's head to a thin, tanned blonde sitting on the beach with a poodle. Caesar looked at the beach. "Come on buddy, live a little bit. Whether that cute poodle is a boy or girl doesn't really matter, you're in Key West."

Jason opened the door to the Hemingway Suite. *You outdid yourself this time Zac.* A wide hallway led to a spacious sitting area. It was elegantly appointed with high-end design elements.

On a table was a folded note and two rectangular blue velvet boxes, the size of a hardcover book with Jason written on one and Caesar on the other in gold, embossed lettering. Jason opened the note:

> Jason, my old-friend, glad you made it. Enjoy your stay, everything is on me this weekend. Come to the Bull & Whistle at exactly 8:30. Come up to The Garden of Eden on the third floor at 8:30 and KEEP YOUR CLOTHES ON :). You and Caesar go relax by the beach and enjoy the gifts I left. Tell my lil'buddy I can't wait to see him and scratch his belly!
> Your most grateful client,
> Z.

Jason put the note down on the desk and checked his watch: *3:00 P.M.* He opened the blue velvet box for Caesar and smiled—it was full of an assortment of dog treats. "Come here, your best bud got you a present." Caesar was about to jump on the expensive-looking couch; he quickly turned his head and waddled over to Jason who was on one knee holding out a couple of treats.

Jason stood back up and opened his box: two Cohibas, two joints, and a bottle of Havana Club Maximo Rum. Jason's smile now engulfed his entire face. The stress tornado of the trial was still there, but it was temporarily out-to-lunch. He took one of the joints and put it in his shirt pocket. He walked over to an antique rolltop desk. Across the top of the desk, between two bookends that were shaped like Ernest Hemingway busts, were some of Hemingway's greatest novels: *The Old Man and the Sea, For Whom the Bell Tolls, A Farewell to Arms,* and *The Garden of Eden.* Jason unclasped his briefcase and took out his laptop and the DVD marked *Government Exhibit 1.*

He walked across the expansive living area of the suite to the floor to ceiling double set of French doors, which were beset by ceiling-to-floor windows, making up the rest of the outer wall of the suite. Jason opened both doors and stepped onto the white tile balcony. To the right was a Jacuzzi made of porcelain with relief etchings of different types of palm trees on its surface. To the left were four low chairs around a table. Two bamboo-framed lounge chairs with white cushions and white umbrella rounded out the patio furniture. Jason's eyes transfixed on the real star of the suite—the 180-degree view of the clear, blue water of the Gulf of Mexico.

The stress-tornado created by the *David & Goliath Trial,* as some in the media dubbed it, unexpectedly reared its head and Jason's stomach tightened as he broke from his stare. *David was getting crushed under Goliath's foot, about to tap out,* he depressingly thought. He walked over to one of the lounge chairs and plopped down. *The video? . . . I hope Zac can help me.* He leaned back in the lounge chair and opened his laptop. He slid *Government Exhibit 1* into the DVD/CD slot. *We're almost at the end of trial—Antonio has done everything to make me defend him with my hands tied behind my back for some unknown reason,* Jason thought. *But with this video, he's adamant?* "I didn't say that. This is bullshit, those bastards at the FBI doctored this video," he routinely exclaimed every time the video came up. "I told my guys *NOT* to do that shit, didn't need to."

Trial prep meetings, when Antonio decided to show up, consisted mostly of Jason trying to convince Antonio that, even though he didn't face the death penalty, facing *life* in prison was just as serious and he needed to help Jason prepare. *He made me waste so much damn time on misinformation.* A dialogue box popped up on the screen: *Play with Windows Media Player.* Jason clicked *OK.* . . . He looked up from the screen; a few sailboats were now in his view—their colorful sails adding to the uber-relaxing view. The sun's rays glistened like diamonds on the calm water. Jason closed the laptop. "Hey, Caesar?" Jason yelled back through the open French doors. "I agree with you; it's time to relax." Jason reached into his shirt pocket and pulled out the joint.

78

TREVOR PROPPED HIS feet up, barely reaching the edge of his desk, and his feet fell heavily to the ground. Embarrassed, head down, he murmured, "Stupid chair." Herb, Tim, Jackson, and Lisa were sitting across from him, each suppressing a smirk. He tried again—this time his feet hit their mark. "Is it too early to smoke a victory cigar?"

"It ain't over yet," Jackson cautioned in his baritone voice, which made his warning sound ominous.

"I agree with Trevor, we should get some victory cigars . . . Trevor's got this in the bag," Tim "Butt-Kisser" Barnes cheerily chimed in. The trial team started calling him that after the first meeting.

Spoken by a guy who never tried a case, Lisa thought, but she didn't have the energy to correct these two fools. "Regardless," she said, "let's prepare for the defense case."

Trevor ignored her. He could taste victory and the free national press coverage he was about to get. . . . *governor's mansion here I come . . . I should probably get the address of the governor's mansion, so I can have my mail forwarded.*

Herb broke the silence. "I must admit, we seem to have the defense on the run without any chance of getting back into this thing. I don't know why Antonio hired that ridiculously inexperienced—"

"And *untested*," Jackson added.

"—lawyer, Jason Noble . . . it's making this too easy. On the video alone, he didn't even do a cross of our tech expert." Herb shrugged his shoulders as he finished.

"He's so ineffective," Tim absently offered.

"It even looks like Antonio is against Noble, *his own lawyer*, the way they interact," Lisa offered. "It's like Antonio intentionally hired him to have an . . . *ineffective counsel* claim for the appeal knowing the evidence was overwhelmingly against him." She raised her head as she spoke, eyes growing wide like a lightbulb just went off inside her head. They all locked eyes except for Trevor, who was still staring off into space daydreaming of his next job.

"Bingo," Jackson said, cracking a slight smile at Lisa.

Herb added, "That's why he fired Peter."

"Or maybe, just maybe, Peter still got paid his huge fee because this was his plan to protect his amazing win/loss record and give his client a legitimate issue on appeal," Lisa added, rounding out the theory.

"Ineffective? Appeal? What?" Trevor said, snapping back to reality. He dropped his feet off the desk and leaned forward. "No way that Boble kid—"

"It's 'Noble,'" Jackson corrected.

"Whatever," Trevor said, dismissively waving his hand. "The kid has a heartbeat, hasn't fallen asleep once, and Quarter asked Antonio several times: 'Is Jason *Noble* your lawyer of choice?' and Antonio said 'yes' every time. There is no way the Eleventh Circuit Court of Appeals will find him 'ineffective'. It's above your pay grades to know that." Trevor spoke with a smug tone as he looked directly at Lisa and Jackson who were sitting next to each other. *Who cares anyway,* he thought, *I'll be in the governor's mansion by the time the case comes back on appeal.*

"Besides, I disagree with all of you. I think Jason has been a very worthy adversary thus far. It's my prowess as a trial attorney that is making this victory a foregone conclusion. . . . Now, I'm going to prepare for closing argument. Get out."

"Closing argument?" Lisa questioned. "What about the anticipated defense case."

"I'm not too concerned. I will handle any defense witnesses. You guys don't need to worry about that. I hope Antonio takes the stand." Trevor rubbed his hands together. "Jason's got nothing. This case is over. Slam dunk. BOOM!" Trevor crumpled up a piece of paper and shot it into the trash can that was about six feet away . . . it missed.

JASON LEFT THE Pier House for the short walk down bustling Duval Street to The Bull & Whistle. *Hope I'm not late*, he thought, as he looked at the time on his iPhone, 8:25. Jason was dressed in Key West black tie: tan shorts, without cargo pockets; a short sleeve light blue, button-down Tommy Bahama shirt with a palm tree print, as opposed to a tank top; and boat shoes instead of flip flops.

To Jason's right was a marina and Sunset Pier. To his left was the North mouth of Duval Street. Jason headed to the left passing the world-famous Sloppy Joe's—its white stucco and brick building with a large red neon sign beckoning to all the tourists. As Jason walked by on the opposite side of the street, he noticed a temporary sign: Twentieth Annual Running of the Hemmingways. A sea of Hemingway look-alikes holding glasses, no doubt filled with rum—Hemmingway's favorite drink, milled about a mock starting line. An announcer said, "If you fall, you're out, and, most importantly, if you spill your drink, you're definitely OUT!" The crowd cheered. "Now let's toast to *The Old Man and The Sea*". Jason smiled and continued on down Duval Street.
. . .

He passed t-shirt shops, bars, restaurants, and ice cream shops. The sounds of live music from each bar mixed in the air—crooner after crooner belting out summer hits from an acoustic guitar. He stopped in front of The Bull & Whistle Bar, which occupied prime real estate on the corner of Duval and Caroline Streets. It was open air all the way around and had a biker-bar look on the first floor. It was packed to capacity with people spilling onto Duval Street.

The first floor was "The Bull". Every inch of the walls had painted murals of 1960s Key West and Caribbean life: a pink Cadillac with JFK,

Castro, and Khrushchev, a Spanish Galleon, Jose Marti, couples kissing on the beach, people dancing, and the like. The second floor was "The Whistle", a sports bar with a wraparound balcony—great for people watching.

The roof was "The Garden of Eden" where clothing was optional.

Jason looked at his phone, 8:34. "Shit," Jason said. The bouncer, sitting on a stool at the foot of a staircase, looked at him. Jason pointed to his phone. "I'm late." He walked over to the bouncer, who looked annoyed that he was interrupted watching the show. "Going to the Garden of Eden." He attempted to step on the first step.

The bouncer stood up and blocked his path. "Five-hundred-dollar cover, cash only."

Jason looked stunned; he tapped his short's pockets like he was checking for the five hundred, which he definitely didn't have in cash. "Uh, uh . . . I'm here to see Zac. My name's Jason Noble . . . maybe I'm on some list where the cover is waived."

The bouncer looked Jason up and down, looked at something on his phone, then back to Jason. "Go on up." He put a red wrist band around Jason's left wrist and pointed up the stairs with a hitchhiker thumb.

"Thanks," Jason said then walked up the dark, narrow staircase. He passed right by The Whistle Bar and up a second flight of stairs, although this time, the two bouncers let him right through the glass door, which made a sucking sound when one of the bouncers opened it. Jason stopped in the doorway and glanced around the doorframe; it had tiny blue lasers emitting all the way around. *Zac . . . what are you into that you need this type of security?* The door automatically vacuum sealed shut after he walked through.

Jason hesitantly took a step forward into the surprisingly large foyer, about twenty by twenty. The area was pitch black, the only light came from an extra wide staircase across from Jason—the stairs had a bright strobe-light effect that were pulsating in a heartbeat pattern. The foyer was dead silent. When Jason's eyes adjusted, he could see a bright arrow pointing to the stairway. As he got closer to the stairs, he noticed that hands and bodies seemed to be pressing against a white skin that made up the walls on either side of the stairway. *You've outdone yourself, Zac.* Jason cautiously began his ascent. . . .

Jason could here EDM pulsating from speakers somewhere behind the walls that somehow did not escape into the foyer. The hands, faces, and bodies that tried to push though the white skin, which was gauze like when up close, brushed Jason as he ascended—he tried to stay in the middle. Silhouettes of naked men and women imprinted on the gauze like walls as the strobe light blinked.

Jason stopped at the top of the stairs and took in the scene. "This really is a *Garden of Eden*," he said aloud to no one in particular.

"Must be your first time . . . trust me, it gets better as the night goes on," a petit brunette in a turquoise thong and bra said. "You're cute . . . maybe I'll see you later." She winked then disappeared into the crowd.

On Jason's right was a bar with about ten stools—the bar was made of a clear, plexi-glass like material, he could see right through the bar to the man and woman bartenders in nothing but their birthday suits. At various points around the rooftop were four private alcoves shielded by tropical plants with bamboo furniture. A DJ was in the corner to the left with only headphones on. The center of the rooftop had a checkered tile floor that lit up like the one in *Saturday Night Fever*. Across from the entrance, on the far side of the dance floor, stood a small structure that looked like a room, but it appeared to have no doors or windows and was made of a mirrored glass. The light from the full moon mixed with the pulsating lights to wash the rooftop in a seductive glow. There were about fifty nude and almost-nude people enjoying themselves. Jason didn't want to stare so he looked down at his feet a lot. Besides, the fantasy of what the girls would look like at a nude bar was very different from the reality. *A lot of these people should have kept their clothes on*, Jason thought, as he looked at a woman and man dancing who clearly didn't miss too many meals.

Jason felt his wrist vibrate. He looked down. His wristband lit up with digital words: walk across the dance floor to the mirror room.

As Jason reached the room, one of the mirrors slid open. "Not early, not late, on-time like a computer—why is that so hard for humans to grasp!" Zac said, tapping his watch.

"I know, buddy, it's a cruel world we live in." Jason reached out and embraced Zac, but quickly backed off. "Sorry, I forgot . . . germs."

"I guess you can come in. You're free of all viruses and bugs, man-made and organic. You were scanned and cleaned on your way up the stairs. What do you think my people behind "The Forbidden Wall of Sin" were doing?" Zac winked and cracked a smile.

Jason cautiously stepped into the room, fully expecting some type of laser scan to engulf his body. The mirror wall automatically closed.

Zac was a small man—maybe a hundred twenty pounds soaking wet. He wore thick black glasses and had shaggy blonde hair that peak-ed through his hoodie. Patchwork scruff on his face rounded out his look. "What do you think of this hoodie? It's a custom-made *Armani*." Zac opened the hoodie and did a little twirl like he was on a runway at NY fashion week. "It's in honor of Cuba; Castro used to have Armani make him military uniforms."

"Looks great. It's been a long time, how are you doing?"

"Never better. I only have warrants in five countries, only one drug cartel wants me dead, and the U.S. Government has me on the "no-fly" list and probably a few *lists* I don't know about. Oh, yeah and I have a warrant in Idaho. Can you take care of that for me? No, wait, you're not a lawyer in Idaho, so forget it." Zac jumped all over the place and was prone to answer his own questions. He was the product of the ADHD computer generation.

"I'll see what I can do. Where can I get a drink?"

Zac said into his watch. "Tina, get me two Hemmingway specials from my private stock."

Jason looked around the sparse room except for a round metal ta-ble with a solid cylindrical base and three chairs in the center. On the table was a wireless keyboard that looked nothing like Jason had ever seen before, it was clear and had no keys just a flat glossy surface. The office was built of one-way glass all around including the floor and ceiling. "Interesting place for an office. And what a view—three hundred sixty-degree view around Key West . . . and naked people. I look at a rusty parking garage from my office." Jason slumped his shoulders and looked down at the thought.

"Let's have a seat and enjoy some rum." Jason was stunned to see two crystal rocks glasses with rum on a silver tray in the middle of the table.

"Where'd they come from? I didn't see anyone come in?"

"Magic. Poof!" Zac waived his fingers over the glasses for effect. "I built this place to see everything. A man in my business can't be too careful. I saw you when you left the Pier House, followed you all the way here. See that green band on your arm, lets me track you and jam any electronic devices you have. The naked part makes it more likely I'll spot someone trying to kill me—nowhere to tuck a gun if you aren't wearing any clothes." Zac took a sip of rum then continued. "Plus, sometimes I enjoy looking at the female form . . . but not tonight." Zac looked out on the dance floor, which had two people grinding—they looked like two bowls of Jello colliding.

Jason looked at Zac, one eyebrow raised, and said, "What if there's a fire or some assassin hides a gun in his ass and busts through the glass? What are you going to do then—you've always prided yourself on creating the perfect system every time you *hack*. . . . Sorry to say, pal, but I think you failed to create the perfect system for your own protection." Jason smiled as if he had just cured cancer, picked up his rum, and took a triumphant sip.

Zac covered his mouth, feigning defeat. He even seemed to retreat into his hoodie a little bit. "Do you mind," Zac handed Jason his glass of rum, a sly smile forming at the corners of his mouth. He moved the silver tray from the round table and touched the silver keyboard thing. "*Voilà.*" Zac swept his hand over the now open center of the table. A rush of air shot up as a platform filled in the black void. "I had it installed as a dumb waiter, that's where the rum came from, but it doubles as an escape route to the second and ground floor. Why do you think I stay so skinny." He opened his hoodie and patted his stomach.

"Cheers," Jason said, raising his glass to toast. "You sure think of everything." They clinked their glasses.

"Now, why does the best lawyer in the world need to see me so badly?"

"Yeah right." Jason shrugged. "I'm getting my ass kicked in this trial. I'm lucky I can find the courthouse each day. This case has really exposed my inexperience for the whole world to see." Jason leaned back, looked up at the moon, and sighed. He looked back at Zac, picked up his glass, "And my damn client is a nightmare." He drained the rum, caught an ice cube between his teeth, and chomped on it.

"I don't know about all that garbage output you just spewed, but, to me, you're the best. I owe you my life, buddy. The way you protected me when we were growing up in that concentration camp New York City called a 'group home.'" Zac looked at Jason with admiration.

"I was just lucky I had fast hands and a strong chin for a skinny kid."

"The way you took care of that little problem I had in North Florida when I changed the election results of that mayor's race and made a black guy win even though everyone voted for that redneck Chuck 'White' Powers."

"I got lucky again. Anyway, here's my problem." Jason handed Zac the DVD.

"A coaster is your problem?"

"It's a DVD."

"I know what it is. That was a computer joke. No one puts anything on a DVD or CD anymore—it's all thumb drives."

"Well, the Feds do." Jason shrugged. "It's a video of—" Jason turned and looked at the glass wall to his right that went black. The video started playing.

"How'd you load that so fast? Its password protected." The DVD was lying on top of the keyboard.

"You really think a DOJ password can slow me down. Give me more credit than that, I hacked the NSA computer 'vault' that holds the nuclear codes in less than thirty seconds, while I was drunk."

"Good point. You don't have to put it in a tray to play?"

"No. I built this *'data sucker'*—I don't like the name, but I haven't really thought of anything better."

"How about . . . wait for it . . . *data drainer.*" Jason nodded his head and pointed at Zac like he just came up with the greatest name for a product ever.

"I don't think so, but nice try. It instantaneously reads data from anything."

"Cool."

"Now what's the deal with this twelve second video?"

"At eight seconds in, Antonio says 'however' and it seems out of place to me, it doesn't belong in the sentence . . . it makes no sense," Jason explained.

"Let's watch and see. . . ." Antonio and his capos in high definition with crystal clear sound appeared on the blacked-out glass wall.

"I know Antonio 'Magic Man' Barrera. I've been following you in the news—you've gone global at twenty-nine. I'm proud of you, Jason. From where we came from, you turned out pretty good—beat the odds."

"Nah, I'm just lucky and, like I said, I'm in way over my head here. You're doing way better than me, look around . . . you got the world by the balls."

Zac laughed at the notion of *him* having the *world by the balls*. "I'm what you'd expect from an orphan kid, I'm a criminal, I just use a computer."

"Anyway, the video. My client has been a pain in the ass the entire trial . . . sometimes I feel like he's helping the government convict himself. But with this damn video, which is the government's main piece of evidence, he is adamant that he never told his guys to get involved with human trafficking. He remembers this meeting and he says he told his guys *he would kill them if they continued with the human trafficking and forced prostitution of kids."*

"A mobster with a conscious . . . I like this Antonio guy," Zac interjected.

"I can't figure out where the camera is that it gets all those different angles—it looks like Martin Scorsese shot the damn thing. I figured, if anyone would know if this video was doctored like Microsoft tried to do with Windows when they were sued for antitrust violations, you would. So, what can you tell me about the video?"

The video on the wall was now replaced with lines of code, which looked like gibberish to Jason. "There it is," Zac said, highlighting a line of code. "It's a mosquito-cam. The DOD developed these mosquito sized high definition cameras about five years ago—they actually look like a mosquito and even make a buzzing sound. Zac tapped the keyboard a few times and another section of wall turned into a video screen, but this time a document appeared that had *CLASSIFIED DOD* across the top and below it was a picture of a mosquito with engineering specs overlaying it.

"Wow . . . how'd you get that classified document?" Jason asked with a measure of concern.

"Why do you think I'm in Key West? I'm not here for the weather."

"I don't know, why?"

"The Navy base here has one of the most advanced, ground-based satellite systems in the world, thanks to the cold war and Cuba. Didn't you notice the gargantuan, white satellites when you drove on the Island?"

"No."

"I simply piggyback on their system and BOOM!" Zac made a mock explosion with his hands. "I can access pretty much anything our government tries to hide in an instant . . . or any government around the world for that matter. You want to hear what Putin is saying right now? I can listen in like we're in the room with him."

Jason's face tightened and his eyes went wide; he started to sweat a little. "um . . . na-na-no. Are the Ma-Ma-Marines going to bust in here any minute?" Jason wiped the sweat from his brow.

"You still stutter when you're nervous, chill, of course not. Even if the government knew what I was doing, they would think I was across the globe, most likely in Africa. Give me some credit, I'm the world's best hacker. I can hide my digital location with ease."

"Let me do a couple of simple things to check if the video has been doctored," Zac touched the keyboard. The screen blinked a few times.

Jason looked around the room, under the table, then asked, "Where's the computer that keyboard connects to?"

"You're looking at it," Zac swept his hand over the top of the keyboard like he was showing off a product on *The Price Is Right*. Zac touched the keyboard and a constantly changing number appeared on one of the walls.

"Why are you showing me the national debt counter for the U.S.?"

"The U.S. government only wishes that number represented the national debt; it's way bigger than the thirty-eight billion on the wall. That's how many devices and computers are connected right now on the entire planet. I crowd source everything. IBM keeps building what it calls a *supercomputer* . . . that's bullshit. I built the greatest supercomputer ever right here in this little 'keyboard thing' as you call it. I harness the power of every device in the world without anyone realizing it or leaving a trace. A computer with that much processing power would be the size of Florida. I call it *The Ghost Ship Virus*."

"Man, you're a genius," Jason said, marveling at his friend.

The wall-screen with the video of Antonio now had *NO ANOMA-LIES DETECTED* on it. "Doesn't mean anything," Zac said. "Tech has come a long way in manipulating digital video." Zac played the video two more times without saying a word.

Zac touched the keyboard—everything on the video faded out except for Antonio. Zac stood up and went over to the video wall and stood a few inches from Antonio's face. "Play . . . rewind three seconds . . ." Zac said into the air without moving his eyes twelve times. *Don't continue to make money*—Antonio said twelve times over. . . .

Zac walked back over to Jason, sat down, and took Jason's rum from his hand and gulped the rest down. "Ahhh . . ." Zac put the empty glass back in Jason's hand. "They made the most obvious mistake. *The first principle of the art is not to rely on tricks of technique. Most swordsmen make too much of technique, sometimes making it their chief concern.* Master Samurai Swordsman Odagiri Ichiun's said that."

Jason looked at Zac with a blank stare.

"Our government, and most around the world, only think about the source code when they manipulate digital processes. They forget about the *art* of digital manipulation."

"I love it when you wax poetic about hacking," Jason chided, his blank stare now replaced with excited eyes. "That's why you're the best at what you do . . . you look at a computer like Van Gogh looked at a canvas."

Zac ignored the compliment. "Come here and see for yourself."

Jason walked over to the video wall. "Stand closer," Zac commanded. Jason was only a few inches from the screen. "Watch Antonio's face, especially his cheeks and eyes. Play, no sound." Zac said into the air. The three second clip played five times.

"Uh . . . okay," Jason said. "I'm not sure what I'm looking for . . . looks like a video of Antonio Barrera speaking."

"That's just what your brain expects you to see, so that's all you will see. Pull back and look at the surface of Antonio's eyes." Zac played the video three more times.

"Will you just tell me already."

Zac rolled his eyes. He had no patience for people who couldn't see what he thought was the obvious. "You've got to look at the surface, man, not the eye. Watch the overhead light reflection on Antonio's pupil." Zac played it three more times.

"Sorry, buddy, still nothing."

"Don't you see how it moves with his pupil when he says the word *however* and *I will kill you* . . . look again." The video played two more times.

"Oh yeah, the light sort of flutters."

A smile started to spread across Zac's face. "Now, look at his left check." Played the video once more.

"Same thing . . . so how does that tell you it was doctored?"

"Haven't you ever been around drag queens like Rue Paul?"

"Huh?"

"Some of my friends here work at the 801 club down the street—it's a great drag show, you should see it while you're in town. What I learned from hanging out backstage with them is they take their makeup and lighting very serious. Drag queens have to keep the illusion that they are woman—how they tuck their you know what, I'll never know." Zac grabbed his crotch at the thought of the pain of a good tuck.

"What the hell does this have to do with the video . . . I'm lost."

Zac looked dismayed at Jason's interruption. "The Queens I know could get a PhD in how light reflects and forms shadows on the face and how the facial muscles and eyes move when talking and singing. I paid attention when they would put on their makeup to account for the lighting. See, when we speak, hundreds of tiny muscles in our face and eyes move involuntarily. Naturally, the light stays constant, it's the face and eye movements that creates shadows, unlike this video.

While the main source code manipulation of this video is top-notch, you can't stop there. You must adjust the source code for each layer. Most people think if you make an exact digital replica of the section of video you want to manipulate and then, like here, find what you want to add from the same source and just merge the two clips—like here with Antonio saying *don't* at a different time in this video—no one will ever know, because the main source code doesn't show any anomalies like my initial analysis verified. The detection tools get fooled because the source code is readjusted to appear in complete unedited sequence in a *read-only* file. But the output isn't right—you must go in and change each element of the video—digital layer by digital layer. You can see that the word *don't* was removed because the overhead light moves on the pupil and the shadows are off on the left cheek. It appears that what Antonio really said was: *However, DON'T do that human and sex trafficking shit or I will kill you where you stand, Capisce!"*

"Sonofabitch! Antonio says the exact opposite . . . that Trevor is a slimeball," Jason said.

"As a bonus for you, look at what else the government cut out of the video": *We don't need to make money that way, we make enough from our legitimate businesses.*

"Man, the government really tried to pull a fast one! They were literally going to try and kill my client with this doctored evidence."

"Now, how are you going to get the bastards?"

Jason thought for a moment, paced around the room, and then snapped his fingers, "Bingo. Can you testify about how this was manipulated? I should be able to get you in as a late witness because of a fraud on the court."

"Me?" Zac pointed to himself. "I don't think so. The only way I'll ever be in a courtroom again is if I'm shackled."

"Do you know someone I could use? A computer expert that's cheap would be great."

"I think that's an oxymoron: *computer expert* and *cheap*. But I know someone who owes me a favor in Miami who I don't think has any active arrest warrants at the moment."

"Great. Thanks. I wonder who did the video for Trevor—FBI, NSA, CIA?" Jason rubbed his chin.

"Let's see if we can find out," Zac said with a mischievous grin.

80

"WE GOT WORK to do, Caesar." Jason said as he helped Caesar into the front seat of the car. "Don't get comfortable, buddy . . . tomorrow we take the fight to that prick Wittingham—FU Goliath!" Jason pumped his fist in the air. He had a spring in his step for the first time all trial. He looked at Caesar who was already sleeping, drool forming at the corners of his mouth. Jason patted his head. "Thanks for your help." He pulled out of the Pier House at 4 a.m. and rushed North to Palm Beach.

Four hours later, he called Rufus Code from his office. "Hi, Mr. Code? . . . Hello, Mr. Code?"

"Shhh, hang up now or I will erase all the data on your phone."

Jason took his phone away from his ear and looked at the screen and confirmed the number was the one Zac gave him. Suddenly, his phone went blank and shut down . . . A look of horror spread across Jason's face. "Son-of-a-bitch!" He kept pressing the side button on his iPhone . . . nothing. After about three minutes, his phone came on, then his A-Team ringtone alerted him to an incoming *FaceTime* call. "Uh, hello? . . . Mr. Code? . . . Is that you?" Jason's screen now showed only green "0s" and "1s".

"Well, well . . . it's the famous Jason Noble I've been reading about online. Hotshot lawyer repin' Mafia Don Scumbag."

"What did you do to my phone?" Jason demanded.

"Your ultra-crappy Apple product. I did you a favor and uploaded an encrypted operating system instead of Apple's IOS that a kindergartner could have coded. Trust me, you'll be happier with my IOS, all your stuff is there . . . plus some nice extras."

"Um, okay. Why are you *FaceTiming* me but not showing your face?"

"No one sees my face . . . ever. What's important is that I can do a face and retina scan on *you*. Zac sent me your biometrics; we're cool. A friend of Zac's is a friend of mine. I hope your calling about that Mafia Don guy. Whatever you need, I'm in. I can last at least another five days without sleeping. Just send me a couple more cases of Red Bull . . . and, if I have to leave my bunker, I need a driver in a black Tesla model-X with one hundred percent tinted windows. Absolutely no substitutes or I won't come—I have to control the autopilot in case you're trying to assassinate me."

This guy must have already drunk a case of Red Bull. He's talking like an auctioneer. "No, that's okay, you can sleep. I'd actually prefer it if you got a few hours of shut-eye, but thanks for the offer. And I can assure you, Mr. Code, I'm not trying to assassinate you; I desperately need you to save Mr. Barrera. Here's what I need. . . ."

81

"HERMAN? CAN YOU hear me, now?"

"He—o . . . Herman Tinsdale, formerly Tinowitz, here, hello."

"I'm driving on the seven-mile bridge back from Key West, so it might be a little noisy on my end, just listen, buddy. It's Jason Noble. We met outside Judge Quarter's courtroom a few weeks ago. I'm representing Antonio Barrera."

"Oh, right, I remember."

"I need you to help me out in my big case." Jason pulled into the Starbucks parking lot just past the bridge.

"Okay, buddy, I'm game. Any money in it for me?"

"Well, no, but you might get on TV if you do this for me . . . think of all the free advertising you'll get out of it. Listen closely, I need you to pick up a surprise witness exactly, and I mean *exactly* as I tell you. One detail out of place and you'll be responsible for helping send the most powerful mob boss, *allegedly*, to prison for life . . . *no pressure*, just get it done for me . . . get it done for JUSTICE!" Jason added for a little more motivation.

— 82 —

JASON FINALLY STOPPED working at 2 a.m. He had spent a few hours preparing Rufus Code for his surprise trial testimony. He felt pretty good. He caught Trevor red-handed, fabricating critical evidence. As a defense lawyer, he only needed a tiny crack in the government's case to create reasonable doubt . . . he hoped. *Don't get too cocky—the remaining evidence against Antonio was so overwhelming that getting the video stricken from evidence may not matter.*

He walked along Flagler Drive to clear his head. He stopped dead in his tracks as a car with no lights on came barreling toward him on the wrong side of the road.

— 83 —

PAULIE "LEAD FOOT", the driver, pulled the Cadillac into a small clearing in the Everglades and turned his lights off. "Get him out," Paulie barked at Luca "the Latin", who was holding a black semi-automatic gun pointed at Jason's chest.

"Outside. Now!" Luca said as he motioned with his gun. Jason noticed Luca's hand was trembling and he was concerned he'd get shot by mistake. Jason didn't move at first; he thought it might be a good opportunity to grab the gun. Luca's eyes were nervously darting from Jason to outside to Paulie.

Just as Jason was about to make a decision, Paulie made it for him. He slapped Jason hard in the face with his catcher's-mitt-sized hands. "Get the fuck out. NOW! Before you make a mess all over the backseat of my car with your brains." Paulie's eyes dared Jason to test him.

As Jason was opening the door, Luca said in a high-pitched, trembling voice, "Fuhgeddaboudit! I'm not go-going out there!"

"Get the fuck out, you idiot!" Paulie barked at Luca.

Jason's right foot stepped on the soft earth that made up the Everglades—one of the natural wonders of the world. Jason knew there were only two reasons to be in the Everglades at night: pick up square grouper or kill someone and let Mother Nature take care of the body. Since square groupers hadn't been airdropped since the late 90s, he wasn't feeling good about his prospects. From the smell in the air, he knew he was deep in Belle Glade. The uniquely sweet smell in the air came from only one thing, sugarcane—Belle Glade's slogan: *Her Fortune is Her Soil.*

It was a full moon and the natural moonlight washed the Everglades in an eerie, supernatural glow. The air was still and silent. Jason knew better than to think nothing was out there in the blackness. Everything within a mile radius stopped and trained its ears on the foreign sound of the car. The gators, pythons, panthers, herons, rats, and everything else that called the swamps of the Everglades home were focused on the three of them.

"Move! Let's go!" Paulie instructed as he pointed toward what looked simply like a black void in the night. One wrong step and they would be alligator food or drown in a massive tangle of mangroves that lined the water's edge.

Jason would come to the Everglades with some charity program every summer when he lived in the group home in New York City, so he knew it well. He knew the first thing he needed to do was acclimate his eyes to the natural light, and since it was a full moon that would be easy. He stayed away from Paulie and Luca's flashlight beams that would only distort his vision. He wasn't worried about Paulie and Luca as much as what lived in the Everglades. He would beg for a bullet if a gator or python got a hold of him.

"Git the fuck over there. Let's move!" Paulie said, losing his patience.

Jason picked up the pace as he headed into the dark void. His eyes had adjusted and he could make out the beginning of a rickety, old dock as he got closer to the dark void. The dock stretched along the swamp's edge for at least twenty-five yards and was completely open on the water side and partially covered by mangrove trees on the other side. One fall into the mangrove trees, with all of their spindly roots, and you were dead meat. The more one would fight to get out, the more tangled he would become. It was the perfect trap to catch dinner for a hungry gator or python.

Paulie was in front with his flashlight, sweeping back and forth across the dock. The dock sagged under his heavy frame as he stepped on it and creaked with every step. Jason was slowly walking a couple feet behind Paulie and Luca was right behind him, pushing the gun barrel into his back—Jason could feel Luca's hand shaking more now.

Jason noticed, out of the corner of his eye, the quick glint off the water. It was only there for a second. The glint was a little behind him, parallel to the dock. Luca definitely didn't see it; he was too scared to notice anything. Jason recognized what made the glint, a good-sized gator, about nine feet long, he estimated from the size of its eyes. It was silently swimming toward them—only its eyes above the water.

Jason saw the source of the gator's interest. Luca was dripping sweat from his hand with the flashlight into the water. Jason slowed up even more and waited for his moment. Drip . . . drip . . . with each drop, the gator moved closer, silent as an assassin.

"Come on, let's get this done already," Paulie snapped, turning back toward Jason and Luca.

Just as Jason stepped forward, it happened; the gator launched itself three feet into the air, jaws open wide and came down on Luca's hand with a sickening crunching sound. His scream pierced through the night air like a siren.

Luca lost his hand with the flashlight and dropped his gun. His balance was off. He tried to shift his weight back onto the dock, but he just pirouetted on one leg and fell into the murky water with a thunderous splash.

Two more gators joined their friend and they violently chomped down in rapid succession on Luca whose screaming was muted by the water rushing in his mouth and the punctures in his torso.

"Holy shit!" Paulie yelled as he turned around, freezing at the site of Luca who now had a gator on either end of him and they were about to twist in opposite directions. A muffled sound came from the water . . . than nothing.

Jason crouched, then stepped back quickly, picking up the gun as he moved to the left. Since his eyes were adjusted to the natural light, he had no problem seeing Paulie, who was the size of a house. He raised the gun and fired two shots in succession.

The first shot missed. The second shot hit Paulie's right knee. He spun around, away from the water, and let out a deep groan as he fell into the mangroves.

Jason slowly walked toward him to make sure he wasn't a threat anymore. "Get me out! Help! You son of a bitch!" Paulie yelled while flailing his arms and legs. With each kick and swing of the arms, Paulie sank deeper and deeper into the mangroves.

Jason looked down and saw the source of Paulie's new, terrifying scream—a massive python was slithering through the mangroves toward him.

— 84 —

"The Defense calls . . . Rufus Code to the witness chair," Jason stood tall and announced.

Trevor jumped out of his chair. "I object, Your Honor, I don't know who this witness is."

"So what, this is a federal trial. You know you don't get 'notice' of potential witnesses until they testify, so sit down, Mr. Wittingham." Trevor sat down in a huff. He wasn't used to rulings not going his way.

Rufus took the stand. Jason qualified him as a computer expert: he had four PhDs from Harvard, Yale, MIT, and Oxford, all obtained before the age of twenty-two.

Trevor bolted upright and objected again. "Your Honor, this is an expert witness, pursuant to the rules of—"

"I know the rules of procedure," Judge Quarter admonished. "Parties approach."

Trevor charged up to the bench, Herb in tow, while Jason casually strode up—white noise filled the air.

Before Jason actually got to the bench, Trevor seethed, "Judge, this is a blatant disregard for the rules of procedure . . . I doubt he—" Trevor pointed with his thumb at Jason who was to his left. ". . . even knows the rules of procedure. I think—"

"I don't care what *you* think. What matters is what *I* think. Got it?"

Trevor, like a child scolded for not cleaning up his room, replied, "Yes, Judge, but—"

"*But*, nothing, I'll inquire with the defense."

Don't like when the shoes on the other foot, huh? Jason thought.

"Mr. Noble, why didn't you notice the government of this clearly expert witness as required by the rules of procedure? Unless I hear a fantastic reason, backed up by case law, I'm inclined to strike this witness."

"Well, Judge, I didn't know I would be calling him until yesterday and, pursuant to *U.S. v. Viszcya,* an Eleventh Circuit case, I can call a witness without notice if the witness will rebut false testimony or an attempt to commit a fraud on the court, which is why I'm calling Mr. Code. *I'm on a role . . . this feels good.* Additionally, Mr. Wittingham never actually served a *Demand for Disclosure of Experts* pretrial. So, I believe his testimony is admissible for those reasons." *Thank you Jeannie Francis.*

Trevor's face was red, his eyes narrow, and his jaw clenched.

Judge Quarter was a bit surprised by this intriguing turn of events in what had been a pretty standard blood bath by the government thus far. "Mr. Noble, do you mean to tell me that you have information that someone for the government offered 'false' or 'materially misleading' testimony and is attempting to, or has already committed 'a fraud' on this court and my jury?"

"Yes, Your Honor." Jason was now leaning on Judge Quarter's bench like a courtroom veteran.

"Those are some very serious allegations, Son." Quarter looked at Jason, the corners of his mouth wanting to break through his constant scowl. "You haven't said much during this entire trial, but this is some powerful evidence if you can back up what you're alleging."

Trevor couldn't contain himself any longer; his voice started to rise above the white noise playing through the courtroom speakers. "This is preposterous. I will file a bar complaint against Mr. Noble after I get my guilty verdict for these materially false allegations to the court. Neither myself, nor anyone on my team offered anything false or misleading in this case . . . why would we? It's been an easy slam dunk." Trevor made the fatal mistake of slapping his hand down on the bench.

Judge Quarter looked at Trevor's hand like it contained a grenade. "I will deal with *that* later." He turned to Jason. "Alright, Mr. Noble, tell us what the fraud is before Mr. Wittingham does something even more stupid and winds up in jail."

Jason took a deep breath and charged forward through the proverbial doors of *great lawyering*. "Respectfully, Your Honor, Mr. Rufus Code is going to testify about Government Exhibit One—the video."

Trevor actually thought he was going to have a heart attack. He became lightheaded and started to sweat, the ability to speak escaped him. All he kept hearing in his head was *fraud* and *video*.

Judge Quarter detected his discomfort. "You okay, Mr. Wittingham?"

Trevor managed a, "Uh, Uh, Yeah." *Fraud* and *video*.

"I'm going to overrule your objection. Mr. Noble may proceed with Mr. Code's testimony. But, you better get somewhere fast," Quarter said as he stabbed his finger at Jason.

"Yes, Your Honor," Jason thought he detected a tiny smile forming on Quarter's face.

Rufus spent the next two hours explaining to the jury how the video of Antonio was doctored. By the time he was done, the jury was glaring at Trevor and the entire prosecution table. Herb and Lisa wanted to hide under the table.

Everyone in the courtroom was stunned—Judge Quarter was visibly angry at the government. "Any cross examination, Mr. Wittingham?" Judge Quarter venomously asked.

Trevor looked at Herb for help, who wouldn't make eye contact with him. "Uh, Uh . . . no, Judge."

— 85 —

TREVOR STOOD, NOT as confident as when he gave his opening statement, but he recovered nicely from Rufus' surprise testimony, and was about to bring it home . . . then on to the governor's mansion.

He concisely laid out, brick by brick, the evidence that supported each element of each crime charged, focusing on the live testimony; for fifty minutes of his allotted one hour for closing argument, he saved ten minutes for rebuttal, another unfair advantage for the prosecution—last to speak with the jury before deliberations. ". . .You don't even need to consider the video, it was unnecessary . . . I didn't even need to introduce it . . . my unforced error—no harm no foul. *Remember* when Alphonso "the Whale" Tomisini was heard, for seventy-five total hours, talking about giving money to that man." Trevor turned and jabbed a finger in Antonio's direction, who stared back with the same neutral expression he had all trial.

". . .*Remember* the heart wrenching testimony of Li Jing . . . *brother twelve year old when die in container . . . no food or air . . . my grandma . . . dead by fat man with gun. . . .*"

"The only just verdict, the only verdict that will protect society and the children, who's going to protect the children if YOU don't, is a GUILTY verdict. Thank you." Trevor sat down.

JASON'S CLOSING ARGUMENT lasted just fifteen minutes—he spent twelve on the video. Rufus created a dazzling PowerPoint for him. The first slide was Government Exhibit One with the text of the statement that was manipulated *flying* into the foreground of the screen in red: *However, do that human and sex trafficking shit or I will kill you where you stand, Capisce!*

The second slide was the defense's only exhibit—Defense Exhibit One, the real video with what Antonio actually told his guys *flying* into the slide in white font: *However, DON'T do that human and sex trafficking shit or I will kill you where you stand, Capisce! We DON'T need to make money that way, we make enough from our legitimate businesses.* "How can you trust any of the other 'evidence' the government introduced if Government Exhibit number *One* was phony, a fake . . . tampered with by that man." Jason turned from the Jury and pointed at Trevor, who looked like he wanted to hide under the table.

Jason continued while still pointing at Trevor, "How dare *he* try and trick you . . . how dare *he* try and kill my client, Antonio Barrera, or try and send him to prison for the rest of his life . . . and lie to y'all to try and do it." Jason stabbed his finger at Trevor again, "That man, representing the almighty and powerful *Government*, thinks y'all are stupid!" Jason always threw in a "y'all" or two—Miami was in the South after all.

Trevor meekly stood and tried to say, "Obje—"

"Overruled! Sit down." Judge Quarter ruled and rebuked without even blinking.

Jason turned back to the jury and showed his third slide: A picture of a red and yellow hot air balloon. "The state's case is like a hot air balloon, if they proved their case against Mr. Barrera, then the balloon floats." Jason clicked his computer remote and the hot air balloon turned into an animated gif and began to float. "But, if they did not prove their case, beyond and to the exclusion of all reasonable doubt, then the balloon crashes back to earth."

Jason clicked to the next slide, which showed the balloon still floating. "The manipulated video," Jason said then clicked the remote again and the word "VIDEO" *flew* onto the screen and created a huge hole in the center of the balloon, which crashed back to the earth with a loud thud through the courtroom speakers. "Case closed . . . the government failed miserably in proving their case. In fact, if the government had any evidence of the crimes which Mr. Barrera is charged with, they would not have found the need to create fake evidence."

Jason clicked the remote one more time. "The government also failed to produce any evidence whatsoever DIRECTLY connecting Mr. Barrera to any of the crimes charged." The phrase "NO DIRECT EVIDENCE" flew onto the screen and put another hole in the balloon while it lay in a heap in the ground. "With the only two UNDISPUTED FACTS in this case: No direct evidence against Mr. Barrera, only circumstantial evidence, and the fake, tampered with, video, the Government's case doesn't even get off the ground." Jason closed his PowerPoint presentation to focus the jury exclusive on him.

Jason looked *his* jury in the eyes. "The only true and just verdict in this case is NOT GUILTY."

— **87** —

It took the jury twenty minutes to come back *NOT GUILTY* on all counts—the fastest *not guilty* in Trevor's career, and the first *not guilty* of Jason's.

— 88 —

TREVOR WENT TO Luke and Mollie-June's house to hide after his embarrassing and highly public defeat. He became the number one trending meme on the internet and every late night host worked a joke about him into their monologues. No governor's mansion for him. Trevor was sitting at the kitchen table with Mollie-June.

"It'll be okay, Son," she said in a soft, empathetic tone. "You'll get through this. Do you want another piece of blackberry pie? Pie makes everything better."

"No thanks, ma . . . pie can't fix this." He put his head down on the table.

Luke was in the living room watching CNN. Anderson Cooper just said: *A Chief Assistant United States Attorney in Miami was served with divorce papers at his press conference where he was explaining his embarrassing loss after a high-profile mob trial. The judge held this bozo in contempt of court after the trial and the Department of Justice will likely indict him for evidence tampering and obstruction—talk about a bad day!*

"Dad, turn the TV off . . . I hate the news media."

— 89 —

THE MARCHING BAND inside Jason's head finally took a break. He was in the backseat of Vinnie "the Bag" Respi's Lincoln Town car. Vinnie was driving and Chrissie "Meatloaf" Stephani was sitting shotgun. No one said a word the entire ride. Vinnie pulled up to Antonio's main gate at his home on Palm Beach, a ten minute ride from Jason's condo. Vinnie put down his window, looked at Johnnie who was standing at the main gate, and nodded.

The gate opened. Jason looked at Johnnie's face from the back seat as they drove by. Johnnie had a solemn look on his face. Jason nervously shifted in his seat. *I guess they wanted me to wear my best suit so I'd look good in my future casket.*

"You smell that, Chrissie," Vinnie said as he put his nose in the air and sniffed hard.

"What the fuck do ya smell, boss? Did I step in dog shit?" Chrissie started to look at the bottom of his shoes.

"No, you moron, I smell death in the air—the Grim Reaper is near," Vinnie said in an ominous tone.

"I-I-I'll ge-get out here," Jason choked out of his dry mouth.

Chrissie turned around and looked Jason in the eye with a snarl and said, "You'll sit there and shut the hell up or I'll shove my fist down your throat into your goddamn stomach."

"I don't care what you're gonna do . . . I'm going home, so fuckin' stop this car!" Jason shot back.

Vinnie and Chrissie just ignored his pleas. . . . The Lincoln pulled up to the front entrance. "Get out," Vinnie ordered.

Jason opened the door and nervously stepped out of the car. He kept telling himself to *relax, why would Antonio want me killed? I did the impossible for him.* Although, he still had the uneasy feeling that his days were numbered. Jason thought about running, but there was nowhere to run to.

"Walk," Vinnie prodded Jason in the back.

"You go first," Jason said.

Chrissie pushed him forward toward the front entrance. Jason started walking, as he was about to reach the front door, Vinnie said, "Not the front, around back."

Jason hesitated then turned to the left and followed a stone pathway around the house. *This is getting worse by the minute, now I'm certain I'm going to die—Dear God, please forgive me for my sins.*

When they arrived around back, Vinnie directed Jason to steps that went down into the ground. Jason couldn't see into the dark void at the bottom of the steps. He thought about protesting or even fighting, but he knew it would do no good.

Jason started descending the dark steps with Vinnie and Chrissie right behind him, almost touching his back. The steps were slippery from the salt air. The walls were thick, smooth stone with a light coating of mist on them from the ocean spray. Jason stepped onto the landing into a wide-open space, probably twenty by twenty. Directly in front of him, across the room, were dozens of candles casting an eerie glow. Jason squinted his eyes and as he felt Vinnie about to step into him, he took a step forward and was immediately stopped by a man with a medium build standing in his path, almost nose to nose who was dressed in a white suit with a thick red sash. *The Italians probably made a ritual out of killing their lawyer like they did everything else,* Jason thought.

Just then the man spoke as he stared into Jason's eyes with a solemn look.

"Who offers this man for entrance?"

"I do," Vinnie said. "He's a *friend of mine.*"

"Who accepts this man to be a *friend of ours?*" the man in the red sash asked without moving an inch. Just then dozens of men stepped from the shadows of the room, encircling it, and creating a pathway to the candles.

"I do," Antonio announced, as he emerged from the shadows and stood in front of the candles. "Sargent-at-Arms holster your weapon and let this man pass," Antonio commanded.

Jason looked down and saw the tip of a gold dagger with a red handle pointing into his stomach, the tip barley touching his clothes. He didn't even know it was there. *Smart,* he thought, *the candles drew his attention away from what was right in front of him.*

The man swiftly placed the dagger under his red sash and stepped aside. "You may proceed."

Jason's mind was racing trying to make sense of this. He slowly stepped forward and walked toward Antonio. The men around the room filled in behind him. He stopped in front of Antonio. *I feel like I just walked down the aisle at a wedding.*

Antonio intensely stared into Jason's eyes. "Jason Noble, the books have been opened." Antonio declared. "Your ancestors have been determined, your blood lines are pure, and you are worthy of entrance into *La Famiglia."*

Jason finally figured out that *he* was being inducted into *La Cosa Nostra. This might be worse than dying,* he nervously thought.

"Does anyone object to Jason Noble's entrance into this family?" Antonio asked. Antonio waited a few seconds but it seemed like hours to Jason. . . . "Hearing no objections—Jason, hold out your hands."

Jason held up his shaking hands like he was about to receive communion. Antonio placed a plastic mass card with a picture of an angel into his cupped hands. He then lit the angel on fire. "As this card burns, may your soul burn in hell if you betray the oath of *Omertà.* You enter this family alive and will leave dead. Do you accept these terms?"

The heat in his hands was getting intense. He knew if he said *no,* which he wanted to say, he'd probably be killed right there. "Yes."

"*Salute!*" The crowd of men yelled. Antonio held out a silver chalice for Jason to put the remnants of the burning angel in. He then embraced

Jason and kissed him on each cheek. "Welcome to *La Famiglia*. You're one of us now."

"Check his pants, he was so scared, I think he shit himself, foghetta-boutit," Vinnie yelled with a howling laugh.

I don't want to be in the Mafia. I just want to be a lawyer, Jason thought forcing a smile.

— 90 —

"Can I talk to you privately?" Jason quietly asked Antonio.

"Sure, let's go in here." They walked into a room off to the side that was also lit by candles. Antonio walked over to a leather couch and sat down, Jason followed.

"No electricity in the basement; you can't drill through these walls," Antonio said as he slapped the wall behind them. "No place for wires. This is a big night for you."

"I appreciate the party, but I don't want to be a mobster, no disrespect. I was just your lawyer . . . and got lucky. That's all I want to be; although, I am going to increase my fees in the future."

"Jason, my friend, take it easy, you're going to have a stroke," Antonio said with a hearty laugh. "You are not a mobster, but you will always be a *friend of mine* and part of both of my families."

"But, the oath, and, and, the burning angel, what the hell was all that?"

"You took an oath to remain silent, basically the lawyer/client privilege, which you have to adhere to anyway, right?"

"Uh, I guess."

"You really think the powers that be would allow you into the *La Famiglia*, come on, get real. I thought you were a smart lawyer," Antonio laughed.

"But why did you show me your secret ceremony?"

"Jason, you didn't need this to know that, it's on *Wikipedia* for Christ's sake. Besides, we didn't show you everything. I thought this was a good way to show you how much I really appreciate what you did for me. I owe you, Jason, and I don't owe anyone. You're a damn good lawyer . . . no fear."

Jason raised his glass, *Salute* and took a gulp of champagne.

"How much did Peter pay you to represent me?"

"Fifty thousand with twenty thousand for costs—more than my yearly salary when I worked for the Public Defender's Office."

"Son-of-a-bitch, I knew Peter was one cheap Jew, but Fifty-K . . . that's ridiculous! I paid him five million dollars."

Jason was taking another gulp of champagne as Antonio said "million" that came flying out of his mouth and all over what looked like a very expensive carpet—good thing he turned his head or it would have been all over Antonio. "Five million dollars! Peter told me you barely paid him anything. Sorry about the carpet."

Antonio reached into his pocket, pulled out his phone, and tapped on the screen for a few seconds . . . "Welcome to the millionaire's club, I just transferred one million dollars to your bank account. I think that's a more appropriate fee for what you've done."

"Th-Th-Th-Thank you . . . thank you very much. I guess fighting "the man" does pay. . . . At least now I can buy some bodyguards to watch my back."

"About that, I've already taken care of it. You won't be bothered again by any of Alphonso 'The Whale's' crew . . . I've sent a close friend to have a, uh, talk with them . . . trust me." Antonio winked.

Jason let the moment pass. As a criminal defense lawyer you learn a lot of secrets. Unless a client specifically tells you that *they are going to cause serious bodily harm or death to someone in the future,* you have no legal or ethical obligation to say anything—just lock it away in the attorney client privilege vault, which, under the law, is stronger than a bank vault and survives death.

"Let me ask you something else, you said my blood lines are pure . . . how do you know that? I was an orphan; I grew up in one bad foster or group home after another. I don't know really anything about my ancestors."

"I had your blood tested. Go ahead, open this." Antonio picked up a manila envelope that was on the coffee table and handed it to Jason.

"If you want to know who you are and where you're from, take a look, I think you'll be pleasantly surprised."

Jason looked down at the envelope in his lap with curious anticipation. He folded the mental clasp and opened the envelope and pulled out a stack of papers that had some photos attached. He started reading the pages with a look of excitement that could only be created by one's discovery of a long-awaited secret.

"You're actually one hundred percent Italian, from Naples—you're *Noblidon!* Your real name is Nobleoni. Your great, great grandfather on your mother's side was the first generation to come to America. I presume the State of New York changed your last name when they took you into the foster care system. There's also two first class tickets to Naples in there, go find out who you *really* are . . . and take that pretty sketch artist, Inaya, with you. She should be here by now."

—91—

Tuxedo Tommy handed the dry cleaner his tuxedo. "I need this back in two hours."

"Tuxedo stain all over. Hard clean," the small Korean lady said as she took the tux. "What kind stain?"

"Blood," Tommy said, the corners of his thin lips curling up. "I cut myself at a party." He fondly reminisced in his head how he spent the last twenty-four hours with Alphonso "the Whale" Tomisini's remaining crew.

-THE END-

— Acknowledgements —

A special THANK YOU to Barbara Cronie and The Writers' Colony.

PLEASE take a minute to leave a review on Amazon, Apple Books, Barnes & Noble, or your favorite book retailer.

Visit gjampublishing.com to view the movie of the first chapter of *The Untested* and learn about the Author. Follow G-JAM Publishing House on social media @gjampublishing for the release date of Greg Morse's upcoming novel: *CONNECT*.